Juliette Hyland began crafting heroes and heroines in high school. She lives in Ohio, USA, with her Prince Charming, who has patiently listened to her many rants regarding characters failing to follow the outline. When not working on fun and flirty happily-ever-afters, Juliette can be found spending time with her beautiful daughters and giant dogs, or sewing uneven stitches with her sewing machine.

Shelley Rivers is a Bournemouth girl who spent most of her childhood reading. Married with a family, she now splits her time between reading, writing, and pandering to the whims of her hilarious greyhound. Her hobbies include lopsided sewing, holey knitting, and collecting old stuff that no one else sees the beauty in.

Also by Juliette Hyland

Unlocking the Ex-Army Doc's Heart
Falling Again for the Single Dad

Also by Shelley Rivers

Tempted by the Brooding Vet

Discover more at millsandboon.co.uk.

A STOLEN KISS WITH THE MIDWIFE

JULIETTE HYLAND

AWAKENING HIS SHY VET

SHELLEY RIVERS

MILLS & BOON

First Published in Great Britain 2021
by Mills & Boon, an imprint of HarperCollins*Publishers*
1 London Bridge Street, London, SE1 9GF

A Stolen Kiss with the Midwife © 2021 by Juliette Hyland

Awakening His Shy Vet © 2021 by Shelley Rivers

ISBN: 978-0-263-29753-9

MIX
Paper from
responsible sources
FSC® C007454

This book is produced from independently certified FSC™ paper
to ensure responsible forest management.
For more information visit www.harpercollins.co.uk/green.

Printed and bound in Spain
by CPI, Barcelona

A STOLEN KISS WITH THE MIDWIFE

JULIETTE HYLAND

MILLS & BOON

For my sister—my confidante and co-conspirator. Here's to more fun and crazy days!

CHAPTER ONE

CERTIFIED NURSE-MIDWIFE Quinn Davis refused to look out the window, even as a few of the other nurses gaped at the orange blaze on the horizon. The wildfire had been burning for almost three weeks; she didn't need to see the damage. Quinn knew what the fire looked like, knew where it was heading, knew what was at risk.

"I can't believe it's still burning."

"I heard it's less than fifteen percent contained."

"No! I was listening to the news this morning, but I changed the station before they talked numbers."

It was twenty percent contained. Quinn had been monitoring the blaze since it began, but she kept the news to herself. She didn't want to join the conversation. Didn't trust herself not to break.

If she could only drown out their words.

She had a patient in labor; she couldn't afford to be distracted right now. At least, not distracted any further.

Quinn slid into a chair and tried to block Rhonda and Sherrie's exclamations from her ears. Both nurses commuted in from the south. This fire wouldn't touch them— not directly. But no one in this area of California ever truly believed a wildfire couldn't reach them.

Georgia stuck her head into the lounge. "Rhonda, Olivia is at nine centimeters."

"Guess that puts us on deck." Sherrie turned from the window and nodded to Quinn as she and Rhonda left to tend to their patient.

Quinn was grateful that work had called them away before they'd asked her about the destruction in the hills.

Or if she was worried.

Her phone pinged with a text message from her landlady, asking if she was safe. She managed to type a short affirmative without tearing up—barely. The evacuation notice for Quinn's neighborhood had shifted from voluntary to mandatory during her shift. A sob pressed against the back of Quinn's throat, but she refused to let it out.

Tapping her foot against the small table in the lounge, Quinn rolled her neck from side to side and tried to think of anything besides the bungalow being in the fire line.

It was just a place...

But it wasn't. The longest lease Quinn had ever signed before she'd seen the bungalow was for six months. During her decade as a traveling nurse, she'd lived out of two duffel bags. She didn't get attached to places—or to people. She'd learned the hard way that just because she connected didn't mean others did. Picking up and moving was ingrained in her.

Or, it had been, until the position at St. Brigit's had opened.

Maybe this was punishment for her giving in to the desire to finally claim something as her own. For painting walls and pretending the bungalow was really hers. *No!* She would not let her brain accept that possibility.

Quinn also refused to look at the opportunity to work with her best friend as anything other than a blessing.

She'd planned St. Brigit's to be a temporary place,

too—a year-long contract at best—but something about that bungalow had called to her.

Or maybe it was being back in California.

When her landlady had told her she'd wanted a long-term tenant, Quinn had readily agreed.

Still, she hadn't bought new furniture. Renting had seemed safer. Easier to dispose of if things didn't work out.

Yet, the bungalow, even with its rented furnishings, had felt like hers. *A home.* She'd never felt at home anywhere, not even as a child. She'd seen so much of the world but never found a place to really call hers. It didn't make sense that it was happening here—the home she'd escaped as soon as she'd graduated college. But no matter how much Quinn pushed back, the seed of a possible forever here in California had refused to slow its bloom.

But now her home was turning to ash.

She swallowed against the tightness in her throat. The yearning for a home, a real home, was uncomfortable. Maybe her biological clock was ticking—a primal desire urging her to plant roots so she could start a family—but that seemed too superficial. Coming back to California had felt different than she'd expected.

She felt different.

Why now? There'd been upheaval in her life before. So many times. And it had never made her want a home or a family. Quinn shifted. Trying to find a comfortable position on the plastic lounge chair was a lost cause, and her body was restless.

She absently rubbed the skin on the finger of her left hand. She'd worn James's engagement ring for less than three weeks before he'd confessed to cheating on her with one of the other itinerant nurses. The worst part was that she hadn't even been all that surprised. Her birth mother hadn't wanted her. Quinn hadn't lived up to her adoptive parents' dreams—so why had she thought James would be different?

She hadn't been angry, hadn't yelled or thrown anything. Quinn couldn't even remember crying. She'd simply packed her bags and moved on. A wildfire in the hills of California—something she'd seen far too many times growing up—wasn't unexpected, but it was throwing her out of sync.

It was her own fault. She knew better than to surrender to sentiment.

Quinn bit her lip and wiped her hands on her thighs as she tried to push away the image of her home on fire. Squeezing her eyes closed, she crossed her arms and willed the tears away.

Before rushing into the birthing center last night, why hadn't she thought to grab the things she'd packed a week ago? She'd boxed the few items that she cared about and carefully stowed them where she could snatch them up in less than ten minutes if the evac orders came down. She should have brought them with her.

"If your face gets any longer..."

A hot cup of coffee pressed against her fingers and Quinn lifted it to her lips without opening her eyes. The black coffee was bitter, and a bit burned, but the caffeine kick was what she needed. And she was grateful for any distraction.

"Seriously, Quinn. What's going on?"

A knee connected with hers as Milo slid into the chair across from her, and Quinn ignored the tingles that slid along her leg. She was tired, worried, and her emotions were tangled. That was the only reason she was reacting to Dr. Milo Russell this morning, she told herself, ignoring the fact that she'd felt those same tingles yesterday morning…and every other day since she'd walked into his arms at the airport eight months ago. Such a simple welcome that had shifted everything in Quinn's soul.

Almost a year later and she still couldn't explain the feelings.

Or why those emotions hadn't made her pack her bags and flee.

Luckily, Quinn's brain was too full of other worries to let that one take residency in the front of her mind today. Not that it ever wandered away for long, though…

Opening her eyes, Quinn tipped her cup at Milo as he took a seat beside her on the lounge chair. His jade eyes bore through her and she barely kept herself from leaning into him. Milo was her friend. Her best friend. He was the reason she'd leaped at the opportunity to work at St. Brigit's.

Sure, he was gorgeous. *Stunning.* His deep dimples were the stuff of legend. She'd heard more than one single lady talk about what it might take to get those dimples to appear outside the birthing center. But Quinn never swooned over anyone. Not over her cheating ex-fiancé and certainly not over Milo. At least, that had been true until she'd moved back to California. Now she yearned for any contact with him.

Quinn and Milo had always just been Quinn and Milo. They'd been best friends since grade school when Quinn had refused to name the person who had started the epic food fight. She'd stood in the principal's office, refusing to out the new kid, when Milo had marched in and declared that he'd thrown the first nugget. In truth, neither had thought tossing a few hard chicken nuggets would result in pandemonium and pudding on the walls—but they'd cleaned it together. And they'd had each other's backs ever since.

Even when wanderlust had taken her to the other side of the country or the other side of the world, she and Milo always kept in touch. Video calls, emails and social media had meant they were only ever a GIF away. He was the one constant in her rambling life. Always there to make her laugh, to bounce ideas off about her next move, to make her happy.

He'd always just been her friend Milo and working together at St. Brigit's was a first for them. She'd enjoyed every minute of it, even if she was in a constant battle to get her body to stop substituting friendly feelings with romantic ones.

"My neighborhood was placed under mandatory evac." She ignored the shake in her hand as she lifted the coffee cup to her lips again. One of the packed boxes was filled with pictures of her and Milo, his sister, and his mother. Diana Russell had never made Quinn feel unwelcome—despite being a single mom and a hardworking physician—unlike Quinn's own family. If that box of memories was lost... Quinn mentally kicked herself. She was *not* going to travel that well-worn path again this morning.

"Do you need to leave?" Milo leaned forward and the soft scent of his cedar shampoo blended with the smell of her coffee.

What was wrong with her? Before she'd returned to California, she couldn't have told anyone anything about Milo's shampoo. Though she could have told them that the scrunch of his nose meant he was concerned. And that a twitch in his left cheek meant he was holding in a laugh, but a twitch in his right cheek meant he was angry.

Maybe the lines between friends and more had blurred long ago...

They'd spent almost all their free time together since she'd arrived, enjoying the opportunity to be together in person rather than on the screen. He'd helped paint her bungalow, and they'd watched silly romantic comedies while sharing giant bowls of popcorn. But he'd never mentioned wanting more.

And Milo always knew what he wanted.

Focus!

Shaking her head, Quinn shrugged. "Molly's in labor. You know her history." Molly had struggled with infertility, and she and her partner had had more than their share of losses over the past five years. After so many disappointments, they'd adopted a son a few years ago—a gorgeous little boy they were both devoted to—and had been stunned when she had conceived naturally.

"I think Molly would understand." Milo gripped her fingers.

The simple gesture made Quinn's heart rate pick up, but she didn't pull away. She didn't have the strength to put distance between them today—even if she wanted to. Glancing out the window, she shuddered. "If I left right now, I wouldn't make it home before the roads closed. I'm just mad I didn't throw stuff in the car before I left last night."

She forced her gaze away from the orange glow creeping along the hills. Her home was really in danger. The place she'd felt called to might vanish.

"Why not?" Milo's lips formed a soft smile that any other day would have sent her belly tumbling with need. "The reports coming in—" He caught his final words.

She knew all about the reports. Knew that if it had been Milo's home, he'd have already prepared a five-page emergency plan. Heck, he probably had one anyway.

Her chest constricted. Plans provided safety and security. But they could be weaponized, too.

Used to control.

Her hair, her room, her clothes, her activities had all

been controlled—micromanaged. Her mother had kept a weekly calendar on the fridge. It was adjusted every Sunday morning—but only with activities deemed important to her parents. And deviation was *not* allowed.

Quinn had learned to hide her true self. To build walls to protect that precious self. The world hurt less if she kept the well-constructed barriers in place.

She'd done what had been expected of her. It hadn't mattered that her toes screamed through another ballet practice. It hadn't mattered that she'd absorbed the cutting remarks with a smile and the criticisms without argument. Walls hadn't provided happiness, but they had kept her safe. Besides, a false smile achieved more than tears.

She'd been the docile daughter until she'd refused to let her parents control her career choices. That one rebellion had led to her being cut out of their lives—all because she'd wanted some say about her future.

But that one mutinous act had granted her freedom. The right to pick up and move to where *she* chose. To cut her hair. To dress how she wanted. To never have a planner!

And when she had her own family, they were never going to feel like their life was scheduled. Her children, if she ever settled anywhere long enough to meet someone and have children, were going to know her love didn't depend on following a plan.

"I figured I had at least another day or two." Her throat closed as she fought off tears. She never cried in front of anyone—and she wasn't going to start today. Plus, denial was easier than focusing on disaster. But Milo wouldn't understand that. He was always at least three steps ahead of everything.

It was too late to do anything about it now, though. "I'll be fine," she assured him. "You know me. If necessary,

I'll find a new place." The thought of moving again made her heart sink. That was new…and not welcome.

Leaning forward, Quinn squeezed his hand.

Why was she always reaching for him?

"Maybe somewhere that gets snow," she quipped, pulling back, "where the summers don't make me worry about melting into the pavement."

Milo's lips turned down. He'd never liked her talking about new places. He'd cheered when she'd announced that she wasn't going to work in her parents' law firm, but then he'd frowned when she'd said she was leaving California. He always frowned when she mentioned moving. She wasn't even sure he was aware he did it.

Though he hadn't frowned when she'd told him she was coming home to join him at St. Brigit's. The memory of his bright smile on that last video call still sent thrills through her.

She hated his frown—hated causing it. Her fingers itched to smooth away the small lines at the corners of his eyes. "Want to see if there's a clinic in Alaska that needs a midwife and stellar ob-gyn? We could buy some snowmobiles and race around the Arctic."

His mouth moved but no words came out. Quinn could feel the heat in her cheeks as Milo's gaze met hers. She hadn't meant to ask that and certainly hadn't expected how his stunned silence would cut across her.

"Quinn…" The question she should never have asked him hung between them as his voice died.

Concern coated Milo's features and she feared pity. That was the last thing she needed or wanted.

Especially from him.

"I'm kidding, homebody." She laughed, hoping it didn't sound as forced to him as it did to her. Maybe Milo would chalk it up to her fear and exhaustion. "I know I'll never get you out of LA. One day you're going to run the maternity ward at Valley General. I've seen the planning boards." She patted his hand.

Milo carefully managed his life. He never jumped from one contract to another. The man developed a plan. And he followed it.

No chasing a shiny, unexpected adventure.

"Enough about me." Standing, she downed the rest of her coffee. "What we should be worrying about is if those winds shift and we have to evacuate the birthing center."

"Quinn…" Milo stood and pulled her into a quick hug.

The heat from the brief connection evaporated before Quinn could blink. But the ghost of his strong arms clung to her. She wanted to step back into the embrace. She wanted to run from the room. But her feet refused to follow either order.

"It's okay to be worried about both the center and your house. I know what that tiny, falling-apart bungalow means to you."

Crossing her arms at her chest, she glared at him. "No knocking the bungalow, *Dr.* Russell. We can't all live in a fancy downtown high-rise." It was her normal retort, but her tone was sharper today. The pain of not having a home, a family, a place to belong to, stabbed her. And somehow she'd lost the ability to bury that emotion behind her walls.

"I'm sorry," Milo muttered. "That was beyond a poor choice of words." A dimple appeared in his left cheek as he stepped up to her.

They were at work, but with the stress of the day, all Quinn wanted to do was to lose herself in Milo's arms. Let him hold her to see if that would make the stress and pain float away. They were close friends; everyone knew it. No one would raise an eyebrow if they found them embracing. But Quinn's heart wanted more.

And she wouldn't risk that.

Quinn's parents hadn't wanted her. She and her brother, Asher, hadn't talked in years. Even her ex-fiancé had found her lacking less than a month after getting down on one knee. If her relationship with Milo changed, would his need to plan everything out clash with her desire to go with her gut?

Their different approach to life worked while they were friends. But if she lost him, Quinn would be completely alone. And she couldn't stand the thought of losing the one person she'd always been able to count on.

She just couldn't.

Putting a bit of distance between them, she held up her empty coffee cup. "Thanks for the caffeine rush." Ignoring the flash of hurt that crossed Milo's features, Quinn moved for the door. He clearly didn't understand why she was being awkward, and there was no safe way for her to say *My heart's confused—sorry.*

Swallowing a pinch of panic, Quinn dropped her coffee cup into the recycle bin. As it hit the bottom, she looked over her shoulder. "I need to check on Molly."

Whatever was going on with her when she was near Milo needed to stop. They were just friends. Best friends. They'd stuck together through their awkward teen phases, all their different jobs, her failed engagement and the end of his short-lived marriage. No one knew her better. No one made her feel more grounded.

More cared for…

Her chest seized. Quinn was just lonely, longing for a place of her own. Her heart was confused. It was reaching for the comfortable. That was all.

Milo's arms were heavy as the light scent he associated with Quinn lingered in the air around him as he stared after her. She was hurting and needed a friend. Why had something that had always been so easy become such a challenge once she'd started working with him at St. Brigit's?

What if she noticed how his embraces lingered a bit too long? How he had to fight to keep from leaning his head against hers? That he longed to be near her?

It had taken over a decade for them to land in the same place at the same time. But the excitement he'd felt when she'd stepped into his arms at LAX eight months ago hadn't been grounded in friendship. He'd wanted Quinn Davis for years. He wasn't sure when the friendship they'd shared had transformed for him, but it was there in every bright smile and subtle touch. Yet she'd never indicated she wanted more. And losing her friendship wasn't an option.

He'd worked up the courage to ask her out once, years ago. But when he'd arrived with flowers, she'd been dancing with her roommate, screaming about signing her first contract with the traveling nurse agency. She'd looked so beautiful and happy. Milo had claimed "best friend telepathy" as he'd passed her the sunflowers and congratulated her on the new job.

Then he'd locked the question he'd wanted to ask deep in his heart. She had talked about putting space between her and California since elementary school. And he'd been determined to never throw a wrench into those plans. Dreams and goals were important—his father had taught him that.

Milo wanted Quinn to be happy. Wanted her to get every stamp in her passport, no matter how much he hated the distance between them…

He swallowed the desire that was his constant companion. Now wasn't the right time to ask Quinn out.

And it wasn't ever going to be right.

St. Brigit's was just a stopover for Quinn. He knew that.

Every time he sat on her lumpy, rented couch, it was a reminder that this was a landing zone after a decade on the road. And he knew the road would eventually call to her again—it always did.

It didn't call to Milo, though. He loved California and never considered relocating. His mom and his sister were in California, as were all his goals.

Still, every so often, Milo would catch a look in Quinn's eyes or a touch of a smile that made him wonder if she'd also considered exploring the possibility that there might be more between them. His brain screamed that he was imagining it, but he couldn't kill the pang of hope his heart felt each time. Last week, their hands had brushed as they'd walked to the movie theater and she'd smiled at him in a way that had Milo barely managing to prevent the words from flying out of his mouth.

These thoughts, the bloom of heat in his belly when she was near, the dreams he woke from, still feeling as though he was holding her close—he'd always been able to suppress them. But now, working with her every day, the thought that she might complete him—might patch the empty space in his soul—was growing ever stronger.

But that void had existed long before he'd met Quinn. It had been ripped open the night his father hadn't come home from the store with the supplies for his science project. His mom had done her best, but Milo had been so lonely.

The comfortable conversations he'd had with his dad hadn't been the same with his mom. He'd missed the feel of their complete family. The hole his father's passing had created still ate at him and he clung to his few memories and the emotions they stirred in him.

But if his short-lived marriage had taught him anything, it was that another person couldn't fill the void of his father's loss. That was far too much to ask. And that disaster had proved that impulsive acts just caused chaos.

And heartbreak.

Milo had always been impressed with Quinn's ability to start over. To pick up and leave the past behind when a new opportunity presented itself. She saw a new thing and ran toward it, confident that the details would sort themselves out. He let his eyes wander to the fire on the hills in the distance and sighed. But if she'd planned better, packed her car when the fire blazed closer last night... He let the thought float away.

As a kid, he'd left everything until the last minute, especially school projects. The week before he died, his dad had bought him two small whiteboards. He'd written Short Term on one and Long Term on the other—just like the headings on the boards his dad kept in his office. Then he'd explained that he wanted Milo to at least plan a few things out.

But Milo hadn't. And the night before his science presentation was due, he'd panicked because they didn't have the supplies he needed. His father had marched him upstairs and taken the money for the supplies from Milo's piggy bank, telling him he would have to do what he could but he was not to stay up past his bedtime.

While Milo had started the research, his father had gone out for supplies. A drunk driver had collided with him as he'd left the grocery store. Poster boards for Milo and flowers for his mother had been found in the car and dutifully delivered by a policeman days later.

Milo, suddenly lost, had been a mere shadow of himself. Adrift in a world where the man who'd made him feel tall, important, special, had vanished. In the grief-filled days that followed, he'd finally started using the planning boards his father had given him. The routine they'd provided had eased his pain. It never entirely vanished, but he found that rigidly structuring life left him open to fewer surprises. It gave him a bit of control in the chaotic world.

Milo was never going to be that person who had no idea what the next six months would hold. Where Quinn needed freedom, he required control. She wasn't going to stay in California, and the goals that would make him whole were set in stone.

And he was so close.

Milo made his way over to the window. Smoke had descended over LA a week ago, but the light of the fires had stayed away until now. A bead of worry moved through him as he stared at the glow just beyond the horizon. Wildfires were an all too constant threat in California and he'd experienced life with voluntary evacuation notices a few times. But he had never received a mandatory evacuation notice.

Would Quinn's house survive? He hoped so. He remembered questioning her decision to rent the rundown property when he'd helped her move her limited belongings inside almost a year ago. She'd just smiled and said she'd loved the place.

They'd spent weekends painting the gray walls of her bedroom a bright blue and her kitchen walls the color of the shining sun. If coffee didn't wake her up, the sunflower color would. Milo hadn't teased her that bright colors were out of fashion—at least according to his interior designer sister—because Quinn deserved to have walls whatever color her heart desired. He'd never understood her mother's refusal to allow Quinn to paint her childhood room, even when Quinn had offered to pay for all the supplies. But there was a lot about the Davis family that Milo hadn't understood.

The only problem Milo had with her bungalow was its

distance from his place. It was forty minutes away from
St. Brigit's on a good traffic day.

Forty minutes away from him…

Maybe it had been ridiculous to think she'd want to be
neighbors. But he'd looked for places near him as soon
as Quinn had told him she'd accepted the position at St.
Brigit's. He'd plotted the best areas and done a ton of research for her. She'd signed her lease on the bungalow
without ever looking at any of it. He knew she'd always
trusted her gut over research, but had thought she'd want
to be closer for the short time she was going to be in LA.
It had hit him surprisingly hard when she'd chosen somewhere so far from him.

She'd signed a two-year lease on the two-bedroom bungalow. He should have rejoiced. But then she'd rented all
her furniture. And his small piece of hope that she'd stay
had died. He'd counted on having two years. But now, if
the bungalow burned, would she leave again?

Even with her lease, Milo had started looking for hints
that she might run off on another adventure. The nursing
agency still sent her job advertisements, and he was aware
that she talked to her clinic colleagues about the travel
opportunities when they arose. Her excitement was con-
tagious, and he knew at least one nurse from St. Brigit's
had put in an application.

But she'd asked him to go to Alaska— No, Milo corrected his heart, Quinn had joked about finding a place
somewhere else if her home turned to ashes. She'd just
thrown him in—probably without thinking. After all, her
cheeks had burned as soon as the question had left her lips.

He'd teased her about her tendency to blush for years
and when her cheeks lit up, he'd wanted to lean forward
and rub his hands over them. To pull her close.

Instead, his tongue had refused to mutter even a basic response. And then she'd confirmed that it was only a joke.

Which he'd known…

So why was his heart still wishing she'd meant it—even if he never planned to leave?

Pushing a hand through his hair, Milo tried to rope in his wayward emotions. An offhand comment when Quinn was stressed didn't mean anything.

But what if it did? What if it was a sign she wanted more from him too? The loose plan he'd thought of for asking Quinn out formed at the back of his brain again.

Why was it refusing to stay buried?

"Molly's crowning and the baby won't drop!" Rhonda shouted from behind him. She was gone before the lounge door slammed shut, giving him the perfect excuse to bury the lingering questions and thoughts, and focus on his work instead.

"I can't," Molly sighed and leaned her head back.

"You can. Just breathe. And when the next contraction comes, I need you to push with all your might." Quinn kept her voice level as Molly let out another low cry.

She'd been pushing for over an hour and was growing tired and frustrated. Quinn dropped her eyes to the baby's heart rate monitor. It was still holding steady, but the longer Molly's son refused to enter this world, the greater her chance of needing an emergency cesarean.

"I'm tired." Molly's voice ached with exhaustion.

"I know," Quinn commiserated, but only for a minute. Her nursing mentor, a former army medic, had taught each of his students that sometimes a patient needed a command. Meeting Molly's gaze, Quinn channeled her inner drill sergeant. "Your job isn't done," she reminded her.

"So, Julian, help Molly sit up a bit. And Molly, get ready to bear down."

Molly's partner helped her up and rubbed her back. He whispered something in her ear, low enough that Quinn couldn't hear him. Whatever the words were, Molly set her lips and nodded at Quinn.

Good. She needed Molly focused. Bringing life into this world was hard work, but Molly could do it.

The monitor started to beep and Molly's face screwed tight. "Oh, God."

"Here we go. Push!" Quinn ordered.

Molly let out a scream as she held on to Julian's hands, but she didn't stop pushing.

And Quinn breathed a sigh. *Finally.* His little nose and lips were perfect. "Good job, Momma. One or two more pushes, and we should have him."

The air shifted next to her and Quinn knew Milo had joined them, but she didn't look up. She'd asked Rhonda to grab Milo after they'd passed the forty-minute mark of pushing. If the baby hadn't descended… Quinn swallowed. The baby had—that was all that mattered now.

Quinn was pleased that Milo's presence wasn't needed, but she knew he wouldn't leave now. Not because he didn't trust her ability to safely deliver a child, but because he cared for each of his patients. And Milo tried to be present for as many births as possible. Quinn liked to joke that he lived a block from the birthing center so that he could welcome as many little ones into this world as possible.

"Looks like I got dressed in my fancy scrubs for nothing."

Quinn could hear the smile in Milo's voice as she focused on Molly's little one. This was the part they all loved. The reason every midwife and ob-gyn entered the profession. There was no better joy than to watch new life enter this world. Sharing a few minutes with loving partners becoming first-time or fifth-time parents… It never got old.

The monitor beeping picked up and Quinn offered Molly a quick smile. "One more time, Momma."

Molly's eyes were a bit watery, but she gripped Julian's hands and pushed as the next contraction cascaded through her. "Fine!" Molly bit out. "But I am definitely telling his first date about how much trouble he put me through."

"That is every parent's right. I think it's in a handbook somewhere," Milo agreed.

Quinn laughed and then smiled as the tiny guy slid into her arms. He was perfect. Ten little toes and fingers, and a set of very healthy lungs, as evidenced by the fact he immediately erupted in a screech.

Perfect.

For just a moment, Quinn wished the child was hers. It was a need that she was having trouble ignoring lately. But it encompassed so much more. A desire to find someone. To walk through life with another, someone who'd try to keep a straight face while she crushed his hands and brought their child into this world.

Someone who would choose her, just as she was…

As she laid the still-screeching little one on his mother's chest, Quinn grinned at her patient. "Congratulations, Molly. You're a mom—again."

Molly and Julian were good people, a loving family. Surely their hearts were big enough to include the new baby *and* their adopted son, even if he didn't share their DNA. Unlike her own parents…

The placenta was delivered with no complications as Molly and Julian bonded with their newborn—each counting his toes and fingers—before letting Milo take the baby to check him over while Quinn took care of Molly.

A few minutes later, Quinn watched as an exhausted

Molly kissed the top of her son's head and then kissed her husband.

"He's beautiful," Quinn said with a smile. It was true. Their little man was adorable—like all new babies.

Molly let out a sigh. "He is. So beautiful. He looks a bit like Owen. I know technically people would say that's not possible, but look at his little nose." Molly's fingers traced a line down the boy's nose and laughed. "Such a cute nose."

Julian kissed his wife. "I agree. Though maybe that is because all baby boys seem to look like little old men when they're first born." Julian laughed and pulled out his cell phone.

A small boy appeared on the screen a few seconds later. "Am I a big brother? Am I?" Owen beamed at the baby on his mother's chest.

"Yes," Molly whispered. "This is Adam—your little brother." She let out a yawn and waved to her oldest.

Julian took over, his smile wide as he looked at Owen. "Mommy is tired, but Grandma is going to bring you to visit in a little while."

"Promise?" Owen queried.

Quinn wondered if the small boy was worried. At four, a bit of sibling jealousy was to be expected, and he was likely too young to understand that his world had altered forever. *Please...* Quinn sent out a silent prayer to the universe that it was altering for the better.

"Promise." Julian gave him a thumbs-up. "I love you, big brother."

Quinn sucked in a breath as her heart clenched. She needed to leave—now. Molly was fine, and the family needed some bonding time, anyway. She wanted to believe that was why she was ducking out. But Quinn had never been good at lying—particularly to herself.

The echoes of her past chased her as she exited the birthing room.

This wasn't her life. The reminder did little to calm her racing heart. Molly wasn't her mother and Julian wasn't her father. These parents would love both their children equally.

They would.

She'd wanted to return to California, had felt drawn here. Working with Milo had been the biggest draw, but LA was also her hometown. Where she'd been raised. She had hoped that maybe enough time had passed. But in the short time she'd been home, she'd realized the pain of her childhood refused to bury itself in the hole in her soul.

Rolling her shoulders, she tried to find a wave of calm, but it eluded her. Her parents had struggled to conceive, too. After years of trying, they'd adopted Quinn a newborn abandoned at a fire station.

If they'd loved her then, Quinn had been too young to remember. Her brother, Asher—the miracle child they'd always wanted—had been born when she was not quite two. Overnight, Quinn had become an interloper. If they could have returned her...

Leaning against the wall, Quinn inhaled a deep breath, trying to fend off the past. Today had been too emotional. But the tiny part of her heart that wasn't happy on the road, that craved permanence, that got louder with every move... And screamed loudest when she was near Milo—

"She looks just like my mother." The soft coo of a new mom walking past with her newborn sent Quinn spiraling further.

Every time someone had commented on how her jet-black hair and dark eyes were so different from her family's blond hair and baby blues, she'd wish her mother would laugh it off. Make up a great-grandfather. Or say that she was her daughter by choice instead of by birth—other adoptive families believed that. But no matter how hard Quinn had tried to follow the family's strict rules, to abide by her parents' wants and desires, it hadn't been enough.

Instead, Carolyn Davis would calmly explain that Quinn wasn't really hers.

Not hers...not a full member of the family.

When her parents had died in a car crash right after she became a nurse, she found out that they'd left everything to her brother. She hadn't even been mentioned in the will.

Though they'd never been close, her brother had tried to make it right. Asher had divided the estate evenly. Quinn hadn't cared about the money or the real estate—her parents had stopped supporting her financially the day she'd declared that she didn't want to be a lawyer. She'd realized that that wouldn't have gained her acceptance, so why give up her dreams of being a nurse?

It wasn't his fault, but Asher had gotten the things that mattered. The letters. The keepsakes. The acknowledgment. Quinn shouldn't have expected anything. Still, part of her had hoped that one day she might be welcomed into her own family. With her parents' passing, that dream became impossible. And to not even be mentioned in the documents they'd meticulously prepared in case they died unexpectedly, was a wound she still didn't know how to mend.

Then she'd lost her brother, too. Not physically. At least, she didn't think so. But Asher had stopped returning her phone calls and picked up the reins at their parents' law firm. Their lives had always been separate, but without their parents between them, she'd hoped they might be friends, or at best, not competitors. She'd been disappointed—again.

But she'd found her place—at least professionally. Nurs-

ing was her calling and she'd never regretted choosing it.
She'd carved her own path, focusing only on the step right
in front of her. But nursing didn't take away her desire
to be accepted, to be loved, to have a family that wanted
her—just as she was.

"Molly and Julian are going to be excellent parents,
and their boys are going to keep them busy." Milo's words
floated over her.

"Of course they are." Quinn opened her eyes and looked
toward the door where Rhonda was hanging the welcome
stork. The spindle-legged creature was hung on all the
doors, and Quinn's heart ached with the worry that she
might never experience that joy. She was less likely to find
it if she moved every year—or sooner. "I'm fine."

Maybe if she repeated the phrase, it would bloom into
truth.

"I didn't ask." Milo leaned against the wall and wrapped
an arm around her shoulders.

At least he hadn't directly called out her lie. Pushing
away from the wall, Quinn offered him a smile, doing her
best to make it seem unforced. "You were going to." She
tapped her head. "Best friend telepathy."

Milo grinned. The dimple in his cheek sent a tiny thrill
through her. Between working with him and hanging out
with him, it was getting harder to keep the lines of friendship from blurring.

Particularly when she didn't want to.

Hurrying on before he could add any commentary,
Quinn knocked a finger against her watch. "I'm off duty.
So, I'm going to—" Her words died as she remembered
that she couldn't go home.

"You want to crash at my place? I'm off, too."

His heat warmed the cold that refused to leave her.
But if she said yes when her emotions were so close to

the surface, it could be a disaster. "No." The rushed word was clipped, and her heart sank as Milo's nose scrunched.

He was worried and hurt, and there wasn't a good way to walk her tone back. She hadn't meant to hurt his feelings.

Trying to sound bright and cheery, Quinn offered, "I'll crash here, and one of the on-call midwives can have a date night!"

Someone should.

Bumping his hip, she ignored the gibe and added, "I'll certainly be on time for my next shift. Maybe even early, given the commute."

Milo nodded, but the ghost of hurt still hovered on his face. "The commute will certainly be quick."

Pursing her lips, Quinn watched him go. Longing pushed at her chest, ordered her to chase after him, to tell him she'd love to go home with him. In so many different ways…

But that was why she couldn't do it. He was her friend. If their dynamic changed, she could lose so much.

But what if she gained everything?

Until she could quash her heart's cry, she needed to keep a bit of distance between them. No matter how much it hurt.

CHAPTER TWO

QUINN'S DARK HAIR spilled across her cheeks, her breaths were slow and her feet hung from the couch. Pulling at the back of his neck, Milo sighed at the sight of the crumpled pillow she was using. He'd taken more than one nap on that monstrosity. She was going to wake with a stiff neck.

If she'd come home with him last night, she'd have been comfortable, well rested. *Cared for.* But he knew Quinn's independent side well. She'd been taking care of herself for most of her life. But she didn't have to do *every*thing herself. Relying on each other was an important part of any friendship. She could ask him for anything. Anything.

Besides, there was independence and then there was stubborn. One night on that couch was more than enough. If the evac order hadn't been lifted on her home by the end of their shift today, he was going to find a way to make her agree to stay at his place until this was over.

His heart rate picked up, and Milo wanted to slap himself. He should not be happy that she might have to stay with him.

Get hold of yourself.

Her home might be engulfed in flames at this very moment. A sobering thought...

Milo's hand shook as he reached for her shoulder, but at least she couldn't see it. "Quinn." She'd never been a quick riser. He set one alarm and never allowed it to snooze, but Quinn relied on at least three. A small smile touched her lips and she rolled toward him—as much as the couch would allow anyway. "Milo, I want…"

I want… What? He wanted to know the final part of that statement. Desperately.

She wasn't really awake. And he knew that dreams offered scattered bits of information. After all, Quinn had been a regular fixture in his dreams for years. And since her return, those dreams often woke him with decidedly less than friendly thoughts.

But that didn't mean he was a feature in her dreams. She could be dreaming of painting, cooking or any of the multitude of activities they'd done together over their two decades of friendship. Still, the small bursts of hope cutting across his heart refused to be quashed.

What if she was dreaming of more too?

He didn't have time for introspection this morning. Gripping her shoulder, he shook harder. "Quinn."

Ainsley Dremer's husband had called to report that his wife was in labor. She'd worked out a plan for a home birth, but the midwives they'd worked with were currently dealing with mandatory evacuation orders. St. Brigit's standing rule was that two midwives attended home births, but no midwives other than Quinn were available. So, Milo was going to act as the second.

If the fire expanded, their patients might have trouble reaching St. Brigit's. He knew the first responders were doing their best, but months of drought had created the perfect landscape for the fire to grow. And grow it had.

According to the news, homes in Quinn's area had been destroyed, though he still didn't know for sure that Quinn's bungalow had been one of them. He didn't want anyone's house destroyed, but Milo especially wanted Quinn's house to stay safe. That way she wouldn't have an excuse to leave.

She belonged here…with him.

Why the hell wouldn't that thought disappear?

Warm fingers grazed his and heat rushed through Milo's body. Those little touches meant far more to him than they should. But that didn't stop him from craving them.

"Milo?" Quinn's lips turned up and her cheeks pinkened as her eyes landed on him. "What time is it?"

"Time to get to work!" Milo winked, hoping his face didn't show the multitude of contradictory emotions floating through him. "Ainsley Dremer is in labor. Sherrie and Heather are both dealing with mandatory evac orders, so you and I are up to the plate."

Quinn flinched as she straightened and rolled her shoulders.

"This couch isn't built for long-term slumber." Milo barely resisted the urge to reach out and rub her shoulders, even though he'd performed the action dozens of times over the years—after long study sessions in college or in the weeks she'd be passing through LA before heading off to her next contract.

It was a simple gesture. One a friend could easily offer. But it felt far too intimate when his body craved so much more than just a friendly touch.

"I've slept on worse." Quinn's hand ran along her neck as she massaged the knots out. "Nothing a few pain tablets and a hot shower won't fix. Though only one of those is an option this morning."

It was her standard reply. She'd said the same thing after sleeping on the floor of a makeshift hospital in Haiti during a cholera outbreak. She'd also joked about the tiny cot she'd fallen into while living in a rural area of Maine where the roads nearly vanished in the winter. The woman seemed capable of falling asleep anywhere, but that didn't stop muscles from complaining, no matter how much she tried to hide it.

At least he was prepared this morning. Milo reached for the glass of water and passed her two pain-relief tablets. Then he held up a small bag with a toothbrush and toothpaste. Small comforts went a long way.

"Milo—" Quinn smiled "—you're the best."

The small compliment sent more than a few shivers down his spine. She was being Quinn. His wonderful, amazing, best friend. But it wasn't enough.

Hadn't been enough for years.

"The service here is going to be hard for my next locale to live up to." Tipping the water bottle toward him, she grinned. "To friends."

"Friends," Milo repeated, bitterness coating his tongue.

Her "next locale." Such a simple phrase. *An expected phrase.* This was just a waypoint. And he needed to remember that.

He tried to force his voice to sound normal. "I am pretty amazing." Milo wished he had more caffeine in his system.

"And so humble." Quinn laughed as she set the water bottle down and grabbed the bag of toiletries. "How far along is Ainsley? Sherrie was her primary. Thankfully, she said Ainsley's pregnancy was textbook."

Home births were rising in popularity in the US, and Milo fully supported them. But he did not recommend them for women with possible birthing risks. Milo loved that St. Brigit's offered both options for his patients. Just like his mother's clinic did.

His heart compressed a tiny bit. He hadn't worked at that clinic in nearly five years. St. Brigit's was great, but it wasn't Oceanside Clinic.

No place was.

And five years ago, when his mother had married Felix Ireman, another ob-gyn at the clinic, the place had taken on an even more homey feel. Milo'd spent most of his teen years volunteering at Oceanside and, during his under-grad years, had even sketched out an idea to add a natural birthing center, which they'd started building the year he'd worked there.

Oceanside Clinic was special and he'd only experienced the feeling he got when he stepped into Oceanside at one other place. Valley General.

Three weeks before his father had passed, he'd had a meeting at Valley General. He'd taken Milo along so he could interview a surgeon for a science project. The one Milo had put off.

As they were leaving, his father had slowed next to the chief of obstetrics' office. He'd smiled at Milo and said, "One day, this will be my office." The memory of the confidence in his father's voice still caused goose pimples to rise on Milo's skin.

It was the clearest memory he had of his dad. His father's voice might have been lost to the waste bin of memory, but that day, that perfect day and all its feelings, Milo remembered. His dad had never achieved that goal—but Milo would. And each morning, when he walked through the door, he'd feel close to his dad again.

"Milo?"

Ignoring the ache in his chest, Milo focused on Quinn's original question. "She is forty weeks and two days. When her husband called, the contractions had been holding steady since a little after three. So it's showtime!"

Milo glanced at the window. The sun wouldn't rise for another two hours, but the glow of orange still lit up the hills in the distance. "Ainsley and her husband are a few miles from the voluntary evacuation zone."

Quinn's eyes hovered on the hills through the window. "Did the winds shift overnight?" Her lips tipped down before she shook herself. "I meant…are they expecting them to shift? Morning brain."

The attempt to cover her worry didn't fool him. Of course she was wondering if her home had survived the night. And he didn't have an answer for her. But rather than pull on the first thread, he addressed her second question. "Have to ask someone more versed in fire control than me." He knew the department's director was in regular contact with the city fire brigades and that conditions had been deemed safe enough for them to head out.

Quinn moved toward the bathroom. "Give me five minutes to take care of necessities, and then we'll be on our way." Before she closed the door, Quinn added, "And don't eat all the croissants. I saw the bag behind your back."

Milo laughed. "I make no promises."

Their director opened the door to the employee lounge just then. "Dr. Russell, if the fire shifts and there are complications with Ainsley Dremer's delivery, I've instructed Kevin to run you south to Oceanside Clinic."

The bag nearly slipped from Milo's hands as he tried to steady the beat of his heart. *Oceanside.* Did they really expect the fire to shift? And if so, why were they not directing Ainsley and her husband to either head to St. Brigit's now or to go south to Oceanside? Plans and routes ran through Milo's head.

"Dr. Russell?" Martina stepped into the room, lines crossing her forehead.

She met his gaze then let her eyes wander to the window. "They aren't anticipating the fire shifting. We would never risk anyone's safety. But it's always good to have a backup plan."

"Of course," Milo agreed. Plans were how he lived his life. He just hated the small bead of want that always pressed against his soul when he thought of the Oceanside Clinic. He'd loved working with his mom, but with each passing year, his connection to his father slipped farther away, making him more determined to get the job at Valley General. For a kid that had been his dad's shadow—to not even remember his dad's voice…

Pain rippled down his neck as he tried to recall it, but it refused to materialize. Valley General offered Milo an opportunity no other place would. If he could reestablish that connection to that last blissful day they'd shared, then maybe the loneliness he hadn't fully conquered since would dissipate.

It might vanish completely if Quinn stayed. Suddenly his body was on fire for a different reason. He couldn't go down this path. She'd mentioned her "next locale" less than fifteen minutes ago.

"Didn't realize we would need to go that far south. Caught me by surprise. That's all."

Martina nodded. "Ainsley and her husband are halfway between here and Oceanside. Easier to head south from there. You know how it is. No one can afford the city rents. And since you still have visiting rights at Oceanside, it makes the most sense."

He'd maintained his position as a visiting physician at his mother's clinic, but only in the event of an emergency or if his mother and Felix were unable to work. Thankfully, that had never happened. Though, if his mother kept talking about him coming back, he might need to end it. She knew what Oceanside meant to Milo, and she also knew about his dreams for Valley General. "Glad it's finally come in handy." Milo lifted his cup of coffee. "Quinn and I will be ready to go soon. Is there anything else you need from us? We'll probably be with Ainsley for most of the day."

"Since you asked… Dr. Metri is looking over a few résumés for the open OBG position. When you get back, I'd like you to look them over, too. See if there is anyone you think would make a good addition to our team. There's even one from a senior Valley General ob-gyn. Guess she's looking to slow down a bit."

Valley General. An open senior position.

His tongue stuck to the roof of his mouth as he glanced toward the door where Quinn was getting ready. Working with Quinn was one of the top highlights of his career. He'd assumed she'd be the first to leave, but could he leave before her?

Mercy General had approached him a few weeks ago about a potential senior OB position. The opportunity would've enhanced his résumé for any potential opening at Valley General, but he'd passed. His credentials were already impressive, and Quinn might never make it back to California once she left. Their working relationship had an expiration date, even if neither of them discussed it, and he just wasn't willing to cut things short.

Valley General! his brain screamed. *It's only ten miles up the road.* But his heart was less willing to celebrate the potential coup. Still, he could look at the résumés.

"Of course." Milo nodded and smiled as Martina walked out. If a senior OB was looking to leave Valley General, perhaps he could accelerate his plan. It would make Quinn's transition back to the road easier to accept.

Maybe keep him from making a fool of himself, too.

"What's up?" Quinn asked as she grabbed the white bag from Milo's fingers. "You look like you're planning something."

"How can you tell?" Milo grabbed a croissant from the bag.

She hit his hip with hers as she raised the pastry to her lips. "The far-off look and rubbing your chin. It's cartoonish but adorable."

She'd been able to read him like that since they'd been teenagers. It was comforting, but what if she saw the swirls of emotion directed at her? Milo's throat tightened as he purposely removed his hand from his chin. "I see."

Quinn's fingers burned as she gripped his wrist. "It really is a cute trait. So, what are you planning?"

"Nothing major." Milo started for the door. "Martina wants me to look over a few résumés. Apparently, one of them is from a senior OB at Valley General."

Quinn fell into step beside him. She was tearing off pieces of her pastry, but her eyes had a faraway look in them. "So, you're plotting how to become their replacement at Valley General?"

"It's not plotting." Milo sighed and hated the flash of hurt that hovered in Quinn's eyes before she strode past him.

Following her to the van bay, Milo opened the back door as their driver, Kevin, started the engine. "I'm sorry. But 'plotting' sounds so much more sinister than 'planning,' which is what I always do. Stay the course." He chuckled, but it sounded false, even to him.

Quinn nodded as she finished her croissant. "Plans can shift. You're the only one writing them in stone."

"What is that supposed to mean?" Milo's stomach hollowed as her gaze met his. Their ability to read each other could really be a curse.

"Milo." Quinn raised a brow. "Ever since Bianca left, Valley General has become your obsession." She leaned her head against the wall of the medical van as it turned out of the parking lot.

"Planning is not an obsession. It gives you control." Milo frowned as Quinn's dark gaze held his.

"Control doesn't—" Quinn bit her lip so hard he feared she was tasting blood, but she didn't continue the well-worn argument.

Quinn moved with her heart; she didn't look for stepping stones in her career. And she didn't understand why he was so focused on Valley General when St. Brigit's and Oceanside had made him happy, too.

He'd been lost after Bianca's infidelity less than six months into their impulsive Vegas marriage. It had been ridiculously cliché and completely out of character, but when Bianca had said it would be nice for them to be bound to each other forever, it had called to the lonely place inside him.

They'd been together for almost a year at that point, and he'd considered proposing, but the time hadn't ever seemed right. Still, he'd rationalized that they'd have done it eventually, so he'd said yes and they'd walked down the aisle.

And in the end, not waiting, not planning, had cost him. He might not be able to remember his father clearly, but the image of his ex in bed with another man was certainly seared into his brain.

He'd stepped off the path he'd outlined and chaos had erupted. In less than a year, he'd gone from married doctor to the source of gossip, particularly when Bianca had announced her pregnancy less than three months after she'd left him.

Luckily, his mother had offered him a position at Oceanside. He'd spent a year there regrouping, and the memory of his father at Valley General, and how right everything had felt in that moment, had begun to consume him. He needed to make it a reality. *He did.*

Quinn kept her eyes closed, but he could see the twitch of her lips. She wanted to say something, probably wanted to run through the pros of letting his heart lead. But it was. It was leading him to Valley General.

It was ironic for a traveling nurse to seem so invested in him staying in one place, something he'd kidded her about a few times. She liked to say that it would be nice if one of them settled down.

Why couldn't it be her?

Ainsley and her husband, Leo, met Quinn and Milo at the door with forced smiles. "Who would have thought we'd be bringing a babe into the world as it burns?" the mom-to-be quipped nervously.

"Well, this isn't California's first drought. We'll be fine. I'm sure," Leo said, kissing Ainsley's head, his gaze not leaving the smoke that was much heavier than even Quinn thought it should be.

They'd checked as they'd driven, and the voluntary evacuation zone was less than fifteen miles north of Ainsley and Leo's neighborhood. Unless luck shifted for the firefighters, this area was going to be under voluntary evacuation orders eventually. Quinn hadn't known much luck in her life, but maybe today…

Ainsley gripped her belly with one hand and the doorknob with the other.

"Breathe," Milo offered as he stepped up beside Quinn.

"I…know." Ainsley's eyes were firmly shut as she forced the words out. When the contraction loosened, she met their gazes and stepped aside. "Sorry. Welcome to our home."

"It's not a problem." Quinn smiled as she gripped the

strap of her midwifery bag and stepped across the threshold. A birthing pool was ready in the center of the living room, and a pile of towels lay next to it. But it was the stack of boxes sitting next to the front door that caught Quinn's eye.

"I thought it might be good to put a few things together...if..." Leo's words were soft as he looked from Quinn to the boxes. "It's mostly baby stuff and paperwork. I've almost put them in the car a dozen times today. Every time I start, I think I'm tempting fate if I do, then worry that I'm tempting it by not. Crazy thoughts while my wife is giving birth, right?"

Quinn understood Leo's rambling logic. She offered the expectant father a smile. "I think you should go ahead and pack it." There was little that a partner could control during a birth. Quinn had seen more than one spouse spiral as they tried to find something to do to help.

And she couldn't push away the bubble of fear in her mind that wanted to scream at her for not doing the same. Her boxes may have turned to ash, but Leo and Ainsley's were still whole.

When Leo hesitated, Quinn added, "You can always take them out later. But if you don't do it, you're just going to keep worrying. And Ainsley will need all your focus soon."

Leo stared at the boxes for a moment longer before looking down the hallway to where Ainsley was pacing. Then his eyes moved to the center of the living room where Milo was pulling supplies from his medical bag. "You're right. Can't hurt."

Moving toward Milo, Quinn set her midwifery bag next to his. The supplies in one kit should be enough, but each practitioner carried their own bag when they went to home deliveries.

"Nice job. Having those boxes in the car will relax Leo a bit." Milo's voice was low as he checked the oxygen and syringes from his bag. Every person she'd worked with had an item or two that was always triple-checked. For Milo, it was oxygen and syringes. For her, it was the maternal and infant resuscitators—items she always prayed would stay packed. "You have a gift for finding the right words."

"Thanks." Quinn nodded. The tiny compliment was nice, but did little to fill the hollow in her stomach that just wanted to know if she still had boxes. If the few precious items she loved were intact.

"It'll be okay." Milo's voice was soft as he kept an eye focused on Ainsley as she paced the hallway.

"What if it isn't? What if everything is gone?" She wanted to kick herself, but there was no way to reel the words back in. Now was not the time or the place.

"Then we buy new things." Milo looked at the oxygen tank for the third time. "And make new memories together. Like helping bring a baby into the world while a fire rages on the doorstep."

Together. Such an easy word with so much meaning. How did he always manage to find the right words? A calmness pressed through her as she stared at him. Milo always put people at ease. It made him a wonderful friend and a great doctor. How many people would have thought to bring water and pain tablets to make the start of her day easier?

But it was more for her. Quinn knew that. Milo grounded her. He was her point of reference. The haven she knew she could come home to anytime, but also the one who would always cheer her on as she found her next adventure.

She wished there was an easy way to return the favor. She might not understand his connection to his father, but she could see how important it was to him. Yet she was terrified he wasn't living his life, not really.

How could he when he was so focused on a memory?

But maybe her desire to run from nearly everything about her past was what fogged her brain— Right now wasn't the time to focus on that. When her mind was more at ease, and less prone to jumping to inopportune thoughts about her best friend, Quinn would find a way to at least mention the cons of running a large unit like the one at Valley General.

He'd miss things like home deliveries and spending extra time with patients—and Quinn didn't think that would make Milo happy.

Was a memory enough to carry him through? Was it worth it?

"I'm going to go wash up and see how far along Ainsley is." Quinn tapped Milo's shoulder as she grabbed her box of gloves and headed for the kitchen. Her fingers tingled from the brief contact, but she ignored that feeling as Ainsley came to stand beside her.

"How far apart are the contractions?"

"About four minutes." Ainsley's face contorted a bit as she gripped the edge of the counter. "Nope, three and a half."

Quinn held out her arms and gestured for Ainsley to grip her forearms as she breathed through the contraction. "Three and a half minutes is good. Breathe. As soon as this one ends, let's see how far along you are. Then, if you want to get into the birthing pool, now would probably be a good time."

"Okay," Ainsley whispered as she released her grip on Quinn's forearms. She looked at the pool and let out a sigh as they walked toward her bedroom. "I planned to spend most of my labor there. But when it started, walking felt better. Leo spent so much time setting it up for me."

"Labor often throws plans out the window." Milo's grin was brilliant as he joined them in the hall.

Quinn shot him a quick look as she followed Ainsley into the bedroom. He was quite willing to grant everyone else the grace to change their plans. Shame he couldn't offer the same grace to himself.

"Dr. Russell is right. If you want to keep walking, that is fine. Leo will understand." Quinn kept her voice level as Ainsley slid onto the bed, which had been prepared with medical-grade covers and protective layers. Many mothers planned out their home births for months. And they became very attached to specific ideas that might have to be adjusted or just weren't what they wanted during labor. There was no shame in changing plans, though.

"I hope so." Ainsley lay back and gripped her belly as another labor pain started.

That one hadn't taken three minutes. "Milo!" Quinn called.

"This…one…is…bad!" Ainsley's face contorted.

She was likely moving into transition labor. There was going to be a little one here shortly.

Milo stepped to the door and took in the scene before him. "I'll get the bags."

As the contraction ended, Quinn checked Ainsley. "Nine centimeters. It won't be long now. I think we need to just stay here and not worry about the tub."

"Here…works." Ainsley shook her head as another contraction started. "Leo?"

Milo returned, dropping the bags next to the bed. "I'll go grab him."

Before Milo could leave, Leo stepped into the room with a police officer.

Quinn felt her heart drop. Milo caught her gaze and she saw fear in his eyes too, though he didn't adjust his position. If the officer was here, the winds must have shifted again. Luck really wasn't on their side, but Milo clearly wasn't going to panic.

"See, we can't leave." Leo's whisper wasn't low enough.

Milo's face paled, but he moved quickly. "I'll go get the stretcher and Kevin." Milo nodded to the officer as he darted from the room.

"No." Ainsley's lip quivered. "Please…"

"Sorry, ma'am." The officer nodded. "But the fire is moving faster than expected. This area is under mandatory evacuation and you need to leave. *Now!*" He tipped his head toward Leo. "I need to see to the rest of the neighborhood."

"Leo." Quinn kept her tone firm as she looked between Leo and Ainsley. "We are headed to Oceanside Clinic. Meet us there."

"I can't leave my wife." Leo's cheeks were red and tears coated his eyes.

"We do not have room for you in the van. Dr. Russell and I need to focus on your wife. Plus, you need to get those boxes to safety." Quinn was surprised her voice was so steady, but she was grateful.

Adrenaline was coursing through her. She'd been in several crisis situations—though never this close to home.

And never fire.

At least it was Milo here with her now. They worked seamlessly as a team, and this delivery was going to be difficult just because of the circumstances. If anyone could handle delivering a baby while on the run from a wildfire, it was Milo.

"I need you to go, so I can take care of your wife and baby." Quinn walked over to Leo but didn't touch him with her gloved hands. She needed to remain sterile. "Ainsley needs all our focus, and she needs to know that you are safe and will be there to meet her at Oceanside."

"Give me a kiss and then go!" Ainsley said, her voice strong despite the tears slipping across her cheeks.

Leo shuddered, but he walked to his wife and dropped a kiss on her forehead. "Race you south, sweetheart."

"I'm right behind you." Ainsley's hands were shaking.

Quinn knew she was trying to hide the contraction. If Leo knew how much pain she was in, how close their child was to this world, he'd never leave. She glanced at her watch—less than a minute since the last one. Transition labor was the shortest phase, and she wished Ainsley had spent just a bit more time in it.

Ainsley laid her head back as Leo left. "I have to push."

No! Quinn rechecked Ainsley, and fear skittered across her skin. They needed to move her. But Ainsley was right, the baby was crowning.

"We need to move." Milo's voice was controlled as he pulled the stretcher into the room. His nose was scrunched tight.

How close is the fire?

"She's crowning. How much time do we have?" Quinn asked, then looked back at Ainsley. "I need you to do your best not to push for me. Don't hold your breath," she added as crimson traveled across Ainsley's cheeks. "Pretend that you are blowing out a candle."

It was a trick Quinn had learned in Puerto Rico during a category four hurricane. They'd had to deliver patients in near darkness with the howling wind pulling at the roof. She'd used it a few times to slow quick labor since, though never in such dire circumstances. She didn't like having to use it during a crisis again.

"All the time we need." Milo smiled, but Quinn saw

his jaw clench as he maneuvered the stretcher closer. He was lying.

Dear God.

Her lungs heavy, Quinn forced herself to breathe evenly. They needed to get Ainsley, her baby and themselves to safety. "Okay."

Milo gripped Quinn's arm and looked at her gloved hands. Lowering his voice, he motioned to the stretcher. "I'm not gloved. If I move her, are you okay to handle delivery?"

"Of course," Quinn stated. "But we could stay until she delivers. It won't be…"

Milo's gaze softened, though he barely shook his head.

"Dear… God…" Ainsley muttered. "I need to push."

"Breathe for me until it passes." Quinn held her finger up, mimicking a candle, and breathed with her. Everyone needed to be calm for what was coming next. This trick worked around sixty percent of the time in Quinn's experience. The longer they waited…

As the contraction receded, Quinn let out a soft sigh. If they were going to move her, it had to be now. "Dr. Russell is going to get you onto the stretcher. Then you can push. I promise," Quinn reassured her. Ainsley nodded, but Quinn could see the fear dancing across her features. Her birth plan had just gone up in smoke, and the disaster that had seemed a bit distant was now on their doorstep.

"All right, Ainsley." Milo's voice was low and steady as he slipped an arm under her shoulders. "Wrap your arms around my neck—just like you see in the movies."

Ainsley let out a tight laugh and did as Milo instructed. "At least I'll have a story to tell this little one."

"She'll love hearing about it, I'm sure. At least until she's a teenager." Milo winked as he put his other arm under Ainsley's knees and lifted her quickly. He wasn't even breathing deeply.

Quinn had seen him work through difficult deliveries—always focused on his patient—but this delivery was one of a kind...she hoped. During her travels, she had witnessed more than one medical professional stumble when the world seemed intent on putting every obstacle in the way. But Milo was in complete control.

As he clicked the emergency belt into place, Ainsley let out another ragged breath and lifted her knees. "I can't stop—"

Quinn understood. Eventually, the body refused to delay the birthing process. At least she was on the stretcher. "Give me a push then. Just don't use all your force. We're saving that for the van."

"I wish... Leo...was here," Ainsley muttered.

"He'll meet us at the..." Quinn's voice dropped away as they stepped out the front door. The orange glow was just over the hill.

Dear God...

"The smoke..." Ainsley coughed as Milo raced them toward the van.

Wrenching the doors open, Milo lifted the stretcher and motioned for Quinn to get in. "Let's roll, Kevin!" Milo's voice cracked as the first bit of strain broke through his composure.

The doors slammed shut, and Quinn repositioned herself to be able to take care of Ainsley. The van started moving, and Quinn braced her feet against the doors the way they'd been trained to do in an emergency situation.

She'd been through a few instances where a home birth became critical and they'd had to transport the mother to the hospital. But the world hadn't been engulfed in flames then. Quinn took a deep breath as the world now dimmed to just her, Ainsley and Milo. She couldn't control anything about the fire.

The van's siren echoed through to the back, and Quinn met her patient's gaze. "Okay, Ainsley. Time to go to work."

In no time, Quinn was holding a beautiful, perfect and very angry baby girl. As her screams erupted in the van, Quinn smiled and laid the baby on Ainsley's chest. "Good job."

She finally let herself start to relax as Milo cleaned the baby as much as was possible given the circumstances. The baby was here and safe. Ainsley's delivery had been textbook—minus the evacuation.

Everything was fine...

As soon as that happy thought exited Quinn's mind, Kevin slammed on the breaks. Quinn lost her footing. She tried to grab herself, but the edge of the gurney connected with the side of her temple.

Pain erupted up her arms as her knees and palms connected with the floor of the van. "Oh!" Quinn blinked, trying to force the black dots dancing in her eyes away.

"Quinn!" Milo's fingers were warm and soft against her forehead as he reached for her. "Hell, Kevin!"

"Sorry!" Kevin shouted as he threw the van into Reverse. "A tree limb fell across the street. Hold on!"

"Is she all right?" Ainsley's voice was taut as the tires squealed again.

"She's going to be fine," Milo said with more certainty than he felt. The cut above Quinn's eye was bleeding, but her pupils were focused. He wasn't sure what the world outside looked like, but he *was* certain he didn't want to know given Kevin's muttered curses.

"Of course I am." Quinn's smile didn't quite reach her eyes, and Milo was stunned when she offered Ainsley a thumbs-up before grabbing gauze and pressing it against the wound. This was the woman who ran into crisis situations, who was comfortable—or at least didn't mind—small cots in areas damaged by natural disasters or ravaged by disease.

He'd seen her in action at St. Brigit's, but the true core of strength running through Quinn hadn't been visible until now. No wonder her nursing agency still sent her open positions, and the contacts she'd made while serving with Doctors Without Borders regularly called or texted her.

"How bad is it?" Quinn leaned forward, "Give it to me straight, Doctor." *And* she was trying to put him and Ainsley at ease, even as blood dripped from the bandage she was holding.

The side of his lip tipped up as he pushed a strand of her dark hair back. She was something else.

"The cut is going to need stitches, but it could have been worse." Milo swallowed as he grabbed another sterile pad and pressed it over the one that was against her forehead. If she'd fallen differently or if the van had hit the tree Kevin had swerved to miss…

Focus on the now!

Milo leaned back and sighed. "Well, this has been quite the day."

"Nothing preps you for running from a wildfire." Ainsley kissed the top of her baby's head and pushed a tear away.

"Nope." Quinn's voice was steady. "But I've served in several crisis zones, and it helps to focus on what you can control. And you did beautifully, Ainsley."

"My heart refuses to stop pounding." Ainsley let out a nervous chuckle. "You and Dr. Russell make this look easy."

"I am just following Quinn's lead. This is, fortunately,

my first time running from a crisis." Milo offered a playful salute, hoping he came off as collected as Quinn.

"But he's fantastic in all situations. There were multiple times when I was with Doctors Without Borders when I wished Milo had been there to help stabilize a tense situation." Quinn grinned as she pressed another gauze pad to her forehead. "And apparently head injuries make me talkative. So, Momma, what's her name?"

Milo tried to focus on the conversation floating between the women as the van raced south, but he kept coming back to Quinn's words. Had she really wished for him to be with her while she'd been working with the humanitarian medical group?

Or was she just trying to project calm in this rapidly changing situation? And why did the idea of serving in such a manner send a thrill through him?

Milo sucked in a breath and ignored the subtle glance Quinn gave him. They needed to get Ainsley checked in at Oceanside, and then to figure out their next steps. And those steps involved getting back to LA, with the fire blocking multiple routes, not addressing the unwelcome desire to follow up with Quinn on her statement.

CHAPTER THREE

"It's a good thing you kept your town house in Oceanside," Quinn said, leaning against Milo's shoulder as he put the key in the lock. They smelled of smoke, and it had taken them nearly twice as long as it should have to reach Oceanside. Then Milo had insisted that she let him check the cut on her forehead after they'd gotten Ainsley and her daughter checked into the Clinic and said a brief hello to Milo's stepdad, Felix.

Now she had six stitches above her eye, and she couldn't remember the last time she'd been this exhausted. She'd been in tense situations multiple times during her career, though, so Quinn knew from experience that her brain was too wired to let her drift into oblivion.

Her stomach growled—another function the body forgot about during stress.

When had they last eaten?

"Tell me you have food in the fridge!"

"Nope." Milo swung the door open. "It's fully furnished, since I rent it out most weekends as a vacation spot. But the rent doesn't include food. Luckily, it's not due to be occupied for the rest of the month. Wildfire concern caused my last two renters to back out."

Her stomach roiled with emptiness, but she ignored it.

Focusing on her hunger wouldn't make food magically appear. "At least I can get a hot shower," Quinn sighed.

"And our Thai food should be here by the time you're done. I ordered it while you were saying hi to Felix."

"You are the best!" Quinn wrapped her arms around his neck without thinking. Today had been hell, even though it had ended well on all fronts. She didn't care that they were both starving and in desperate need of showers. She just wanted to hold him, to remind herself that they were fine. Her body molded to his as Milo's strong arms pulled her closer.

Her day's fears melted as he held her. This was where she wanted to be *so badly*. Her fingers itched to run through his short hair. To trace her lips along the edge of his jaw and see what happened. Sparks flew across her back as his fingers tightened on her waist.

If she held him any longer… Quinn swallowed. This embrace had already gone on for too long. She needed to stop this before Milo started to think she was crazy.

Her cheeks were warm as she pulled away. "I promise not to steal all the hot water."

"Wait." Milo grabbed her hand.

Her body vibrated with need as Milo ran his fingers along the bandage on her forehead. His touch burned as she stared at his lips.

So close, and yet so far away.

."The bandage I put on seems watertight." Milo's husky tone raced around her.

"Since you put it on less than an hour ago, I would hope so."

Was he looking for reasons to touch her?

"Yes, but it's important the wound doesn't get wet." His words were so matter-of-fact.

Of course they were.

He was a good physician and her oldest friend.

But just for a moment, she'd thought he might need to touch her, need to be near her, to hold her, too.

"I should clean up." Her throat was dry as she pulled away, but Milo didn't stop her again.

When humans were stressed or escaped catastrophe, they often sought comfort in the arms of another. A reminder that they'd lived to fight another day. She'd seen it happen when she was serving in areas that had been hit by earthquakes and floods. It was standard. But Quinn had never felt the urge to seek out that comfort—until tonight.

Until Milo…

Milo cleared his throat as he started to follow her. "There should still be some of Bianca's old clothes in the back closet. They got left behind when we separated, and she never picked them up. I'll see if I can find something you can wear."

Bianca… That name sent a cold splash down Quinn's spine. Quinn had never gotten along with the woman. She'd tried, but Bianca always seemed cold to her—unwelcoming. But she'd been Milo's choice, so Quinn had kept her mouth shut.

When he'd called to tell her that they had gotten married in Vegas, she'd cried for almost a week. For a man who planned everything, she'd been stunned that Milo had run off with Bianca for the weekend—even if they were overdue for a vacation after their residencies—and to get married on a whim?

Quinn had also been hurt that he hadn't at least told her beforehand. She'd have video-called to support him. Even if she'd thought Bianca hadn't been worthy.

She'd been right about that and hated the small part of her that had been happy when Milo had told her it was over. He'd been hurt—and happy shouldn't have been an emotion she'd felt. But maybe a small part of her had wanted him even then. Quinn was certainly not going to examine that thought tonight.

Milo was the best part of her life. He had deep roots in this state, and he deserved someone who would walk beside him as he followed his plans.

Someone who supported him.

And Bianca had not been Milo's match even before she'd cheated on him.

Quinn's throat closed at the realization that she wasn't his match, either. Her parents had ensured she'd known exactly where her faults lay. Too flighty. Too needy. Impulsive. She led with her heart. She'd always support Milo's dreams, but checking off items on a list, trying to control everything? That wasn't something Quinn could do.

She should be happy just being best friends with Milo. Her heart skipped around him, but she could put it back in its place. Maybe returning to California had been a mistake. But she'd felt called here. Like she needed to come home—at least for a little while.

It was a feeling she still couldn't explain, but Quinn had always chosen new locations and jobs by what felt right. And working with Milo had felt right—still felt right.

So why was it so hard?

Turning on the shower, Quinn quickly stripped off her scrubs and tried to push away the thoughts of the man just outside the door.

How does Milo kiss?

She shivered despite the heat of the water.

"Quinn?" Milo's voice raced across her and goose pimples rose on her skin. "Can I put the clothes on the counter?"

"Yes." Her tongue felt thick, but she forced the word out.

"Quinn?" Milo's voice echoed in the small bathroom, and Quinn held her breath. What was he going to say?

Part of her brain screamed to be bold. To stick her head around the curtain and suggest they conserve water. But that was just the craziness of the day talking.

Quinn had never been bold in her relationships. She always looked for the reasons why they would fail. Even when James had proposed, she'd wondered when her world would upend…though she'd expected it would be longer than three weeks.

Her guard had been up ever since.

No matter how often she told her brain to stop, it always tried to identify any signs that a partner was getting ready to leave her.

When would they throw her out of their life?

If her parents could discard her so easily, then anyone could.

She'd become an expert in identifying the subtle shifts in people. Noticed the moment the nurse she'd met in Puerto Rico discussed moving and asked her opinion as an afterthought. Her brain had tweaked the first time the oil manager she'd dated in Alaska canceled a date and mentioned his full schedule. So Quinn had ended the relationships. Better to leave first.

If you left first, the hurt wasn't as deep. Her family had drilled that lesson into her. But that did not lend itself to sultry risk-taking.

When he didn't say anything, Quinn worked up her courage. "Still out there?"

"Food is here." Milo's husky voice drifted over the curtain, an emotion she couldn't place deep within it.

Quinn wondered if he'd wanted to say something else.

Get it together!

"Remember, you promised not to use all the hot water," Milo joked.

"Well, I'd be done faster if you'd take your leave." She heard him chuckle and forced her shoulders to relax. They were both exhausted from the day, burning through the last reserves of their adrenaline. After they'd showered and had food, their bodies would sleep for the next ten hours.

Focus. Stop letting adrenaline control your hormones.

She raced through the rest of her shower and quickly dried off. Pulling on the shorts he'd left on the counter, Quinn's heart raced as she held up the green tank top. It had a built-in shelf bra, which meant that she wouldn't have to put on her smoke-scented bra, but it was a much lower cut than she usually wore.

It would have looked great on Bianca. She'd had full breasts and a curvy frame. On Quinn's athletic figure, it was much more likely to highlight her lack of assets. She sighed as she pulled it on.

Then she began to remove the bandage on her forehead. Stitches needed to be kept dry and uncovered for the first forty-eight hours, but she'd needed to shower to wash away the day's grime and smoky residue.

Between the dark circles under her eyes, the wet hair, the borrowed clothes and the cut, Quinn looked less than desirable.

Which was fine.

But she also felt downright pathetic. Were the borrowed outfit and the smoky scrubs the only things she had to her name?

"I'm going to eat all the pad thai if you keep hogging the bathroom!" Milo called out.

The ghost of a smile pulled at her lips. She'd told Milo that she'd had nothing when her parents had disowned her following her admittance to UCLA's school of nursing. He'd put his hand in her hand and said, "Nope. You have me."

"You better not!" Whatever tomorrow brought, she could handle it. As long as she had her friend by her side.

Milo's gaze fell on her as she stepped up to the kitchen counter. Heat tore across Quinn's skin, but she refused to acknowledge it. "I will not apologize for eating all the food if you're just going to stare at me. I know I look like I need a belly full of food, followed by ten hours of sleep."

"You always look perfect." Milo grinned. "Or at least presentable."

Presentable... That was a word.

"Well, hop into that shower so we can dig in." Picking up one of the boxes, she nodded in the direction of the bathroom.

Why was he just standing there? Did she look that bad?

"Go shower, Milo. I promise there will be enough here for you to have dinner."

"I'm counting on you to share." He paused right in front of her.

His face was so close. What would he do if she lifted her head and kissed him? Just as Quinn started to follow through, Milo stepped back.

"I plan on taking the quickest shower ever!" Milo raced down the small hallway.

Quinn let out a breath as she stared at his retreating form. His smoky scent still clung to her senses. Grabbing plates from the cabinet, she began to set their dinner out. Anything to try to keep her mind from wandering to thoughts of how he might kiss.

The shower shut off in record time, and Quinn jumped. She could do this. It was just Milo. Except there was nothing *just* about Milo. At least, not anymore.

* * *

Presentable. He'd called her presentable!

What the hell, Milo?

Perfect, wonderful, sexy—all of those were descriptions for Quinn. *Never* presentable.

He wanted—needed—to get back to her. Today had been an emotional roller coaster. When he'd watched her fall, his heart had stopped. It had only been a minor cut, but his need to hold her, no matter how unprofessional, had been overwhelming. He'd barely managed to keep it together.

He needed a plan. Plans gave him peace, a sense of order—control. He could follow a plan. Quinn was at St. Brigit's for at least another few months. Maybe she'd stay if he asked her to. Was that what he wanted?

Yes!

True, she loved being a traveling nurse and working around the world. But life was here. Could he ask her to give that up? *Sure.* But should he? Maybe not. Yet suddenly he wasn't sure that he cared.

As that selfish thought rolled through him, Milo promised himself he'd find a way to broach the topic. Not tonight. Their day had been too hectic. Their emotions were still packed too tightly with adrenaline and fear to really know what they wanted. And even if he did know, Milo needed to sort out the best way to approach all of this.

Coward! his brain shouted as he toweled his short hair dry. His heart knew what he wanted.

But Quinn always left. She chased adventure and never stayed in one place for too long. What if they started dating and a new job—a better job—materialized half a world away?

Could he handle losing her?

He shivered as the silence of the town house registered.

They were all alone. That wasn't new—yet the lack of distractions felt dangerous. His stomach skittered.

It was just him and Quinn. His tongue was tied around her, and his body wanted to act. When she'd walked out in that low-cut green tank top, Milo had ached to pull her to him. His fingers had pulsed with the need to run along her sides. He'd had to grip the side of the kitchen counter just to keep from rushing toward her.

How could he address these racing thoughts with Quinn?

No immediate answer came to Milo as he dropped a shirt over his head. He would think better after dinner and some sleep. Maybe tomorrow? No. He wouldn't rush this. It was Quinn. So the plan—if he used it—had to be perfect.

"Did you eat it all?" Milo picked up an empty container on the counter. Then he froze. The table was set and Quinn was pouring wine. The shorts he'd grabbed for her hugged her derriere and highlighted her long, slim legs. His mouth watered as he imagined trailing kisses up her thighs. "I figured we'd just eat out of the paper cartons."

Quinn's dark eyes met his and her lips pulled up into a smile. "We spent the day outrunning a fire while helping a new baby into the world. I think that calls for actual plates and a glass of wine. You'll have to get another bottle for your next renters."

"It's fine." Milo walked to the table. His property manager always dropped off a bottle of red for the occupants. Milo would let him know that they needed another. It was the least of his concerns as Quinn's knee knocked against his.

Her shoulder-length hair was damp, and she was wearing borrowed clothes, but she was perfection. Her high cheekbones had a few freckles that his thumb ached to trace. How could he ask her if she'd ever thought of chang-

ing their relationship? If her heart had yearned like his for
something more?

They ate in silence. The tension made Milo ache. Or
maybe he was imagining it. After all, they hadn't eaten
anything other than a few granola bars since their croissants this morning.

Once her plate was empty, Quinn leaned her elbows
on the table, propped her head in her palms, and stared at
him. "We have a problem, you know."

Milo smiled. "We do?" Her full lips were calling to him.
If she brought up the emotions charging the air around
them, would it save him from having to find the right path
to address their relationship? No. Thinking it through still
held more appeal. Rushing only messed things up.

How many times did he have to prove that?

"Dishes!" She winked and pushed back from the table.

"Dishes?" Milo's head spun. "Dishes?" He hadn't meant
to repeat the question, but his brain was incapable of finding any other response. He was thinking of kissing her,
of changing everything, and Quinn was thinking about
dishes?

Could he have misread the situation more?

Quinn leaned over and pecked his cheek. It was an innocent action. One she'd done hundreds of times over the
years. "Yes." Her gaze held his as she gathered the plates
and rose. "If we'd just eaten from the cartons, the cleanup
would be so much easier."

"But the dinner would have been less satisfying," Milo
murmured, standing, as well.

Like that peck?

It wasn't what he wanted. What he craved.

"Exactly!" Quinn's smile sent a thrill through him. "I've
eaten off disposable plates in so many places. You don't realize what a luxury such simple things are until they aren't

an option." She yawned, raising the plates over her head as she tried to cover the motion with her arm.

Milo took the dishes from her hands and laid them in the sink. "We've had a long day. I think they can wait until tomorrow."

She leaned against the counter, millimeters from him. "Today was certainly something."

Pushing the hair away from her left cheek, Milo nodded at her stitches. "And you got a permanent souvenir."

"A minor flaw. At least I'm presentable."

"No." Milo shook his head. "You are gorgeous." Without thinking, he let his fingers brush the softness of her cheek. Her skin was cool, but his fingers burned as he—finally—traced the line of freckles on her jaw. "Breathtaking. Smart. Courageous." *Sexy.* He barely caught that word. Over the years, he'd tried to combat the negativity he'd heard Quinn voice when she'd talked about herself. If only she could see what he saw. But tonight, so much more rested on his compliments.

Before his brain could comprehend what was happening, Quinn's lips connected with his.

Milo's arms wrapped around her waist and he pulled her to him. He didn't want any distance between them. Her fingers slid up his neck, ran through his hair, and Milo felt the world shift.

This was right. Quinn in his arms, her lips pressing against his. It made all reason leak from his brain.

Her mouth opened and a whole new level of sensations pulsed through him. She tasted of wine, Thai food and perfection.

His Quinn.

Wrapping a hand in her hair, Milo deepened the kiss. loving the small moans escaping her lips. He'd wondered how she kissed for months. Years…

Quinn...

Need pulled at him.

She pulled back a bit, her lips swollen. Her eyes were hooded with desire as she ran a finger down his jaw. "What are we doing?"

He couldn't read the expression floating through her eyes, and the first trace of doubt ripped down his back. What if she was just reacting on the adrenaline from today?

"I don't know. Maybe making a mistake." Those were the wrong words. *Again.* He'd wanted this for so long, but her kiss had been so unexpected, so unplanned. He needed a plan—needed to know that she wanted more than just one night.

He knew Quinn didn't move from partner to partner. But he also knew she never stayed in one place too long, and he was tied to California. The day had been crazy. What if…

"I—" Quinn stepped out of his arms. "Right." She shook her head. "Long day."

His arms felt heavy without her.

Why couldn't he say the right things?

"Quinn." Milo started toward her, but she put the counter between them.

"I'm going to…" Quinn looked to the back rooms. "Bed. Yep. I am going to bed. It was such a long day. I'm not acting like myself. Sorry."

Quinn rushed off before Milo could find a way to fix the mess his overthinking brain had caused. "Quinn." But she'd already fled down the hallway and closed the bedroom door.

"Dammit!" Milo gripped the counter, his brain too wired, too focused on Quinn, to let him sleep. Grabbing the wine bottle, he poured the last bit into his glass and stared at her closed door. Tomorrow... They'd sort all of this out tomorrow. At least he had a few hours to figure out a plan.

Quinn pushed a tear away from her cheek as she stared at the shadows cast by the rising sun along the beach. She'd left Milo's town house quietly, wishing there was some way she could make it home on her own. But her vehicle was back at St. Brigit's, almost two hours away.

How could she have been so stupid? It must have been the long day. And Milo telling her she was gorgeous. Leaning close...touching her cheek...

His compliments and touch had flooded her system. Flowed into the cracks her parents' harsh words and James's betrayal had worn on her soul. For just a moment, she'd believed Milo had been thinking the same thing she had been.

Quinn never let her guard down. She kept her shields up with everyone.

Everyone but Milo.

She could still feel the brush of his fingers along her cheek if she closed her eyes. *Gorgeous.* Had anyone ever called her that?

The emotion and desires that had raced through her since she'd landed in LA had propelled her forward with just a few compliments. Milo had always seen the best in her, looked past the flaws her mother and ex-fiancé had constantly pointed out. She was being needy, and she'd misread Milo's concern after a long day.

She wasn't bold with her partners. So Milo's rejection was the first she'd experienced—at least, before anything had actually happened. That was the only reason it burned so deeply.

She scoffed as the lie tripped through her brain. The

truth was that it hurt because it was Milo. Because no matter what she tried to believe, Quinn wanted more.

And she hadn't even been able to seek refuge in her bungalow. Couldn't pretend to be busy for a few days while she licked her battered emotional wounds. Instead, she'd lain in bed knowing he was on the other side of the wall. So close and yet so far away.

Quinn hugged her knees as she buried her toes in the sand and stared at the ocean waves. She hadn't managed much sleep, but at least she'd worked out a plan to address last night's indiscretion. It would be easier if Milo didn't bring it up. She'd dated several men who would have let it go, but that was not Milo.

Milo planned everything. He'd want to talk about what had happened—make sure that she was all right. And he was going to apologize.

Shame tore across her. That was the part Quinn feared most. The "I'm sorry I don't feel the same. You're my best friend." She could hear the entire speech already, and the last thing she wanted was pity from Milo.

"You know, I tore through the place, afraid you'd started walking back to LA without telling me."

She started before offering a smile that Quinn prayed looked real in the early light. "How often do you get to watch the sunrise at the beach?" She gestured to the incoming waves as she accepted the travel mug of coffee he held out to her.

"You could have left a note." His voice was gruff as he slid down onto the sand beside her. He was grumpy this morning.

Not that she could blame him.

"A note? To walk four hundred feet from your front door to the beach?" She hit his shoulder with hers. If her plan was going to work, she needed to act as naturally as possible. "Really, Milo. I've come down here early before. Nothing has changed."

She said the final words and took a deep sip of her coffee, refusing to let her gaze leave the waves. He'd been her friend for decades and knew her better than anyone. If she looked at him, he might see the hurt pooling in her soul, and she couldn't let that happen.

"Nothing?" Milo's voice was soft. "We kissed last night."

"Actually, I kissed you." It hurt to say the words, but she kept her tone bright. For a minute last night, he'd responded to her. For that brief flicker, everything in her world had seemed right.

Quinn shook her head. She couldn't think of this now, not while sitting beside him. Not if her plan was to work. "I guess racing through a wildfire made me lose my head, huh? Flighty Quinn!"

"I hate it when you call yourself that." Milo's voice was ragged.

He'd loathed her family's nickname and despised the fact that she'd adopted the moniker. But that didn't make it untrue. Quinn never stayed in one place too long. She made decisions based on a feeling in her gut, not rational thought. If a job felt right or didn't, she acted.

Even if everyone said it was a bad move.

She flew from relationships before she could get hurt, too.

That made it impossible to settle down and start a family.

Why wouldn't that chirp in her brain shut up? Quinn didn't have the close family she saw so many of her patients were blessed with. She'd never felt truly part of one, so she shouldn't miss it.

But she did.

And that was an ache that Milo's presence soothed.

But he'd pulled away from her last night. She wasn't sure that pain would ever vanish, but she couldn't lose Milo. He was the closest thing she had to family. She couldn't—wouldn't—risk that because her heart wanted something more. "At least now when people joke that they can't believe we've never kissed, we can say, 'Oh, we did once. We're just better as…friends.'"

She'd practiced that line before the sun rose this morning. Even with all that rehearsal, her voice still shook a bit.

"Better as friends," Milo murmured.

"Do you think I'm wrong?" She did look at him then. Wished he'd contradict her. But Milo just stared at the incoming waves.

He hadn't shaved. The morning stubble along his jawline gave him a rugged look that made Quinn's stomach clench. Why did she have to be so attracted to him?

"You're all control and I'm all heart. You're planted here and I have rented furniture. We're opposites—perfectly balanced, but opposites." She kept waiting, hoping he'd interrupt her. He didn't. "I love St. Brigit's, but eventually…" She shrugged as she watched the waves crash against the beach.

"You do love finding new places." His head rested against hers as the sun cast its brilliant rays across the water.

You could ask me to stay…

She kept that desire buried deep inside. No one had ever asked Quinn to stay. Her family hadn't cared when she'd left for college and never come home. The men she'd dated had hardly batted their eyes when she'd taken a new position and packed up her things. Even James had barely blinked when she'd handed back his ring, no pleas for forgiveness or claims that he still wanted her. No one ever seemed to want her to stay.

"You have a world of adventures left," Milo said with a sigh as he straightened. Then he smiled and threw an arm around her shoulders. "And my life is in LA."

Quinn wanted to yank his arm away from her. Maybe that would stop the longing flowing through her. But he'd always touched her like that. In small ways that didn't mean much, even if she now wished they did. Leaning her head on his shoulder, Quinn sighed. She'd always planned to leave LA.

Hadn't she?

She'd rented her furniture but signed a two-year lease. The contradiction hadn't bothered her at the time. But leaving when her contract was up didn't feel like seeking adventure. Now it felt like running.

Maybe distance was what she needed, even if it was the last thing she wanted. If she stayed, she'd eventually make the same mistake she'd made last night. Let her feelings get too close to the surface and kiss him. She couldn't stand the thought of Milo pulling away again. That might just destroy her. For now, she would soak up as many of these moments as she could get. Maybe they'd be enough to last a lifetime.

Milo hadn't known the heart was capable of breaking before you actually dated someone. But as they walked the short distance back to his town house, that was the only description for the aching hole deep in his body. Quinn's actions had been impulsive. Brought on by yesterday's extremes.

He blew out a breath. How was he supposed to pretend that her touch hadn't electrified his soul? By remembering that this was just another stop for Quinn on her adventures and he was just lucky to be part of it. The reminder did little to quench the pull of need racing through him.

As they reached his door, Milo inhaled. The scent of the ocean gripped him. California was home. He'd never be the man who could pick up a phone and say yes to a job halfway around the world. He needed plans, schedules, five-year goals.

And he had those. All anchored in LA. He should focus on them. But right now, it was only Quinn that his brain wished to think of.

Quinn's ability to jump to a new adventure, to explore the next big thing, impressed him, even if he didn't understand it. But the realization that she would pack her bags again—maybe not today, or even this year, but someday—ripped him up.

He'd thrown his arm around her this morning because he'd wanted to touch her. To sit beside her for a few more minutes. As if his touch could anchor her. And because he was terrified she'd run from him after telling him that their kiss had been impulsive. When she'd leaned her head against his shoulder, it had taken every bit of his willpower not to kiss the top of it.

Her phone was ringing as he opened the door and she raced for it. Good, he needed a distraction.

"Hello?"

Milo walked over and poured himself another cup of coffee. He wasn't sure there was enough caffeine in the world to get him through the rest of the day. But he had to act unaffected by their morning chat. Otherwise, she might pick up and leave sooner—and Milo needed more time with her.

"Really?"

A smile tore across Quinn's face and Milo grinned despite himself. A happy Quinn thrilled him. No matter what happened between them, he wanted her to smile like that all the time. She clicked off the phone, and he raised an eyebrow.

"That was Martina. They're advising patients outside the LA city limits to seek care at our community partners, so they don't have to find a way around the evacuation zones—just to be safe. That means, until the all-clear comes through, all patients south of the city are advised to go to—"

Milo gripped the coffee cup, trying to ignore the twist in his gut. "Oceanside Clinic."

"Yep!"

"You seem surprisingly excited about this." He wanted to kick himself as Quinn's lips turned down.

Why was his brain refusing to find the right words?

"Sorry, Quinn. I didn't mean to make it sound like you were happy about any of this." Milo turned and started fixing another pot of coffee. At least his property manager stocked the cabinet with coffee and tea for the tenants. Otherwise, Milo would have been even more prickly this morning.

"You're right. It is a terrible time. But I've never gotten to work with your mom and Felix, assuming they want a few extra hands. Martina says we should exercise extreme caution in returning."

"I am certain my parents would love to have you help out."

And me, too.

His mother had tried repeatedly to get him to spend more time at the birthing center he'd helped design. She didn't understand his need to follow his father's dream, no matter how many times he'd discussed it.

It had led to a few tense arguments when she'd pointed out how happy the Oceanside Clinic made him. She was right. Milo enjoyed being there. But the closer he got to Felix, his mother's husband, the further his father slipped away. He was desperate to recapture the feelings he'd had so long ago.

Oceanside made him happy, but it would never bring him the same feeling he'd had with his father. He wasn't willing to give up that dream.

He couldn't.

"Are they as easy to work with as you?" Quinn's eyes were bright as she sidled up beside him and inhaled the scent of the brewing coffee.

"Easier," Milo remarked. It was the truth. His mother and Felix were the best physicians he'd ever worked with. The year he'd spent in their clinic following his divorce had been the happiest of his career—until Quinn had arrived at St. Brigit's.

Quinn's hip bumped his, and his body sang with the brief connection. "I'm not sure anyone is easier to work with than you. Any chance your mom might have scrubs I can borrow? She is almost as tall as me." Quinn folded her arms. "And we need transportation."

"Let me get another cup of coffee in me, Quinn. Then my mind will work a bit better. The sun's barely been up for more than an hour, in case you've forgotten."

"Nope," Quinn sighed. "I haven't forgotten." There was such a weariness to her statement.

Was she not as okay as she was pretending to be?

They'd always seemed to know what the other was thinking. But he couldn't stop second-guessing himself. Then she grinned, and Milo pushed the bead of hope from his mind. She was just Quinn. His perfect, fly-by-the-seat-of-her pants, explore-every-new-option, best friend, Quinn. And somehow that had to be enough.

CHAPTER FOUR

HIS PARENTS' CARS were already in the staff parking lot when Milo and Quinn's Uber driver dropped them at the back door. Quinn had traded the low cut tank top from last night for one of the T-shirts he stashed at the town house for the few times he came down to surf.

His gray T-shirt was too big for Quinn. But she'd tied the corner of it, so it hugged her waist. It was a simple look, and it made his mouth water.

He needed to get control of himself. He'd lain in bed all night, aware that she was only a wall away, desperately trying to will his mind to do anything other than relive that kiss and his overthinking, disastrous words.

Or fantasize about what could have come next.

"Quinn!" His mother raced for them and wrapped her arms around Quinn. They'd always been close, and he knew that Quinn had come to Oceanside several times since she'd moved to LA. They'd even come together— though not to the clinic.

When his mom stepped away from Quinn, she hugged him. "It is so good to see you—here, too." Her breath was warm on his chin as she kissed his cheek. "This is..." She paused, her lip wavering slightly. "Nice."

It wasn't what she'd meant to say. And Milo didn't have any problem hearing *This is where you belong.* It wasn't.

But for the next few days or so, some of St. Brigit's patients were likely to show up at Oceanside.

"It's good to see you too, Mom." Milo threw an arm around her shoulder and squeezed it firmly before following her inside. "I fear we do not have anything other than us and our midwifery bags."

"Felix and I have scrubs for both of you. He drove his car today, so you can take mine back to LA."

"We can't—" Milo started.

"Are you planning to make Quinn walk back to LA, then?" His mother laughed as Quinn smiled.

"I... I hadn't figured that out yet." The phrase felt weird.

His mother's eyes widened. "You didn't spend all night working out the details?" She playfully put the back of her hand against his forehead. "You don't *feel* feverish."

Milo's gaze flitted to Quinn before he shook his head. "Nope. Yesterday was a bit of a beast. You may not have heard, but we outran a wildfire." His voice didn't sound as relaxed as he'd hoped. "I fell asleep as soon as I laid my head on the pillow."

Quinn's eyes flashed as the lie slipped from his tongue.

Rubbing his arms, Milo looked past his mother and Quinn. There was no way he was going to mention he'd spent the night replaying Quinn's kiss. That his brain had been incapable of focusing on anything substantive since their early-morning beach conversation.

"Well, lucky for you, I do have a plan." His mother wrapped an arm around Quinn. "Ladies' changing room is this way."

"You okay?"

Felix's deep voice made Milo jump. "You startled me!"

The lines deepened on Felix's brow. "Are you okay?" he repeated.

There wasn't much that got past Felix Ireman. He'd married Milo's mother not that long ago, and Milo and his sister, Gina, had been thrilled to welcome the man into their small family. But Milo wasn't going to talk to Felix about his roaring emotions for Quinn.

Substituting another concern, he shrugged. "I'm worried about my patients. Some of the staff will probably go to Bloom Birthing Center to help our patients that live north of the city, but it's a stressful time for everyone."

Felix nodded, though Milo suspected he didn't quite believe him. Luckily, Felix wasn't one to pry. "Well, we're glad you're here. Did your mother mention that Dr. Acton's husband was transferred last month, and they're away on a house hunting expedition in Ohio? She'll be hard to replace."

The statement hit Milo in the chest. "I'm sure you'll find the right person," he said, turning to find his own set of scrubs before Felix could raise the subject of Milo returning to Oceanside.

Quinn and Milo had been assigned to the birthing center and Sherrie had joined them from St. Brigit's. At least Milo's parents' clinic was well equipped to handle the influx of patients.

Soothing music played in the hallways. The walls were painted a light gray, but Gina, Milo's sister, had ensured the effect was calming, not sterile. Having an interior designer in the family had clearly come in handy when Milo had developed the plans for the birthing center.

Quinn could still remember his excitement as he'd laid out the basic plan when they were undergrads. He'd even asked Quinn to sketch a few of the ideas for him, even though her drawing skills favored landscapes.

The architects had adjusted the design, but the basics of what Milo had imagined were all here. She'd been in

Hawaii when they'd broken ground on the facility, and on the island of Tonga when they'd held the ribbon-cutting ceremony, so she'd only seen it in pictures.

It was perfect. A calmness settled through her that was so at odds with the craziness of the last day. This place was lovely. A truly great accomplishment. And yet, Milo hadn't stayed long enough to see the ribbon-cutting two years ago. Quinn shook her head.

"Something wrong?" Milo's voice was soft as he stepped beside her. What was it about places where babies were born that made everyone, even the midwives and doctors who routinely saw births, lower their voices?

Yes, her heart screamed. So many things were wrong. He didn't want her. He wasn't working in the center that he'd helped design. And she felt like this was home.

All those things bothered her, but that final piece struck her harder than she'd expected. She'd worked many places. And enjoyed something about all of them. But she'd never walked into a birthing center, hospital or field hospital, and felt a sense of peace. A sense of rightness.

Like this was where she was meant to be.

It was ridiculous, of course. This was Milo's place, even if he didn't work here.

Yet…

He'd do well at a large facility, maybe even run Valley General's OB unit for a few years, but this was the place he'd come home to eventually. She knew it deep in her soul.

She belonged here, too. But she didn't know what that meant for their friendship after last night. *If anything.* But she couldn't push the feeling from her heart.

"Just marveling at your work." Quinn sighed as she looked at him. Her arms ached to reach out to him. To smooth the creases from his forehead. At least at work she could focus on keeping a professional distance.

"It's more my mother's work and my sister's interior decorating. I think it could use a splash of color. Maybe not bright yellow, but…" Milo's words ran out.

He rubbed the back of his neck before smiling. He was trying to be normal, too. Maybe in a day or two, it wouldn't feel so awkward between them—though she knew that was just wishful thinking. Nothing would ever be the same.

At least not for her.

"No picking on my kitchen." Her throat seized. What if her kitchen was gone? "That color makes me happy."

Straightening her shoulders, she forced the subject back to the Oceanside Clinic. "But this is your accomplishment, Milo. It wouldn't be here without you."

Milo's lips turned up as he looked around. "It is nice."

Nice? Was that the word he associated with it? This place was wonderful. A birthing center that gave mothers more choices in their delivery options, run by OBs, with a surgical suite tucked out of sight in case of emergency deliveries. Already a few hospital administrators from California, Ohio and Texas had visited to see if they could mimic Oceanside's successes. *Nice* didn't begin to cover this achievement.

The buzzer at the front of the building rang out and she was grateful for the interruption. "Incoming." Quinn smiled. She loved deliveries. New life was the best part of her job. And it was the perfect distraction.

A woman wearing a floral-print dress walked in holding the arm of a tall man who was clearly more distressed than his partner. "Hello." The woman smiled and gasped in a breath as she started to work through a contraction.

"We're having a baby!" her partner nearly shouted.

Quinn smiled. "Are you sure?" She walked over to the woman and playfully looked at her belly.

"I think so." The woman let out a giggle and tapped her

partner's side. "You have to let go of me for a few minutes, sweetheart." She rose on her tiptoes and kissed his cheek.

He laid his hands over her belly, and Quinn's heart leaped at the simple motion.

This was what her life was missing. Family.

Her friendship with Milo was nice—better than nice when things weren't so tense between them—but it wasn't the sense of belonging she experienced with her patients. Wasn't what her soul yearned for.

Pushing the feeling away, she gestured for the mother to follow her while her partner checked them in. The young woman looked back at him, and Quinn squeezed her hand. "Dr. Russell will settle him down. I promise."

Milo was already talking to the father while the admitting nurse kept passing him electronic forms to sign. By the time the father was ready to join them in a few minutes, Milo would have soothed all his worries.

If only Quinn could soothe away her feelings that way, too.

"You're not Dr. Russell or Dr. Acton." The man looked around him. Milo could see the happiness and hope bubbling through him. All new parents seemed to wear that expression. But there was a layer of fear beneath the surface, too. Many first-time parents were fearful, but anxiety poured from this man as he bounced on his heel and kept his gaze on the hallway where his partner had disappeared.

"Actually, I am a Dr. Russell. Dr. Milo Russell. I'm an OB, like my mother. I'm filling in for Dr. Acton while she is out today. And you are?"

"Trey Kenns."

The man bit his lip as he stared at Milo. Keeping his voice low, Milo leaned closer. "Trey, your wife will be fine."

"Fiancée." The man's fingers trembled as he electronically signed another document. "We…we…" He sighed loudly. "None of this was planned. But it's amazing."

Milo blinked. He'd attended more than one birth where the partner didn't seem as thrilled about the birth as he'd thought they should be. But this man was clearly excited… and terrified. "What wasn't supposed to happen?"

"Carla and I were best friends. *Are* best friends." He looked toward the hallway where his fiancée had disappeared. "Took me months to convince her that we should be…" He pushed his hair back. "Sorry, I ramble when I'm nervous. I never planned to have children. If I lose her…"

Recognition flew through Milo. "You lost someone in childbirth?"

Trey nodded. "My mother and baby sister. It's been years, and I know the technology is better. But you ever had someone that meant the world to you?"

Yes. And she was with Trey's fiancée right now.

Milo nodded. "She'll be fine. I promise. Quinn Davis is one of the finest midwives in the world. And that is not me exaggerating. She's served all over the globe. Carla is in excellent hands. And if, for some reason, we need it, we have a surgical suite for emergency C-sections, if necessary. But less than six percent of birthing center deliveries result in C-sections. She and your baby are in excellent hands."

Slapping Trey on the back, he motioned for the soon-to-be dad to follow him. "I think Kelly has had you fill out all the paperwork for admittance. Why don't we go see how Carla is progressing?"

Quinn stepped out of Carla's room and wiped a bead of sweat from her forehead. Milo started toward her without thinking. Carla had been in labor for most of the day, but Quinn hadn't raised any concerns to him. The two times he'd checked on her, Carla had been progressing slowly, but progressing.

"Everything okay?" Milo saw the tightness in Quinn's shoulders. They'd been running on full steam since Molly's delivery. How was that only two days ago?

"She's finally at seven centimeters. With any luck, Carla will move into transition labor soon. But she's been laboring for almost twelve hours already. Not counting the six hours she did at home. She's getting tired."

Milo knew that was an understatement. Carla had to be exhausted. A woman's ability to deliver after a long labor never failed to impress him, but if she got too tired...

"Are you worried?"

He hadn't lied to Trey. Quinn was an excellent midwife. She'd been on multiple tours with Doctors Without Borders, spent more than a decade as a traveling nurse, and always seemed to find her way to where she was needed most. She'd delivered babies all over the world and in conditions far less comfortable than this. Her instincts were almost always spot-on.

"No." Quinn shook her head. "At least, not yet. If she doesn't move into transitional labor in the next hour or two, I may adjust that statement."

Milo nodded as he leaned against the wall beside her. His skin vibrated at the closeness, and his palms ached with the desire to reach for her. Holding her hand, putting an arm around her shoulder or her waist—anything. Even after what had happened this morning, he couldn't stand the idea of being away from Quinn. Thank goodness, they were at work or his heart might just give in.

Putting distance between them would probably be a good idea. And a hell of a lot easier if they weren't working and staying in the same apartment. But Milo didn't want to change things. Maybe when she took off for parts unknown again, he'd find a way to adjust. Right now, though, he couldn't bear the thought of it.

"How is Trey?" He'd only seen Carla's fiancé a few times as he'd run for ice chips—literally run! One of the floor nurses had warned him to use his walking feet, and Milo had laughed.

"They are adorable," Quinn breathed. "They have been best friends since high school. I swear they even seem to be able to read each other's thoughts. Just like…" She turned her face from his and let the words die away.

Just like us…

The unspoken words hung in the space between them. Milo swallowed the lump in his throat as he tried to force air into his lungs. He should say something, but his brain disconnected from his tongue as the silence dragged on.

She cleared her throat. "Anyway…they started dating about nine months ago." Quinn grinned as she tried to rub the knots out of her neck.

"Ah." Milo chuckled. "Well, they seem very happy." He hated the twinge of jealousy pooling in his gut. He just needed to focus on his goals, his plans, focus on the feeling they gave him. Except, for the first time, planning out his life didn't offer him any comfort.

"Breathe," Quinn ordered Carla as Trey held her hand.

Milo had entered when Carla had started pushing. The baby's heart rate had dropped the first time she'd pushed. Early decelerations often happened when the baby's head was compressed in the birth canal.

The heart rate had stabilized, and it hadn't happened again. But Milo was on standby, monitoring for any sign of fetal distress. He had also ordered the surgical suite readied—just in case.

He was probably overthinking this delivery, but the

hairs on the back of his neck were rising. He'd promised Trey that Carla would be fine. A promise he made to all his patients, but the reality was that labor could be dangerous. There was a reason it was still the highest cause of death for women in underdeveloped countries. Technology lessened that burden, but it didn't decrease it altogether.

Milo had lost a few patients during his career. It was impossible to work in this field for years and not have at least a handful of deliveries go wrong. But today was not going to be one of those days.

"The next contraction is coming, I need you to push, Carla." Quinn's voice was tight as she looked at the maternal and fetal heart rate monitors. "Dr. Russell."

That sent a chill down his spine. During deliveries, Quinn maintained an informality with him. Except when there was a problem. Then he immediately became "Dr. Russell." It was her tell. He wasn't even sure she was aware of it.

His eyes flicked to the heart monitor. The baby's heart rate had shifted from early deceleration to variable deceleration. The baby wasn't getting enough oxygen.

"Carla, I want you to lay back until the next contraction comes." Milo nodded to Trey. "Help her lie back."

"What's going on?" Trey's voice was shaky as he looked from Quinn to Milo.

"The baby's heart rate is fluctuating in a way that I don't like," Milo said. "The little guy has been holding steady throughout labor, so adjusting your position a bit might be enough to give him the room he needs."

"And if it doesn't?" Carla's voice was firm as she gripped Trey's hand and looked at Quinn.

"Then Dr. Russell will perform an emergency C-section." Quinn's voice was low as she stared at the monitors.

She looked at him, and Milo saw the steel in Quinn again. But a subtle peace pressed against him. They were partners, maybe not romantically, but for the first time since she'd walked away from him last night, Milo felt like he could truly breathe.

She held up one finger. This was where their closeness, their friendship, and the layers beneath it collided. The benefits of being able to read each other so easily. Quinn was willing to let Carla push one more time, but if the baby's heart rate dropped again, they'd transfer her to the surgical suite. He nodded and she turned back to their patient.

"All right, Carla. Push on the next contraction, but if your baby's heart rate drops, Dr. Russell will get ready for a C-section."

"My baby?"

"Can be here in less than fifteen minutes, if necessary," Milo stated as he watched the monitors.

"Don't tell him I said so, but Dr. Russell is one of the best in the business." Quinn smiled as she fake whispered the compliment.

He felt his lips tip up. Quinn didn't issue false praise. Her confidence in him sent a wave of strength through Milo. She'd never doubted his ability to accomplish anything. She'd always been his biggest cheerleader. Maybe they were opposites, but they complemented each other— she was right about that.

"Try to breathe regularly," Milo instructed. The baby's heart rate shifted, and Milo exchanged a look with Quinn. The rate hadn't dropped nearly as much on that contraction as it had on the previous one, but it had fallen. They needed to get Carla and Trey's son out now.

Quinn nodded at Milo, and he took a deep breath. "Carla, we are transferring you."

"This wasn't part of the plan." Trey's voice wobbled as he watched Quinn prep Carla's bed for transfer.

"Trey, a nurse will be back to get you in a few minutes." Quinn pulled Carla's bed forward.

Milo didn't have time to comfort the man, but he offered a small smile to Carla's fiancé.

Trey dropped a light kiss on her forehead. "I'll see you soon."

"I'll be the one on the operating table." The love radiating between them was so apparent.

"Here we go," Quinn called as she guided the bed out of the room.

Fifteen minutes later, Milo listened to the monitors as he lifted Carla's son from her exposed womb. The umbilical cord was wrapped around the boy's neck and his skin had a blue hue. Milo unwrapped the cord, but still, the little guy made no noise.

"He's not crying." Trey's voice echoed in the room.

"Trey…" Carla's voice wobbled through the curtain separating them. "Why is he not crying, Quinn?"

"Give the little guy a minute. He's been through a time." Quinn's voice was low but comforting as she took the newborn from Milo, wrapped him in a warm towel, and started rubbing his back.

Come on, little one.

Milo kept his eyes on Carla's incisions and his ears tuned to the baby and Quinn.

After what seemed like an eternity, but was probably no more than a few seconds, the tiny man let out one of the angriest wails Milo could ever remember hearing. Quinn's gaze met his as she laid the baby on Carla's chest.

"He's got a full head of hair." Quinn grinned as she looked from Carla to Trey to Milo.

There was no one he'd rather be in a delivery room or surgical suite with than Quinn. No one he'd rather be with anywhere. Milo let out a breath and smiled as he finished closing Carla's incisions.

Looking over the curtain, he stared at the small family. Trey looked at them with such love that Milo felt his chest clamp. He loved helping deliver new life, and he'd never felt envious of anyone before, but as he looked from Carla and Trey to Quinn, he was surprised by the twinge of the emotion pulling at him.

Maybe her kissing him had been impulsive, but Milo suddenly didn't care. In that moment, she'd wanted him. There were tons of adventures they could have together in California. Milo just needed to find a way to make her want to stay.

With him.

CHAPTER FIVE

"If this goes on much longer, we will need to get a few more clothes," Quinn joked as she dumped the small load of laundry on Milo's leather couch. Her shoulders were knotted, and she flexed them twice before picking up the gray T-shirt Milo had loaned her. Between monitoring her phone for any word that she could return home, and trying her best to act normal around her best friend, Quinn's entire body felt like it might snap.

Milo picked up another shirt and started folding it. "That is true, but this has been nice, too."

Quinn raised an eyebrow. Nice? That was not a description she'd use to describe the last three days. Though last night, when they'd watched a movie, it had almost felt like old times.

Except it hadn't at all… Her heart had screamed as her brain tried to rationalize the hour and a half she'd spent wondering if she was acting normal enough. Or too normal. Or any of the other myriad thoughts that had run through her head.

This was what needy felt like, and Quinn hated it. Her mother had called her "needy" if she broke any rule or asked to do anything other than approved extracurricular activities. Her wants were too much. And each time she'd failed to follow her parents' exacting rules, she'd been belittled. Her schedule and her life had never truly been her own.

Even the drawing classes she'd begged for had only been granted after her art teacher had told them she was skilled. However, instead of taking classes at the local community center, her mother had set her up with a private art teacher four times a week. The thing Quinn had loved most became a controlled item on her schedule, not an activity she could actually lose herself in.

Yet as each day of uncertainty with Milo dragged on, Quinn wished she had some way to manage the chaos.

But would it ease the uncertainty or make her feel trapped?

Softly exhaling, Quinn forced those thoughts to the side. "'Nice'? How do you figure?"

Milo dragged a hand across the back of his neck. "Quinn…"

His deep voice sent a tingle down her back. He leaned toward her, and she held her breath. The drop of hope that he might kiss her had refused to die. It was ridiculous, and if she was able to spend more time away from him, then she might be able to bury it completely. But as his green eyes held hers, she couldn't quiet the want pulsating in her chest.

"I like spending time with you." Milo's words were soft.

Quinn let out a nervous laugh. She liked spending time with him, too, always had. He'd never made her feel unwanted…until two nights ago. Her stomach flipped as she focused on the laundry again. "Milo, we are always together. *Literally.* We work together, and you were at my bungalow almost every weekend."

"Yes." Milo's hip connected with hers. The touch was too much and not enough all at once. "I had to come to the bungalow," Milo continued, oblivious to the turmoil roiling through her, "you never came to my place."

"That is not true." Quinn's head popped back. She'd gone to his place when she'd first returned. And been anxious from the moment she'd stepped into it until she'd left.

The downtown high-rise unit looked like something out of a design magazine. Its light gray walls were devoid of pictures. Flower vases, filled with fake arrangements, hovered in the corners, adding the appropriate hints of color against the perfectly oiled hardwood floors. It screamed success. But it wasn't personal.

Her mother would have loved the place. She'd have oohed and aahed at the full-length windows that overlooked downtown. Complimented the well-thought-out vases and minimalistic decor that made the space look bigger than it was. *Upscale...* That was the description she would have used.

Quinn had felt out of place in her torn blue jeans and T-shirt. A lackluster accessory to Milo's life on the fast track to success. After all, what did she have to show for the last ten years? All her worldly possessions had fit into the two canvas bags she'd carried when she'd landed in LA.

Sure, her bank account was healthy, but it couldn't afford the rent for a downtown unit like Milo's. Not that she'd told him that. The few places that he'd scoped out for her had been nice, but they'd also been too much for her—too upscale.

"Really?" Milo's lip quirked. "I don't think one time counts, Quinn."

Why was he pushing this?

He'd always seemed fine coming to her place. "I was there at least twice." When Milo playfully rolled his eyes, Quinn shrugged. "It's too clean!"

"You're complaining about my cleanliness?" Milo

laughed. "Should I have had dirty laundry draped over the couch or dirty dishes in the sink? Somehow I don't think that would be very enticing."

His voice shifted; its deepness almost felt like it was stroking her. The gleam in his eye and the dimple in his cheek sent thrills through her.

Was he flirting with her?

It was a ridiculous thought, but as his gaze held hers, she almost thought he was.

"No!" Quinn lightly slapped his shoulder. And her fingers burned from the brief connection. She needed to stop touching him. But that was an edict her body refused to follow.

"I should've picked a different adjective. It's perfect. Airy." She put a finger to her chin. "Picturesque. That is the word for it. I worry that if I spill anything, I might destroy the esthetic. Then I won't be invited again."

Milo's strong arms encompassed her. And before she could catch herself, Quinn leaned her head against his shoulder. "You are always welcome at my place, Quinn. Always and forever."

Forever. A term Quinn never associated with anyone.

No, that wasn't true.

She'd always associated it with Milo.

Milo's fingers moved along her back, and Quinn sighed. This hug was dangerous. His heat poured through her as she cataloged each finger's small stroke. She inhaled, letting his scent rip through her.

Milo…

She looked up and met his eyes, but he didn't release her. His gaze hovered on her lips.

Or maybe she just wished it would.

She tried to force her feet to move, but they were unwilling to follow her brain's command.

She sighed as Milo smiled at her. Just a moment longer…
"Quinn—"

Before Milo could finish whatever he'd planned to say, Quinn's phone rang. Grateful for the distraction, she pulled away.

The area code sent waves of excitement and dread racing down her spine. This was the call she'd been waiting for. But her fingers cramped as she stared at the answer button. The oxygen had evaporated from the room. The issues with Milo…the fire…all of it was just too much.

She slapped the phone into his hand. "I can't answer. Please."

Milo pursed his lips then lifted the phone to his ear.

Before he could do more than just say hello, Quinn bolted. It was childish, but she needed a moment to prepare for whatever Milo learned. Prepare for where she'd go if the tiny number of personal items she'd treasured were gone.

Her toes hit the sand of the beach and Quinn leaned over her knees. "Get yourself together. Get yourself together. You can handle this. You have to."

Quinn repeated the mantra to herself over and over, trying to put her feelings back behind the walls she'd carefully constructed since her childhood. Why were they cracking now—when she needed them the most?

Milo clicked off the call and looked toward the door. Her shoes were still there, so she couldn't have gone anywhere other than the beach. He couldn't blame her for not wanting to hear the message. Though the recording hadn't said much, the fire was now under control in her area and residents could return starting this afternoon.

Miranda had also called to let them know that St. Brigit's was no longer referring patients to other clinics. They could head home to Los Angeles.

He just didn't know exactly what home looked like now.

But they'd figure that out together.

He headed for the beach.

Quinn was standing at the edge of the ocean, her back to him. He stared at her for a few minutes. Her shoulders were tight, and he knew that he'd added to that strain. But everything had shifted and he didn't want it to go back to normal. Not with Quinn.

They belonged together. She knew everything about him, they completed each other's sentences and the first call they made when their worlds exploded was always to one another. Maybe his brain had overthought her impulsive kiss, but Quinn moved with her heart.

And it had reached out to him.

There were still a few months left on Quinn's contract with St. Brigit's. There was plenty of time for him to make her realize she belonged here—*with him*. But first, they needed to go to her place and see if there was anything left.

"One step at a time," Milo muttered as he stepped onto the beach.

"How bad is it?" Quinn's voice was ragged.

She turned to him as she brushed a tear from her cheek. The single tear tore his heart. Had he ever seen Quinn cry? No.

Quinn refused to show that weakness. Even when her parents had been awful, and then when they'd passed and the opportunity to ever achieve some reconciliation had evaporated, no tears had spilled from Quinn's eyes. He'd known that the bungalow meant a lot to her, but Milo hadn't realized how much the place had touched her.

She wrapped her arms around his waist. "Just tell me."

"I don't know." He laid his head against her head, wishing he could put an end to the unknown. Hating that this horrible situation she was facing gave him an excuse to touch her.

He dropped a kiss to the top of her head without thinking and was grateful when she didn't pull away. If they could stand on the beach holding each other forever, he'd be the happiest man ever. But life called, and they needed to see to the next steps. "That was just the notification that the fire is contained enough for us to return this afternoon."

Quinn ran her hands through her hair and cringed. "This is the worst Schrödinger's cat situation. Is my house still around? Or do I have nothing? Nowhere to go?"

"You will *never* have nowhere to go, Quinn." Milo squeezed her tightly, wishing there was a way to take all the pain and worry from her.

How could she think about going anywhere but to his place?

"I hope your bungalow is unharmed. But Quinn—" he squeezed her tightly "—you will always have a place with me."

"I know." Quinn smiled, but it didn't quite reach her eyes. The wind caught her hair as she stared at him. "I'm just worried and trying to bury my neediness."

Her eyes widened, and Milo doubted she'd meant to say that. "Being worried about your home isn't neediness, Quinn. And everyone is needy sometimes."

"Thank you," she sighed.

"Miranda called, too. Looks like we've worked our last shifts at my parents' clinic. The fire is contained enough for everyone to make it safely to St. Brigit's." The words were sooty in his mouth. He'd enjoyed working at Oceanside again. Loved being near his family.

"Well, right now, I am trying to figure out how to get

back to the town house without dragging sand everywhere. Standing in the ocean seemed like such a good idea a few minutes ago."

Milo had worn sandals down to the beach. This was something he could fix. "Hop on!" He turned and pointed to his back.

"No!" Quinn laughed. "I'm too tall and heavy."

"Are you calling me weak?" Milo grinned as he looked over his shoulder at her. These were the moments he lived for; being with her, making her laugh even as life's chaos twisted around them. He wanted years of laughter and fun with her.

"Very funny." Quinn glared at him.

Another wave rolled over her feet, and he hopped just far enough away to keep his feet from getting wet. He was going to have a bit of sand on his sandals, a small price to pay for living so close to the beach.

Except you don't live here anymore, his brain reminded him.

"Either you're going to have to walk through the sand with wet feet, or you'll have to get on my back. Come on, Quinn."

"Fine. But if I break you, you can't complain about it." Quinn wagged her finger before accepting his offer.

"You could never break me," Milo stated with more bravado than he felt. Quinn was light enough on his back. But she had the power to destroy him.

They were best friends, but so much more. She was the person who knew him better than anyone else. The woman who had made him smile when his marriage had failed. The person who'd answer his phone calls no matter which time zone she was in. She could tell his moods and always find a way to make him feel better. Quinn was the other part of his heart.

But what if she didn't feel the same way?
Milo pushed that worry away.

Hope slipped away as Quinn stared at the ashes around them as she and Milo made their way toward where her bungalow should be. The hills that had once been dotted with older homes and small lawns were now unrecognizable. Quinn was grateful that Milo had insisted on driving. Not only because her hands were shaking, but because she wasn't sure she could have found her way here.

All the landmarks she'd associated with the area were gone. She could have relied on GPS, sure, but she probably wouldn't have thought to turn it on until she'd been turned around a few times. Quinn had worked in multiple disaster zones, seen people deal with the trauma of losing everything, but she hadn't been prepared for this. No one could be.

Milo's hand reached for hers and Quinn held it tightly. "I am so sorry, Quinn."

As he slowed the car, Quinn realized they'd turned down her street. Everything was gone. A small sob escaped her lips. Her parents hadn't allowed her to have many possessions as a child. At least, not things that mattered to a small child, like drawings from school or pictures she liked. She'd never developed a desire for worldly goods. But seeing what little she did have turned to gray dust stung.

She had renter's insurance and—thankfully—had added wildfire protection, but the pictures of her and Milo all dressed up for their undergraduate graduation, pictures and notes from friends around the world, the few mementos she'd saved from her childhood. No amount of insurance could replace those.

She leaned her head against the headrest. Her body was

heavy. Quinn had thought she was ready for this. She'd known what might happen when the mandatory evacuation had been issued. But seeing the destruction sent waves of panic through her.

What was she going to do?

"Do you want to go?" Milo's voice was gentle as his fingers stroked hers. "We don't have to look through the ashes. At least, not today. If anything is left..." His voice died away, but he didn't release her hand.

She wanted to run—wanted to get away from the week's stresses and hurts. But the sooner she got through this part, the sooner she could start to grieve for what was gone.

At least Milo is here.

"No, let's get this over with. I don't think I can do this alone." The confession slipped through her lips. She'd traveled the world, landed in new places and handled all of life's challenges alone. It was something Quinn took pride in.

But her ability to control herself, to lock away her emotions, had evaporated. Her face heated, but she kept her eyes firmly closed. It was the truth, and her walls were piles of ash at this point anyway.

"You never have to do anything alone, Quinn." Milo's arms suddenly enveloped her. "Never."

The car was small, and the action felt awkward, but comfort swam through her. She only allowed herself a cycle of breath before she pulled back. "Thank you."

Gripping the door handle, she looked at the destroyed lot that had once been her bungalow. "Let's go see if the fire left anything. Then, do you mind dropping me at a clothing store? I'd like something other than Bianca's leftovers."

"Of course." Milo nodded. "But I am not dropping you

anywhere. If you need to go to twenty different stores, I will go to each one with you."

She should say something, thank him for the kind statement, but her tongue was heavy and her brain lacked words. Opening the car door, she let out a soft cry. The world smelled of smoke and destroyed dreams.

But Quinn forced her feet to move forward. She could do this. Had to.

Walking up the singed cement walkway, Quinn stared at the fallen stucco walls and wet soot. She stepped over a pile of debris as she stood in what was once her living room, though there was nothing to identify it.

Swallowing, she turned to find Milo. His face was long, but he was pushing at the ashes with his feet. She needed to do the same, to see if there was anything that she might be able to salvage. But where to start?

The garage… The boxes she'd set there and then forgotten in her rush to get to Molly's delivery had been full of papers and trinkets that wouldn't have stood a chance in the blaze. But she had to check.

Please…

The metal door frame that had led to the tiny garage was still standing. A spooky host to a door that had burned. A doorway to nowhere. Quinn shivered despite the afternoon's heat. Watching her step, she moved toward the marker.

Squatting, she brushed away the ashes that had once been her most precious things. Biting her lip, Quinn sucked in air. They were just things… The phrase felt hollow. They were her memories, and now they lived entirely in her mind.

Her fingers caught on something sharp and Quinn let out a small cry. Pulling her hand back, she looked it over. No blood or scratches.

"Quinn?"

Milo's voice carried across the damage, but she ignored him. Something besides soot and ash was there. It was probably part of the ceiling or a chunk of wall, but...

An ironwork frame emerged from the destruction and she let out another low cry. This time her heart was rejoicing. The frame was singed, and the glass darkened, but there in the frame was the image of her and Milo holding up her nursing diploma.

Her family hadn't attended her graduation. Her father had claimed a big work meeting that he couldn't miss and her mother had made an excuse so ridiculous that Quinn had long ago dumped it from her memory. But Milo had waited for hours before the civic hall opened to make sure he could sit in the front row.

Her lip trembled as she stared at the photograph. It was dirty, the corners burned. It would never look pristine again, but it was safe.

"I still remember how big your smile was when you walked across the stage." Milo's voice was low as he knelt next to her. "You were radiant. I remember the exact moment your gaze caught mine." Milo smiled as he looked at the photo.

Radiant... Her throat tightened as she clasped the picture to her chest. *What was he doing?*

She kept that question buried in her heart as she stared at the rest of the debris pile. "I think this is the only thing that survived."

"I found a few pots, though they are a bit less cylindrical now. And one spoon." Milo wrapped an arm around her shoulders. "But I didn't make it back to your bedroom. Did you have any pictures there?"

"No." Quinn blinked back the moisture coating her eyes. She was not going to cry, "I put all the photos I treasured by the door. When Molly went into labor, I left. Guess I figured I'd get another chance."

Milo's nose scrunched. She pressed her hand against his cheek, not caring about the soot stain she was leaving. Quinn needed to touch him, needed to ground them. "What's wrong?"

He raised an eyebrow. "Speaking of another chance—" Before he could finish, a scream went up from the house, or what was left of it, a few doors down.

"Help!" The call was cracked and laced with terror.

Milo took off. Quinn laid the picture down and raced after him.

Mrs. Garcia was hovering over her husband near the front steps of what had once been their well-maintained porch. Her hands were covered in blood.

Milo reached them, and Quinn pulled out her phone to call 9-1-1 as she turned and raced back to the car. There was water there, and they'd brought their midwifery bags with them. They had sterile gauze and a few supplies that might be useful until the ambulance arrived.

By the time she returned, she had a stitch in her side, but Mr. Garcia was sitting up. The right side of his face was streaked with blood, and the cut running up his leg would need to be cleaned at the hospital and closed with at least a dozen stitches. It was still seeping blood.

"Is it slowing at all?" Quinn asked as she slipped in next to Milo.

"No." He took the water and hand sanitizer she offered. It wasn't much, but it was better than nothing. Milo laid several gauze pads across the wound before pulling off his T-shirt and pressing it against the wound, as well.

She glanced at Milo as she sanitized her own hands and donned gloves. His muscles were taut as he kept pressure on Mr. Garcia's wound. He hadn't hesitated to act. His quick thinking would have been a benefit in many of the field hospitals she'd served in.

And they were a giant benefit here, too.

"The ambulance is at least fifteen minutes out." Quinn kept her voice low, but she heard Mrs. Garcia whimper. In an area with well-known traffic issues, fifteen minutes wasn't terrible. Still, everyone knew that it might take longer.

Milo nodded. "I think the bleeding is slowing, but there is at least one vein open, up by the knee."

Pulling out the surgical tape that they carried in their bags, Quinn wrapped it tightly around the shirt. She and Milo needed both their hands. This way, pressure would remain on the wound.

"What happened?" Milo asked as he moved his attention from Mr. Garcia's leg to his head.

"He insisted we come back for some silly trinket that he forgot to pack." Mrs. Garcia bit her lip as she stared at her husband.

Quinn offered her a forgiving look. "I think Milo was asking about what happened with the injury."

"I…" Mr. Garcia huffed as he gestured to the house and started over. "The steps were loose and crumbled when I stepped on them. Guess the fire was hot enough to weaken the cement." He blinked and moved to touch his face before Milo caught his arm.

"Let me." His voice was low and soothing, but still authoritative. Even in this destroyed area, shirtless, with nothing but a midwifery bag and bottles of water, Milo was the consummate professional.

Quinn bit her lip as Milo carefully cleaned the cut on Mr. Garcia's head. His gentle touches made Quinn's heart clench. She'd loved working with him. It wasn't St. Brigit's, or the wonderful work being done there, that had called her home. It was Milo and how complete she felt when she was near him.

Milo was the reason her walls were in such shambles. She'd never kept them up around him. She'd always been herself. Maybe it would be safer for her heart to find a way to erect them, but Quinn didn't want to. Not now or ever.

"And it wasn't a trinket." Mr. Garcia's voice was strong as he looked at his wife. "It was your anniversary present. I spent months making…"

He looked over Quinn's shoulder. "I didn't expect this level of destruction. Even with the news reports, somehow…" He closed his eyes.

Mrs. Garcia's eyes widened. "We are here for an anniversary present? I could throttle you." Then her gaze softened. "Right after I kiss you."

"I almost lost you once, honey. I won't risk it again." Mr. Garcia's eyes were full of love as they looked at his wife.

"Almost lost her?" The question slipped from Quinn's lips as she checked on Mr. Garcia's leg. It was still bleeding, but blood wasn't seeping through Milo's T-shirt. Though Quinn had waved to Mrs. Garcia whenever she saw the woman puttering around in her yard, they were not close. Certainly not close enough for her to pry into their private lives.

Mrs. Garcia laughed as she folded her arms. "It's his running joke. I asked him out first. I was very brazen in my youth, although I'm more so now, if I may say so." She winked at her husband. The silly gesture felt oddly intimate. The kind of inside joke that long-married, happy couples enjoyed.

"Gumption," Mr. Garcia corrected. "She had—*has* so much gumption."

"Anyway…" Her eyes never left her husband's face as

she retold what was obviously a well-discussed memory between them. "I asked him out, and he said no."

Milo's breath hitched and Quinn's chest tightened. She made sure to keep her face averted.

What was he thinking?

"I was so surprised that the prettiest girl I'd ever seen wanted me. I thought it was a joke. Biggest mistake of my life." Mr. Garcia sighed as he stared at his wife.

The sirens rang out in the distance, and Quinn saw Mrs. Garcia's shoulders relax. She understood. She'd be glad when they were on their way to get his leg properly looked at, too.

"It took me almost a month to work up the courage to own up to the mistake." Mr. Garcia wrapped his hand around his wife's wrist.

Quinn felt moisture form along the ridges of her eyelashes—again. She was in danger of becoming a real watering pot.

She saw Milo catch her gaze and watched an unknown emotion play across his face. She wanted to believe that it was desire, hope for a different future than they'd discussed on the beach. A second chance...

She'd played his little touches and jokes from this morning over in her head. She was almost positive he'd been flirting. Milo never did anything without thinking it out.

There'd been so much going on the day she'd kissed him. What if she broached the topic again when life wasn't so hectic? When he could think about it for a few minutes? If he turned her down then, at least she'd never wonder what-if—even if it left a crater in her heart.

"What was the present?" Milo's question stunned her as he waved to the incoming paramedics.

Mr. Garcia shook his head. "If I tell you, it won't be a

surprise, son. I figure I got a few months to recreate it. Maybe in time for Christmas."

Milo laughed as he stepped to the side and started talking to the paramedics.

"Your boyfriend is quite the looker." Mrs. Garcia smiled at Quinn.

"He's not my boyfriend." The words tasted like soot as she stared at Milo. He made her feel important. He wrapped her in comfort and had always cheered her on, no matter the places she traveled or the jobs she took. And he'd guided her home. "He's my best friend."

But those words didn't feel right anymore as Quinn wrapped her arms around herself. Milo was her compass, the person who kept her on course.

Mrs. Garcia raised an eyebrow but didn't say anything before hustling off after her husband.

Quinn wasn't needed here anymore. Letting out a sigh, she walked back to her destroyed bungalow. She picked up the photo and smiled at the happy memory before turning her focus to the ruins around her.

It was all really gone. Outside of filing insurance paperwork, this wasn't her home anymore. The one place she'd felt like she could let all her walls down, be herself.

Strong arms wrapped around her, and Quinn leaned back against Milo.

"Ready to go?"

"Are you sure you want me to stay with you, Milo? I'll admit, the idea of walking to St. Brigit's from your apartment is nice." Quinn turned in his arms. She should step back, but she had neither the strength nor the desire to. This was where she felt safe. "But I doubt I will be great company."

"You'll be you. And that is priceless." Milo rested his forehead against hers for a moment. "We'll figure out all the details when we get to the apartment. I actually have a plan I want to run by you."

"A plan?" Quinn let out a soft giggle despite herself. Of course Milo had a plan for what happened if she couldn't come home. "I can't wait to hear it."

"It may be my best plan ever." He smiled, and warmth crept through her belly.

CHAPTER SIX

QUINN'S HAIR WAS WET, and her new tank top clung to her waist as she pulled out the chair at his kitchen island. She smiled as she accepted the glass of wine. Her eyes closed as she took a long sip.

Milo stared at her neck. He wanted to plant kisses there, trail them down her shoulder and lower. Wanted to hold her, to wake up next to her. He wanted so many things.

"So, what is your plan?" Quinn's voice carried through the kitchen.

Her dark eyes called to him. He'd looked at them so often, he knew where each of the gold flecks were.

Quinn called to him.

Her spirit made Milo's soul cry out with need. Her unfailing desire to help, to run from her destroyed home to aid a neighbor… Her ability to pick up and start anew… Everything about her made his heart leap.

"Milo?" Her hand ran along his knee, and he jumped.

"Sorry." Quinn's voice shook. "I… I…" Her eyes raced across his face. "I didn't mean to scare you."

"You didn't." Milo shook his head. "No, you did. But not just now. I mean, I jumped, but…" He shut his mouth. Rambling was not how he'd meant to have this conversation.

"When you kissed me…" Milo bit his tongue. He'd planned this talk and now he was starting in the middle?

"I scared you when I kissed you." Quinn's fingers reached for her wineglass, but she didn't look away.

Milo looked at her and his heart cracked as her bottom lip trembled. His script had flown from his memory. Taking a deep breath, he started again. "I made a mistake." The words were simple, but they were the truth.

"A mistake?" Quinn took another sip of wine before setting her glass down. "Do you want me to leave? I can…"

"No." He reached for her hands. As her fingers wrapped through his, his soul calmed. Quinn grounded him. "I am saying all the wrong things. And I even had a plan."

He gulped and started over.

"When you kissed me…" Quinn looked away, and Milo couldn't stand that. Running a finger along her cheek, Milo waited until she looked at him to continue. "I've dreamed of kissing you for years. Since our undergraduate days. Even before. The time never seemed right to ask, or maybe I was just worried you'd say no. But when it finally happened, my brain went into overthinking mode. Because—"

Quinn laid a finger against his lips. "Years?"

"Years," Milo confirmed.

Quinn's mouth fell into the cutest O shape.

God, she was adorable.

"I want you. But not for just a night or a few months, Quinn. I've spent the last two days trying to figure out how to get you back into my arms. I have a whole plan, but honestly, you've driven it from my mind. All I can think of is kissing you." He leaned forward. "I want to kiss you. Desperately. But if you need time to think—"

Her lips were on his before he could finish.

Quinn…his Quinn.

Pulling her to him, Milo deepened the kiss as the chairs they were sitting in locked together. Quinn in his arms was simply right. Life slowed as he reveled in the taste of her. The feel of her heat pressed against his chest. All of it was intoxicating.

There was more to discuss, to figure out. But when she was in his arms, none of it seemed to matter. Her fingers traced up his neck and Milo let out a low groan. How had he waited days to have this conversation? Years? Those were days, hours and minutes of kisses he'd thrown away.

"Quinn." Milo let his fingers travel down her sides. "I want you. But if you don't want me to carry you to bed right now, we need to stop."

She pulled back momentarily.

He meant it. If she wanted to take their physical relationship slowly, he'd wait as long as she needed him to.

"I've wanted you since the moment I landed in LA."

The sultry words undid him. There would be time to discuss his plans later. Right now, he needed Quinn.

Sliding from his chair, Milo wrapped his arms around her and lifted her. She let out a light squeal and he kissed her neck. "I've got you, Quinn."

And he was never going to let go.

He dropped kisses on her lips as he carried her to his bedroom. He laid her gently on the bed before reaching for the small lamp. The first time he made love to Quinn was not going to be in the dark.

Her fingers reached for his shirt and he let her pull it off, relishing the desire pooling in her eyes. Had anyone ever looked at him like that? Like they needed him and only him?

Sitting beside her, Milo ran his fingers under her tank top, listening to every tiny change in her breathing. Cataloging where she responded. When his fingers finally worked their way to her breast, Milo's heart raced. He didn't want to rush this, but his body was taut with need.

Quinn's eyes met his as she lifted her shirt over her

head. She wore no bra. She bit her lips as she stared at him. "Milo…"

"You are so beautiful," he murmured as he stared at her. He wanted to know exactly how she liked to be touched, the noises she made. But he could see an emotion hovering in her eyes that he couldn't quite read. "Do you want to stop?"

"No." She kissed his chin.

"Tell me what you're thinking, then." Milo licked the hollow at the base of her neck, loving the groan that echoed in the room.

"That this doesn't feel weird." Quinn's hand trailed along his stomach and down his thigh. "After so many years of friendship—this feels right."

"And how, then—" Milo kissed her lips "—does this feel?" Dipping his head, he sucked one nipple before turning his attention to the other.

"Amazing…"

Quinn's voice, was threaded with need, and it made Milo's own desire pulse more.

She was so beautiful.

Gripping her shoulders, Milo guided her onto her back. Lowering her shorts, Milo let out a soft groan. She wasn't wearing any panties. Quinn, his perfect Quinn, was naked on the bed.

"I don't sleep in underwear," Quinn stated as he ran a finger up her thigh.

"That is something I didn't know." Milo held her gaze for a moment before lowering his head. "I love learning new things about you. Like how you taste…"

His senses exploded as he savored her. Her body arched, pushing against him.

This was perfect.

"Milo." He doubted there was a sweeter sound than his name on Quinn's lips when she was in the throes of passion.

He let his fingers trail her calves as he teased her, driving her closer to the edge with his mouth. Her hands running across his shoulders, rolling through his hair, were enough to make him want to bury himself deep inside her. But he was determined not to rush this. They had all night—and all the days after.

"Milo." Quinn gripped his shoulders, and he felt her reach the edge. "Please, Milo. Make love to me."

The plea undid him.

He dropped his jeans to the floor, grabbed a condom from the side table and returned to her.

Quinn's arms wrapped around his neck as she pulled him close. "I need you."

Her mouth captured his as he drove into her. "Milo!" Her fingers raked his back and he held her tightly.

Nothing in the world mattered more than this moment. This perfect moment. He felt her start to orgasm again and, this time, he didn't hold back. "Quinn."

Her fingers traced his back as he lay in her arms afterward. "That was…" She sighed against his shoulder. "Not sure the words exist." Her voice was lazy with pleasure and exhaustion.

"I agree." He kissed her, his hand caressing her chin. She was so wonderful, and she was here in his arms.

His Quinn.

The sun was rising over LA as Quinn stood in front of the planning boards in Milo's study. He'd outlined his life for the next fifteen years. Something that her parents would have been impressed by. *And* it was impressive—and daunting.

He'd said that he'd worked out a plan for them. But

her name was nowhere on any of the lists. So, where did she fit? And did she really want everything planned out? *Controlled?*

She'd lived like that for years. Plans and schedules were one of the things she'd left behind when she'd fled her parents' home. Quinn only planned for her current job and one follow-on assignment. There had been a few times when she hadn't known what was going to happen, yet she'd found that life generally worked out. But she knew Milo needed these.

Lifting the mug of coffee to her lips, she took a deep breath and tried to reorient her mind. She'd spent the night in Milo's bed, though they hadn't slept much. Her body tingled as she remembered the feel of Milo's fingers on her skin. His kisses trailing along her belly. Last night had been lovely. So why was she standing in his study before dawn, unable to quiet the chatter in her mind?

Rolling her neck, Quinn let out a sigh. Milo planned. He thought things through. And he followed through with his plans, no matter what. When he'd decided to resign from the Oceanside Clinic, nothing she or his mom had said had mattered. He was determined.

It was one of the things Quinn loved about him. The word had floated around her last night as he'd held her. Quinn loved Milo. Loved his thoughtfulness, his open heart, his determined spirit. When had her love shifted from that of a cherished friend to romantic?

Did it matter?

Milo had wanted her—had said he'd wanted her for years. But what if she failed to fit into his plans like she'd failed to fit into her parents'?

Her knees trembled. No. Milo was not her parents, and she was not going to imagine the end of this relationship before it even began.

She wasn't.

Quinn forced herself to walk into the kitchen. Placing the mug on the counter, she moved to grab the coffeepot. She poured the coffee then turned to rinse out the pot. Yawning, she reached for her mug, but her fingers didn't quite catch it. The cup tumbled to the floor and she let out a cry. The ceramic shattered at her feet, the sound echoing through the room.

Heat raced along her toes as coffee splashed. "Shoot!" She hopped onto the counter. The coffee spreading across the tiles, clinging to the previously perfect grout.

"In his apartment for less than twenty-four hours and already destroying stuff." Quinn sighed. Somewhere her mother's ghost was saying, *Told you so...*

"I don't care about a mug, Quinn." Milo spoke from the doorway. He wore only boxers, and he looked from the floor to where she was perched on the counter. "Are you okay?"

"Burned my toes, but otherwise fine." Quinn looked around the kitchen. She'd kept towels in the drawer by the sink at the bungalow, and Milo knew where everything was. But she had no idea where he kept his towels.

Because she'd avoided his upscale apartment.

Avoided things that reminded her of her past. But Milo was part of her past, and good. So good. And she was done running.

She was…

Her heart beat with a certainty her brain didn't quite feel, but the rush of emotion was enough to propel her mentally forward. "Where are your towels?"

Milo didn't answer as he started toward her.

"Wait!" Quinn held up her hands. "You're barefoot. The shards…" She didn't want him hurt. And she could see the same emotion wavering on his face. "I promise to stay right here while you get shoes."

He raised an eyebrow as he looked at her. "If you get down, we will have our first fight."

First fight... They were silly words, but they made her smile. She wanted a whole world of firsts with him.

Milo returned quickly. "You're smiling."

"You mentioned our first fight. I am pretty sure that we had our first major fight over your refusal to sit as a subject in my art class in high school."

Milo chuckled as he walked over and pulled two towels from a drawer. He dropped them on top of the mess before lifting her off the counter and carrying her into the other room. "You were mad at me for almost a month. All because I didn't want to pose in a toga."

"It seemed important at the time. Although, if you want to pose for me now..." She kissed the delicate skin behind his ear, enjoying the soft groan that escaped his lips as she slipped down from his arms. Flirting with Milo was fun and easy. But they needed to get the mess she'd made cleaned up, and then discuss what had happened last night.

"I don't think any of the ceramic shards traveled this far." Her fingers tousled his hair as she leaned against his chest.

"I like holding you." Milo sighed. "Though I guess we do need to clean up the mess."

She slipped her flip-flops on and followed Milo back into the kitchen. "I really am sorry. I guess I wasn't too far off when I said I'd make a mess of your place."

"Don't do that." The broken pottery clinked as it hit the bottom of the trash can, but Milo didn't break her gaze.

"Do what?"

He raised an eyebrow before bending to grab the towels from the floor.

Quinn bit her lip. She knew what. He'd gotten on her for years about her self-deprecating jokes. She'd used them to survive in her family, and now her brain just automatically supplied them.

"I know." Quinn shook her head. "My coping mechanism is not the best."

Milo pulled her into his arms and kissed her forehead. "You've had a lot to deal with over the last few days. But you belong here with me. I don't care if you destroy every single mug in the cabinet." He paused for a moment before adding, "Except my favorite mug. It's special."

Milo opened a cabinet and pulled out a slightly misshapen mug.

Her mouth fell open as he held it up for her inspection. "You kept it!" Quinn laughed. The mug was the only thing to survive the twelve weeks of pottery courses she'd taken years ago.

The traveling nursing agency she'd contracted with had mandated the three-month sabbatical after she'd worked in three different disaster zones in nine months. She'd rented a small unit over a pottery studio and taken classes each day—never managing to make more than one lopsided cup.

Drawing and painting were skills that came more or less naturally to her. Her work was pretty, and she'd even sold a few pieces. But no matter what she'd done, the clay refused to turn into anything. The cup was too short, and its handle was misshapen.

"I can't believe you kept that." She'd given it to Milo right after his marriage had ended. He'd held it up and smiled. The first smile she'd seen on his lips for weeks. She'd meant the cup to be a joke, a brief spotlight of happiness before it landed in the trash. But it was in his hands now, being held with such reverence that she thought her heart might explode.

"You worked hard to make this. I remember you cursing about the 'stupid pottery wheel.' Very colorful language, if I remember correctly." Milo put the mug away and then pushed a piece of hair away from Quinn's eyes. "You can break everything in this place, Quinn, and it still won't make me think you don't belong here."

"You never told me your plan." Quinn looked up and the emotion traveling across Milo's face made her heart race. "We got distracted." Quinn grinned. "A few times."

"Yes, we did." Milo dropped his lips to hers.

Quinn's skin tingled as he deepened the kiss. She'd been in relationships; but this sense of rightness, of being in the arms of her match, had never been present. Even during her short engagement, Quinn had never reacted to James the way she reacted to Milo. Her body sang every time he touched her.

"Was your plan to only be distracted a few times?" She held her breath.

"No." Milo's tone was firm as he stared at her. "And after last night, if you still think we're better off as just friends, then I have a whole other plan to make you change your mind."

Her words from the beach felt like another lifetime ago. And maybe they were. She'd kept a part of herself locked away in every relationship. Even James had complained that Quinn never let him all the way in. He'd said that if she loved him, he wouldn't have to guess what was going on in her mind. Though *he* hadn't loved *her* enough to stay faithful, to choose her. The wounds across her heart may not bleed anymore, but they'd never fully healed.

But this was Milo, and he already knew so much about her. She could let him into the few places she kept only for herself.

She could.

Grinning, she ran a finger along the outside of his thigh. "I want us to try being us."

"How did you manage to make the word *us* sound so intimate?" Milo's eyes sparked as he pushed another wayward strand of her hair behind her ear.

Milo bent his head, but she stepped back. There was clearly still something she needed to say. "I have two conditions, which I probably should have laid down last night. But you are very good at distractions."

"Name them," Milo stated. "Whatever they are, I'll do it."

"Really?" Quinn raised a brow. If she said she wanted to take a job a few thousand miles from here, what would he say?

No! That was the fear she'd always let worm its way into her brain. *Look for the way you might get hurt, how it might end.* Then she could be prepared. Protected. But she refused to do that with Milo.

"No matter what happens, we stay friends." Quinn gripped his fingers. "I couldn't stand it if I lost you forever. I want this to work. But if it doesn't…" Her breath caught as Milo pulled her forward.

"I want it to work, too." Milo's lips grazed hers. "But I promise, Quinn. No matter what, I am in your life forever. What's the other condition?"

"You can't plan out everything." Quinn paused as a shadow passed over Milo's eyes. "I don't want to live by an outline, Milo. Let's see where these feelings take us— with no plan."

"No plan?" Milo's voice was tense. "I am not sure I can do that, Quinn. What if I make you a deal?"

She tried to ignore the button of fear in her belly. "What's the deal?"

"I can plan a week at a time—that at least gets us a date night once or twice a week," Milo countered.

"A week at a time..." Quinn nodded. "Deal, but if something fun comes up, we are jumping at it—even if the weekly plan says we're booked."

Milo shook his head before smiling, "Do we settle this with a handshake...or?" Wrapping his arms around her waist, Milo's lips captured hers. "Or would you prefer another action to seal the deal?"

She sighed as he deepened the kiss. If there was a better way to start the morning than kissing Milo, she didn't wish to find it.

She moved her lips down, kissing the delicate skin along his neck. She loved the way Milo responded to her touch. "Do you want breakfast? Or are you up for more 'distracting'?"

Milo kissed her, his hands wandering to her hips. "I plan to spend most of the day 'distracting' you."

Quinn sighed as his lips trailed to her chest. She kept her gaze off the coffee stain on the kitchen tile. She'd make sure the lingering evidence of her mishap was mopped up later. It wasn't important right now.

CHAPTER SEVEN

THE LAST WEEK had flown by in kisses and a fog of happiness. Quinn smiled as she exited the employee lounge. She couldn't seem to stop smiling.

It was intoxicating and a bit unsettling. Milo raised his head from the end of the hall before heading into a patient's room. The subtle acknowledgment sent a burst of happiness through her.

Glancing at the next patient's chart on her tablet, Quinn frowned. Tara Siemens had checked the "extreme stress" box on the survey they gave to all their patients before their appointments, which didn't make sense to Quinn. Tara was one of her happiest clients.

Many first-time mothers got worried toward the end of their pregnancy. Still, extreme stress could have detrimental effects on the mother and child. Quinn sent an electronic note to Milo, requesting he stop in if he was available. Milo and Dr. Greg had both done additional training on maternal mental health care. It was therefore standard procedure to ask one of them to see any patient who'd checked the extreme stress box.

Quinn opened the door and a sob echoed from the room. "Tara?" Setting aside the tablet, Quinn grabbed the rolling chair and slid in front of her patient.

Her eyes were swollen and red. She wiped at her nose and then took the box of tissues Quinn offered. "So...sorry."

Quinn tapped Tara's knee. "You don't need to apologize. All feelings are allowed in here. What is going on?"

"Brandon." Tara hiccupped and closed her eyes.

Quinn slid her eyes to Tara's hand and noticed her engagement ring was gone. Brandon had attended a few of the appointments with Tara. He'd seemed distracted, but he wasn't the only partner that Quinn had thought was less than enthusiastic about the prospect of parenthood. Most of the time it was nerves, or a coping strategy, particularly in the early days, in case something went wrong. Sometimes, though...

"I am so sorry." Quinn made sure to keep her voice low and soothing. There was never a great time to end an engagement, but when a child was involved, it added a significant amount of stress.

"Want to take a look at your baby?" When a mother was frantic, or concerned, seeing her child often offered a bit of calm. When Tara had checked the stress box on the survey, it had ensured she was placed in one of the rooms with a portable ultrasound machine.

Tara nodded and leaned back on the table. She let Quinn raise her shirt, but silent tears still streamed down her cheeks. "Brandon said he liked the fact that we were so different."

The phrase caught Quinn off guard as she grabbed the gel. She wanted to calm Tara, but relationship discussions were not Quinn's forte—even with the few people she knew well. She made a low noncommittal noise as she dropped a bit of gel against Tara's belly.

"Opposites attract. That was the joke he made when he proposed. He liked my need to order my life, said it balanced his free spirit. Until it didn't..."

The baby's strong heartbeat saved Quinn from trying to find an answer. What was she supposed to say? Opposites sometimes attracted—look at her and Milo. But they'd only just started dating.

"That sounds like a strong heartbeat." Milo's deep voice echoed through the small room. "And you look gorgeous as always, Tara." His voice was soothing as he met Tara's gaze.

"If you like snotty noses and red eyes." Tara sniffled into her tissue.

"Your daughter looks very healthy," Quinn added as Tara stared at the monitor. The monitor that Quinn had hooked up as she'd readied the ultrasound machine showed Tara's heart rate was slowing, too.

Milo caught Quinn's eye, and she carefully rubbed her ring finger. He looked from her hand to Tara's, and she saw recognition flare in Milo's eyes. This wasn't the first time a couple had broken up before the birth of their child, but it was never easy.

"Did you eat breakfast this morning?" Milo asked.

"Egg sandwich," Tara answered.

"Good." Milo nodded. "I had a giant plate of pancakes!"

It was a lie. Milo had eaten a granola bar and a yogurt-to-go, the same as Quinn, as they'd raced out of his place this morning. But he was putting the patient at ease as he asked a series of questions designed to assess her well-being without raising suspicion. Tara's shoulders started to relax as Milo talked to her.

He was gentle but made sure that Tara answered the questions. Pregnancy was a stressful time. Add in trying to find a new place to live and getting over a broken engagement, and you were dealing with issues that could feel overwhelming.

"I think you are going to be just fine," Milo said. "But

we are going to give you an emotional check sheet before you leave today. Most people are aware of postpartum depression, but some women will suffer from antepartum depression or depression during pregnancy. Major life changes and the hormone changes going on in your body can make you more susceptible to this kind of depression. And there is nothing wrong with you if it happens."

"Nothing," Quinn reiterated. Many women believed they were supposed to be happy no matter what during their pregnancy. That line of thinking could be dangerous.

Milo nodded. "I need to see to another patient. I enjoyed our chat, Tara."

Quinn talked to Tara about the rain that had started this afternoon and their plans for dinner as they wrapped up the appointment. Easy topics, but Tara didn't cry. That was a good sign.

"You think she'll be okay?" Milo caught Quinn as he exited another patient's room. His thumb rubbed against the back of her wrist.

"I hope so." Quinn quickly straightened the collar of his shirt.

How had he not noticed that?

"She seems so heartbroken."

"Breakups are never easy." Milo flipped through a few screens on his tablet before looking at her.

"She said her ex loved the fact that they were opposites...until he suddenly didn't." Quinn huffed out a breath. It was ridiculous to make comparisons, but she'd always imagined that was how her family had seen her. A perfect, dark-haired opposite to them...until that wasn't good enough.

"Well, that old wisdom that opposites attract is pretty inaccurate."

"It is?" Quinn's heart spun as she stared at him.

If he thought that, what were they doing together?

She picked up and moved when the call came. Milo had moved less than a hundred miles from where they'd grown up. She loved bright, obnoxious decorations and letting life take her where she was supposed to go. Milo liked neutrals and planning everything. He had one-year, three-year, five-year, ten-year and twenty-year plans written on his wall in the study. Quinn didn't even know what three years from now would look like for her—except for the certainty that she wanted Milo in her life.

Milo pushed a piece of hair behind her ear, "I've always thought so. Eventually, the differences drive you apart. Unless the partners can adjust."

"Adjust?" Quinn's skin felt like ice. How was he so casually discussing this? *With her?* Did he not see how different they were? Was the first hint of emotional intoxication overwhelming his rational planning self? And when would he decide that her differences were too much?

"Sure. Everyone adjusts in a relationship. But in an opposites situation, the adjustment has to be larger. I don't know many couples that can overcome that. Though, ideally, you figure that out before starting a family. Plans…" He shrugged. "But life happens." Milo looked at her, his smile gone.

Was she part of life happening? Something that went against Milo's plans? Her mouth was dry as she tried to think of something to say to turn this conversation to something else. Anything else…

"Quinn?" Milo's hand reached for hers. He grasped it briefly before he dropped it. The floor knew that they were dating, but professionalism still needed to be maintained. "I know what you're thinking, but we balance each other. And we have a lot in common. We both love bad movies, hate cooking, love our jobs. We make each other laugh."

But were those enough?

"You're right," Quinn finally murmured, trying to stop the twist of her stomach as it rumbled. "Those pancakes are sounding better by the moment."

Milo raised an eyebrow, but didn't call her out on shifting the topic. "Do you want to do breakfast for dinner? We can make pancakes drizzled with maple syrup, and I am pretty sure that I have some bacon in the fridge. But we could also swing by the market before we go home."

Home. That was a word that struck Quinn. She wanted a home, and Milo including her in the simple statement meant the world to her. But what if their differences set them apart eventually?

"Quinn?" Milo's voice broke her woolgathering.

"Pancakes for dinner would be lovely." The words slipped from her lips without much thought.

"Okay." Milo squeezed her hand one more time before he turned to head to his next patient's room.

Quinn crossed her arms as she watched him go. Milo was right; everyone had to make adjustments in relationships.

They could make it work…couldn't they?

"I'll see you when I get ho—back." Quinn kissed his cheek as she carefully held on to her to-go cup of coffee. She'd purchased the travel mugs the day after she'd spilled the coffee across the kitchen. At least today, she was actually going somewhere with it. No matter how many times Milo told her that he didn't care if she dumped coffee on the floor each morning, she refused to use the ceramic mugs.

It was a silly thing to worry about, but Milo couldn't press the fear from his throat that Quinn was maintaining a bit of distance. Not much, just a thin veneer around her heart—enough to protect herself. Like she didn't think this was permanent. Like *he* might not be permanent.

This wasn't Quinn's home. Milo understood that. And if her bungalow hadn't been a casualty in the fire, they wouldn't have transitioned to living together so quickly— though he'd probably would've stayed at the bungalow as often as possible.

He enjoyed having her here. Loved waking next to the tangle of dark hair on the pillow beside him. But he hated the fact that Quinn didn't feel completely comfortable in his home. Hated that the gray walls brought forth ghosts better left buried.

With Quinn in residence over the last two weeks, he'd watched her carefully slip into the quiet, palatable Quinn she'd been when living with her parents. Her Quinn shell.

That was the term he'd coined years ago. It had made Quinn laugh, though he knew that she hated that it was necessary to maintain the peace in her home. She'd dropped her defense mechanism once she'd moved out. And he hated that it was currently being used on him— even if she didn't realize she was doing it.

He wanted the real Quinn. The woman who'd bloomed in her own space. Who wore what she wanted, not outfits selected by her mother. The woman who flew wherever was necessary and served everyone. The woman he was in love with.

Love... The word struck him. He'd been dating Quinn a few weeks; that couldn't be right. It was too soon. He'd been with Bianca nearly six months before they'd broached the topic of love.

But as the word settled around him, Milo let it warm him. He loved Quinn. *Loved Quinn.*

He'd never considered theirs a short-term relationship, but as the word rattled around his brain, Milo felt the completion of it. The joy such a simple phrase projected into all the pieces of his soul.

Still, it was too soon to tell her. Quinn had briefly dated a banker in Georgia, and he recalled her breaking it off the minute the guy had hinted at seriousness. She'd said, "Relationships need to be cultivated, not rushed." He was not going to screw this up by moving too fast. Though he wasn't planning to wait too long, either.

Despite her edict to only think one week ahead, his brain had instantly started putting plans together. In another month, it wouldn't seem too rushed if he announced his love. Hopefully, that would give Quinn enough time to realize that they belonged together. If not...? Well, Quinn was worth waiting a lifetime for.

But right now he needed to find a way to make this place feel more like a home for Quinn. Make her realize that he didn't see it as a temporary space for her. He wanted—*needed*—her to want to stay in Los Angeles. With him.

Particularly since Miranda had decided to interview the senior OB from Valley General. Milo had quietly reached out to a colleague in the unit and inquired about potential openings. They'd told him that they expected an opening in the next few months, which suggested that Dr. Torres was planning to leave, even if she didn't get the position at St. Brigit's. All Milo's plans were falling into place; he just had to make sure Quinn wanted to stay.

Crossing his arms, Milo stared at the kitchen. An idea flew into his mind. And with Quinn on a ten-hour shift, he had just enough time to pull it off.

Picking up the phone, he dialed his sister's number.

"It's not even eight, Milo! Some of us start our mornings a little later." Gina yawned, but she didn't hang up.

"I need paint. Bright yellow paint and sunflower pictures." His fingers itched to get to work. To make the feelings bursting through his heart erupt onto the walls.

"You are calling before eight to talk about redecorating. I thought you wanted all calming tones in your place. Yellow—"

"Is bright and fun. *And* Quinn's favorite color." Milo smiled as he stared at the kitchen walls. The bungalow was gone, but he could bring a bit of it here for her. His chest swelled as he mentally ran through the checklist. This was perfect, and Quinn was going to love it.

"Quinn." His sister sounded much more awake now. "I'll make some calls."

"I'm headed to the hardware store. You know where the key is." Milo grinned as he said a quick goodbye. He loved Quinn, and this was going to make her smile.

Quinn belonged in a yellow kitchen with bright pictures. And she belonged with him.

Quinn flexed her shoulders, glad her shift had finally ended. She'd overseen two deliveries that had begun long before her ten-hour stint had started. Both mothers were fine, but they'd labored for more than twenty hours and were exhausted, as was the staff. And she'd wished Milo had been there to help.

It was silly to miss him when she'd seen him just this morning. She'd known a few people who claimed working with their significant other was stressful, but working with Milo was invigorating. He challenged and supported her.

Her stomach grumbled. The two deliveries had kept her from being able to run out to the food trucks that always parked across from the medical park that housed St. Brigit's, and the few items of questionable sustenance she'd procured from the vending machine had not staved off hunger for long.

Her belly growled again, and the gentleman on the other side of the elevator car looked at her. So many people didn't realize that hospital employees rarely got full lunch or dinner breaks. This wasn't the first time she'd come home with an empty stomach. But it was nothing that a sandwich and a hot shower couldn't fix.

The door to the apartment opened as she stepped out of the elevator. Milo leaned against the door frame, exhaustion coating his eyes, too.

"Are you okay?" Quinn asked as she kissed his cheek. "And how did you time opening the door for me when I got off the elevator?"

"I'm great." Milo dipped his lips to hers just as his stomach rumbled. "A little hungry. I lost track of time and missed lunch. And I asked Jamison to let me know when you got here."

"You asked the doorman to look out for me?" Quinn smiled. "What did you get up to today?" Her stomach growled again. "And please tell me it involved cooking dinner."

"It didn't." Milo grinned. "But the pizza and beer I ordered were delivered ten minutes ago."

"Bless you." As Milo moved aside, Quinn stepped into the apartment and stopped. Her purse slipped from her fingers, landing with a thud.

She covered her heart with her hands as she stared at the bright yellow kitchen and the sunflower pictures hanging above the sink. It was the exact same color as her kitchen at the bungalow. Her pictures had been ones she'd painted, but these were wonderful, too.

All thoughts of her grumbling stomach flew from her mind as she looked at the happy kitchen.

This *gesture was…*

Her brain couldn't find the right word. It was the most thoughtful thing that anyone had ever done for her.

Turning, she stared at Milo. "You painted the kitchen." Her lip trembled as she looked at him. How did she thank him for this? It was too much and so perfect.

His smile was huge as he stepped closer to her and wrapped an arm around her waist. His lips brushed her lips as if he couldn't stand another minute of being apart, either.

Running her free hand over the countertop, she gazed at his hard work. He'd spent the entire day doing this—*for her.* "How did you manage to paint and decorate this all in one day?"

Milo dragged a hand through his hair as he looked at her. "I had a bit of help. I called my sister, and she found the drawings for me. Gina used a few of her designer connections and had them delivered while I was painting." Milo opened the cabinet. "She even found some of those sunflower mugs that you had." He paused. "I know it's not quite the same—"

Quinn kissed him. It wasn't her bungalow—it was better. It was a gift. The most perfect gift. Happiness raced through her, a delirious sensation after a long day. She deepened the kiss, enjoying the low moans echoing in Milo's throat.

He pulled back and gave her a warm smile. "I'm glad you like it. Maybe we should paint the bedroom, too."

She laughed as he held her close. How could she not love it? "Blue and green can be very relaxing."

Milo traced kisses along her jaw before capturing her mouth.

She could melt into him, sink into the wonderful feelings racing through her. Quinn threaded her fingers through his hair. "Thank you."

He dipped his head to her neck. "I need to hop in the

shower before I eat. You don't have to wait for me. I won't be long."

"Or I could join you." Quinn laughed as he grabbed her hand and headed for the bathroom.

"This is one room that I wouldn't change a single thing about." Quinn sighed as she watched Milo lean in to turn on the shower. His backside was a work of art.

She licked her lips as she slid her hands down his tight butt before unbuttoning the top of his jeans. She unzipped his pants and loved the shift in his breathing—loved knowing that she turned him on so easily. Quinn stared at him as she pulled his pants off and stroked him.

Milo's fingers grazed her stomach as he tugged her T-shirt off. Her bra dropped to the floor next. "If you want to focus on a shower, you need to step into it—now." His voice was deep as he ripped his shirt over his head.

"And if I don't want to?" Quinn smiled as she kissed him and then slowly trailed her mouth down his magnificent body.

"Quinn…" Milo's moan sent goose bumps across her skin. She enjoyed nothing more than the sound of her name on his lips as she turned him on.

She kissed her way along his thighs, coming close to his manhood, but then moving away each time. Quinn smiled as Milo's large hands cupped her head.

"Quinn, love…"

She took him in her mouth then, loving the control. She gripped his butt and sighed at the sounds of pleasure echoing through him. He pulled her up and kissed her.

"God, Quinn." Milo shuddered as he sat her on the counter. "You are too amazing."

"Imagine if you'd let me finish." Quinn was surprised by the boldness in her voice. She had never been a bold lover, but with Milo, everything felt so easy.

Milo kissed the tender spot below her ear he'd found their first night together. "I have every plan to finish," he vowed, his thumb pressing against her nub as he watched her. Milo took one of her nipples between his lips as he continued to use his fingers to drive her closer to the edge.

"Milo…" Quinn's body moved against his. The way he was teasing her felt glorious, but it wasn't enough. She needed him. All of him…now.

"Milo," she repeated.

His tongue flicked her nipple, and her body erupted. "Want something?" His eyes dilated with pleasure as he met her gaze. "All you have to do is ask. I'll give you anything, Quinn. Anything."

"I need you." Quinn ran her hand down his length. "Now!"

Milo grabbed a condom from the drawer and sheathed himself quickly. Pressing against her, he captured her lips. He put one hand around her waist and pressed the other to the mirror as he buried himself deep inside her.

Quinn gripped his shoulders, completely lost to the oblivion that was she and Milo.

"There's a new patient asking for you," Sherrie said, nodding to room six.

Quinn looked toward the room, then back at Sherrie. Patients often asked for specific midwives, but St. Brigit's had a rule that all midwives and OBs saw all patients because when a woman went into labor, a particular midwife or doctor might not be on call.

"A new patient?" Quinn looked at Sherrie. "Why is she asking for me?"

Sherrie shrugged. "Not sure. But her husband asked if they could speak to you before they left. I can always have Heather tell them you aren't available when she goes in to schedule their next appointment. But figured if you had a moment, I'd pass along the request."

"I have a moment." Quinn smiled. Maybe a friend from overseas had moved into the local area. More likely, one of her former patients had recommended St. Brigit's because of working with Quinn.

She opened the door and froze. A woman with curly dark hair was sitting on the edge of the exam table, a brilliant smile on her face. But it was the presence of the man in the room that kept her feet planted at the entryway.

"Quinn." Her brother's voice faltered a bit, but his eyes were soft as they met hers. "It's good to see you."

"Asher." Quinn stepped into the room and shut the door. Her chest was tight, as if she couldn't get enough oxygen. He'd been a teenager when their parents had cut contact with Quinn. She'd briefly hoped they might reconnect after Asher had divided their parents' estate, but her phone calls and texts had gone unanswered. She'd looked him up on social media a few times since, though not recently. But she'd never reached out—it was clear from his silence that he hadn't been interested in having a relationship with her.

What was he doing *here*? *Having a baby.*

They'd never been close, not even as children. She couldn't remember them playing together more than a handful of times. It could have been a survival technique. Since her parents' focus had always been on what she did wrong, Asher had had a bit more freedom. Now that he was here, all that distance didn't seem to matter so much.

He had a brilliant smile as he looked from Quinn to the woman on the table. "This is Samantha." Asher gestured to the woman before gripping her hand. She wasn't visibly pregnant, but St. Brigit's typically started seeing patients around the ten-week mark. "My wife," Asher added, beaming as he looked at her.

"Congratulations," Quinn murmured. She meant the words. No matter what, she would always want the best for her brother. And she couldn't remember ever seeing him smile like this. It made her smile, too.

"I couldn't find your address or phone number when we were sending out invitations. It was a tiny ceremony, about two years ago." Asher rubbed the back of his head. "Family stuff has never been my strong suit." His jaw hardened as he squeezed his wife's hand. "Though I'm learning."

They'd hardly had good role models to follow. "It is good to see you, Asher. And to meet you, Samantha." The moment was awkward, but how could any moment with a sibling be normal after so many years of no contact?

He swallowed. "I know this isn't the time or place for a reunion. But I saw your picture on the wall in the waiting room and I couldn't believe it." Asher shrugged. "I thought you were overseas. I checked a few times online. Even started a letter to you once, but I didn't know what to write."

So she hadn't been the only one unsure how to reach out. Pushing through the discomfort, Quinn smiled. "I was. But I've been back for almost a year. It is good to see you, Asher, but I can't treat your wife. Not as a family member." Quinn looked at Samantha. "Not that I wouldn't like to..."

The door to the room opened and Milo stepped in. His fingers pressed briefly against her back as he said, "Asher." His tone was polite but firm.

"Milo." Asher nodded at him. "I must have been too focused on Quinn's picture to notice you worked here, too. This is my wife, Samantha."

Samantha waved. "It's nice to meet both of you, but we've probably taken up enough of your workday."

Samantha was right, but Quinn didn't want to waste the opportunity. She grabbed a paper towel, and wrote down her number. "Just in case."

Asher smiled as he stared at the number. "I'll text you. It was really good to see you, Quinn."

"You, too, Asher, and nice to meet you, Samantha. Your midwife will be in to see you in just a moment."

Once outside the exam room, Quinn leaned against the closed door for a minute before she looked at Milo. "Running to my rescue?"

"Yes." Milo dropped a quick kiss on the top of her head. "Though you seemed to have it under control."

"My heart is racing, and my brain still hasn't fully figured out what is going on. So much has happened so quickly."

Her hands were shaking, but she felt good. Surprisingly good. "I think I'm fine. Guess I'm going to be an aunt! Though I'm not sure how much Asher will want me to be involved. Probably not much."

"Or maybe he would love for his children to get to know their beautiful, smart, fun aunt Quinn. He didn't tell Samantha they should cancel their appointment and run when he saw your picture. Focus on the potential good outcome. At least for now."

Milo offered her a quick hug before rushing off down the hall to his next appointment.

So much had happened in the last month and a half, Quinn was realizing that LA could be just as much of an adventure as any of the places she'd worked before. Her skills were just as useful here as they'd been anywhere else. She smiled as she watched Milo duck into another patient's room. Her heart had been right to pull her here. Despite the fire, the sweet definitely outweighed the sour.

"Did he call?" Milo knew the answer as Quinn looked away from the phone and plastered on a fake smile. If Milo could thrash Asher, he would. "I'm sorry, Quinn."

What was wrong with her family? Why couldn't they see the incredible woman she was?

"It's fine." Her voice was tired as she slid down beside him on the couch. Her shoulders sagged. "At least he sent me his number. Maybe asking if he wanted to grab dinner was too much." Her lip trembled as she flipped her phone over. "No one ever wants to keep me."

The final phrase was so quiet Milo didn't know if Quinn realized she'd said it aloud. But it ripped through him.

How could she think that?

Her family, and that lout James, may have thrown away one of the best things to happen to them, but so many others hadn't. "That is *not* true," he whispered as he kissed her forehead.

Milo sat up and pulled her hands into his lap. He waited until she looked at him. "I have always kept you. Ever since you started that food fight, it's been you and me."

"Pretty sure *you* started that food fight." She smiled, but it didn't quite reach her eyes.

"I'm not the only one, either." Milo kissed the tip of her nose. Her parents' desire to make her into something she wasn't, to force her into their mold and then withhold love when she didn't meet their impossible standards and routines, bordered on evil, in Milo's opinion. Especially because they'd doted on Asher. They had been capable of being loving parents and yet had chosen not to be with Quinn.

"Thanks, Milo." She kissed his cheek. "I shouldn't have said it, and certainly not to you. You're always there for me."

But her voice wasn't steady and the tears he saw her trying to hide nearly broke him. She didn't see herself the way others saw her, and that ended tonight.

"Your phone has the number for the head of Doctors Without Borders, right?"

"Yes, because I worked a few missions for them." Quinn shrugged.

"No. Julio has your number because you bonded late one night in some out-of-the-way place while he was still just one of their regular physicians. He calls you to ask your opinion because of how impressed he was with you." Milo paused. "And what about the hospital in Boston that has twice offered you a position as a senior midwife in their unit? And that's just in your professional life…

"There have been cards arriving here for the last two weeks from your friends around the world sorry to hear that your bungalow burned. Not to mention the box of clothes and photos that arrived yesterday, from someone named Christine, to replace some of what you lost."

Quinn's lips captured his, and Milo held her for a minute before pulling away. "Trying to silence me with kisses?"

Her lips tipped up as her dark eyes held his. "Maybe." Quinn leaned her head back. "It's uncomfortable to hear so many good things about myself."

Particularly when you grew up hearing so many bad things.

Quinn left those words unstated, but Milo knew she was thinking them. "If Asher doesn't want a relationship with you, that is *his* loss." Milo kissed the top of her head.

"I know." Quinn leaned against him. "I really do know that—objectively." She was silent for a minute before adding, "But he's my family, and it just hurts."

Rubbing her arm, Milo held her close. He'd grown up in a loving family. They'd supported him and never made him feel like he was anything other than a beloved son. He'd never felt like his mom loved him more or less than his sister. In his mother's eyes, they were equal.

"I'm here for you," Milo added, hoping it was enough.

"Thank you." Quinn sat up and smiled. "I lo—"

Her cell interrupted her, and Milo glared at it. What if Quinn was going to say I love you? But if Asher had interrupted… Well, it would be worth it to make Quinn happy. Though he'd give the man a hard time about it at some point.

Quinn answered, and he saw her eyebrows twitch before she smiled. It wasn't the giant smile that always sent such a thrill down his body, so it probably wasn't Asher. At least someone else had brightened her mood. She kissed his cheek and then stood up, walking into the kitchen as she continued the call.

"Florida?" Quinn laughed before looking over at him.

Florida? Milo's mind spun into overdrive. This was the call that he'd been terrified of since they'd started dating. She'd made connections all over the world—literally. It had always been only a matter of time before her phone rang again with news of a new opportunity, a new adventure.

Milo hadn't been kidding when he'd spoken about how many people wanted to work with Quinn. Even if her family had been unable to see the wonderful woman she was, her colleagues admired her greatly.

"I'll think about it."

Those words sent a splash of pain racing through him. Florida was on the other side of the country. An all-day plane trip away from him. His stomach knotted as she grinned and put her phone in her pocket.

"How do you feel about the Atlantic Ocean?" Quinn asked, handing him a beer.

"I've never really thought about it." That wasn't completely true. He'd rolled the idea of living and working somewhere else around his brain a few times since they'd started dating. He'd even stood in front of his wall of plans

a few days ago. But the image of his father's face and his
hand pointing to the nameplate kept floating in Milo's
mind—a beacon that stayed his hand whenever he picked
up the eraser, thinking about changing his plan.

"But I like California." That was true. He'd always felt
his path was here, even as he watched Quinn plot her
course around the world.

Quinn held up a finger. "Don't worry. I'm not actually
planning on taking this position."

His heart lifted with joy before crashing. *This position.* She hadn't said that she wouldn't consider moving
at all. His gaze flew to the yellow kitchen, and he racked
his brain, trying to think of a way he could compete with
the likely possibility that an offer would come that she
would want to take.

"Why?" He hated the selfish thoughts running through
his mind. But that didn't stop his need to know the answer.

Quinn paused as she looked at him. She opened her
mouth, but closed it a second later. Then she shrugged.
"Because I like where I'm at right now."

That wasn't what she'd thought about saying; he was
nearly certain. Milo's heart yearned to hear what had been
on the tip of her tongue before she'd swallowed it. He
should be happy, thrilled, but the words *right now* pounded
in his brain.

Quinn's gaze wandered to the window behind him. "But
I have always wanted to run my own unit…"

"Is that what the job is? Does that mean you *are* thinking about it?" Milo tried to gauge the look in her eyes. She
almost looked like she was trying to talk herself out of it.

"No, I'm not considering it. But thinking about running
my own unit makes me smile." Quinn tapped his knee.
Her voice was bright, but he could hear the bit of longing
in it. "But I'm not moving to Florida. So, you don't need

to worry about it. Florida's not high on my list of places I want to work."

List of places?

His throat constricted as he looked at her. How long was that list? His brain was spinning as he tried to focus.

"But you said you'd think about it?" Milo knew he shouldn't press, but there was something about the glint in her eye when she'd mentioned running her own unit. The head of St. Brigit's had at least another ten years before she retired. That was a long time to wait. If Quinn really wanted to run her own unit soon—it wouldn't be here.

"Terri is persistent!" Quinn laughed. "If I'd said no right away, he'd say I hadn't thought it through and my inbox would be full of emails detailing the wonders of Orlando. I bet he'd even offer Disney World tickets."

"Anaheim is less than thirty miles from here. We can see Mickey anytime." Milo hated the defensiveness in his tone.

"When did you become such a Disney fan?" Quinn smiled as she set her beer down. "I seem to remember you complaining about the ticket prices, parking and lines when we went as teenagers. It was a very grown-up complaint, if memory serves." Her lips pressed against his cheek as her fingers tracked his thigh.

"The lines *were* long, and it *was* hot. But we still had a great time." Milo had taken her for their sixteenth birthdays, excited to be able to drive them there himself. For a moment that day, he'd considered kissing her. He'd looked at Quinn and wondered what if…? But the moment had passed.

But she was here now. Her fingers slid up to the waistband of his jeans, and the memory flew from his brain. "You're trying to distract me," Milo murmured as Quinn placed light kisses along his jawline.

"There is nothing more to discuss. I'm not interested in the Orlando job. What I am interested in…" Her fingers slid inside his pants, and Milo lost his ability to reason. There would be plenty of time to work out a plan.

Plenty of time.

CHAPTER EIGHT

"Quinn!" Opal called from the registration desk. "Can you do a quick review of this transfer chart?"

"Sure." Quinn took the tablet from Opal's outstretched hand. It was unusual for a patient to transfer their care from St. Brigit's, but sometimes the facility wasn't a good fit. Or, if the pregnancy was high risk, they'd recommend delivering at a nearby hospital instead. But before they transferred a patient's records, a midwife or OB had to do a quick review of the chart to make sure everything was in order.

Her stomach shook as she stared at the name on the chart: Samantha Davis. "I can't do the review." Even if it wasn't against policy for her to review her brother's wife's chart, Quinn couldn't have stomached it. Why had Asher asked to see her if he was just going to ghost her again?

Pain trickled across her skin. She knew it wouldn't be visible to anyone, but her whole body ached at th…th… the… Her heart screamed *betrayal*, but her mind refused to accept the word. *Denial.*

Asher had never spoken up on her behalf. Never interjected to support her as she'd argued that she didn't want to do the activities her parents thought were best, even though she'd seen him roll his eyes at her mother's daily schedules, too. She could forgive him for not realizing how differently their parents treated them when they were children—no child should think their parents capable of only loving one of their children—but the inequity in their family had been so glaring, he had to have seen it as a teenager and as a young adult. And yet he'd said nothing; he'd just accepted it.

She couldn't have treated his wife. As a family member, the relationship was too personal.

Even for a family that never spoke.

But apparently just being in the same facility as Quinn was too much. The hurt spun through her as she stared at her brother's name on the forms. They had the same last name, had lived in the same house for sixteen years, but that hadn't been enough to bind them.

"Quinn?" Opal's question drew her back to reality. "Are you okay?"

No. She was going to lose it, and she couldn't do that here. Not now. "Yes, but Samantha Davis is my brother's wife. So, you will need one of the other midwives or doctors to review this before the transfer." She was impressed that her voice didn't break, even as a piece of her spirit shattered.

"Ah-hh." Opal's eyes widened. "I didn't know you had a brother."

Why wouldn't your brother want his wife to deliver here? That was the question hovering in Opal's eyes, but Quinn knew she wouldn't ask it. At least, not to Quinn. This was going to be fodder for gossip, but what answer could Quinn give?

"Oh, Dr. Russell." Opal's eyes brightened as Milo joined them. "Since you're here, can you do a quick patient review for me?"

Milo's gaze slid to Quinn. She saw the recognition flash across his face as he made the logical leap to why she wasn't the one reviewing the records.

Milo knew Asher hadn't returned her invitation to dinner. Hadn't even texted a polite "too busy." He knew it hurt, even if Quinn tried to pretend that it didn't. His hand brushed her back as he leaned over to take the tablet. It was a small motion, one that no one else would notice, but it sent a flood of comfort through her, and her heart clung to it.

He'd been a bit odd after Terri had called to offer her the job in Orlando, though she'd tried her best to quiet his fears. Before coming back to California, Quinn would have jumped at the offer—the adventure of running her own unit.

But moving didn't hold the appeal it once had. Milo's closeness settled her. From the moment she'd arrived at LAX, the pull of the road had relaxed. The driving need to move, to find a new place—her place—had almost vanished.

Her place was here.

That probably would have terrified her if it wasn't for Milo. Maybe his need to control life's chaos really did balance her need to be propelled by her emotions and gut instinct.

The idea of running her own unit was appealing, but another opening would present itself eventually. That was one lesson she'd learned. Life had a habit of providing opportunities that surprised you. Maybe not always with happiness and joy, but those things would be mixed in, too.

"Molly is in room two for a postpartum follow-up." The nurse's aide's voice was taut as she walked toward them, looking from Quinn to Milo. "She checked off three items on her postpartum depression survey, and she's trying to hold back tears."

"Okay." Quinn took the tablet and headed toward room two. At least this gave her something to focus on. More than fifteen percent of women suffered from postpartum depression, but many still felt there was shame in admitting it.

In Quinn's experience, if a recently delivered mother was acknowledging there was a problem, that was a win. But if they checked more than two boxes, they were also probably experiencing additional symptoms.

"Molly." Quinn smiled as she walked into the room. Her son was asleep in his carrier and Molly was chewing on a fingernail. "How are you feeling?"

"Fine!" Molly's response was too bright. Her hair was unkempt, and there were bags under her eyes and spit-up on her clothes. All symptoms of having a newborn at home. But the watery eyes, anxious glances at her son and nail biting sent a bead of worry through Quinn.

"It's okay if you're not."

Molly's eyes darted between Quinn and the door.

"What's going on?"

She tapped her chewed fingernails against her knees before letting out a sigh that was nearly a sob. "I wanted to be a mother for so long." Molly's lips shook. "Then we adopted Owen. It was amazing. *Is amazing.* But when we found out I was pregnant..." Molly closed her eyes and hugged herself tightly. "It felt like I was going to get to experience something I missed with Owen." Molly hiccupped and wiped a tear away.

"If I can't be happy now, what kind of mom does that make me?" Molly looked at Quinn, and the dam of emotions broke. Tears cascaded down her cheeks, and she sucked in a breath.

"It makes you a mom who is dealing with the stress of having two children and a body that's been through a trial, because birth is hard. There's a reason we call it labor!" Quinn patted Molly's knee. "This is not uncommon. It isn't."

"I want to run away when Adam cries." Molly's cheeks flamed as she told the dark secret. "I never felt that way with Owen. And Owen is clingy, which I know is to be expected with the new baby. But after what feels like marathon breastfeeding sessions with Adam, snuggling with Owen is too much. That isn't how a good mom responds."

"Yes. It is, sometimes." Quinn looked at Molly. "This is postpartum depression, and you cannot just force it away. There is no shame in saying it. You're very brave for telling me these things."

"Owen is into everything, and I am trying to make sure he doesn't feel left out, but Adam is up all the time, and breastfeeding hasn't been super easy. My mother took Owen last weekend to give us a bit of a break. It's easier with one." Molly let out an uncomfortable laugh as she stared at her son.

That statement cut at Quinn's heart. She'd heard the same from countless mothers. The fact that her own mother had only wanted one, and would have liked to return her adopted daughter, didn't have any bearing on what was going on with Molly.

"I bet it was," Quinn agreed and nodded when Molly's mouth gaped.

"I'm terrible." Molly wiped a tear away.

"No, you're not." Quinn kept her voice level but firm. "There is nothing wrong with the truth, Molly. You've gone from having a wonderful, lovely toddler—who, by your own description, is into everything—and added a newborn to the mix. And your body is still healing. How did you feel when Owen was gone?"

"A little more relaxed. But I missed him terribly. He only stayed one night before I asked Mom to bring him home." She ran the tissue under her nose and then sighed. "I can't stop crying, and I feel like a failure."

Reassuringly, Quinn tapped Molly's hand. "You are a good mother. Do you know how I know?"

Molly shook her head, but didn't answer.

"Because you love your children. That is what matters. It's what they…" Quinn swallowed the lump that had unexpectedly materialized in her throat. "It's what they remember most—the love."

Especially if it isn't given.

But she left that last thought unstated.

"Now, let's get *you* taken care of."

"Are you okay?"

Milo's question hit her as she stared at the charred hill in the distance. She didn't have an easy answer. How had it been less than two months since she'd sat and avoided looking out this window while her home burned? And how had so much changed?

"I don't know." The truth slipped through Quinn's lips. After discovering that Asher and his wife had transferred their care, and dealing with the emotions of Molly's postpartum issues, Quinn felt drained. Her tank was empty.

Milo's arms wrapped around her, and Quinn sighed but didn't step away. "We're at work."

"And you've had a long day," Milo kissed the top of her head as he released her. "I am sorry about Asher."

"It's not just him." Quinn hugged herself.

"Is it the Orlando job?" Milo's voice was tight.

"What?" Quinn frowned. This was the fourth time he'd brought it up over the last three days. Why would he not drop it? She'd sent a polite refusal to Terri this morning. Though he'd sent back the standard request to give it one more thought, Quinn knew Terri wouldn't press. "No, it's that Molly has postpartum depression. She made some comments about it being easier with only one kid. She loves her children, and with medication and the support group Sherrie set up several years ago, she is going to be fine. But with Asher's refusal to contact me and her having an older adopted son, my brain is just spinning."

"That's to be expected," Milo stated. "The last two months would have overloaded anyone. It doesn't make you weak for being tired—and maybe even a little furious at the universe."

She shook her head as he offered her a lopsided smile. "Maybe I need to get away." She looked at the hills and sighed. A small holiday would be nice, and they both had a healthy amount of vacation days stocked up.

"Away?" Milo's voice caught as he looked at her.

"Sure, running away—" The unit alarm interrupted her. She looked at Milo. "Who is in labor?"

"No one," Milo called as he raced for the door.

Was there no time for anyone to breathe?

Maybe it was too soon, but they were going to take a vacation together. Maybe she could convince Milo to throw a dart on a map and just go.

"It's time to push," Milo ordered as Tien gripped Quinn's hand. The woman had labored at home for almost nine hours and she'd been eight centimeters when she'd walked in. Her husband had boarded a plane on the east coast as soon as he could once her labor started, but he was still at least two hours out. Milo understood why she was so distraught, but babies waited for no one.

"My husband isn't here." Tien let out a wail as Quinn helped her get into position. She'd repeated that line every few minutes since arriving. Probably hoping that the mantra would either speed up his arrival or delay the baby's.

"I know." Quinn's voice was soft as she held Tien's gaze. "I know he wants to be here, too."

That was true. Milo had served as Tien's primary OB over the last nine months. Her husband had been to every appointment but the last one, when his job had sent him to DC for a week, but he'd video-called. Tien had still had four weeks before her due date—but babies rarely adhered to scheduled dates, unfortunately. If Milo had been a betting man, he'd have bet that Tien had at least two more weeks before delivering her first child.

Quinn pressed a cloth to Tien's forehead. "Your son or daughter is going to be here soon. And then you'll get to introduce your new child to your husband when he arrives." Quinn took a deep breath. "But right now, it's time for you to do your job. Dr. Russell and I are here for you."

Her voice was the perfect mix of comforting and authoritative. Tien let out a small cry as she sat up.

Milo nodded to Quinn. She was impressive. Even after the long day, and the shock of learning that Asher's wife had requested to transfer her care, Quinn was taking care of another mother. With no hint of the turmoil that Milo knew she must be experiencing.

"All right, Tien. Push!" Milo ordered.

Milo found Quinn cooing over Tien's tiny daughter as she sat with the new mother. They'd been off the clock for almost two hours, but traffic from LAX was so bad that Tien's husband still hadn't made it to the hospital. So, she'd stayed at St. Brigit's to keep her company while Milo ran home to get some dinner ready.

He'd done his best to make sure everything at home would be just right when he finally managed to get Quinn to leave St. Brigit's. Her quip about running away was still sending chills through him. After the day she'd had—hell, the last several weeks she'd had—he could understand the sentiment, but it still frightened him.

They both needed a hot meal and a full night of sleep. Quinn should be dead on her feet after the day's emotional roller-coaster ride, but you would never be able to guess it from the happy laughs coming from Tien's room. How was he so lucky to have found such a terrific partner?

Milo's heart ached as he watched Quinn take the little girl from Tien. She cuddled the baby, and he saw her shoulders relax just a bit. She'd discussed children a few times over the years. Always wistfully, like she didn't know if she'd ever get the chance.

But staring at Quinn with a child in her arms, Milo felt the future tug at him. She'd be an excellent mother. She'd fight for her children and make sure they never doubted her love.

And he wanted to be the one standing next to her through all of it. Wanted to plan a life that included family and fun, and endless happy memories.

"Dr. Russell!" Tien's husband, Jack, ran toward him with a man who was nearly his mirror image. "Where's Tien?"

"Deep breaths, son," the other man said.

"Room five." Milo nodded toward the doorway.

"Thank you." Jack's father grinned as he watched his son run into the room. "The nurse at the front desk told him the same thing, but I'm not sure his brain fully heard it in his rush."

"Understandable." Milo nodded to Quinn as she exited the room and gestured to the employee lounge before heading to grab her things.

Jack's father leaned over and peered through the door. "I can't wait to meet my granddaughter, but I think my son and daughter-in-law deserve a few minutes before Papa intrudes." The pride radiating off the man was intoxicating. "Not sure there's a better moment than seeing your son hold his own child."

The words hung in the space around Milo, pushing at him as he watched Jack's father wipe a tear from his eye and turned to go meet his new granddaughter. This was a moment Milo's father had never had—and would never get. The small ache that never left him throbbed and a wave of unexpected grief passed over him.

For a moment, Milo was a kid again. Reaching for his dad. But the memory was foggy, like so many of them were. And his voice refused to come to Milo.

Quinn's hand was warm as it slipped into his. "What's wrong?"

The quiet words drew him back to the present, and her presence grounded him. How did you explain that you'd lost your dad's memory? That it was easier to draw his face to your mind only after you looked at his picture? That you felt like a failure for not keeping his memory closer?

The right words didn't appear, and Milo wasn't certain he was strong enough to utter them if they did.

"Long day." He threw his arm around Quinn's shoulders. "But it's nothing a plate of hot food, a shower, and a night in your arms won't fix."

She raised an eyebrow, and Milo could see her desire to call out the lie. Instead, she patted his chest just over his heart and kissed his cheek. "Let's go home."

Quinn was curled on the couch reading when Milo's phone buzzed. He'd been in his study for most of the afternoon. He'd said he was catching up on paperwork, but the two times that Quinn had peered in the door, he'd been staring at his planning boards. She'd asked if he needed any help, but he'd just kissed her and told her he was fine.

Ever since coming home after Tien's birth, Milo had been… Her brain searched for the right word. *Reflective.*

If she asked, he said it was nothing, but she knew that wasn't true. Something was bothering him, and he hadn't told Quinn what it was. It felt like he was actively keeping it from her.

Milo had maintained his planning boards for as long as Quinn had known him. They gave him a sense of peace, of control. He only adjusted them when he was certain of the plan he wanted to follow.

And her name hadn't appeared anywhere on them.

It was selfish to want it when she'd ordered him not to plan out their relationship. Told him not to focus too far into the future. But she was surprised by how much she wanted the confirmation that he saw her there, wanted the security of knowing what five years from now looked like. It was terrifying for a woman who'd spent the last decade carefully avoiding any sort of long-term plan. Yet she couldn't force the desire away.

When the phone buzzed again, she pushed away the prickle of panic as she answered. "Hi, Diana. Milo is in his study doing…" Quinn hesitated. She had no idea what was keeping him so long. "Something," she finished lamely.

Milo's mother let out a soft laugh. "Knowing my son, he's probably planning something. Or adjusting a plan, or thinking about adjusting a plan."

Quinn chuckled, too, but the sound was false, even to her own ears. She was certain that was what Milo was up to, and part of her wanted to ask what changes he was making. Most important, if they included her.

They'd moved in together before they'd even officially started dating. They were happy. *They were!* But occasionally he looked at her and she could see the doubt hovering in his eyes. And it had been there several times since she'd been offered the job in Florida.

Was he waiting for her to leave?

Pushing the thought to the side, Quinn stood up and wandered to the kitchen. "I suspect you're right about the plans. It's his favorite hobby."

"Yes," his mother stated, an underlying note to the word that Quinn couldn't place.

"Is there something I can do for you?"

"Felix and I are having a barbecue this weekend. We usually try to plan these things out. Otherwise, Milo or Gina—or both—are busy. But the weather is going to be so nice."

There was something she wasn't saying… Quinn was almost certain, but then she shook herself. Now she was looking for things to worry about with Milo's mom? She needed to get control of herself. "We aren't on call this weekend. What should I bring?"

"How about some dessert? Gina's already promised the dip—which I know Milo hates."

Quinn laughed. "Well, dessert is easy enough."

"Wonderful!" She could hear Diana's smile through the phone. "I can't wait to see you, Quinn—and Milo, too."

Diana had been thrilled when they'd told her they were dating. Quinn had always felt comfortable around his mother and sister, but they were really making her feel like part of the family.

An important part, not just Milo's girlfriend.

"Your parents are having a barbecue this weekend," Quinn stated as soon as she stepped into his study.

Milo turned in his chair, and Quinn looked at the wall behind him. The plans hadn't changed. There was still nothing to indicate he saw her as part of his five- or ten-year plan.

Stop it!

Her heart pounded at her brain's warning. She was not going to fall into the trap she'd fallen into so many times. She wasn't going to look for things that might mean she'd get hurt.

She wasn't.

"And I'll bet Gina's bringing that dip I hate. Well, this time, we'll bring our own," Milo said with a rueful shake of his head.

"I already promised we'd bring dessert." She giggled as he threw his hands in the air. Quinn had heard his dip rant several times over the years. She wasn't even sure Gina liked the dip she brought, but she loved seeing Milo act overly put off by it. And Milo enjoyed the show as much as his sister.

What would life have been like if Quinn and Asher had had inside jokes like that? Had made silly games that annoyed their parents but made each other laugh? Had been partners *and* siblings? It would have been a whole different world. A fun world.

If Milo and Quinn had kids, she hoped they'd be friends, too.

The air rushed from Quinn's lungs as she stared at Milo. Children were a topic Quinn had always tried to push to the back of her mind, but whenever she held a newborn, part of her briefly wondered what it would feel like to cuddle her own.

And now, even though she and Milo had only been dating a few weeks, she could already imagine him snuggling with a little one that had her dark hair and his nose. Could imagine him playing games and encouraging their kids to get along and be friends.

"You okay?"

Milo pulled her close and she sank into his heat. Her

heart pounded as the desire for a family—her family—nearly overwhelmed her. "I feel like I should be asking you that."

Milo kissed her cheek, but didn't comment.

"Maybe one day I'll have an inside joke with the Russell family, too."

Milo chuckled and dropped a kiss across her temple. "Challenge accepted."

She laughed as she laid her head against his shoulder. It was a simple statement, but she heard her future in it. Her name might not be on any of those boards—yet—but one way or another, she was going to add a few items to those boards. Items that would fulfill both their dreams.

"You look so happy." Milo's mother squeezed his hand as she looked at Quinn.

Quinn was rocking a friend's baby on the porch. He felt his mind start calculating. If he told her he loved her in three weeks, proposed in six months, then they married six months from that, they could be parents in the next three or four years.

He'd almost adjusted his list a few times over the past week. But each time he'd raised his eraser, his hand had refused to move. Quinn had a list of places she wanted to work. Milo had *a* place he needed to work. There had to be a way to reconcile the two, but he hadn't found it yet.

His mother started pulling fruit trays from the refrigerator. She looked out the window over the sink and smiled. A faraway look came over her features as she stared at the gathered mass outside. "I love having everyone here. Love having the entire weekend off."

"It's nice," Milo agreed as he took a sip of his water. Her distant tone sent shivers along his arms, but he didn't know why.

"I want to do it more often." His mother crossed her arms and looked at him.

He looked out the window and grinned. Today had been close to perfect. The weather had been fine, the food delicious. He wasn't sure he could have planned a finer day if he'd had weeks to do it.

Milo shrugged. "Sure. A little more planning might be a good idea. We got lucky this time, but there is no telling when we might all have the day off again. Babies don't generally hold their deliveries for barbecues."

"Sometimes it's nice not to plan." She looked at him and leaned close. "I want to clear my schedule a bit."

Milo looked at his mother. Her smile was bright, but she was bouncing on her heels.

What was going on?

"Meaning?"

"Felix and I are planning to retire."

"Really?" Milo was stunned. His brain clicked through a multitude of responses as it reeled at the news. This couldn't be—his mother and Felix loved their clinic. They'd just started the birthing center. "I'm…" His mouth seemed stuck. "Stunned," he finally managed.

"I know. But we don't want to work for the rest of our lives. And it seems like the right time to start dialing back."

"Wow," Milo breathed out. He'd always seen his mom at the clinic, had always thought of it as hers. He'd never considered that she and Felix would want to move on. In his mind, that was where they belonged. *Always.*

"So, what are you doing about the clinic, the birthing center?" His throat burned, and Milo took a sip of water to force the uncomfortable sensation away. His mother had taken the job at Oceanside Clinic just after his father died. Her professional relationship with Felix had bloomed into friendship that had eventually turned to love. Milo couldn't imagine Oceanside without them. Didn't want to imagine a stranger running such a special place.

"We were hoping you might want to take it over." His mother's eyes shimmered as they looked at him.

He could see the hope in her gaze. The need. She expected him to take it. To want it. And part of him did.

"I know your father would like the idea, too."

The words set his heart racing. He tried to pull on that thread. Tried to imagine what his father might say, but all he could pull up was the trip to Valley General. His dad bending close to him, saying something about running the unit. Even now, with everything his mother had said, the shadowy image sent chills down his back.

"Milo, you are the best person I can think of to run Oceanside Clinic." His mother smiled. "You helped design the birthing center. It should be you."

Why was she making this so difficult?

She rubbed his hand, and hundreds of memories of them working together at Oceanside jumped into his mind. His first and last day, the babies they'd cooed over, the difficult days when everything had gone wrong. He had a lifetime of memories there.

And only one solid one of his dad.

His mother nodded toward the window. "The birthing center needs a head midwife, too." Her eyes were bright. Maybe she'd expected him to scream no immediately. He should put her hope aside and explain his decision, but the words were caught in his throat.

"Nancy only planned to get it off the ground. She's been talking about retirement for the last three years. I'd planned to talk to Quinn about the position—even before I knew you were together. She's perfect for it."

"She is," Milo agreed. His tongue felt tied. He knew

Quinn would love being the head midwife at the birthing center, and that she'd excel at it.

"I know you've dreamed of running a big hospital unit—"

"I haven't *just* dreamed of it," Milo interrupted, and immediately felt heat travel up his neck, but he continued. He had to make his mother understand why his answer had to be no. "I feel called to it. Led to it…by dad."

His mother sighed, but she didn't look away. "Are you prepared for everything you will have to sacrifice?" His mother's eyes darted to the back patio.

Turning his head, Milo couldn't stop the smile spreading across his face. Quinn was dancing barefoot in the grass with the neighbor's granddaughter. She was laughing as they spun around, and his heart expanded as she collapsed on the grass with the young girl.

"I'm not going to have to sacrifice anything." Quinn knew about his plans. She'd seen his boards. She knew what a life with him looked like.

Didn't she?

"With the right plan, you can avoid—"

"Life doesn't always care about your plans," his mother snapped. "As you are so fond of saying, babies don't care about schedules, or birthdays or anniversaries. Children don't care that you're on call. They have dance recitals, baseball games, all sorts of activities. As a physician, you are already going to miss some, but if you run a large unit…" She shook her head. "At Oceanside, you and Quinn could control more of your schedule, your life."

Why was she pushing this? How could his mother not understand? "If you could have seen him that day at Valley General, felt what I felt—what I still feel—you'd understand."

"Milo, you are allowed your own dreams." She smiled.

It was the look she'd used when he was a kid and she was trying to coax him into finding the right answer on his own.

"This is my dream." Milo shook his head. How could she not understand? Part of him needed this. And it was larger than the unruly piece of his heart that screamed he belonged at Oceanside Clinic.

"Is it?" She stepped closer. "Or are you trying to make up for something that was never your fault?" Her hands trembled, and she wrapped her arms around her waist. "Listen to me. Your father died in a car accident. That was *not* your fault."

"If I hadn't put off my science fair project..." He hated how small his voice sounded. How it made him face the feeling of failure that had never fully left him.

His mother's warmth seeped into his chest. He wasn't sure when she'd reached out to hug him. Still, he let her hold him as the energy and anger drained from him.

Milo blew out a breath. He loved his mother. But the hole his father's death had left could never be filled. That was the way it was with his grief—it never fully went away. He just learned to move around it, to walk with it.

After several minutes, she raised her head and stroked his cheek. "Milo, for the hundredth time, it wasn't about a poster board. And it wasn't about the flowers he went to get because of our fight, either. It was bad timing, and another person's poor decision-making." She held him tightly.

"Your father loved every minute of his life. He loved you and me and Gina. And he understood that you don't get guarantees." She smiled as she looked at Milo. "The last thing he would have wanted was for you to be unhappy."

Milo shook his head. "I'm not unhappy." It was true. He enjoyed his work at St. Brigit's, was looking forward to competing for the Valley General position when it opened.

Just because he loved Oceanside didn't mean he had to give up the dream he'd had for so long.

She kissed his cheek. "Your father would have loved Oceanside, too. He sometimes talked about owning his own practice."

"He did?" That revelation stunned him. He racked his brain, but he couldn't think of a single time he'd heard that before.

His mother sighed, and her eyes drifted to the side. "Parents are always more than their children see, at least when they are young." Her hand wrapped around his. "On rough days, your dad even talked about becoming a full-time writer. I always thought he was joking, but there were three unfinished fantasy manuscripts at the bottom of his filing cabinet that I found…" She bit her lip and waved a hand. "The point is, he had many dreams. And he would want you to live yours."

Running the Valley General unit was his dream…wasn't it? The thing that promised him comfort? The thing he wanted terribly? It was. "My career is in LA."

Her fingers patted his cheek before she turned to grab the fruit platter. "I know that's what your plans say, sweetheart. Just make sure it's what *you* really want." Then she headed back out onto the patio, leaving him alone with his thoughts and memories.

CHAPTER NINE

MILO HAD KISSED her and then disappeared into his study as soon as they got home. Did he know that his mother had talked to her about running the birthing center at the Oceanside Clinic? Surely, she'd discussed it with him. But each time Quinn had tried to broach the topic on the ride home, Milo had changed the subject.

He hadn't even attempted to be subtle about it. She knew he liked working together at St. Brigit's. But he wasn't going to stay there forever. He'd brought up St. Brigit's new hire and the empty spot left at Valley General only once, but she knew how much he wanted that position.

If she accepted Diana's offer, they could live halfway. But that meant at least an hour and a half commute with traffic for each. And if they were on call, it would be easier to stay at the hospital than to come home.

How long could they last living that way?

She preferred the hominess of birthing centers. The personal care she got to give with only having a few women giving birth on any one day. She'd been at hospitals where she'd helped deliver a dozen babies during her shift. There wasn't time to enjoy the newborn's snuggles, to help a new mom acclimate to breastfeeding, or to answer the dozens of questions that arose in the first hours of new life.

None of those needs had gone unseen. But *she* hadn't

been able to take her moms from prenatal to postpartum care. And Quinn loved that aspect of the job. It was what put the bounce in her step when she went in for each shift.

Milo loved it, too. Loved watching the joy that came with new life. And he was going to miss it terribly if he ran the ob-gyn unit at Valley General and had to focus much of his time on the minutia of making a unit run well.

Resolved, she started for the study. If they were to have a future together, they needed to get on the same page. And Quinn was done letting him change the topic…and done avoiding it herself.

He didn't turn around as she entered the study. He'd been in here for almost an hour, but none of the tension she'd seen in the car had leaked from him. Whatever was going on, she could help him—talk him through it, like he'd talked her through so many things in the last few weeks alone.

"So, I take it my mother told you that she and my stepfather are planning to retire?"

His voice was distant as she stepped up beside him. Quinn knocked his hip with hers, trying to push a bit of the rigidity from him. "She did. I expect that we shall be getting a lot more barbecue invitations in the future."

He nodded, but his eyes never wavered from the wall before them. "They want me to run Oceanside Clinic when they retire."

The words stunned Quinn. Diana hadn't mentioned that when she'd discussed the midwife job with her. Her heart pounded in her chest. That would solve all the problems she'd been worrying about for the past ten minutes. "Really! That would be perfect. You would be so good—"

"I told her no." Milo's words were flat as they fell between them.

Quinn was shocked. "No? Just no? Without even telling

her you'd think about it?" She knew he had his plans. But this was the chance to run his own clinic. A place he loved.

"I don't need to think about it." A nerve twitched in Milo's jaw as he stared at the wall of goals in front of him. "I've already made the necessary decisions about my future," Milo said, gesturing to the words scrawled in front of him.

"Your future?" The words slipped through Quinn's numb lips.

Not *our* future…

Stepping between him and the boards, Quinn waited for Milo to look at her. Her chest was knotted, but her voice was steady. "These are whiteboards. Do you know what is wonderful about them?" She ran her hand across one and held up her finger stained with red ink. "You can figure out what you want and alter the plan."

She trembled as she stared at him. She'd never touched his boards. They were sacred to him. A physical homage to his father. She'd crossed a line, but she couldn't go back now.

Her heart stung as she looked at him. Her parents had been rigid. Milo wasn't a rigid person—he planned, liked to know what he was doing, but he could adjust.

Couldn't he?

"Why can't you even consider changing them for this opportunity?"

"Because I'm not impulsive! Not…" Milo pulled his hand across his face.

"Not flighty. Is that what you mean? Never flying off to parts unknown for a position, right?" Her lips trembled as she wrapped her arms around her waist.

"That wasn't what I was going to say." Milo's voice was firm, but he still wouldn't look at her.

She wanted to challenge him, and her heart ached as

he stared at the erased marks on his board. They were just notes, writings that could be replaced.

She waited a moment longer, wishing he'd look at her. Just her. Then she turned. If she spoke, Quinn worried it was going to be something hurtful.

Bottling up the pain pushing through her, she headed for the door. She knew he wouldn't follow her, and that crushed her spirit a bit further. They each needed some time to blow off steam, but she still wished that he would run after her.

Her cell phone rang as she grabbed her keys. She hit Ignore as she walked out. She didn't have a goal in mind—she just needed to be somewhere else.

Anywhere else.

She'd walked through the small park by the apartment three times before her phone rang again. It wasn't Milo's ring, and her heart seized when she saw her old traveling nurse agency's number. Swallowing, Quinn answered. It never hurt to listen, to think about possibilities, to have a backup plan.

A backup plan...

The simple thought crushed her soul. But she pressed Answer on her phone.

"Quinn! I have the perfect position for you!" Isla didn't wait for Quinn to say hello. The staffing adviser was one of the bubbliest individuals Quinn had ever met. "It's in Maine, and you don't have to be there for three months. It's a six-month rotation as the lead of a midwifery unit, while the head midwife is out on maternity leave."

Quinn puffed out a breath. It was as far from Milo as she could get and still remain in the continental US. She looked up at the high-rise complex and rubbed a tear away. "I'm not sure. Can you give me a few days?"

"Of course. But there is actually another position I need to fill, too. Do you know a Sherrie Foster? She works at St. Brigit and applied a few months ago. She's very qualified for the other midwife position at this unit. The traveling nurse there now plans to rotate out in a few months, too."

"She's wonderful." Quinn wrapped an arm around her waist. Sherrie had mentioned applying. Quinn had told her that she'd be a reference, but Sherrie hadn't mentioned it again. "She'd be a good fit for the head position, too, if I decide to turn it down."

Quinn kicked a rock. Could she take the position at Oceanside if she and Milo weren't destined for forever?

No.

The word resounded in her head. Her phone beeped, and she quickly told Isla that she'd let her know in a few days.

Come home...please. Milo's text sent chills racing across her heart. Was it her home? All of this had happened so quickly. And she'd erased part of one of his boards.

What had come over her? Fear.

She wanted Milo to choose her. To rewrite his plans or to at least include her in discussions about the future. She needed to know that he saw her dreams as part of his future, too.

Milo paced back and forth, trying to calm himself. His brain had panicked when Quinn had held up her ink-stained finger. No one erased his boards. They were his connection to his father—erasing them felt almost like betrayal.

But in his frustration, he'd lashed out. Impulsive might not sound like a horrid thing to fling into a conversation, but he'd known how she might take it. And then he hadn't been able to do anything but stare at the blank spaces she'd left. She'd wiped it all away so easily.

How different would his life be if he could do that? And why hadn't he chased after her already?

Milo wanted her home. And with each passing minute, his stomach sank further. He'd gone to the door three times, thinking he'd heard her, only to be met with the curious stare of his neighbor.

He'd called, and she hadn't answered. Then he'd sent the text. He looked at his phone. Quinn had read it twenty minutes ago and hadn't responded. What if he'd driven her away for good? He didn't want to lose Quinn.

Pressing his hand to his forehead, Milo hit Call on his phone again. He heard Quinn's phone ring in the hallway outside and tripped over a shoe in his rush to get to the door. His knees collided with the tiled floor, but Milo didn't care. Quinn was here.

"I am so sorry."

"I'm sorry."

They each said the words at the same time as Quinn rushed to his side. Milo stood, ignoring the pain in his knees as he held her. "I should not have let you think that I thought you impulsive or flighty, and I should have immediately come after you. I am so sorry."

"I shouldn't have wiped away part of your board." Quinn rested her head against his shoulder. "I know how much those mean. I just…" Her words were firm. "I just wanted you to think about it."

Milo stiffened. He had thought about it. Maybe not today, or at least not as much today, but years ago. Even if he wasn't trying to honor his father. Oceanside wasn't what he wanted.

At least, it wasn't the only thing he wanted—was it?

Why did his brain keep coming back to that thought? Milo had charged down this path for years. With the potential opening at Valley General, it was finally within his grasp—finally, he could be close to his dad again.

So why did it feel like his heart was leaning away from it now that the opportunity was here?

"What if I consider it for a few days?" He hadn't meant for the question to exit his mind.

Quinn's eyes met his. An emotion he feared was doubt hovered in them. "I promise to think about it, Quinn. It's just... I've had my career path laid out for years. I swore I'd do this for my dad."

"What about what you want?" Quinn's voice was quiet, but he felt her stiffen in his arms.

Leaning back, he looked at her. Why did his heart have to want so many conflicting things? "Give me a couple of days to think about it."

She smiled, but it wasn't quite full. "That's all I'm asking."

She kissed his cheek, but the fear coating his heart didn't disappear.

Was that really all she was asking? And what if he didn't change his mind?

Milo kept those questions buried inside. She was back—in his arms. That was what mattered tonight.

Milo nodded as he handed Quinn a tablet chart. Dark circles underlined his beautiful eyes, and the strum of tension that had connected them over the last week hummed as her fingers touched his. He grinned, but it was taut. When was the last time she'd seen him smile? Really smile?

They'd always remained professional during work, but the little touches and stolen conversations were gone. There was an uncharted space between them now.

And neither wanted to address it.

Quinn wished there was a way to go back to the early

days of their relationship. Then she scoffed. They'd been together less than three months. These *were* the early days.

And if they were already at an impasse?

Since they were teenagers, Quinn had talked to Milo about almost everything. During the first weeks of their relationship, she'd relished how easy it was to talk to him as a partner. To already know his tells.

Now it was a curse. Quinn knew he was stressed. But when she asked about it, he just said it was nothing. And she was hiding things, too. She hadn't taken the job in Maine, hadn't turned it down, either. And she hadn't told Milo—yet. Her heart ached at all the unsaid words between them.

She bit her lip. She and Milo had managed to get through the last few days by ignoring the giant boulder between them. She wanted to run the midwifery unit at Oceanside, and he wanted to be the head of Valley General's obstetrics program.

Were those two things really so at odds?

Quinn tapped a pencil on the nurse's station and tried to catch her breath. Were relationships supposed to be this hard to navigate?

"You okay?" Sherrie asked as she leaned over the nurses' station and placed her tablet on the charging pad.

"Yes." The lie weighed on her heart, but if she opened up about it, Quinn worried that she would burst into tears. Or maybe rage at what she feared were Milo's unyielding dreams.

Sherrie raised an eyebrow, but she didn't press her. "If you decide you want to talk about it, I'm available."

She was pleased by the kind offer. "Thank you."

Her friend nodded. "I suspect Keena will be delivering by the weekend, but Hanna is at least another week away.

We might need to start talking about what happens if we need to do an induction."

Quinn smiled as the conversation turned to work. This was an area where she was comfortable. She didn't doubt herself inside these walls. Didn't doubt that she had a place. In the midwifery unit, she knew what to expect and trusted herself.

Babies might keep to their own schedules, but Quinn knew there were patterns you could recognize, once you'd been a midwife for long enough. "Hanna will not be thrilled with an induction. She's already overdue, and she had to be induced with her first. I remember when she was here for her twelve-week appointment. She wanted to know what she could do to avoid it happening again."

"I know," Sherrie said. "I mentioned it to her today, and her reaction was what you'd expect. After a few sniffles, she squared her shoulders. Pitocin is no one's first choice, but she said whatever is best for the baby."

Quinn smiled. "Right answer. She still has at least another week before we need to start worrying, though. Maybe the little one will grant his mother some grace."

"Maybe." Sherrie turned off her tablet, but she didn't look very confident. "I'm off for the night. And Quinn—" Sherrie crossed her arms "—if you need anything, let me know. I owe you. Particularly if you turn down that head nurse position in Maine."

"They told you they'd offered it to me, huh?" Quinn rolled her eyes. "Isla is bubbly and happy, but she is not known for her discretion. One day it's going to get her in trouble. What if you'd wanted to battle it out with me?" Quinn laughed.

"If you want it, the job's yours. I know that." Sherrie said it with such confidence that Quinn's head popped back. "You've worked all over the place and literally fled a wildfire while successfully delivering a patient. Of course, you're their first choice."

Quinn let out a breath. "My résumé is certainly unique."

"I've never left California. I'm excited about the opportunity." Sherrie swallowed before continuing. "Though it would be nice to know someone in Maine." She waved as she headed toward the employee lounge. "Oh, I didn't see you there, Dr. Russell," Sherrie said as she stepped around Milo—who had appeared at an exam room doorway—and disappeared down the hall.

Milo's face didn't give anything away, but Quinn wrapped her arms around herself as she stared at him.

Had he heard?

Quinn had meant to discuss the Maine offer with him several times, but the tension between them was already high. The time was never right, and the last thing she wanted to do was to make him think she was fleeing. It was just a backup plan—one she wasn't going to use.

She wasn't.

She'd checked his study each day, hoping to see some sort of change on his board, some indication that he saw her as permanent. But nothing had changed. What if she told him about the job offer and he told her to take it? That would make his choice about the Oceanside Clinic and Valley General so much easier.

Before she could gauge his reaction, Tara Siemens walked into St. Brigit's and immediately doubled over, clenching her belly. Quinn and Milo reached her at nearly the same time.

"How far apart are the contractions?" Milo's voice was light, but she could see the small tremor in his jaw. He'd heard Sherrie. Worry cascaded through her, but there wasn't time to deal with it now.

"Five… minutes…" Tara panted. "I tried to get Brandon to come. But he wouldn't answer my calls."

Fury floated across Quinn's skin. It didn't matter what the differences were between Tara and her ex-fiancé—to not answer the call of your pregnant ex when you knew she was close to delivery was horrible. Sucking in a quick breath, Quinn squeezed Tara's hand as Milo led her back to a delivery room.

"My parents are gone, and my sister lives on the other side of the country. She's going to come out for a few weeks next month, but she has two under two so…" Tara looked out the window and wiped away a tear as she rubbed her belly. "Brandon was all I had."

"Well, soon you're going to have a new little member of the family. And Quinn and I will make sure you are never alone." Milo's voice was soft as he started hooking up the monitor to measure Tara's contractions.

Never alone…

Milo had made the promise so easily. At St. Brigit's or at Oceanside, it could be effortlessly accomplished, but such a promise would be a stretch at a large facility like Valley General.

The buzzer on Quinn's hip went off. "I need to see another patient, but I'll leave you in the capable hands of Dr. Russell for now, and I'll be back shortly."

As Quinn stepped to the door, she glanced back at Milo. He was talking with Tara about movies while watching the monitors, fully focused on his patient, on making sure she'd be okay delivering without a loved one. In a larger facility, he wouldn't have the luxury to take his time like this.

He laughed at something Quinn couldn't hear, and she watched his shoulders relax. A facility like St. Brigit's or Oceanside would make him happiest. It was where he belonged. How could he not see that?

* * *

Quinn had been offered a position across the country.

And she hadn't told him.

The thought ricocheted around his mind as he stepped out of Tara's birthing room. He'd managed to trade off care with Quinn during Tara's labor as he wasn't sure how long he could be around her without begging for answers.

Tara smiled as she walked past him. Her contractions had remained five minutes apart for the last two hours, so one of the nursing aids was walking the halls with her now, trying to move labor along.

"I talked to Tara's ex." Quinn's voice was low as she motioned for Milo to follow her into the employee lounge.

His heart leaped as they stepped into the room together. They were at work, but his palms ached to touch her. His arms wanted to pull her close. To kiss away the worry lines marring her forehead. To plead for answers about the Maine job. But none of those things was possible right now.

"You called him?" Milo was stunned. He'd thought Brandon was acting immaturely. Hopefully, he'd change his actions after his child was born. If not before. But there were rules and procedures that had to be followed.

Quinn's eyes widened. "Of course not."

He saw the hurt flash across her features. The words he'd said to her these past few days always seemed to be off. The easiness that had flowed between them had evaporated once the offer to run the Oceanside Clinic had been thrown into the mix. If only she could understand that his plans didn't include a return to Oceanside.

He needed to focus. "Sorry, Quinn." She was an excellent midwife and nurse. She knew the rules regarding patient information.

Her face relaxed a bit, but she didn't touch him. All the

little touches, the small smiles, that he'd taken for granted had disappeared. He craved them.

She sighed as she leaned against the bay of lockers. "He's called the admitting desk every thirty minutes since she arrived." Quinn shook her head. "If he's so concerned with her condition, then he should be here…which is what I told him."

Milo let out a soft chuckle. "And how did he take that?"

"Told me they were too different and hung up the phone." Quinn sighed. "Differences may keep them apart, but they are bound by a child forever. Shame he can't see that right now."

"Differences have a way of piling up." Milo's voice was tight. For a moment, he wasn't sure if he was talking about Tara and Brandon or him and Quinn.

Partners didn't have to be exactly the same. But they did need to want the same things. And if she could still consider taking a job with her traveling nursing agency… The thought tore through his soul.

Why hadn't she immediately told her old agency she wasn't interested in the new job?

Quinn's eyes held his, and he could see the questions hovering there. But now wasn't the time to discuss them. Besides, he was terrified of the answers. Terrified that she wouldn't choose his plan.

Wouldn't choose *him*.

"Tara's contractions are picking up." The aid slipped back from the employee lounge door before either Quinn or Milo could respond.

He watched Quinn swallow before he nodded at the door.

"Shall we go see about a baby, Dr. Russell?"

Dr. Russell? He would focus on what that meant later.

* * *

"Are you coming to bed?" Quinn rubbed her arms as she stood in the doorway of Milo's study. Tara's labor had finally proceeded, and she'd delivered a healthy baby boy. But she'd been alone. Her ex had answered when she'd asked Milo to call and tell him he had a son, but Quinn didn't know if he would come visit the baby. She hoped he would.

There was so much for Quinn and Milo to talk about, but he'd grabbed a quick snack and retreated almost as soon as they'd arrived home. It stung. He was pulling away from her. And Quinn had no idea how to draw him back.

How did she compete with plans he felt he owed his father?

Should she?

That was the question that tore through her the most.

Life without Milo had never seemed like an option before. They'd sworn when this started to remain friends. Quinn now saw how laughable that was. As if there was a way she could act as though her heart wouldn't always cry out for him.

She loved him. Always would. But if this ended, their friendship would be a casualty. Her heart tore as she stared at his back. "Milo?"

"When were you going to tell me that you were considering moving to Maine?" His voice was rough as he looked over his shoulder.

Quinn went cold as she tried to find the right words. They needed to talk. Needed to figure out what was next. If anything...

"I should have told you. But they called after our—" her voice caught "—disagreement the other night, and the timing wasn't right." She felt her throat closing, but she pushed through. "I haven't accepted the position."

"Have you turned it down?" His voice was rough—*hurt*.

"No." Quinn bit her lip, wishing there was a different answer, but it was the truth. "I always think about job offers for a few days." That was her routine. He knew that. She'd always talked to him about where the agency had open positions and gotten his thoughts, though he'd commented more than once that she always went with her gut, so why ask him?

"So what does your gut say you should do? Is the job calling to you more than LA?" The lines around Milo's eyes were deep as he dug his fingers into his folded arms.

"That is *not* fair," Quinn shot back. They were exhausted, too exhausted to have this argument now. "We should get some rest, then we can discuss the Oceanside Clinic, Maine, and everything else."

"I'm not going to take my mom's offer. It's not what I want."

What about what she wanted? What about their future—together?

She had wanted to put off for a few more hours what now felt inevitable. It would be his plan that mattered. His choice that reigned.

"We need to figure out our plan."

"Now, it's *our* plan?" Quinn wanted to shake him. She'd wanted him to start including her in his plan weeks ago. For a man who plotted everything out, she should have seen some sort of change on his whiteboards. Or some mention of their future. So where was she? Where was her place amid his dreams of running Valley General's OB unit?

And if she stayed, would he keep looking at her like she was a flight risk? "Are you expecting me to leave? Ever since Terri offered me the position in Orlando, I feel like you've been waiting for me to say I'm packing my bags."

Milo shrugged, and Quinn felt her heart crack.

"I've been looking for the signs that you're about to leave ever since you moved back. That's what you do, Quinn. You leave. But me? I can't go anywhere. The job for senior OB at Valley General opened yesterday."

So, she hadn't been the only one keeping career opportunities secret.

"And if you don't get it?"

"I will," Milo stated.

To be so confident...

"But if you don't, will you consider your mother's opportunity then?" Pain dug into her palms and she forced her fingers to relax.

"If I don't get it, then I'll look at Mercy General. Valley hires out of there regularly."

Pain ripped through her as she looked at his infernal boards. He'd never thought she was staying—no wonder Milo hadn't adjusted his plans to include her.

Instead, he'd painstakingly rewritten the words her hand had erased two days ago. Though the ink looked different. Her heart sank as she stared at it.

Why didn't it have the silky look of Dry Erase markers?

Stepping up to the board, she ran her finger along it. It came away clean.

She held it up for his inspection. "I was a traveling nurse for more than a decade. It was a job I loved, but I never considered leaving St. Brigit's until you refused to even consider Oceanside Clinic. To consider something different, some other way to honor your father, your dreams, and mine. It doesn't just have to be Valley General, Milo."

"If you had seen his face, Quinn. Felt what I felt—what I still feel. I know objectively that my actions weren't the reason he passed. But I need this, and it is within my reach. If not now, then in a few years."

How did one compete with a ghost?

"I need this."

More than he needed her?

Quinn couldn't ask that question. Couldn't bear the answer.

Her hand shook as she pointed at the boards. "I understand, but these aren't *our* plans, Milo. They're yours. And in the last forty-eight hours, the only change you've made to them is to write the notes in permanent marker."

Quinn closed her eyes and rocked back on her heels. "If this isn't what I want, then I don't fit in to these plans, do I? My desire to run a unit, Oceanside…" Her lip trembled, but she refused to break. Not yet. There would be plenty of time for that later. *Forever.*

"Of course you fit in. You love being at St. Brigit's, And you'd love Mercy General or Valley General." Milo's nose scrunched as he looked at her.

"So, if I make all the adjustments. Change all my plans…" Quinn shuddered.

How come her dreams were so easy to dismiss?

And why was this happening with Milo? The one person who knew her better than anyone.

"You go from position to position, trusting your gut." Milo stared at her. "That isn't a plan."

She'd had a lot of positions over the last decade, but each one had added a valuable piece to her résumé. And each had taught her what she really wanted, and it wasn't to be another face in a large hospital.

"Trusting my intuition on job choices doesn't mean that I don't think things through. Just because I don't need to list out every move for the next five or fifty years doesn't make my choices less valid. It doesn't mean I don't know what I want." Quinn brushed away the lone tear that refused to listen to her mandate.

"I want to belong, to be chosen. For who *I* am. I don't want someone who has to fit me in. I want a man who stands beside me and sees me and my dreams in his future. Who is willing to change his plans if it's what's best for us." Quinn stared at him, willing him to change his mind. To say he wanted her. No matter what.

"Your dreams matter to me. But I need this. I need Valley General," Milo countered, and the final piece of hope died inside her.

"Why? It's just a place. Why does it have to be the only place?" Pain tumbled through her, but she needed an answer.

"I've thought about it for years. I've researched everything." He pushed a hand through his hair.

It wasn't an answer, not really. But she'd heard similar words before, so many times.

Our plan is best, Quinn. We've done all the research and work, so you don't have to. Why can't you just get in line?

"Where do I fit on that list, Milo? Or your family? Or children? What if we don't fall in line with the plan?" Quinn gestured to the boards.

Love, real love, didn't ask you to adjust for it. It accepted you.

"Life can't be outlined like a book. Chaos and change are inevitable." Her heart wept as she stared at him. It had to be this way, but she hated it.

She wished she'd paid more attention to the last time they'd kissed. Wished she could remember the last time he'd held her more clearly. If she'd known it had been the last time, she'd have made sure to let it seep into every edge of her soul.

Pushing the pain away for a moment longer, she met his gaze. "I want you to get everything on your list, Milo.

I really do." She tried to force out a goodbye, but her heart refused to provide any words as it broke.

She turned without looking back. If she looked at him, she'd break.

If he had chased after her, she'd have pledged whatever he'd wanted. But he hadn't. He'd stayed in the study while she'd packed the small number of belongings she'd accumulated during their relationship, the door firmly closed to her dreams and wishes.

She hung her key on the ring by the kitchen and forced her eyes to stare ahead as she closed the front door behind her. It was time to move on. To find the next adventure, even if it never excited her as much as these last few months with Milo had.

CHAPTER TEN

MILO SAT ON the floor of his living room and stared at the bright yellow kitchen as the sun rose. He'd spent the entire night trying to figure out how everything had gone so wrong. How his deepest dream had evaporated in a matter of minutes.

He looked at the small box on the coffee table. After Quinn had left the study, he'd stared at the window, trying to find the right words to explain why he'd rewritten everything in permanent marker. To explain that after his mother had offered him the chance to run Oceanside, he'd rewritten it so he couldn't change his mind. So, it wouldn't seem like an option to derail him from his father's memory. It was ridiculous and childish. But Milo had felt better after the small gesture.

Then he'd stared at the boards rather than run after her. Trying to find an adjustment, so they both got what they needed. A way that didn't feel like he was letting down his father or Quinn. But nothing had come to him.

Finally, he'd grabbed the box from the drawer where he'd hidden it weeks ago. He hadn't planned to buy it. It had happened by accident. *By impulse.* He'd walked past the jewelry store and had just been pulled in.

But after the purchase, he'd started second-guessing himself. Wondering if it had been too soon. If he should have spent more time researching to find the perfect symbol of his devotion. He'd spent so much time worrying over it that he hadn't even managed to figure out the best plan for asking the woman he loved to be his wife.

And then he'd been unable to give her what she'd really wanted—needed—when she'd asked. A chance to be included in his future—fully. Her dreams and his, blended in harmony.

He'd wanted her, but on his terms. By the time he'd grabbed the ring—the symbol that he wanted her forever—Quinn was already gone. And she hadn't answered any of his calls or texts since.

He didn't blame her. Quinn had only wanted to know that she was part of his life. That she'd have a say on their future. And he'd dismissed her dreams. Dismissed her gut feelings.

Dismissed the woman he loved.

He'd clung to an idealized version of a memory and lost the person that made him happiest as a result. And now he had no idea where she was.

Milo laid his head back against the couch and tried to force air through his lungs. She was gone, and he was alone. Everything hurt.

How was he supposed to get through the rest of his life without Quinn? From the moment they'd met, he'd felt like she was family. She'd been his constant. A place of sanctuary. His person. Why hadn't those words materialized when they'd been arguing?

Fear.

Milo pressed his palms against his closed eyes. As soon as she'd landed in LA, Milo had been afraid that Quinn would leave. Feared that he wouldn't be able to compete with the adventures she'd already had and could have in the future. She wanted to work at Oceanside now, but what if, in a few years, another phone call came, offering something even more exciting?

He pressed his palm to his forehead. He had spent all his time calculating how she might leave…but what if she stayed? Milo had never fully considered that. And he'd never forget the look in her eyes when he'd confessed that he'd been looking for signs that she'd leave for almost a year—or the selfish hope that had wanted her to promise that she wouldn't. Relationships took adjustments, but other than painting his kitchen, what adjustments had he made for her?

None! his brain shouted. He'd held back, hoping she'd make all the changes. That way, he wouldn't have to examine what he really wanted. What he really needed. He could just float by on the path that he thought might bring him some form of closure with his dad.

Even if he wasn't sure it was what he really wanted.

God, Quinn was right to leave.

He dialed her number again and bit his lip as the call immediately went to voice mail. What had he expected? She'd asked to have a say in the dreams they followed, and he'd stayed silent, terrified to embrace a future that might mean letting go of the past.

He called St. Brigit's. He wasn't on shift today, but he needed to take some additional personal time. He couldn't see Quinn. At least not yet.

Not until I have a *plan.* The thought ran through his mind, and Milo wanted to bang the rigidity out of his brain.

He'd lost Quinn because of his incessant need to organize his life, to pretend he had some say in life's chaos. Yet, that was where his brain wanted to go, wanted to leap to: the security of plans.

Except nothing in his plans had prepared him for such heartbreak.

He called HR and asked for two weeks off. He doubted

his heart would ever heal, but maybe by then the simple act of forcing oxygen into his lungs wouldn't be so difficult.

Standing, he ignored the pain in his legs. He'd been on the floor for too long, but Milo didn't care. He couldn't stay here, couldn't be where everything reminded him of Quinn. Grabbing his keys, he raced for the door. He didn't have a destination in mind, but anywhere had to be better than the emptiness here.

Quinn stared at the gray walls of her hotel room. When had gray become such a popular color? At least the sad color matched the feel of her soul. The hotel was the first one she'd passed after leaving last night. It wasn't much, but with the rental insurance from the fire and staying with Milo, her nest egg was quite healthy.

Milo…

Her lungs burned, but her eyes were finally dry. No matter what she did, his name kept popping into her mind. Even now, it felt like he was everywhere. Milo had seeped into her soul years ago, and there was no way to remove him. No matter how much it hurt.

Her phone rang, but it wasn't Milo's ringtone. Milo had called repeatedly after she left, but Quinn hadn't trusted herself to answer. As soon as she'd closed the door to the apartment, she'd wanted to turn around. Wanted to say that it didn't matter that his life plan was written in permanent ink—without her—she could accept it.

But she couldn't. She'd lived like that before, and she hadn't been able to bend enough to fit. If Milo ever looked at her like her parents had, like she was intruding…

She wasn't sure she could survive it. It was better to leave before that happened. Quinn tasted blood, and belatedly realized that she was biting the inside of her cheek.

Milo wanted a different dream. It wasn't wrong, and he

should have it because he'd worked so hard to make sure it happened. She just hoped it brought him all the peace he sought, and wished she'd realized that he would never walk away from his dream before she'd lost her heart so completely.

Each time she heard his ringtone, she'd burst into tears, wishing he'd leave her be. When the calls had stopped, she'd cried again. Nothing felt right anymore.

The phone rang again, and she flipped it over. Her fingers froze, but she managed to answer just before it shifted to voice mail.

"Asher?" Quinn kept her voice level.

"Quinn." Asher's voice was rigid, and immediately she knew something was wrong.

"What's wrong?"

"Samantha's been hospitalized. They're trying to stop her labor." Asher let out a soft whimper. "She's only twenty-two weeks along. If she delivers..." Asher's voice broke.

"Where are you?" Quinn slid from the hotel bed. They weren't close, but she could hear the pain in his voice. And Samantha would be understandably terrified.

"Valley General," Asher stated. "You don't have to come." But she could hear the plea in his voice.

"I'm on my way."

"I think you probably don't need me anymore." Quinn stood and stretched. The hours had passed in a stream of nurses, monitors and checks. The doctor had decided Samantha would spend at least the next two days being monitored, and then be on strict bed rest for the rest of her pregnancy. But, at last, it seemed like Samantha was out of danger.

"Thank you so much for coming," Samantha said as

she held out a hand. "Asher, why don't you see Quinn to her car?"

Quinn started to protest, but she caught a look between the two and held her tongue. She and Milo had been able to do that, too. To communicate so much with just a small look.

Her heart bled as she started for the door. Focusing on Asher and Samantha's issues had allowed her a brief respite from her own brokenness. The idea of heading back to her small hotel room held no appeal, but staying here didn't seem like an option, either. Quinn had hovered long enough.

She let her brother follow her to the waiting room then turned to him. "I know that Samantha wanted you to see me out, but it's really okay, Asher. If you have any questions about bed rest or what to expect, you can call."

"I should have called you back." Asher's voice was low as he stared at her. His lip stuck out, and he sighed. "Should have jumped at the chance to have dinner or coffee."

Quinn's heart twisted as she looked at him. It would be easy to offer a platitude. To tell him that it was fine that he'd left her wondering what she'd done wrong and waiting patiently for a response that never came. But her heart wasn't in it. "So why didn't you?"

Her brother pursed his lips before he stuck his hands into his pockets. "I started to, so many times. But I had no idea how to say all that needed to be said. That should be said." Asher rocked back on his heels. "No matter how Mom and Dad tried to change you, you resisted. They tried to mold you into their image, and you refused." Asher ran a hand through his short hair. "You're my hero."

Quinn felt her mouth fall open. Hero? None of that made any sense. "Asher, I think you're remembering everything a bit wrong."

His cheeks heated as he shook his head, "No, I'm not. I gave in to everything they wanted. It was easier— God knows they rewarded me for it—but even after they passed..." He pushed a hand through his hair again. "I became a lawyer just like they wanted me to. Did so many things because—" his lip trembled as he met his gaze "—I didn't know who I was until a few years ago."

His eyes burned through her, but Quinn had no idea what to say.

"You were yourself. No matter how Mom tried to make you blend in, you stood out. You figured out what you wanted in life and left to get it."

"Sure of myself? I was terrified." Quinn shook her head. She'd never felt like she belonged. "I literally ran away."

"Could have fooled me," Asher lightly scoffed. "You set off on an adventure. And then another. And another... I was always in awe of your ability to escape. You never needed anyone."

Never needed anyone? The words struck her. She'd needed Milo, but had she ever told him that? The world spun around her as she tried to steady herself.

Her brother continued. "You see what you want and you go for it. No matter where it means you have to go."

She'd loved being a travel nurse, loved going new places. But it had been lonely, too. Never staying in one place, keeping people at a distance because you weren't sure you'd ever see them again. That was one of the reasons she'd come back to California.

To Milo.

She'd never said it was permanent, though. Milo had been waiting for her to pack her bags because she'd always packed them before.

Even her furniture had been rented.

But she hadn't wanted to get away from Milo.

Had she ever told him that? Ever told him that he was what grounded her, gave her the roots she desperately needed?

No.

Because she'd wanted him to change first. Wanted him to adjust his plans for her, rather than seeing if there was a way they could join their dreams together. Blood rushed through her ears as she tried to focus on her brother.

Asher's warm hand pressed into hers. "I just didn't know how to say how sorry I was for not standing up to Mom and Dad. For just following the safety of the plans laid out before me."

He huffed out a deep breath. "I was jealous of you."

"Jealous?"

He smiled. "When Mom and Dad said they wouldn't pay for nursing school, you told them that you'd already filled out the paperwork for scholarships and applied for a loan. I was in awe of your courage. You set a goal and didn't let anyone distract you or talk you out of it."

Like wanting to run the birthing center at Oceanside. She'd decided that was her next goal—her next adventure. And yet, when Milo hadn't immediately altered everything, she'd run.

Just like he'd feared she would.

But Milo wasn't her parents. His plans hadn't been designed to trap her. *She'd* set that trap, and stepped into it herself.

She knew how important plans were to him. How safe they made him feel. How they brought him closer to his father's memory. Yet she'd asked him to change everything. And it had cost her the person who made her feel whole.

Quinn's heart melted as she embraced her brother. "None of this is your fault. We each made mistakes, but that's in the past now." She meant the words. They'd been children in a home with impossible rules. And each had adapted in their own way. She was too old to keep running from past pains.

"I know it's selfish," Asher said, "but I kind of hope you're planning to stay in the area. At least for a little while. I'd love for our child to spend as much time as possible with Aunt Quinn."

Her heart pounded as she nodded. "I've actually been thinking of making my California residency permanent." The words felt right. She smiled as her brother beamed.

The Oceanside Clinic had four cars in the employee parking lot as he pulled in. But none of them belonged to his mother or Felix. At least he wouldn't have to immediately explain why he was there.

He'd driven here without thinking. But when he'd finally arrived in Oceanside, Milo hadn't wanted to go to his town house. The memory of Quinn kissing him there was imprinted on his brain. Instead, he'd sat on the beach, just thinking until the sun had finally started to sink over the ocean.

Kelly, the nurse at the front desk, smiled as he walked through the front door. "Dr. Russell." She started to stand, but he motioned for her to stay where she was. "We don't have any patients in labor, two patients and their little ones are sleeping, and Dr. Acton is on call. It's her last month before she moves." Kelly stopped chatting. "Sorry, slow night shift."

"I understand. The shifts drag when there's no one to help. I…" He looked at the pictures he'd helped his sister pick out. "I just needed to see this place."

The words left his mouth and he felt a weight lift from

his chest. He needed to walk through this center he'd helped design, needed a chance to say goodbye.

Kelly gave him a strange look, but she didn't say anything as he started down the hall.

Once his mother and Felix retired, he doubted the new physician would want to keep him on as a very part-time employee. His head hurt as he realized he would no longer have a connection to the place.

The thought that this would be someone else's pride and joy felt like a rock in his stomach. His mother and Felix had supported the idea of the birthing center, but it had been Milo's baby. He'd pored over the architect's plans, spent hours researching and investigating how to let mothers birth in complete comfort.

The door to his mother's office was open, and Milo slipped through it. This could be his. *Should be his.*

The thought held him, and Milo exhaled. Peace settled through him. His father wasn't at Valley General. His dad was with him no matter where he served, because Milo carried him with him always. Memories faded, but love carried through time and space. Why had it taken him so long to see that? To accept it?

His cell buzzed, and he smiled as he answered. "I'm surprised it took Kelly this long to let you know I was here."

"Is everything okay?" His mother's voice was tired, but he knew she'd come to the clinic if he said he needed it.

"No," Milo answered honestly. "But it will be. I'm going to run this clinic, Mom."

"And Quinn?"

Just her name was enough to make the blood rush to his ears as his heart ached. He swallowed as he stared across the hall at the office that should be hers. "If I can convince her, this will be our greatest adventure."

"If anyone can figure out a plan for that, it's you."

Milo smiled. "Maybe. But I need a favor."

"Name it!"

He could see his mother's smile in his mind. He hoped that he hadn't pushed Quinn too far. That she'd want to take this new path with him.

CHAPTER ELEVEN

"Why is Milo not on the schedule for the next two weeks?" Quinn's soul shuddered as she looked at Martina. He wasn't supposed to be on the schedule today, and she'd been grateful for the extra day to figure out how to tell him she was staying. And that she wanted to be with him, no matter what his plans were.

She'd turned down the position in Maine last night. For years, Quinn had picked up and moved on when life got tough. She'd controlled life by running from hurt. When she'd faced setbacks, she'd reached for the comfort of knowing that she could escape. But her heart didn't want an escape. There was nowhere better than wherever Milo was. Quinn Davis was done running. She was putting down roots.

The news that Milo was taking an extended vacation had been the talk of the employee lounge when she'd arrived this morning, everyone wondering what he was doing and commenting on the fact that he never normally took leave. She'd caught more than a few side glances her direction, too—though no one had worked up the courage to ask her directly if she knew where he was.

Thank goodness.

"He called in yesterday and asked for some leave." Martina leaned closer. "I bet he's interviewing for the position over at Valley General. If he gets it, he has a lot of unused leave he's accumulated here that he either uses or loses."

"Valley General." Quinn nodded. "Of course."

Martina held up her hands. "I suspect he'll get it. I still remember him telling me his five-year plan during his interview. That man had it all outlined—even then." She shook her head. "I've already put out a few feelers. But if you know anyone who might be interested—send me their name. Oh, and we need to start thinking about your contract, too. We would love to retain you. Let's set up a meeting next week to go over the details."

"I'll get it on your calendar." Quinn smiled.

Her phone buzzed and she froze as Milo's name jumped across the screen.

You left something at my place. Can you come by after your shift?

Left something? Quinn wasn't sure what he'd found, but it couldn't have been anything major. Was this his way of trying to talk...or of pushing the last remnants of her from his life?

I'll be there as soon as my shift ends.

She hit Send and then forced herself to focus on work. Time would move faster if she stayed as busy as possible.

The knock at the door sent tingles across Milo's skin. Quinn was here. She was finally here.

When he'd sent the text this morning, Milo had been prepared to wait exactly one day for her to respond before he took more drastic measures to seek her out. But she'd answered almost instantly. He'd wrapped his mind around all the potential outcomes this afternoon, but he was not going to focus on those now.

Sliding the door open, he took her in. She wore jeans and a loose T-shirt. Her dark hair was pulled into a low ponytail. His body ached with relief as his eyes drank her in.

Quinn…

"Are you going to invite me in?" Her voice wavered a little as she looked past him.

"Oh my gosh!" Milo jumped to the side. "Yes, of course. It's just so good to see you. My brain stopped working." Her lips tipped up, and Milo released the breath he'd been holding. "I was worried you might change your mind about coming."

Her dark eyes raked across him.

Did she want to touch him as much as he wanted to touch her? He refused to examine that thought. There was too much to say.

"You said I left something." Her head swiveled as she looked around the living room. "Where is it?"

"Here." Milo placed a hand to his chest as he let the words flow. "You left my heart."

Milo stepped toward her, grateful when she didn't move away. "It's yours, Quinn, and it always will be. I should have said so many things the other night. I should have promised you forever. I thought my plans grounded me, but they were just a cover for my fear that everything can be ripped away. My life has revolved around plans and control since Dad died. They were my talisman—my protection against the world of unknowns. And my way to keep him close." Milo swallowed, waiting for the grief he always felt when he thought of his dad, but it didn't overwhelm him this time.

"That's understandable."

"Maybe." Milo reached for her hand, unable to keep from touching her. Her fingers wrapped through his, but there was still so much to say. "But I can't lose my dad—he's part of me. And I never meant to make you feel like you weren't part of my future. *You* are my plan, Quinn."

"I know you like to travel—" Milo let go of her hand to trace his fingers across her chin "—but I'm hoping that I can convince you to stay local. I love it here. Love being close to Mom and Felix and Gina. Even if she does make the worst vegetable dip in history. But if you need—"

"I owe you an apology, too." Quinn closed the bit of distance between them as she interrupted.

"No."

Her finger landed against his lips. "Let me finish."

Milo nodded as he relished the heat from her other hand slipping into his. His heart steadied as Quinn held him. For the first time in two days, the pressure in his chest finally evaporated.

"You were right." Quinn pressed her lips to his cheek. "Maine was my backup." A tear ran down her cheek. "After I wiped away your plans…" She sucked in a breath. "I worried that maybe I wouldn't fit into your life. Wouldn't have a place. And I panicked. But I'm done running."

He pulled her close and just held her. Pressing light kisses to the top of her head, Milo waited until she looked up at him. Pushing the tears from her cheek, Milo held her gaze. "I will always choose you, Quinn. Always."

Then his lips captured hers, and her arms wrapped around his neck as she deepened the kiss.

"I love you, Quinn Davis."

"I love you, too."

He got down on one knee and smiled as her fingers covered her lips. "I bought this weeks ago. When you asked me to show you that your dreams were part of my future,

I should have pulled this from the drawer and gotten down on one knee then. You are my plan, Quinn. From now until forever, please say you'll be my wife."

Lowering herself to her knees, Quinn put her hands on either side of his face as she dropped a kiss against his lips. "Yes. Yes." She giggled as he placed the diamond on her finger. "It's perfect."

"There is one other thing we need to discuss. About St. Brigit's…"

"Martina mentioned my contract today. And that you might be taking a position at Valley General." Quinn squeezed his hand.

"You didn't sign a new contract, did you?" Milo's voice was rushed, and he shook his head. "It's just, I made one plan without talking to you. Well—two, but that's all. I promise."

Quinn raised an eyebrow. "What have you done?"

"After you left, I couldn't stay here. I went to Oceanside, I meant to say goodbye to the facility, but…" Milo smiled. "It's where I belong. I want to run the clinic and the birthing center. Do you want to run the midwife unit?"

"Yes!" Quinn's scream echoed in the room, and she covered her lips. "That was a little loud!"

"I loved it." Milo kissed her. "But there is still the other plan."

Quinn's brow furrowed, but she didn't interrupt him.

"I got my mother and Felix to agree to put off their retirement for six months." Milo pushed a loose piece of hair behind her ear.

"Why?" Quinn's eyes were wide as she stared at him.

"In case you wanted to go on one more tour with Doctors Without Borders. You mentioned getting away a few weeks ago. Once we take over the clinic, that option will not be something we can do—at least not without a lot of pre-planning. And if we have a family, then it becomes even harder."

"We?" Quinn's voice was low as she ran her hand along his cheek.

"Figure it might be a good time for an adventure."

Milo's heart exploded as she launched into his arms.

"I love you!" She peppered his face with kisses.

EPILOGUE

QUINN BREATHED THROUGH her contractions as she smiled at Robin. She'd been walking with the young woman down Oceanside's hallways for the last hour, hoping it might speed up Robin's contractions. But all it appeared to have done was bring on Quinn's. When she'd said she planned to work up until she delivered, she hadn't meant it so literally.

She looked toward the clock and frowned. The last three had been exactly five and a half minutes apart.

Milo strolled through the front door of the birthing center as she and Robin rounded the nurses' station. He grinned before stepping aside and letting Kelly through, too. Neither of them was supposed to be on rounds today.

"Who told on me?" Quinn squinted as Kelly took Robin's arm.

"So, you are in labor?" Robin grinned.

"I run to the restroom for five minutes..." Quinn sighed. "I thought I was covering it well, too."

Robin let out a sheepish laugh. "You squeezed my arm almost every seven minutes, then every six. At least our little ones will have the same birthdays." She laughed again before a contraction overtook her.

"I was going to call you as soon as I hit five minutes." Quinn beamed as Milo dropped a kiss on her forehead.

"Right now, all I can think about is that our daughter

will be here soon. I brought the birthing bag." Milo's smile spun up her spine as he held up the bag.

They'd packed it weeks ago. Actually, he'd packed it—carefully going over each item on his list. Quinn had laughed and said all they really needed was an outfit for the baby and car seat, but he'd insisted.

"I think this little one is a bit anxious." Quinn gripped Milo's arm as she breathed through another contraction. "Her due date isn't for another three days. She isn't following the plan."

Milo laughed before he kissed her. "Some plans are meant to be broken."

* * * * *

AWAKENING
HIS SHY VET

SHELLEY RIVERS

MILLS & BOON

For Mum—thank you for always encouraging the weirdness and the love of colour.

CHAPTER ONE

THE SMELL OF steak pie and the repeat firing of a machine gun made no sense to Ruby Day as she dragged open her heavy eyelids. The long drive from Cambridge to Dorset the previous night had left her exhausted and desperate for nothing but indulging in a further twenty-four hours' worth of sleep.

Frowning at the hot breath fanning her suspiciously damp cheek, she focused blearily on the snoring grey Irish Wolfhound stretched out alongside her, hogging a good portion of the already space-challenged double bed. A slobbering pink tongue hung from his mouth only inches from her nose.

'Dog,' she growled softly. 'When are you going to accept that this is *my* bed, not *yours?* I spent a small fortune on *your* bed—the least you can do is sleep on it occasionally.'

She wiped her cheek, wincing as hound saliva dampened her fingertips. Lovely. What every girl yearned for—doggy dribble for face cream. As if waking to the meaty aroma of canine breath wasn't enough.

Sitting up, she reached for the blue dressing gown draped across the foot of the bed, jumping when loud banging suddenly vibrated through the caravan. Well, that explained the strange machine gun noise in her dream. Not a weapon of destruction, but someone knocking impatiently on the door of her home.

Pushing the still snoring long-legged dog to one side, Ruby slipped out from beneath the warm cover, gasping as her feet hit the cold black-and-white vinyl floor. Tiptoeing to the open bedroom door, she hesitated for a moment, hoping the person knocking would give up and leave. Conversation was the last thing she wanted before caffeine perked the sluggishness from her veins and settled her nerves.

'Hello?' a female voice called out, shattering Ruby's hopes, before another round of banging resumed.

Whoever the woman was, she meant to get a reply, and Ruby doubted even the sinful dead charcoaling in hell would be able to ignore the noise.

'Hi, it's Kiki Morsi. I was wondering if you'd like a cup of tea?'

Ruby stared at the door and a kaleidoscope of thoughts kicked her heart into a galloping trot. Wasn't the man she was here to have an interview with named Morsi? Was this woman his wife? Sister? Mother? Someone related to the man, anyway, and not someone she could just ignore.

Slowly creeping into the kitchen, Ruby eased over to the window by the kitchen sink, grateful that she'd lowered all the blinds the previous night. She'd learnt the hard way to guard her privacy over the years, when closing out the world had become a daily habit.

Leaning over the sink, Ruby felt the metal edge dig through the thin layer of her cotton pyjamas and into her stomach. She peeked through the small crack where the blind didn't quite cover the window frame and got her first sight of her early-morning caller.

A small blonde woman wearing a green coat and a blue woolly hat topped with several multi-coloured pompoms stood in the veterinary practice's car park. She cuddled a tortoiseshell cat against her chest, and an Old English Sheepdog sniffed intently at her left coat pocket. Apart from the hat, the cat and the dog, she appeared relatively normal.

'Are you Mr Morsi's wife?' Ruby yelled out, grimacing seconds later at the stupidity of her query.

How dumb did she sound, yelling through a closed door with a question a ten-year-old would cringe at? And it didn't matter who the woman was because she needed to go away—and fast.

The woman chuckled and glanced towards the window. 'I am. Can I come in? I promise I'm friendly. It's my husband who's known to growl and occasionally bite.'

Ruby pulled back, her fingers digging into the sink's sides. No way was she opening the door while she stood there in her Christmas reindeer pyjamas without a lick of make-up covering her skin. She never allowed *anyone* to see her without her face on. Not since her sixteenth birthday, when—

She shuffled away, wrapping her arms around her body, suddenly cold from the memory and the lack of heat in the caravan. *No, don't think about it.* It never helped, and her nerves were already rattled over the upcoming interview without adding painful recollections from her past.

'No!' She winced at her bluntness, her nails digging into her elbows.

How to make friends, Ruby. Just keep insulting them and that should get you hated by even more people.

She sucked in a shaky breath, closed her eyes and tried again, 'What I mean is, I—'

Ruby cursed silently. The woman would think her rude, whatever excuse she used, but too bad. She glared towards the bedroom at Dog, who lay content in the middle of her bed, showing a definite lack of the guard dog gene.

'Wh-what I mean is,' she stammered loudly, 'I'm not dressed and the place is a mess. I'll throw on some clothes and be out in ten…no…maybe twenty minutes.'

A pause followed, before the woman outside chuckled. 'Great. Come and join us in Reception when you're ready. Can't wait to meet you, Ruby. Alex is excited too. And ignore my joke about him being growly. He's a real sweetheart—honest!'

Letting out a sigh of relief at the sound of the woman's retreating footsteps, Ruby slumped against the cupboard. What had happened to her alarm? She remembered setting it last night, after she'd driven into the car park. Alex Morsi had said she could pitch up here in his email, and after travelling for hours the last thing she'd felt like doing was searching for a caravan park. Most would be fully booked at this time of year anyway, with the schools about to break for the Easter holidays.

She straightened and headed for the bedroom, stepping on the crushed and mangled plastic remains of what used to be her alarm clock, scattered all over her bedroom floor. It was a miracle she hadn't stepped on anything when she'd left the bedroom. Thankfully, the battery showed no signs of canine destruction.

Picking up the pieces, Ruby threw them into the wastepaper bin and glared at the sleeping dog. 'I buy you a ton of toys and you eat my alarm clock on the one day I really need it to wake me. Are you trying to make my life harder, Dog? Do you not want me to find a job so we can settle in one place for a while?'

She smiled ruefully at the dog and shook her head.

'You lie there, big boy. Let's hope I can save this cluster of a mess and get through the interview without things getting any worse.'

Tugging a hand through the tangles of the black curly

hair that hung in tight ringlets to her shoulders, she headed to the kitchen and retrieved a can of pre-made coffee from a cupboard. Pulling off the lid, she took a long swig, before moving to the small bathroom at the caravan's opposite end.

Once washed and freshened, Ruby snatched up her make-up bag and a magnifying mirror from the shelving unit behind the door. Life in a caravan had taken some getting used to, but now Ruby loved it. When she got bored with a place, or things didn't turn out great, she just packed up and left. No ties, no problems and no trouble.

Returning to the kitchen, she placed the make-up bag and mirror on the table and sat down on the padded seat. Unzipping the bag, she placed its contents carefully on the table, setting each item out in the order she intended to use them.

Picking up a small pot of concealer, two shades lighter than her own natural skin tone, she quickly and expertly sponged the cream over her face and along the length of her neck, taking extra time to camouflage the pink scarring that ran from underneath her jaw and finished just shy of her collarbone.

Once happy the scar no longer showed, Ruby applied powder in a matching colour to set the concealer. Next, she reached for black eyeliner, and with careful, expert strokes swiped a long thick line along the edge of her eyes, ending with an upward tilt at each corner.

Her fingers hovered for several moments over the various different eyeshadows in colours ranging from dark plum to golden-brown. Finally, she chose and applied a shimmering metallic blue shade. A generous brush of thick black mascara finished her eyes perfectly.

Fluttering her eyelashes, she stared at her reflection for a second before reaching for a blue lipstick. Several slick swipes and her eyes and lips matched. A clean cotton bud wiped superfluous lipstick from the silver ring in the centre of her lower lip.

With a final spray of face mist to set the make-up in place, she took one last glance in the mirror. Transformation completed and armour on. Now she could face the next hour and the upcoming interview.

'Hello, Ruby Day. Time to face the world again.'

She studied her reflection for a moment longer, taking in the black curly hair and the pale skin hiding the scar. Eyes large and dramatic…lips full and plump. A face to show to a cold and uncaring public who loved to revel in other people's misery with morbid interest. The perfect face to hide behind in a world that chose to see only the make-up and not to search further to learn who the woman was underneath.

That suited Ruby. With this make-up nobody instantly recognised her mother's model face in hers. No one compared her to her parent or asked about the father she'd supposedly betrayed. With this make-up people didn't gaze at her with pity, interest or horror.

At sixteen years old, her teenage self had learnt several hard lessons, and one was how to create a defence against the hurt and pain others wanted to inflict on her. Over time her make-up and clothes had become her secure shield.

She turned the mirror upside down, hiding her reflection from view, and stood. She walked into the bedroom and changed into a pair of tight black jeans and a black T-shirt with a large silver cross on the front. After adding several silver bracelets and a necklace with a large silver and blue heart dangling from it, she finally tugged on black leather boots.

If her make-up didn't send Alex Morsi into convulsions, her clothes definitely would.

She finished the outfit off with a fitted vintage black velvet jacket that had once belonged to her mother. She stroked a hand over the soft, smooth material—it was one of the few items she'd kept from the past, and a connection to the woman she loved and missed every day.

With a final quick check in the full-length mirror attached to the back of the bedroom door, she grabbed her black leather handbag and left the room.

Alex Morsi and his staff would no doubt be like all the other practices she'd applied to. Ready to dismiss her application the minute they set eyes on her. After all, who employed someone who dressed with an unmistakable Goth vibe? No one who owned a veterinary practice, that was for sure.

This whole trip to Dorset was nothing but a waste of time and petrol money. Why she had promised her old tutor, Professor Handel, to give it one last go, she didn't know. Misplaced gratitude, probably. The woman had frequently gone out of her way to help Ruby during the years she'd studied at college, becoming more than a tutor— she'd become a real friend.

Ruby already dreaded the evening phone call she'd promised to make, when she'd have to confess that, yet again, she'd not secured the position. Though for some reason, Professor Handel had insisted that Alex Morsi was different.

Yeah, right. No doubt Morsi was another middle-aged vet who wore tweed and fashioned himself on the old television dramas so often repeated on TV.

She was tired of it all. Not just driving miles to each interview, but the horrified expressions that greeted her appearance and the hastily concocted excuses and promises to call back—calls she never received. So what if she dressed differently and liked dramatic make-up? Her clothes made her feel safe and able to face the world.

No one complained or looked strangely at ordinarily dressed candidates when they turned up for an interview.

But no more, Ruby decided, snatching up a bunch of keys from the kitchen table. The events of the past had left her with no choice but to dress and look this way. After this interview she was done trying. Time to finally face reality and pack away the dream of becoming a practising vet for good.

Kern MacKinley lay on the grass, staring up at the sky, almost gagging on the bitter taste of failure. Memories old and painful gnawed and tore at his conscience, burning reminders of a past he'd done his damnedest to bury and forget.

Nineteen years he'd stayed away from this farm. Nineteen long, exciting years filled with the heady, sweet taste of ambition and success. Nineteen years of hard work and determination, during which everything he'd hoped and dreamed of professionally had come true. Wonderful, perfect days, weeks and months filled with glory and triumph as he clawed, climbed and fought to build his reputation as one of the top racehorse trainers in the country—if not the world.

He was a man people admired and looked up to. Someone whose work ethic and training methods they respected and revered.

But now he lay on the Dorset land of his childhood and everything he'd built and achieved during those heady nineteen years sat in failure and decay. Ruined beyond hope or fixing. Thirty-eight years old and he had nothing left in his life but regret and heartbreak after all those years battling to be one of the best in horse racing.

Now he was nothing more than a lousy failure!

The only thing that had survived the bloody carnage was now so broken it might have been kinder if she'd died with the rest. Then at least her pain and sorrow wouldn't be trapped inside her, like a festering wound waiting to explode.

Rubbing a hand over the ache in his chest, he sighed, his eyes following a cloud as it floated above him. There was no one to blame for the whole horrendous mess but his own sweet self. He'd purposely stuck his pig-stubborn head in the ground and pretended not to see the problems stewing in his personal life—or listen to the one person who mattered.

And what had his obstinacy cost him?

Everything.

His reputation, three prized racehorses who'd deserved his protection, and the woman he'd once upon a time promised to love and treasure. The woman who, despite the problems in their relationship, had deserved his help when it might have made a difference. Before it had all finally been amplified into the catastrophe it had become.

Closing his eyes, he refused to picture her face, burying the image in the murky pit of denial. Even now, after everything, it was still a habit he found himself unable to break. Better to hold back than confront the unpleasant facts of what his selfishness had driven another person to do.

Opening his eyes, he forced his mind to the present. All he owned sat in two cardboard boxes on the passenger seat of the old horsebox parked not far away, together with one emotionally damaged horse, five thousand pounds in his pocket, an old inheritance he didn't want and a throbbing hangover courtesy of the bottle of vodka that had kept him company last night.

His life was well and truly stuffed.

Ignoring the pressing discomfort of a full bladder, he continued to stare unseeingly at the sky. What the hell was he supposed to do now? Two days ago he'd come back to Dorset so his wife's ashes could finally be scattered in her family's special spot, and he'd stayed.

Where did a has-been go when the world turned away, determined and eager to forget him?

The recent months had left him with no choice but to sell everything he'd worked for, to pay his debts and walk away. Forcing him to accept charity and hand-outs from people he'd never considered friends, while the ones he'd thought were had deserted him without even a goodbye.

Out of habit, he reached for his mobile, resting in the centre of his bare chest, and checked for messages. His thumb slipped over the screen in pathetic hope. Hope that quickly died after several seconds. Nothing except a message from his service provider, notifying him that he needed credit.

No one called any more. These days his phone stayed silent because his name was shrouded in whispers, gossip and scandal. He was someone no sane person in the racing world wanted to trust with the care of their precious thoroughbred livestock. A trainer no one wanted to touch. The last nineteen years had all been for nothing.

What the hell was he going to do now?

Everything was wrecked because he hadn't seen the damage that chasing after his dreams had caused to the one person he should have protected and helped.

God, what an idiot he was.

A noise drew his attention back to the sky. Three white gulls flew above him, squawking as they went. Their large wings flapped in perfect timing as they headed some place new.

A rare smile tugged at Kern's lips. 'Have a safe journey—'

Suddenly something swooped over him. A second later a small red and brown robin landed on his bare stomach.

'Well, hello,' he whispered, not wanting to scare the bird.

Small dark eyes stared back, before the robin started pecking at the wiry hairs circling Kern's tummy button.

'Ouch! No. That's attached, you little—'

Kern registered something wet and warm on his skin a second after the robin flew off. Glancing down, he saw bird droppings splattered across his stomach.

Great, even the wildlife wanted to echo how crap his life was.

'Thanks!' he yelled to the long-gone bird. 'Like I need the reminder.'

Rolling onto his feet, Kern stared at the river that marked the edge of MacKinley land. Dressed in nothing but blue boxers, he strolled towards it, feeling the damp grass cushioning his footsteps, the green blades tickling his toes.

It was the same river where he'd played and swum during his childhood. He'd kissed his first sweetheart and eagerly tried to lose his virginity behind the bushes that grew in places along the bank. It was where he'd thought up boyhood daydreams and big plans. Back when his mother had run the place and kept his stepfather out of Kern's business.

A time before she'd betrayed him and everything he'd once thought true. Long before he'd fallen in love with a neighbour's youngest daughter and run away with her. Before he'd married her and formed a new life away from their families. A time before he'd bought his first racehorse and won his first major trophy.

Coming to a halt on the bank, he dug his toes into the grass and breathed in a lungful of sharp morning air. Wriggling the gold wedding ring off his finger, he glanced at it for several long seconds, sad that its familiar sight no longer stirred any emotions. Was he so far gone now that she'd ripped even that from him? Killed the last threads of his affection so that the act of removing this ring for the first time in nineteen years left him feeling nothing?

Drawing his arm back, he threw the ring into the air, watching as it flew, then dropped, breaking through the water's surface with a loud, distinct *plop*.

Now that last connection was gone too. Relegated to nothing but a memory to shovel on to the huge pile of disappointment his life had become.

He'd returned to this old run-down farm because there was no other place to go.

With that final thought, he jumped into the freezing water, gasping as it swirled over his skin and froze every inch of his body.

Scrambling back out of the water, his fingers grasping at the mud and grass, he crawled onto the bank with all the style and finesse of a flapping, gaping fish. Bent over on all fours, he dragged air into his shocked lungs as his mind vaguely registered the loss of feeling in his body.

How the hell had he forgotten how cold the river was? His life was already on the slide, without adding the agony of self-inflicted frozen body parts too.

They were staring. After years of enduring similar behaviour from strangers, Ruby had expected it and now fought the urge to stick out her tongue. Every time she arrived somewhere new the stares began, triggering prickles of tension as she prepared for the remarks and insults that followed. The nosy, ridiculous questions that always ended up becoming too personal.

She pretended not to notice as she stepped into the reception area. Closing the door, she caught the faint smell of disinfectant in the air, mixed with the whiff of rich coffee. Two women stood behind the counter. One she recognised as Kiki Morsi—the other was a grey-haired older woman.

'Ruby?' With a smile, Kiki stepped from behind the counter and walked over to greet her. Dressed in blue animal print scrubs, she held out a hand in welcome. 'It's lovely to meet you. I hope you didn't mind my knocking earlier? Only I've been so looking forward to your arrival.'

Not sure what to say, Ruby shook Kiki's hand, conscious of the intense gaze of the woman at the counter.

'My husband's finishing some paperwork and other important chores he apparently has to see to,' Kiki continued. 'I suspect they involve cuddling and singing to our daughter. Come and meet Anne.'

The woman behind the counter leaned forward. Her smile was wide and genuine. 'Nice to meet you, Ruby. Is your hair naturally curly, or thanks to chemicals and a skilled hairdresser?'

Stunned, Ruby stared at the woman before answering. Of all the things she'd expected, comments on her hair wasn't one of them. 'It's natural.'

'It's very pretty,' Kiki agreed, tilting her head to one side. 'Much better than my boring straight blonde mop. I'm going bald, you know—'

'You've just had a baby,' Anne interrupted. 'I keep telling you it will grow back. It's your messed-up hormones.'

'That's what Alex dared to say the last time we disagreed.' Kiki sighed. 'Until I threatened to stick his expert opinion somewhere uncomfortable. Anyway, enough about me and the love of my life. Tell me all about yourself, Ruby.'

'Ignore her, dear,' Anne said. 'She's recently returned from maternity leave and she's trying to get her fix of female conversation and gossip before she starts work for the day.'

Kiki grinned and nodded. 'All true. Though she forgot to mention that I'm incredibly nosy, too.'

Ruby laughed, envying the women's easy camaraderie. Their chattiness was something she wasn't used to and had never experienced for herself. Normally people avoided talking to her or just stared.

'So you live in that box, do you?' Anne asked, pointing out of the large window to Ruby's caravan.

Ruby stiffened, waiting for further remarks about her unusual home. Okay, it might not be everyone's idea of home, but she loved it. It was her sanctuary. Her place to escape when she required a private moment alone. Her 'Ruby' space, where she could lower her walls, wash off her make-up and be her true self.

'Yes.'

Anne shivered and folded her arms on the counter. 'Must get cold in the winter. It would play my old bones up something awful.'

It did get cold, but Ruby refused to admit it and felt a silly need to defend her home take hold. 'Actually, it's quite cosy.'

The sound of someone clearing his throat stopped further conversation.

Ruby turned to find a tall, dark-haired man frowning at the blonde woman at her side. His serious expression was a sharp contrast with the pink baby carrier strapped to his waist, holding a wriggling and softly grunting child.

His eyes flicked to Ruby, lingered for a second before returning to Kiki. 'Our daughter needs feeding.'

Kiki smiled, her expression softening as she gazed at the man and child. 'Stop frowning—you'll scare Ruby away. I'll get Neeve's bottle for you. Be *nice*.'

The man grunted, then returned his full attention to Ruby. His eyes narrowed for several seconds, before he held out his hand. 'Miss Day?'

Seized by nerves, Ruby grappled for her courage before placing her hand in his. She tried to speak, but her voice wouldn't work.

Not the tweed-wearing country vet she'd imagined, but although he was good-looking and young, Alex Morsi still gave off an unapproachable air that told her she didn't have any hope of getting a job at his practice. No doubt he was already figuring out a way to get rid of her and save himself the inconvenience of having to go through with the interview.

'I'm Alex Morsi.' He rubbed a loving hand over the baby's back, glancing to the older woman behind the desk. 'Anne, have you sent anyone to MacKinley farm yet?'

'Nope. Eloise said her nephew wanted you to go.'

Alex frowned and shook his head. 'I'm too busy with Neeve.' He glanced once again in Ruby's direction. 'Miss Day can go. From what I've read and heard, horses are her passion and her area of expertise.'

Kiki returned, carrying a bottle of baby's milk and a cloth. She handed both to her husband with a frown. 'Her name's Ruby, Alex.'

'I know,' Alex murmured, taking the bottle and throwing the cloth over his shoulder. 'Your CV states that you have a strong interest in equine health and have volunteered at several horse rescue centres in order to work with a couple of top specialists. Professor Handel also mentioned your gift.'

Ruby stiffened, unsure how to answer. How much had her old professor divulged about her supposed 'gift'? Neither of them had made it public knowledge during her training. Why had her mentor and friend trusted this man with the information?

Forcing herself to meet Alex's eyes, Ruby found only curiosity in his gaze. Deciding it might be best to blag her way through the rest of the conversation, while she tried to gauge how much he actually knew, she nodded. 'Yes, I loved helping out and I found the work fascinating.'

'Good. I'd like to observe you in action some time.'

Ruby didn't know what to say, so she stayed quiet. Should she trust his apparent interest or not? Did he want to watch her so he could afterwards pooh-pooh her gift as nothing but a charlatan's work? Surely Professor Handel should have warned her that she had told Alex Morsi about it.

Alex nodded, taking her silence as agreement. 'So you're the best person to deal with this visit, Miss Day. Anne will give you directions to the farm. No point relying on satnav—it's useless out there.'

Confused, Ruby asked, 'You want me to go and see a horse?'

Alex nodded. 'Yes. The owner wants a general check done. Nothing you can't manage. His name is Kern MacKinley. Have you heard of him?'

She shook her head. 'No.'

'He's a racehorse trainer,' Anne piped up. 'Damn good one too. Never met him, so I have no idea what he's like to deal with, but he's in the area and he wants his horse looked over. It isn't a good traveller or something. Nothing major or concerning, but best you go out and put the man's mind at ease.'

'Okay…'

'Don't worry, dear,' Anne said, writing something in a notebook. 'You'll be fine. I don't know Kern MacKinley— do know his aunt, though. Wonderful woman. Blunt to the point of rudeness, but honest to deal with. I've seen the nephew on television, of course. Handsome man…if you like them rough and smelling of horses. Avoid the stepfather if he's about. My Harry gets on with him well enough, but I've no time for the man.'

'I'll pop your tea in a flask, shall I?' Kiki asked brightly. 'You can take it with you. I think there are a couple of spare chocolate croissants in the kitchen too.'

Ruby frowned as Kiki rushed off again. Was this some bizarre dream?

She turned to Alex and asked, 'But don't you want to interview me?'

He sighed. 'Isn't Professor Handel's endorsement enough? She spoke very highly of you during our phone call the other day.'

'I—I don't know…' she stammered. 'Is it?'

'Miss Day, can you do the job? Are your qualifications real and up to date?'

Pulling herself together before she ruined this chance, Ruby nodded. 'Yes, of course they are.'

'Then off you go. I've no time to waste on interviewing you when my daughter needs feeding. It's best you learn, Miss Day, that my family always comes first. We can chat later, when you return, and go through everything you need to know. Will that please you?'

Ruby's mouth fell open as he walked away, kissing his wife on the head as they passed each other.

'It's Ruby, Alex,' Kiki reminded him brightly.

He snorted. 'I know. Until later, Miss Day.'

Kiki held out a blue flask to Ruby. 'My husband's really sweet when you get used to him. A year or two should do it.'

Confused, Ruby took the flask. 'He did give me a job, didn't he? I have that right?'

'Oh, yes. Trust me—Alex wouldn't let you near a client if he wasn't sure you knew your stuff. I'm sure he quizzed Professor Handel and checked your qualifications thoroughly.' She smiled once more and shoved a plastic bag holding two croissants Ruby's way. 'Welcome to the family, Ruby. It's good to have you here.'

CHAPTER TWO

RUBY SLAMMED ON the brakes and stared at the sight that had greeted her within moments of turning off the country lane and onto MacKinley land. No sooner had she bumped her way over the cattle grid, then bounced over several stomach-tilting potholes, she'd glanced to her left and set eyes on an almost naked man, kneeling on all fours beside a river.

Screwing her eyes shut, Ruby paused, then opened them again, convinced that the vision was nothing more than an illusion of her mind, brought on by the shock of actually securing her dream job and the peculiar way it had happened.

But, no, there the man knelt, in nothing but tight blue boxer shorts, almost as exposed as the beautiful nature in the field surrounding him.

What the heck had Alex Morsi sent her to deal with?

No one at the practice had mentioned anything about the risk of encountering an unclothed male. Was this some test, specially concocted to mess with the newbie vet? Was there even a horse requiring a visit, or was this all some stupid practical joke on her?

Pushing open the car door, Ruby slowly climbed out, unable to move her eyes from the sensual curve and dip of the man's back above the material so snugly covering the round curve of his very firm backside.

She was embarrassed by her own staring, but she couldn't stop herself. Apart from the countryside, and an old horsebox, there wasn't much else to look at. And from this angle the man appeared to be a perfectly formed specimen of masculinity.

Flushing at her thoughts, Ruby reluctantly moved in the man's direction and called out. 'Hello? I'm Ruby Day. Alex Morsi sent me from the vet's practice in town. Are you all right?'

The man glanced up, water dripping down his face. and puffed. 'I will be in a sec. Just waiting for things to defrost.'

'Defrost?'

'Yeah. My blood, for one, and other more sensitive parts of my body. Right now I'm struggling to feel anything from my waist down.'

'Oh,' Ruby said, wondering if he was one of those endurance swimmers who liked to pit themselves against nature.

Getting awkwardly to his feet, the man stared at her for several moments before demanding, 'Is he on his way?'

Good grief. Ruby glanced away, forcing her gaze to a nearby hedge despite the irresistible and unexpected urge to sneak a second eyeful. Anne had said the man was good-looking, but he made even her handsome new boss look plain. Tall, wide-chested and shivering, the man literally made her mouth water.

The man called out again. 'Hey? Miss?'

With no choice but to look at him, she resisted the childish urge to cover her eyes and croaked, 'Yes?'

'I asked if Morsi is on his way,' the man repeated, walking towards her.

His lack of embarrassment over his undressed state and his determination to talk to her while in it was unsettling. How was she supposed to have a conversation with him when he was so blatantly uncovered and when his swim had left the material of his boxers clinging rather rudely to him?

'Are you going to answer me or simply stand there?' he asked.

Ruby squirmed on the spot, unsure whether to shut her eyes or take off and make for the safety of her car.

Heat warming her cheeks, she folded her arms and admitted, 'To be honest, I'm debating whether to cover my eyes or leave.'

'Why?'

Surely the man knew?

She waved a hand towards his lower body. 'I wasn't expecting to arrive and find you so unclothed.'

Silence followed by a sharp intake of breath came from the man, before he glanced down at himself and said. 'God, can things get any worse?'

He spun round and hurried over to the horsebox and dragged on a pair of jeans. Sliding them on and up over his firm wet thighs with difficulty, he zipped them, before returning to Ruby.

'Sorry about that,' he puffed. 'Truth is I forgot I was only wearing my boxers.'

'You *forgot*?' she echoed disbelievingly.

He rubbed a hand over his head and sighed. 'Yes.'

'Really?' she drawled, doubting the truth of his apology. Who forgot they weren't wearing their clothes? The very fact that everything was exposed to the air proved his words a lie. 'Hmm… Do you often go swimming in the river in just your underwear?'

'Not any more,' he muttered. 'Not until summer, at least.'

She wasn't a prude, but she really hadn't expected her first call to involve an undressed male. Glancing at his still bare chest, she noticed water dripping in rivulets down over the well-defined hard muscles to hang like clear jewels from his dusky nipples. Her tongue tingled at the sight.

Her eyes moved farther down, stopping when they came to a strange patch of sludge splattered across his stomach.

'What's that?' she asked, trying to work out what the strangely familiar-looking muck was. It reminded her of watered-down grease, but it also resembled—

'What?' the man asked.

'There.' She pointed at the offending mess. 'On your stomach, just above your jeans.'

He clenched his jaw. 'It's nothing.'

'It looks like bird's m—'

'It's mud.'

'Mud?' she repeated. 'It doesn't look like mud. It's whitish, for one, and the patterning reminds me of—'

'The soil around here has a high chalk content,' he insisted.

She narrowed her eyes and considered the mess again. 'Are you sure? It does look an awful lot like—'

'It's nothing. I'll wash it off later. Now, about Morsi.'

'Don't you have a shirt or jumper?' she asked, deciding to forget about the muck on his stomach and get on with her job. 'Or is your memory so bad you've forgotten where you've put them?'

His eyes narrowed. 'No, I remember fine, thanks.'

'Then please fetch one and put it on. I'd really prefer to speak to you without any unnecessary distractions.'

He grinned, losing his serious expression for the first time. 'Distraction, huh? I'll take that as a compliment.'

'It's not meant as one,' she bit back, flustered slightly

by the sudden roguish twinkle in his blue eyes and the suggestiveness warming his voice.

It was a voice capable of seduction if he chose to use it. Not that she would ever be seduced by it. But she understood some women would find the effect of his deep silky tones coupled with his attractive body irresistible and maybe a bit knee-weakening.

'Well?' he asked, still smiling. 'Is Morsi coming?'

'No,' she said, wondering if he was some kind of exhibitionist.

Did he get a kick out of cavorting half-naked in his field? Well, he could do what he liked in private, but she wanted him covered. Preferably all over! Head to toe—twice over! Finger to finger and everything in between.

'Alex—Mr Morsi—asked me to call instead.'

His humour vanished at her reply. 'But I need someone with experience.'

'I *am* experienced,' she replied, not about to be bullied or intimidated into leaving before she saw her patient. Alex Morsi had given her the chance to prove herself and she wasn't going to fail at the first hurdle—or the first grumpy man with odd tendencies to nakedness and covered in suspected bird droppings.

He folded his arms and regarded her. 'You're a qualified vet? You're very young.'

Ruby closed the space between them. 'Mr MacKinley? I guess you *are* Mr MacKinley? Only you've yet to have the decency to introduce yourself other than to expose yourself in a fashion I would prefer *not* to see you in.'

'You sure?' he asked, his eyes once again flashing with humour.

'Yes, I'm s-sure,' she stuttered, tilting her chin up. 'Mr MacKinley, I am a qualified vet and more than capable of examining your horse. I have a degree to prove it.'

Crossing his arms, he asked, 'Is that supposed to mean something to me?'

'It means that your horse will be treated not only by someone who knows her stuff, but has the documentation to prove it.' She hoped he wouldn't demand to know how much actual experience she'd had, otherwise she would be forced to tell a little white lie.

He hesitated. 'My aunt gave me Morsi's name. Not yours.'

'I'm afraid he's busy,' she said, picturing Alex Morsi with his baby daughter. How would Mr MacKinley react if she informed him that her new boss put feeding his child before everything—including this man's precious horse? 'He sent me instead.'

'My girl isn't any old nag. She's a top thoroughbred.'

'She's a horse, no matter what her bloodline is or how much she's worth, Mr MacKinley. One whom I will be able to treat. If she's sick, I need to examine her.'

'She's not sick,' he hedged. 'I just want someone to check her over. We've done a lot of travelling over the last few days.'

Ruby nodded, not seeing a problem other than a trainer's protectiveness. 'Fine. If you'll show me where she is…?'

He stared back at her, then grinned. 'You blush when you're embarrassed.'

Gritting her teeth, Ruby replied, 'I am not embarrassed— merely shocked by your unorthodox behaviour. *Annoyed* is a better description of how I'm feeling.'

'You reacted as though you'd never seen a man in only his underwear before,' he persisted, not letting the subject go.

'Your horse, Mr MacKinley?'

Intense blue eyes stared down at her.

'Lady, that horse is all I have left in the world. Only the best vet is going to get anywhere near her.'

'I *am* the best, Mr MacKinley.'

An out-and-out lie, but one day Ruby intended to be. Once she had real everyday experience and a chance to prove herself. Something she was determined to do now that Alex Morsi had given her the opportunity and the means.

Kern MacKinley regarded her for a long moment, then said, 'Then I guess you'd better prove it to me.'

'I intend to, sir,' she replied, but the man had already turned and walked away.

What the hell was Morsi up to? Sending some young woman to do his job? Kern continued to walk in the direction of the back paddock while buttoning his shirt. His mind was still full of the recent exchange between him and the woman trailing several paces behind him. For such a shy woman, she packed a fair slap-down when roused.

He'd asked for the practice's top vet and they'd sent out Miss Ruby Day, with her weird make-up and her hair so thick and curly his fingers begged to slide into it and discover if it really was as soft and bouncy as it appeared. A woman who'd nearly choked on her prissy tongue when faced with a wet naked chest and more.

Irritated, he pushed the notion away. Miss Vet was no doubt waiting for Mr Right to come along and dance her up the altar. Some man who'd make promises he'd struggle to keep.

Once he'd been that man, to his own Miss Right, little knowing that she'd eventually become his Mrs Wrong, who'd refuse to listen to anything but the poisonous whispers in her head.

He sighed, feeling the weight of everything once again settling heavily on him.

To reach the paddock meant passing the old grey brick farmhouse he'd grown up in. Kern had purposely avoided the building since he'd driven onto the land, but now he had no choice.

Memories of his bedroom up in the thatched roofed attic swept over him. He'd moved up there after his mother had married her second husband. He glanced up at the small window in the roof. Did the room still hold everything he'd left behind? Did his once-treasured keepsakes still sit on the shelves? Had his posters yellowed and faded?

A part of him ached to go inside and find out. To reach out and touch the past for just a brief moment.

'Who's she?'

The question interrupted Kern's reminiscing. His stepfather was walking out through the front door of the farmhouse towards them. Well, staggering described his movements better. Kern's hangover was nothing but a minor inconvenience compared to the one he suspected bothered the old man.

Great—dealing with Fin was the last thing he needed right now.

'No one,' Kern answered briskly. 'Leave us to our business. It has nothing to do with you.'

'Wrong,' Fin snapped, stumbling closer. He raised a shaky hand and pointed at Kern. 'If you think I'm going to let you turn up and start ordering me around, then you're wrong. Maybe I need to teach you a lesson, like I did when you were younger.'

Resisting the urge to snap his stepfather's finger, just to stop his ranting, Kern searched and found the last piece of his patience. He wasn't a kid any more, and no matter how low he fell he'd never stoop as low as Fin.

'Forty-five per cent is yours—the rest belongs to me.'

'I'm the one who kept everything going while you swanned around drinking champagne with your fancy crowd. Where are they now, hey? Since your golden crown has fallen off your damn big head? Where are they now, boy?' He cackled. 'Gone. Just like your career. It's the only reason you've come back here to trouble me.'

'Shut up,' Kern warned him, not needing his problems to be shared with the vet. His life's mistakes concerned no one. The woman didn't need to know that failure hung around his neck like an unwanted bridle.

'No one wants to know the great Kern MacKinley now, do they?' Fin continued. 'Your name must really be dirt if the only sort of woman you're attracting is *her* kind.' He glanced at the vet and grimaced. 'A step down for you, boy, isn't she? From all the blondes who used to flutter around you at the race courses. You'd be better off paying for a woman's time than picking up a freak like *her* from the gutter.'

Kern's patience evaporated, and before Fin could utter another insult he grabbed the old man by the shirt. The woman deserved better than bearing Fin's slurs and bitterness.

Temper and frustration pumped through his blood as he faced the man who'd given his mother such a hard time during the last years of her life. 'Shut your damn mouth. There's nothing wrong with her. Got that? She's a queen compared to a nasty old dog like you. At least she doesn't stink of body odour and urine. When was the last time you bathed?'

'Get your hands off me!' Fin cried, all his bravado vanishing beneath Kern's temper. 'Beating up old men impresses her, does it?'

'I wouldn't waste my time.' Kern shoved him away, furious they'd not managed five minutes before they were at each other's throats.

He watched the sour old man turn and head into the farmhouse and slam the door. A black iron horseshoe fell off and hit the stone step with a dull clang. Who knew what state the old place was in after all these years of housing Fin and his addiction?

He glanced at the vet, his heart tugging as he took in her bent head and the way she hugged herself. Clearly a protective stance. How many times had she endured hurtful comments from strangers because she dressed a little differently and wore make-up in unusual colours?

An unexpected urge to comfort her tugged at him, but he buried it, not about to scare the woman further. Although Fin must be blind as well as useless if he couldn't see the beauty in this woman's lines and form. She reminded him of a newly born foal. With long, shapely legs and an unconfident delicacy to her movements.

'Mr MacKinley, are you all right?'

Kern blinked several times as her question penetrated his wandering thoughts. 'I'm sorry about Fin. Ignore his stupidity. My stepfather is a drunk and bitter man. He married my mother expecting to inherit this farm when she died, and turned vicious when he discovered he never would—not completely. It's a family farm and the majority owner will always be a blood relation. Besides, he's an idiot. Any man can see you're a stunner.'

She stared at him as though his words had shocked her. Surely someone—a parent, a boyfriend or a lover—had told her the same? Even an old cynic like him could see that Miss Vet was a beautiful woman.

A deep flush coloured her cheeks beneath her make-up and she glanced towards the paddock. 'Your horse?' she said again.

The sight of her blush pulled at Kern's battered heart and he changed his mind. Folding his arms, he shook his head. 'I think it's best you leave. I'll give the practice a call in a few days if my horse still hasn't settled.'

'But Mr MacKinley…'

'Truth is, Fin will be out here again in a few minutes, once he's drunk some fresh courage. Now's not a good time for you to stay around. Things will get uglier than they already have. I'll call and make another appointment once I'm confident you'll not get caught in the middle of our argument. Okay?'

'But—but…' she stammered.

Kern placed his hands on his hips and sighed. 'I'm sorry—but my property, my rules. I'm afraid it's past time for you to leave, Miss Day.'

What a mess. Kern stared around at the rundown stables, unsure whether to yell until his throat burned or toss a lit match on the whole place and drive north.

Disrepair and neglect stared back at him, no matter where his eyes settled. From the piles of dried manure to the stable doors hanging off rusty hinges.

Paint flaked from walls once adorned from top to bottom with multicoloured rosettes. These derelict stables had once homed some of the best horses in the country. Now they were fit for nothing more than flattening with a bulldozer.

Large cobwebs hung from the sloped beamed ceiling like fragile Halloween decorations, gently moving from side to side thanks to the draughts coming through the roof where there were missing tiles. Thick mould grew in dark corners and heavily scented the air.

Fin had a lot of explaining to do once he sobered up.

Not just about the decay of this building, but the rest of the farm.

Kern had taken a walk up to the old gallops his grand-father had created, back in the 1950s, and he'd had to fight his way through thick overgrown bushes and hip-high weeds just to reach the start. The rest of the course wasn't much better.

'It's a sight to hurt the optics and the heart, isn't it?' a familiar female voice remarked behind him.

Though its tones were aged, he would recognise that accent in a crowd of cheering racegoers any day.

Not sure what to expect from the woman, he slowly turned and braced himself to see her for the first time in nineteen long years. 'Eloise...'

Eloise Blake, his aunt, had collected her share of wrin-kles and shrunk several inches in height, but he could still see the tough spirit of the woman he'd once known in her hazel eyes and straight back. Even now she stood holding the lead rope of a pretty brown mare.

'*Aunt* Eloise, if you don't mind,' she replied, her displea-sure clear in both her voice and gaze. 'I haven't forgiven you yet and I'm not sure I want to.'

Figuring it best to forget polite chit-chat and face the full wrath of his aunt's anger, he asked, 'Why the hell didn't you tell me how bad Fin had let things get?'

Eloise raised a brown pencilled eyebrow and stared down her straight nose. Her right hand gripped a pink walking stick. 'Would you have cared?'

The question hit him right in the chest, where he sus-pected she'd meant it to. Never one to pull her punches, his aunt had something on her mind and he might as well let her spit it out if he wanted answers.

He sighed. 'What's that supposed to mean?'

'Let's not kid ourselves, young man,' she said, disappointment in every syllable. 'I'm no fool and you're no liar... Well, you never were. I called Corinne time and again over the years, and every time she insisted you didn't care. That you'd kicked us and this place from your heels without regret. Yet now you stand here complaining. As though this is all my fault. As though I was the one who walked away.'

Confused, Kern asked, 'She did what?'

'She said you'd left us all behind for a reason and that you had far more important things to deal with than this farm.' She lifted the walking stick and pointed it at him. 'Oh, she enjoyed telling me that, you know. Never could keep the glee from her voice when she did it.'

Kern clenched his hands, absorbing this latest discovery of his wife's betrayal. Never had he said anything about not wanting to hear from his aunt. He'd believed it was the other way around, when after the first year he'd heard nothing from his relative despite the fact he had written with his new address and phone number.

'She never told me you called.'

Eloise sniffed and lowered the stick. 'I bet she didn't. Well, I honestly don't suppose it would have made any difference if she had. You never called me either, did you? No, you turned your back on this place and moved on, just as your dear mother predicted you would. Yes, she was right about that.'

Mention of his mother brought fresh irritation. The woman he'd loved and believed loved him. The woman who'd gambled with his inheritance and then left him with the resulting mess when she'd died too young.

'Do you blame me?'

'For leaving?' Eloise shook her head. 'No. I understood in the beginning. You always had a temper and your mother spoilt you. But I hoped once you'd calmed down and thought about things you would eventually trail home. You didn't—and *that* is what upsets me the most. This place, its history, the people who built it—your own family—you walked away from it all. So, yes, you *are* to blame for the broken roof on the stables and the overgrown, weed-thick paddocks, and the fact that not one horse calls this place home any more. Your mother loved this farm and sacrificed her happiness for it. When she left you her share of the place she did it because she hoped you'd grasp it and make a new history for it. Continue her and your grand-parents' legacy. Yet all you've done is prove her greatest fears correct.'

Mixed emotions gripped Kern. His aunt's words were uncomfortable and true. No one had forced him to leave and no one had kept him away. But even yesterday he'd chosen to leave a message on Eloise's answer machine, asking her to arrange for a vet to come, rather than go and face her in person.

'How could I have stayed when her second husband had a share? A share my mother gave him even when she knew it was a disaster to give anything to someone like him. Fin would have fought me at every turn.'

'So instead you've allowed him to destroy the place, panel by panel, nail by broken nail. Everything my parents and my sister gave to this place. The home and land your mother loved, same as your grandparents. All that history. You walked away from it because of a man not good enough to step onto this land, let alone be left with a free hand over it.'

Kern sighed as he took in his surroundings again. 'Better that than stay and be guilty of ripping it apart through fights and petty disagreements. Fin was never going to go along with anything I wanted or decided without ar-guing over it first. Better to start over than give myself a premature heart attack like the one that killed my mother. Besides, I didn't know it was this bad.'

'You didn't *care*, Kern,' Eloise said sadly.

Keeping a tight hold of the rope, she hitched the curve of her walking stick to the leather belt around her waist and lifted a tender hand to soothe the mare.

'Well, my darling. We know how that feels, don't we? When someone stops caring.'

'It wasn't that I didn't care—' Kern began, and the words were bitter on his tongue. He'd been raised to believe that he would inherit the whole property, but when his mother's will had been read he'd discovered that she hadn't only married Fin to keep his horses, but had also handed over forty-five per cent of the business. A business the man had no interest in building or growing. 'It was just—'

Eloise waved a hand at him, but when she spoke her tone was softer. 'Your dear mother hoped you'd be strong enough to grasp the challenge. Yet you packed up and left the day after the will was read. Sulked like the child you were. Married that cheap little opportunist—'

'Don't call my wife that,' he warned. He was aware that everything his aunt accused Corinne of being was sadly true, but he wouldn't hear a word against her. She'd had faults, yes, but she hadn't been completely to blame. 'She was—'

Eloise sneered, unhooking her stick from her belt. 'Just because the woman's dead, don't turn her into some saint. She saw ambition and talent in your eyes and she wanted to ride your colours. She was always going to be the ruin of you. All those years of work and she wrecked it all—just to spite you. You silly boy. You chose to be loyal to the wrong person, when this place was where you should have been.'

Kern opened his mouth to deny the accusation, but his aunt's words held too much truth. Nothing he said would make her understand his deceased wife's complex nature. Hell, he had struggled with it for most of their marriage.

'I still know people in the game, Kern. Don't try and dismiss what she did.'

Kern lowered his head. His aunt had never liked Corinne and she wasn't going to change her opinion. But she didn't know the whole story—no one did. Only he knew what had really caused his wife's actions that last day. Corinne might have caused the mayhem, but he was the one who'd helped to push her to it. That and the cruel reality that occasionally life denied a person what they truly craved.

'She's dead, Eloise.'

'I know—and I won't lie to you and pretend I cried tears over the news. But it doesn't change the truth that you ran away from your heritage and she made certain you stayed away. Until now.'

Kern swallowed hard, unable to deny it. He *had* run and, as Eloise had already pointed out, he was guilty of never picking up a phone or turning up for a visit.

'Well, I'm here now.'

'Yes, you are—though I do wonder how long for. Is this just a quick stop-off, or are you actually going to stay for a while?'

He didn't answer. If his aunt knew that he planned to leave as soon as possible, he hated to imagine her reaction. 'If you'll excuse me? I'm going to check on my horse.'

She nodded and remarked dryly, 'I'm sure some time outside will help clear that hangover you're carrying.'

He opened his mouth to deny it, but she shook her head. 'Don't be that liar I mentioned earlier.'

He moved towards the entrance, needing fresh air for

more than just to clear his head. The stables, despite their condition, still held memories in every corner he looked. They stifled and taunted him. Reminding him of everything he had lost both recently and long ago.

'Did the vet come yet?' his aunt asked.

Glad for a subject other than raking up the past, he nodded. 'Yes, but Fin came out of the house and played up, so I sent her away.'

Eloise smiled mysteriously. 'She's arrived in Dorset, then? Good. Here—take this girl,' she ordered, holding out the rope. 'I rescued this sweetheart yesterday and I need someone to look after her.'

Kern sighed and reached for the rope. What did the woman expect him to do with the mare? The stables were hardly decent, clean or accommodating. 'Why can't you do it?'

Eloise patted the mare gently on the neck. 'I'm too old and all my barns are full.'

'With what?'

She shoved a hand into her cardigan pocket and turned towards the entrance. 'Things I doubt you'd be interested in. Look after her. She needs someone to care. She used to be a bit of a star once.'

So had he, Kern mused silently. One so bright he'd believed he would be star for ever. What a joke.

'This place is falling down and I have no bedding.'

Eloise raised her eyebrow once more. 'Then you'd best get busy rectifying those issues. You never used to be afraid of hard work. Please don't tell me that has changed.'

'Of course not,' he retorted.

He'd worked his backside off to achieve his dreams and no one could take that truth from him.

She chuckled and walked away. 'Good to see you home, Kern. I truly hope this time you find the gumption to stay.'

CHAPTER THREE

RUBY KNOCKED ON the frosted glass door of the 1960s bungalow, trying to decide if she might be better spending the remainder of the afternoon searching for a caravan site.

When she'd returned to the practice and explained the events at MacKinley farm, and Kern MacKinley's strange behaviour, her new boss had listened, then handed over half his afternoon appointments to her, stating she should consider them part of a practical interview.

Thrilled to finally be working, Ruby had enjoyed every moment of the consultations. And despite a nervous start she'd managed to treat the seven animals without any mishaps.

After her last appointment Anne had handed her a piece of paper with the name of a woman who would be willing to let Ruby park her caravan on her land for a small weekly fee. But then Anne had mentioned it was next door to the MacKinley farm and was owned by Kern MacKinley's aunt.

After this morning's carry-on with the nephew, Ruby dreaded meeting the woman. What if she was as bad as her nephew?

Ruby knocked again, leaning close to the glass to listen for any sign of movement from inside the building. Perhaps Eloise Blake had fallen asleep?

Anne had told her the woman rarely answered the phone, and it would be better to drive out and talk to her in person.

Finally a figure appeared through the glass and the door opened to reveal a dark-haired woman with silver streaks at her temples, leaning heavily on a walking stick.

'Hello. Are you Eloise?' Ruby asked, suddenly hit by an attack of nerves.

The woman lifted her chin and gave Ruby a thorough once-over. 'I am. You must be the new vet from town.'

Surprised, Ruby paused for a second. Had Anne contacted the woman and warned her of Ruby's visit? 'Yes. How did you know?'

'Psychic, dear. I read it in my daily horoscope. How a young beautiful stranger with a lip ring would soon come to see me.'

'Oh,' Ruby said, her good mood evaporating. Obviously the MacKinleys and the Blakes were all bonkers. First the unclothed nephew and now the mystic aunt.

'You think I'm batty, don't you?' Eloise asked with a smile. 'Most people do when faced with a subject they don't understand. Though I'd have thought you might think differently, considering your own special gift.'

Discomfort moved over Ruby for the second time that day. What did this strange old lady know about her gift? Had Alex Morsi spoken to her about what Professor Handel had apparently told him? Did others know too?

'I'm not—'

Eloise huffed and shook her head, giving Ruby the impression she had disappointed the old woman. 'I'm not crazy. It's better you understand that from the start or you and I may well fall out. Now, you want to set up home on my land, do you?'

Ruby wasn't sure any more—but time was getting on

and she needed to find somewhere to park for the night. 'Is it possible?' she asked.

Eloise nodded and stepped out onto the doorstep. 'It is. I suggest you park your caravan along by the river. It's beautiful at this time of the year, and the weather forecast for the week says the sun is staying around.'

'I own a dog,' Ruby said, aware that not everyone liked or allowed animals on their land. She refused to stay anywhere Dog wasn't welcome.

Eloise slammed the front door. 'Not a problem. I like dogs. Better company than humans, in my opinion. Almost as good as horses. Let's take a drive down, shall we?'

She didn't wait for Ruby to reply. Instead, she walked past her and towards the car. With a quick hello to Dog, who'd stuck his head out of the open rear window, she climbed into the front passenger seat and slammed the door.

Deciding she'd better follow, before the old lady changed her mind, Ruby hurried over to the car.

Within minutes they were heading down a dirt track in the direction of the river.

'I ran the place as a campsite until my second husband died and left me with a right mess to sort out, thanks to his aversion to paperwork. Still, he's dead and I survived.' She glanced towards Ruby. 'It's what we do, isn't it? Survive the trauma and move on with our lives.'

Ruby swallowed, but kept her eyes on the track. Something about Eloise Blake unsettled her. It was almost as though she knew things about Ruby's past—which was impossible.

'You'll be able to hook up to electricity,' Eloise continued. 'The old cables still work. Hubby number two had his faults, but he was good at practical stuff.' She pointed out through the windscreen to the land in front of them.

'All this belongs to me, on this side of the river. The other side belongs mostly to my nephew. I understand you met him this morning?'

Ruby nodded and turned through an open gate into a field. 'Yes, he wanted someone to check his horse over but then he changed his mind once I arrived.'

'He was being cautious, sending you away,' Eloise explained. 'Fin, my brother-in-law, is a difficult man when he's sober and worse when he is drunk. Don't worry, Kern would never allow a horse to suffer. He loves the creatures far too much to do anything so cruel. If he says its fine, then it's the truth. But I'm sure you wish you'd seen for yourself.'

'Yes.'

'Well, you'll get the chance soon.' Eloise smiled mysteriously.

A shiver waved up Ruby's spine, increasing her discomfort. Yes, the family was definitely odd.

'I will?'

Eloise smiled again before pointing to a spot not far from the river's edge. 'It's in the chart, my dear. It's all written there if you know how to read it.'

Kern threw a stack of crinkled yellowed papers, consisting mainly of old receipts, bills and circulars for long-finished special offers on equine equipment, into the large plastic bin he'd dragged into the stable office from outside.

Forcing every bit of his attention to the chore, he tried to ignore the complaints coming from Enticing Evie, his four-year-old filly, who was making it clear she wasn't happy about being inside the old building.

Giving the dusty room another weary glance, he felt his heart ache at the sight of all the neglect. This room had been the hub of the yard when he was a child. Often better kept and cleaner than the main house. The shelves had been filled with a variety of books on horse care, veterinary and training manuals. Each upright and in their proper place. Now the books were either missing or lying in discarded piles on the filthy floor.

His eyes rested on a pair of leather gloves abandoned at the corner of the desk. His mother's old riding gloves. He reached for them, feeling the leather dirty and stiff in his palms. These simple gloves had once been so much a part of his mother, he struggled to imagine her without them.

Was she riding around heaven wearing a pair? He liked the idea of her jumping over hurdles, encouraging her favourite horse to do better, while his father yelled out praise from the side.

His eyes stung as he stared down at the gloves. They'd been a Christmas gift from his father before he'd passed away. He'd been twenty-five years older than Kern's mother, but the age gap had never bothered them or caused any issues in their marriage. They'd loved each other so much they'd seen only each other's hearts and love.

How he envied them that easy, natural love. So very different from the one he'd shared with Corinne.

Was Eloise right? Had his mother truly believed he had enough grit and determination to deal with Fin—the man she'd married out of desperation when he'd threatened to remove his best horses from the yard and take them to her nearest competitor unless she did so?

Evie's objections increased, forcing Kern to move to the open doorway. The thoroughbred's head was up, and she was stamping the ground like an equine Irish dancer having a tantrum. She tugged against the rope attaching her to the metal ring fixed into the wall and her eyes rolled as her body trembled and flinched.

'Hey, pretty girl…' he soothed, moving closer until he stood by her side.

She didn't want to be inside the building and she intended to make sure he knew it. She was desperate to return outside to the paddock, where she considered it safer. But a storm was forecast for the middle of the night, and he refused to leave her out in the elements.

'I know you hate it in here. I do too, sweetheart. But you can't stay outside in the paddock. It's not safe, and you're too precious to me.'

He'd hoped having his aunt's mare in one of the recently cleaned stalls he'd spent the afternoon repairing would help calm his girl, but she'd refused even to acknowledge the other horse.

Kern glanced towards the open end of the stable. In the distance he could see the shape of a caravan. His aunt had texted him earlier to let him know the vet would be staying on her land.

Great. Just what he needed. Miss Ruby Day was a distraction he could do without. He'd lost count of the amount of times her image had drifted through his thoughts since she'd left the farm earlier. Those serious brown eyes, her sweet pink mouth and her shocked expression at his undressed state…

He smiled. It was a long time since he'd shocked a woman. Thank goodness she hadn't figured out that the real reason he'd struggled to get his jeans on was due to his trying to hide the evidence of his body's inopportune attraction to her.

He'd considered marching over to Eloise's to demand she send the woman on her way—but he doubted his aunt would listen, and he had no right to dictate who stayed on her side of the river anyway.

He'd lost any rights by leaving and staying silent for

nineteen years. Today, when he tried to justify his reasons for doing so, he couldn't. He *had* sulked like the schoolboy his aunt had accused him of being.

First anger and grief had kept him away from Dorset. But as the years had turned into five, and then ten, and more, it had been embarrassment, shame and guilt which had kept his feet in another part of the country.

The trouble was, not once in that time had he imagined Eloise getting old.

What had happened to her second husband, Ralph? Had he left her too?

Evie snorted in another display of irritation. Kern understood and didn't blame her. After the bloodshed she'd experienced, the last thing she deserved was more stress. The drive to Dorset in the horsebox had been just about all the confinement she could stand.

He patted her neck and made his way to the opening. The coming rain scented the air with a damp fresh chill.

With a final glance back at his distressed horse, Kern stepped out into the night. For Evie he would face anyone and do whatever was needed. He owed her. And for her alone he would eat humble horse crap pie.

Ruby climbed onto the bed, balancing a large glass bowl filled with cheese and onion crisps in one hand. On the bedside table sat a can of ice-cold cola, recently purchased from the town's mini supermarket.

For the first time in years, she felt hope warm her heart. Today had almost been her definition of perfect. She had a job she wanted, where the staff treated her normally, and a beautiful place to stay. How long it would last, she didn't want to contemplate, but tonight she was happy, and she intended to enjoy the rare feeling.

When the time to leave came, she would pack and do

what she always did. Move on without acknowledging any regrets. Start over again the same way she had since the day she'd left home at sixteen.

Only once had she stupidly risked trusting someone with the truth of her past, and they'd repaid her by selling a story to the kind of shoddy newspaper only interested in a sordid headline and lies. She'd stopped trusting people after that.

The so-called friend had tried to make excuses, but Ruby had refused to listen. There was no excuse for breaking a promise. None. What was friendship or a relationship without trust? Since that day Ruby had kept to herself and kept her mouth shut.

Sometimes it had been hard, but thanks to a decent inheritance from her mother, she'd managed to finish school and move on to university. After a couple of years working at a cat rescue centre she'd decided to train to become a vet.

Today had made lots of hard work, eye-straining studying and numerous part-time retail jobs worth it.

Leaning back on the pillows, she gently eased Dog's nose out of the bowl before he swiped a mouthful of crisps. Loving the unusual lightness in her heart, she closed her eyes and smiled.

'Paws crossed, Dog,' she whispered, stroking his rough, furry head, 'that this time we get to stay for a few months…maybe even a year.'

Dog licked her hand as if to agree.

Whatever happened during her time in Dorset, Ruby had this wonderful dog to love. Together they made do. She happily confessed all her secrets, wishes and dreams to him, her best friend, knowing that he'd keep them from the world. He was her perfect confidant.

A heavy knock on the caravan door startled Ruby into spilling half the bowl of crisps over the bed.

Glancing at her watch, she saw it was after seven o'clock. Who was knocking at her door? She knew it wouldn't be her new boss or his wife, because the man had whisked his family out through the practice door as soon as the last client had left, muttering something about a romantic evening. Perhaps it was Eloise? But Ruby didn't see the old woman as the type to go galivanting around at night—even if it was still just about light outside—unless she was ill and needed help?

Ruby opened her mouth to ask who it was when the answer came via a familiar deep voice.

'Miss Day? It's Kern MacKinley.'

She growled and glared in the direction of the door. What right did he have, bothering her after work hours?

Another knock hit the door. 'I know you're inside. I can see a light and I recognise your car from our earlier meeting.'

With an irritated sigh, she rose from the bed, leaving Dog to feast on the spilled crisps. Slamming the bowl down on to the bedside table, she left the bedroom and headed for the door.

Lifting a hand, she hesitated before opening it. 'What do you want, Mr MacKinley?'

'I want *you*, Miss Day.'

In what way exactly did he want her?

She rubbed a hand across her brow. 'What did you say? You're mumbling.'

Silence hung between them for a second, before Kern replied in a much louder voice, 'I need your help. If you'd be gracious enough to forget what happened this morning, I could use your professional advice.'

Ruby bit her bottom lip, not wanting to be gracious or anything else where this man was concerned. Just because she was staying close by, it didn't mean she was offering twenty-four-hour animal care.

'It's late. Can't it wait until tomorrow? Perhaps you'd prefer to speak to my boss—?'

'No, I need someone this evening.'

And then he said the words she couldn't ignore.

'My horse needs you.'

Concerned, she opened the caravan door and looked down at the man who'd messed up her morning and seemed set on ruining her evening. 'In that case, Mr MacKinley, I'll come with you. But you'd better not mess me around again. The first time I could understand, but a second time will get you blacklisted at the practice.'

Kern nodded and placed his hand to his heart. 'I won't. I swear.'

She was pretty in the early-evening light, with her make-up smudged and faded in places. The woman's beauty shone through because of her eyes. Large, shaped like a cat's, and full of emotions Kern knew better than to try to decipher.

If he did, he might risk never being able to get free from the secrets that lay inside this woman's heart. He feared she had the power to bewitch him, and he was determined never to let that happen again. Once burnt, for ever scarred.

'It's a lovely evening,' Kern murmured, staring at the sky as they headed towards the river.

Anything to take his mind from the unwanted attraction he suddenly felt towards the woman walking by his side. His wife had been dead for less than a year—barely time for him to get used to being single again, let alone notice a pretty woman he'd best avoid.

Ruby nodded and shifted her medical bag from her left hand to her right. He'd offered to carry it for her, but she'd refused and gripped it tighter.

'But there's a storm heading for us in a few hours,' he went on, needing the atmosphere between them to ease. The last thing he wanted was for Evie to pick up on it. The sensitive horse was skittish enough.

Ruby glanced up at the evening sky. 'How can you tell?'

'You can smell it in the air,' he said, taking a deep breath through his nose before letting it out of his mouth.

She sniffed the air like a suspicious child might smell an unwrapped sweet. 'Really? All I can smell is grass.'

'It's going to be a heavy one,' he said.

'You get all that from sniffing the air?' she asked, intrigued.

He smiled her way. 'Experience. I'm a country boy, remember?'

She gave the sky another doubtful look, then asked, 'What's wrong with your horse, Mr MacKinley?'

'Call me Kern,' he invited.

'I prefer to call clients by their surnames,' she replied primly. 'You said earlier she wasn't sick. Yet now you're calling on me out of hours to see her.'

'No, she isn't sick. Not in a physical way. My girl's more heart sick.'

Ruby stopped and stared at him. 'What happened?'

Kern let out a heavy sigh. 'Evie has recently developed an aversion to staying inside a stable. I was hoping you might have something in that case of yours that might help calm her for a few hours. Just until the storm passes and tomorrow comes.'

'Shouldn't she be used to staying inside?' Ruby asked.

Kern nodded. 'She was, but a few months ago she had a fright, and since then she hates being anywhere near a stable.'

'How did she cope travelling in the horsebox?'

Kern rubbed his jaw ruefully at the question. 'We

stopped—a lot. But it's not the horsebox that's the problem—just the stable. And despite the one here not being up to much, it has a roof and walls, and smells enough like a stable for Evie to hate it.'

'Sounds like she's suffering from stress.'

'She is. But none of the paddocks are secure enough to leave her there during the night, and anyway my girl deserves better than being left out in a storm.'

'Okay. I'll examine her and see what can be done to ease her trouble.'

'Thank you, Ruby.'

'No need for thanks. Payment to the practice for my visit will be enough. Just call Anne in the morning and she'll tell you what you owe.'

He nodded. 'Of course.'

They came to the edge of the river and stopped. For a moment Kern stared down at the water, trying to think of the best way to phrase his next suggestion. Finally, he decided straightforward bluntness was probably best.

He turned to Ruby. 'Unless you want wet feet and legs, you'd best jump up on to my back.'

Startled, Ruby backed away. 'I beg your pardon?'

Kern chuckled. 'You may want to close your eyes too, because I intend to take off my jeans. I don't want them to get soaked either. It's what I did on the way over to you.'

She hesitated, lifting her bag in front of her like a protective barrier. 'But—'

Kern placed his hand on his jeans button and popped it. Next, he pulled down his zip. The metallic rasp of it echoed between them. Kicking his trainers off, he tied them together and handed them to her to hold.

Ruby gasped and took another step backwards. Eyes wide, she spluttered, 'Honestly, Mr MacKinley. Must you keep doing this? If you dare lower your jeans, I swear it won't be your horse in need of medical attention, but you. Isn't there a bridge or something we can use?'

He almost laughed at the look on the vet's face. God, she was sweet. A man might even believe she was as innocent as she acted. But Ruby Day exuded a fragility that suggested she'd once been deeply hurt. In a way only someone who had meant something important to her could inflict.

'My aunt had it dismantled the day my mother married Fin. I doubt she's had it rebuilt during the last nineteen years. Come on—for you, I will get my jeans wet.'

He fixed his trousers, turned his back and bent down, waiting for her to make a decision. He just hoped it would be the one that would benefit Evie.

A sharp, infuriated sigh signalled her agreement. 'Just until we reach the other side. Then you put me down.'

He nodded. 'Of course.'

The feel of her small hand on his shoulder sent a shiver of awareness and relief through his body. He bit back a deep groan when she jumped up and secured her long legs around his waist. God forgive him for the wicked thoughts going through his head, but he was only a mere man, and it had been a long time since a woman had wrapped any part of her body around his own.

Grabbing one of her legs to shift her into a more comfortable hold, he held on to the arm she'd slipped around his neck. 'Hold on tight. The water's not too deep here, but you don't want to fall in. And try not to hit me with that bag.'

She chuckled low in his ear. 'Make sure you don't drop me, then, Mr MacKinley, otherwise I might do it accidentally.'

Kern swallowed hard and stepped down into the water. 'Oh, I won't do that, Ruby. I'm never careless on purpose. Just don't fidget around and we'll be fine.'

She snorted. 'Make sure you're not. Or I'll make certain you get wetter than you did this morning. You should know I fight dirty when required, and I don't appreciate people who play games and waste my time.'

Kern chuckled and stopped halfway across the river. Water soaked him to just above his knees. This part of the river was shallower than where he'd jumped this morning, but still enough to be uncomfortable and cold, even on a spring evening.

'Are you threatening me, Ruby Day?'

'Just making sure you're the only one who gets wet tonight.'

Kern shut out the dirty thoughts her innocent words aroused and continued through the water to the other side. 'Hold on. The bottom's a little uneven on this side of the river.'

'Is the water still as cold as it was this morning?' Ruby asked, tightening her legs around his waist.

Kern groaned, forcing his footsteps on. Did she even know the effect her actions was causing? 'Yes. It's freezing.'

She laughed impishly. 'Good.'

Yeah, she knew. He'd bet his last pound coin on it.

Ruby stopped just inside the stables, her focus immediately drawn to the horse standing in the centre aisle. Everything about the animal screamed sadness and pain. Not in an obvious physical way that anyone else would notice, but a deeper, emotional agony that few understood or saw.

But Ruby did. And she felt it too.

Moving farther inside she saw Enticing Evie shift, suddenly aware of their presence. Or rather Ruby's unknown one. Her tense, fearful stance and wide eyes were clear indications that she didn't want Ruby anywhere near her.

This horse wasn't going to be an easy patient and she would probably resent any help.

'I'm going closer,' Ruby said, glancing at Kern MacKinley. 'It's probably a good idea for you to go first, though. She knows you and it might help to settle her.'

Kern nodded and walked over to the horse. Stroking a hand down her face, he crooned, 'Hey, girl. How are you doing?'

Ruby walked nearer, until she stood at the horse's side. The nervous filly stepped away instinctively, half turning to Kern for protection.

'First I'll carry out a basic physical examination,' Ruby said, placing her bag down on the ground, out of the way.

She opened it and retrieved her stethoscope. As she placed it around her neck she quickly looked Evie over, checking her general demeanour and alertness. From what she could see the horse seemed fine, other than mistrusting of Ruby's unfamiliar presence.

Stepping closer, Ruby inspected the horse's eyes, nose and mouth. Everything seemed normal and her gums were a healthy pink.

'How's her appetite? Any cough?'

'Appetite's fine and no cough,' Kern answered.

Placing the ends of the stethoscope into her ears, Ruby listened to the sound of Evie's heart. Next she moved on to the lungs and stomach. Thankfully, everything sounded fine.

Fetching a digital thermometer from her bag, Ruby tugged the ends of her stethoscope out of her ears and approached Evie's rear end. This was when she expected the horse to make her displeasure clear. Many horses disliked the intimate invasion necessary for taking their temperature.

Giving the thermometer a coat of lubricant, she glanced

over her shoulder towards Kern. 'I'm going to take her temperature now. Can you hold her steady?'

Kern nodded. 'Of course.'

Standing to Evie's side, in case the horse decided to kick out, Ruby move her tail to one side, gently pushed the lubricated thermometer inside her rectum and held on to the end. After thirty seconds, she pulled it out again and checked it.

'Her temperature is fine. As is her general condition.'

'That's good to hear.'

Ruby cleaned the thermometer and put it away, then turned back to the horse. After spending a few minutes checking her over from nose to tail, she asked, 'Is there anything else that concerns you other than her dislike for the stable?'

'No, not really.'

'Can you move round to her other side?' Ruby asked, needing him out of sight for what she planned to do next. 'I think it will also help if you untie her and hold the rope instead.'

Waiting until Kern could no longer see her, she slowly raised her right hand. Gently touching the horse on the neck, she closed her eyes and whispered softly, *I'm here to help you.*

Evie immediately stepped away, tossing her head in answer to Ruby's words.

'What are you doing?' Kern asked, suspicion colouring his voice.

He reminded Ruby of an over-protective parent. Would he be the same over his child or his wife? What would it be like to have someone act that way over *her*? Would she like it or resent it?

'I'm just making friends,' Ruby said. 'Seems only right

after she's let me examine her. To have a little female getting to know each other time.'

Kern chuckled. 'You make it sound like a date.'

She lightly placed her fingers on Evie's neck again. 'Perhaps it is, in a way. Would you go to a doctor and expect him to just give you medication without talking to you? Or examine you fully and then walk away without a word? I just want her to know that I'm not all bad, even if I did stick my thermometer somewhere personal.'

'I guess you're right…'

Ruby stroked her left hand over the horse's face. Slow, calm movements meant to ease and relax. 'Always, Mr MacKinley. You should remember that.'

Come on, Evie. Let me help you. Ruby closed her eyes once again and mentally repeated the words, wanting to reassure the stressed horse that she could trust her. Some horses gave their trust quickly, whereas others fought against help. It all depended on the horse and what it had been through.

Resting her fingers with the lightest of touches, Ruby continued to talk silently to her patient, shutting out the noise of another horse softly snuffling somewhere in the stables and the birdsong outside. She cleared her mind of everything but the animal beneath her fingertips.

This time she felt some of the tension leave Evie's body. She wasn't fully relaxed, but it was a start.

I just want to help you, I promise.

'Can I do anything?'

Kern's voice penetrated Ruby's concentration like the prick of a pin.

'Like formally introduce you, or something?'

With a sharp sigh, Ruby opened her eyes and stopped herself from suggesting he shut up. She'd had owners like this before. People who struggled to be quiet and not interfere with the process. Worried they were somehow caus-ing their animal harm by having her help them. Of course, Kern didn't know that.

'Would you mind fetching some fresh water?'

'Of course. I'll get some from the farm's well. It's clean and drinkable. It's a fair way from here, though, so I may be gone a while.'

Perfect.

Kern grabbed a bucket and disappeared outside.

Finally alone with the horse, Ruby returned her atten-tion to her new friend.

'Now we can talk properly' she said, patting Evie gently. 'I can make you feel a little better about being in here, if you'll let me.'

A sound came from one of the stalls and a brown head appeared over the door. 'See—even your friend there thinks you should listen. It's good advice.'

This time Evie appeared to consider Ruby's offer, and within moments Ruby's hand started to warm, radiating heat into the horse's stiff, defensive body. Instantly, visions of red and hot pain overwhelmed Ruby's senses. What-ever had happened to this horse had been ugly and raw. No wonder she was edgy.

'Oh, sweet girl,' Ruby whispered, a tear rolling down her cheek as she felt the pain envelop her. She couldn't see pictures, or clear images, but she could feel the fear and the sadness in the horse's heart and spirit. The intense agony.

Evie had suffered real loss and heartbreak.

The sound of footsteps broke into her concentration again, and with one final offer of love from her heart Ruby stepped away, pleased to see her new friend with her head down, looking more relaxed than when she'd first entered the stables. With luck, it would be enough to last for a few hours, until the coming storm had moved on.

'Here's the water,' Kern said, walking towards them.

Ruby nodded. 'Good. I think your girl's ready for a drink. She should settle now.'

Kern placed the bucket down on the stable floor in front of Evie. 'She seems much more relaxed. What did you do?'

'A little bit of massage,' she hedged, not about to admit the truth.

Her kind of healing was seen by many as some kind of hocus-pocus witchery and not proper medicine. But she knew it was. What she did dealt with the damaged spirit inside an animal.

'Some horses respond to it when they're stressed, others not so much.'

Kern continued to regard his horse. 'She's definitely calmer. Massage…?'

Ruby stepped away and retrieved her bag. 'She may sleep for a while. You might want to try her in a stall.'

'I prepared one earlier, just in case,' he said. 'Give me a minute and I'll walk you back.'

Ruby shook her head and wandered over to the entrance. The sun was low on the horizon and casting a pretty pink hue over the sky. 'You don't have to. It's not far.'

Kern led a much calmer Evie into a stall. 'How are you going to get across the river without your local piggyback knight to carry you? We're kind of a rarity in Dorset, you know.'

She laughed. 'I think this time I'll walk across, thanks.'

Kern closed the stable door and followed her outside. 'No need. Where are you from, Ruby?'

'Here and there,' she answered, purposely vague. 'No particular place or town.'

When they came to the river, Kern scooped her up and stepped into the water before she could argue or decline.

'I said I'd walk over this time,' she complained, but instinctively wrapped an arm around his neck and held tight.

'I know,' he said, moving through the water to the other side. Again, he stopped at the centre of the river. 'Of course if you'd rather I dropped you, just say.'

She gripped his neck tighter. 'When you've gone to so much trouble, that would be ungrateful and stupid.'

Kern laughed and shifted her higher in his hold. 'So you're a lady with no set home?'

'None except for the one I take with me.'

Reaching the other bank, he placed her back on her feet and together they moved in the direction of her caravan. 'Well, you certainly have a mysterious aura about you.'

Ruby frowned at his words, not sure how to take them. They sounded complimentary, but she'd never had anyone say anything like that before, so she wasn't sure.

'I do?'

'I'm sorry that I doubted you earlier,' Kern said. 'You must have wondered what was going on after that scene between Fin and I. Truth is, I haven't been home in a long time, and I'm not staying for any longer than I need to.'

'Does your aunt know?' Ruby asked.

He shrugged and turned to her. 'Probably—deep down. For the first time in years I'm in a position to make decisions which affect only me and no one else. My being here is only to tie up loose ends before I move on.' He sighed heavily. 'Doesn't matter where I stand on this farm, I just feel the past mocking me.'

Curious, she asked, 'Why would it do that?'

'Because I have a bad habit of making the women in my life sad. And it's time it stopped.'

Not understanding, Ruby regarded this man whose spirit appeared dejected and tired. As though life had slammed him with trouble too much. It saddened her, because she knew that feeling.

'I don't know what you did to Evie. God knows, I'm going to spend the rest of the night trying to figure it out. But you did something while I was fetching the water. Of that I'm sure.'

Ruby shrugged and glanced away. She didn't like not telling the complete truth, but she refused to give him a reason to dismiss her gift as nonsense when he'd already seen its effect.

'I just talked to her and massaged her a little. It was hardly anything. In fact, forget about making any payment to the practice. Consider it a neighbour's freebie.'

'Thanks, but I know it was more than that,' he said, stepping closer. He touched Ruby's face and turned it to him. 'Your eyes are pools of secrets, aren't they? You're too enticing for a man like me.'

'I am?'

He winked and tilted his head. 'Goodnight, Ruby.'

A shiver ran over her skin as he disappeared back across the river. Kern MacKinley saw too much, and from now on she had to make certain that where she was concerned he saw no more.

CHAPTER FOUR

'OKAY, I'M HERE. What's wrong?' Kern panted, having run over from the stables to his aunt's place after receiving a text message demanding his immediate presence.

Eloise stopped hunting through a bundle of old leather tack and smiled. 'Nothing. I just need your help with clearing this place.'

Kern glanced around the barn, packed with boxes and long-abandoned pieces of furniture, all the tat a person tended to accumulate after years of living in the same place, and almost groaned. *This* was the reason she'd called him over? A barn full of rubbish that had probably sat here for decades?

'Why?'

'Because,' Eloise replied cryptically. 'And as you have time right now, seeing as you're still undecided about your future, I figured you'd be glad to help. Besides, it will save you from having to do it when I depart for the next world.'

Kern sank down on a nearby stool and wiped his sweaty forehead. 'You're not going anywhere, so why the rush?'

Eloise peered at him. 'Who knows what's in store for me—or you—but I want this done. Move this lawnmower, will you?'

He stood and lifted the mower, which looked like a relic

from the Edwardian era, and dumped it out of his aunt's way. 'Why the sudden urge to spring clean?'

His aunt returned her attention to the tack. 'I need the room.'

He again glanced around the barn. 'For what?'

'You are a Nosy Nicholas today, aren't you?' Eloise tutted, tugging on a leather bridle before tossing it back into the box. 'I just want your help, Kern. Not your opinion.'

'Forget I asked.' Kern remembered from his childhood that when his aunt was in this mood it was better just to do what she wanted. 'Where should I start?'

'You can put this old tack by the door,' she said, shoving the box towards him. 'It's old, but with a good cleaning it will be as good as anything you can buy. It belongs to you, anyway.'

He lifted several pieces out of the box and inspected it. His aunt was right. Although it was old, it was in good nick.

He glanced at her with suspicion. 'It does?'

'Yes.' Eloise nodded and waved a hand towards it. 'I borrowed it from your mother, along with a few other bits and bobs, after she died.'

Kern stared at his aunt. '*After* she died?'

Eloise picked at the top button of her cardigan. 'The day after the reading of the will, actually. You'd run off, and Fin was in London, no doubt trying to find some way to break the terms of the will. So I went over to the house and the stables with a van and…borrowed a few things.'

Kern took in all the boxes cluttering the area for a third time. Slowly, he recognised several pieces of furniture that had used to belong to his mother. Family heirlooms from his grandparents' time. 'You *borrowed* them?'

'Just until you came home,' Eloise said, flashing him a bright smile. 'Well, I wasn't going to leave it all for Fin to sell off, was I? You can go through it and decide what you want to keep and take back to the farm with you. The rest you can chuck out. Of course I never imagined I would be storing it for so long.'

Kern decided it was time for him and Eloise to get a few things straight.

'It wasn't that I didn't care about the farm. I just had to get away. Without Mum it felt wrong to be here. And, even though I was young, I had sense enough to understand that trying to run a business with Fin would never have worked. There was also a part of me that wanted to prove I could make it on my own. I worked my way from stable boy to boss and I'm proud of that fact.'

'Your mother would have been proud too, you know,' Eloise said. 'Of everything you've achieved. Even though it wasn't here at the farm, she still would have been proud.'

A hard lump formed in Kern's throat at his aunt's well-meant words. It was praise he didn't want to hear—not when he had fallen so far.

'Well, she would have something to say about where I am now, I'm sure.'

'She would have said that at the bottom of nowhere there's only one way to go. Back to the top of somewhere. Where you really belong.'

Kern sighed and focused on the box of tack. 'Who says I want to go back?'

'Horses and racing fuel your blood, Kern,' his aunt insisted. 'No point in denying that truth. What are you going to do if not train horses?'

That was a question he had no answer for. 'I'm not sure. I haven't decided.'

'There's nothing to decide. Can you really see yourself in a nine-to-five job, stuck in an office somewhere? You're down, Kern, but you're not finished. Not you—never you.

You have land, the farm and a good horse. One from good stock, from what I can see. I'd say you have it pretty fine for a man about to rebuild his life.'

Kern shrugged, not sure he wanted to hear his aunt's words of encouragement. Right now, the whole idea of returning to the racing world left bitterness in his mouth.

'Maybe.'

'No maybe. Training is what you were born to do. It's what your parents taught you. Stop wallowing in the past and get on with achieving the glory days of tomorrow.'

'Ah, here she is. Ruby, come in and see how little my nephew has accomplished in the hour he's been here. He needs organising and I bet you can do it.'

Kern glanced up from searching through the umpteenth box of rescued belongings, to see the woman standing with her dog on the threshold of the barn. Dressed in black cut-off jean shorts and a black T-shirt with hearts, roses and skulls all over it, she should look like a Goth, but the red and white scarf tied in her curly black hair gave her a fif-ties rockabilly cuteness instead.

Eloise walked over to Ruby. 'I have some shopping to do, so I'll see you two later. If you're good, I'll bring you both back a treat.'

Kern waited until his aunt had disappeared before speaking. 'I think she still thinks of me as a child. Though I'd best prepare you—my aunt's idea of a treat is never the expected.'

'Not sweets, then?' Ruby asked, shoving her hands into the pockets of her shorts.

Kern did his best not to take in her slim legs and the pretty curve of her calf muscles. But he was male, and Ruby was an attractive woman. And it had been so long since he'd thought of a woman as anything but an unfixable dilemma…

He chuckled and shook his head. 'No. Far too conventional for Eloise. Years ago she brought me a children's book I was desperate to own. She gave it to me to read, but when it was time for her to go home she took the book with her, stating that she had to take it back to the library the next day.'

Ruby stared at him. 'She didn't tell you it was a library book when she gave it to you?'

'Nope. Eloise was always kind of crazy like that. And when you're raised with the unconventional, you miss it when it's no longer around. Though there's other people's type of crazy to deal with instead, I guess.'

Ruby moved towards him, her dog following at her heels.

'Has she always been interested in astrology?' she asked.

'Oh, yeah. My aunt is as bright as a wolf moon. Don't be fooled by the scatty act she likes to use when it suits her. She's clever, tough, and she has a heart so soft it makes whipped cream look hard. I'd hate you to think differently. How did she talk you into helping with clearing the barn?'

Ruby stroked her dog's head and smiled down at him. 'She offered to have Dog one night a week, so I can do a late shift at the practice.'

Kern lifted a plastic tub filled with horse brushes and carried it over to the entrance, where several other containers and boxes were stacked. 'Are you always happy when you talk about your work?'

She nodded. 'What's the point in working at a job if you don't love doing it?'

Her words reminded him of his aunt's earlier ones, but he pushed the thought away. The future could wait until another day. Right now there was a barn to clear. Though where he was going to put everything he wanted to keep, he'd yet to figure out.

'What should I do?' Ruby asked, reaching out to pick up an old book. She blew the dust off the jacket and smiled. '"The Long-Abandoned Farm".'

'How apt,' Kern mused. 'Start anywhere you want. I have a feeling I'll be packing it all in the horsebox and carting it back to the farm with me, anyway.'

'You've been quiet for a long time. What have you found over there?'

Kern jumped down from the chair he was standing on, coughing as dirt rose up from the floor after his landing. Walking through the dust cloud, he wove between several crates to where Ruby sat on an old pine box at the back of the building, sifting through a dark wooden trunk.

'I'm looking at this,' she murmured, her concentration on the piece of paper in her hand.

Intrigued, Kern reached Ruby's side and crouched down. 'What is it?'

Ruby handed him a faded old newspaper cutting. 'This must have been important to someone. And look at these photos. Aren't they wonderful?'

Kern took the black-and-white cutting from her, immediately recognising the image. A larger one used to hang in the stable office—a proud token from his grandparents' time. In the photo, they stood on either side of a horse. The horse he knew had been his grandparents' first National Hunt winner.

'Do you know who they are?' Ruby asked.

Kern nodded and smiled. 'Let me introduce you to my grandparents—Tom and Ada MacKinley.'

Ruby took the piece of paper back and smiled brightly.

'Hello, Tom and Ada. I'm pleased to meet you. You look a little like your grandfather, you know?' she told Kern.

He glanced at the photo again, searching for similarities with the old man he remembered only as a booming voice and a loud laugh but seeing none. 'Yeah?'

Ruby traced a finger lightly over his grandfather's faded black-and-white image. 'Here in the jaw and the eyebrows. In the eyes too. You both have determination in your gaze.'

Kern didn't see it. Everyone had always commented that he took after his father in looks and his mother in temper. Perhaps now he was older it had changed.

'My grandmother would have said bloody-mindedness. They married when they were both eighteen years old. They bought this land with a dream in their hearts and a willingness to work for it.'

Ruby glanced up. 'Did the dream come true for them?'

'Yes, for their lifetime it did. Grandfather Tom bred and trained winners. My grandmother ran the business side. The old man won nearly every cup and award you can imagine. They were talented and a team. It makes a difference working towards success when two people are willing to work for the same goal. They were good people.'

'They sound it.'

'They were each other's backbone and reassurance when times were tough or lean. My mother was the same with my father. But when he passed, I suppose she lost her anchor. She struggled to keep the place going. She only married Fin because he threatened to take away his seven racehorses unless she did. The farm was going through one of its lean times, with Dad and Grandfather dying within two years of each other and new trainers coming into the business—young and keen, full of enthusiasm and false promises. In the end there were too many obstacles for her to fight against. She lost a couple of big owners to men who were not only the preferred sex, but who also spouted the guarantees of wins they wanted to hear.'

'So she married your stepfather to save the business?'

'Yeah—a man she couldn't stand, but needed. I told her on their wedding day I would never forgive her—that I'd rather she lost everything than be married to someone who wasn't Dad.'

'You were close to your father?'

'I was his shadow from before I could walk. My relationship with my mother was never the same after he died. She might have saved the farm and the business, but she lost my respect.'

'That was harsh,' Ruby muttered.

He sighed and reached for a photograph from the trunk. One of his mother and father on their wedding day. 'It was. And, do you know, if I was standing in her boots today I'd marry someone to keep what I'd worked for. I know that now. I'll always regret not being able to tell her so.'

'She probably understood your anger.'

He nodded, then grinned. 'But I bet she wondered how the hell she'd managed to raise such an obnoxious, self-righteous brat.'

Ruby laughed and handed him another photograph. This one of a pretty grey horse. 'I'm sure she did that on a daily basis anyway.'

Kern touched the photo but didn't take it. 'Are you insinuating something, Ruby?'

Shaking her head, she struggled to stop the corner of her mouth from twitching. 'Never.'

Kern leaned closer, his shoulder bumping hers. 'Are you sure?'

Ruby met his gaze, a twinkle of mischief shimmering in her eyes. 'Well, I have noticed you do have a bossy way about you that I suspect you also had as a child.'

'I do?'

'Mmm.' She nodded. 'You're something of an acquired taste, Mr MacKinley.'

Not able to resist the challenge in her gaze, Kern murmured, 'Am I really?'

As though realising the danger her honesty had placed her in, Ruby returned her attention to the trunk. 'Perhaps we should see what else is in here?'

'Trouble, I suspect.'

Those brown eyes came back to him. 'Sorry?'

'Nothing,' he said, reaching for another newspaper cutting and purposely brushing the back of her hand with his fingers. This woman was far too tempting to ignore. 'Just talking to myself.'

CHAPTER FIVE

RUBY WAITED UNTIL Kern's full attention was focused again on the papers and photos before examining the strange buoyancy in her chest. She'd tried to ignore its presence while they talked, had determinedly fought it when his long fingers had accidentally touched the back of her hand, but now she had no choice but to acknowledge and investigate the strange, frothy fluttering in both her stomach and her chest.

It reminded her of the times when her mother had twirled her around in a circle and her stomach had rocked and swirled throughout. She'd hated and loved it at the same time. Half scared and half excited by the unfamiliar sensation. It was exactly the same feeling as the one caused by the man crouched next to her.

Was this what people called attraction? A stupid physical reaction that didn't deserve anything more than a quick acknowledgement before she forgot about it again?

Why did Kern affect her so strangely? Was it because she had seen him without many clothes on, or because he was one of the few people who treated her as a normal person? He didn't seem to see her make-up and clothes the same way others did.

It was a strange feeling to be regarded as ordinary. But since she'd come to Dorset it was slowly becoming her new normal. Kern and everyone at the practice acted as if she was just a regular person. They were not put off by the way she dressed.

But deep down she knew she couldn't risk trusting them, or falling for the niceness of their words and actions. Too soon the disappointment would follow, and with it would come the pain. There was always the dreaded pain. Better to protect herself from it—even if it did mean missing out on this wonderful lightness in her heart.

Attraction wasn't for her. In the past she'd purposely avoided such emotion, preferring to keep acquaintances—male and female—in the friend zone. At first because she'd feared her past would become known, but eventually because it was easier just to place everyone in the same group and leave them there. Anyway, between studying and working, what little spare time she'd had left had tended to go on sleeping and eating.

Besides, she wasn't even sure she liked Kern MacKinley very much. The way he sneered every time he opened a box or unearthed a piece of furniture was a clear indication that he saw this afternoon's work as nothing but a chore.

For a moment, though, when he'd studied that old newspaper cutting, she could have sworn she saw something like regret in his expression. She'd probably imagined it. Thought she'd seen something in him just because she wanted to believe that, despite his odd behaviour at times, he was a decent person.

'You okay, Ruby?' Kern asked.

Startled from her musings, Ruby glanced up to find him regarding her.

'You appear to be off in a private dream world.'

No, not dreaming—just reinstating some common sense. Attraction to anyone was a weakness which led to mistakes. She didn't want to repeat the hurt of misplacing

her trust. She'd survived it once—better not to test her resolve a second time.

He reached out and touched her chin. His long fingers
were warm against her skin.

'Hey, where's your smile gone?'

She tilted her head thoughtfully. 'Smile?'

'That pretty one you showed me last night,' he said
softly. His thumb slid along the curve of her jaw before
he let it fall away.

She returned her gaze to the box and frowned down at
the contents. 'I did not smile at you.'

'Yes, you did. Almost stopped my heart, it was so unexpected.'

'Shh,' she hushed, embarrassed by his words and the
idea that she had done such a thing. She never smiled. She
wasn't the smiling type. Never had been. 'Don't you know
Goths never smile?'

'You did,' he argued, and leaned closer to whisper in
her ear, his breath hot and ticklish against her skin. 'Maybe
you're not a real Goth. Perhaps there's another woman inside you who wants to smile, but your strict Goth rules
are suppressing her.'

She sniffed and wrinkled her nose. 'The same way
there's a normal man inside *you*, I suppose?'

'Oh, Ruby,' Kern said, placing a hand to his chest. 'Are
you being sarcastic and mean just because I know you
have a secret smile?'

'Just making an observation,' she insisted, reaching for
a large black photo album.

She flicked over several pages, waiting for his reply. Her
neck was still tingling even though he was no longer close.

'Oh, no. I know sarcasm when I hear it,' he argued.
'And your words were thick with it.'

She flicked over another page. 'Maybe you need to test

your hearing, Mr MacKinley. Unless, of course, your problem is age-related—then there's really no hope. Though I did recently read that hearing aids have improved. Perhaps you should check them out.'

'Why, you...'

Before she could see the danger, Kern stood up, scooped her up off the pine box, threw her over his shoulder and headed to the entrance.

'What are you doing?' Ruby yelped as they headed outside into the sunshine.

'I think I'll take your advice and see if my ears need cleaning. A good, thorough wash will do the job perfectly.'

'Put me down!' Ruby cried. Whatever he was planning, she guessed she wasn't going to like it. 'Dog, help me!'

Her traitor of a pet leapt around beside them, barking with excitement. Instead of saving her, he just wanted to enter their game.

Kern laughed. 'I think he plans on joining us in our dip.'

'Dip?'

The swine laughed again, wickedly. 'Brace yourself, Ruby. Because it's going to be cold.'

Freezing water engulfed them both within seconds, covering them completely as they sank to the river's depths and then rose back up again. Splashing and barking nearby let Ruby know that Dog had joined them in their dunking.

Spluttering, and filled with thoughts of revenge, Ruby splashed out for the man who'd caused this impromptu wash. 'I'm going to get you, MacKinley!'

Kern laughed and stumbled back out of reach. His dark hair was plastered to his head and his shirt clung to his body.

Flicking more water in her direction, he chanted, 'Look at you...all dirty. Let me help clean you off.'

'Keep away,' she growled, wiping water from her eyes. 'I can't believe you did that.'

Shrugging, Kern playfully splashed more water at her. 'I only wanted to cool down that hot, cruel tongue of yours.'

'Oh, I'm going to make you pay,' she threatened, moving towards him. 'You're going to suffer, second by second.'

'Come on, then,' he teased.

She charged towards him, but her soaked trainers sank into the river's muddy bottom and made hard work of it. Before she had a chance to reach Kern he dodged out of her way for a second time, causing her to spin and fall back into the water.

'Missed!' he taunted, laughing. 'Try again, Miss Wet Vet.'

She did. And failed once more. The man moved like a fish, not at all hindered by his wet clothes.

'Ah, come on, Ruby,' he mocked. 'You can do better than that.'

'I'm going to get you back,' she swore, already imagining the vengeful retaliation she would inflict upon him once they were back on dry land.

He chuckled and shook his head. Waddling over to her, he grabbed her hand and dragged her towards the bank. 'Come on, Ruby. Let's go to your place and dry off.'

She seethed, glaring at his back as he tugged her through the water and up onto the grass. 'I don't recall inviting you.'

'Surely you don't begrudge me a towel to dry off?'

'Actually,' she mused darkly, 'I think I do.'

He turned back to her and pouted. 'But I could get a chill…'

She bit her lip to stop herself from grinning at his fake pathetic expression. This man was just too adorable. That cute boyish face he worked weakened her resistance and anger.

He could have a towel—but he could use it outside on the grass. The last thing she wanted was Kern inside her home, dripping, teasing, and utterly far too charming.

'This is nice,' Kern said, looking around her caravan with obvious curiosity.

Every now and then he would pick something up, study it for a moment, and then return it to its place.

'Thank you,' Ruby said, self-conscious of how small the space was with the two of them and Dog inside the kitchen area.

Her attempt to keep Kern outside had failed dismally when he had dived through the door before she could prevent him, and now he stood in the centre of the kitchen, surrounded by pale pink cushions and mint-green-painted kitchen cupboards, trying not to bang his head on the dangling crystals of her mini chandelier.

Opening the cupboard where she kept her clean linen, she reached for the top towel, smirking as she turned and handed it to him. 'Use this before you drip water all over the floor. Why you couldn't stay outside as I suggested—'

'Because then I wouldn't be in here and seeing another side to you,' he murmured. He glanced down at the towel, then back up at her before taking it.

She glared at him and tried to hustle him towards the door. He had a towel, so now there was no reason for him to stay inside. Besides, her own clothes were sticking to her, and probably revealing too much of her body.

'I get the feeling you want me to leave,' he said.

'You threw me in the river and pushed your way into my home. You're not exactly my favourite person right now.'

He nodded to the dog stretched out at his feet, looking

up at him adoringly. 'Dog's happy I'm here—and besides, I'm still looking around your home.'

She folded her arms. 'It's just a caravan. Nothing much to see.'

'It's more than that, Ruby,' he dismissed. 'It's your home and there's everything to see.'

He wiped the towel over the side of his face, leaving a trail of tiny pink threads where he'd rubbed against his stubble, while reaching out for an old postcard stuck on a board near the kettle. It showed a picture of a famous race course. One she suspected he would recognise.

Kern pulled it off the board. 'Cheltenham. Nice course. Have you been there?'

'Yes, years ago.'

She moved away and picked up the fluffy lilac throw she liked to snuggle into while reading at night. Folding it in half, she turned away from him and the questions she sensed brewed in his too-clever mind.

She should have thrown the stupid postcard away years ago. She regretted not doing so now.

'I never took you for a racing girl. Show jumping, maybe, but not National Hunt.'

'You hardly know me,' she reminded him curtly.

She was uncomfortable with how close he was to the truth. What would the man say if she listed the number of other racetracks she had visited as a child, or the less public names of well-known people involved in the sport? Names only people deeply immersed in the scene would recognise.

'True.'

She glanced at the card, fighting the urge to snatch it from his fingers. 'I was taken there a few times as a child by my parents. It's just a silly souvenir. Nothing more.'

'They like horse racing, then?' he asked. 'Your parents, I mean.'

'They used to,' Ruby said with a shrug. 'They're both dead now.'

Kern placed his towel on a seat and sat down on top of it. Twisting the card in his fingers, his expression serious, he stared at it. 'Sorry to hear that.'

'It happened a long time ago,' she said.

Sensing he planned to grill her further, Ruby pointed towards her bedroom door, judging avoidance and escape to be the best idea. 'I'll just go and change. I won't be long.'

Kern glanced again at the postcard, his eyes narrowing. Nothing was written on the back, and yet it added another thread of mystery to Ruby Day.

He'd tried to ignore her, but every time they were together it was as though they had known each other for longer than a few days. Time with her felt comfortable and easy. He'd forgotten how relaxing being with another person—a woman—could be. His marriage hadn't felt that way for years.

Yes, Ruby was a riddle. Her reaction to the card told him there was more to it than just a few fun days watching the gee-gees with her parents. This postcard meant something to her—something important and not something she intended to share with him.

Why? What was it about this card or the place on it that she didn't want to talk about? Was it simply that the card caused her to remember happier times with her parents, who were no longer around?

Well, they all had secrets and past experiences they wanted to keep hidden, but for some strange reason he was curious about Ruby's.

Why had she been so secretive about her background

the other day? She clammed up every time he asked something personal. Why hadn't she mentioned her parents had died when they'd been discussing his own, earlier in the barn? And how had she got that scar on her neck?

Their dunk in the river had removed some of her make-up and exposed jagged pink flesh. Was the story behind the wound what she wanted to keep quiet? Or was she just shy and wouldn't feel comfortable opening up to him?

MacKinley, stop letting your imagination play just because the woman doesn't want to share her life story with you. It's not as if you're sharing your own, is it?

God, no, he didn't want to scare the woman off with his tales of marital woe.

Hang on—what the heck was he thinking? He didn't want to do anything where Ruby Day or any other woman was concerned *full stop*. He'd learnt that lesson for life.

He'd returned to Dorset because he had nowhere else to go and he wanted to take some time to work out his next move. For the past few months he'd dealt with the fallout of everything Corinne had instigated and, despite what his aunt thought, he wasn't sure horse racing was how he wanted to spend the rest of his days.

Perhaps this was fate's prod to rethink and change course? Maybe there was something else for him? Though winning races hadn't been a complete waste of his time…

Kern looked at the postcard once more and frowned. He'd never won the Gold Cup, though. Cheltenham's coveted top trophy had never sat in his collection.

A collection he no longer owned.

He stood and tossed the card down on to the tabletop. With a final glance round at the warm and cosy caravan, he strolled to the door.

Getting mixed up with a woman, no matter how cute and tempting, was not for him. Women caused nothing but strife and heartache. It would be easy to want to get to know Ruby better, to try and uncover her riddles and study her secrets, peel away the coverings around her heart, but he refused to hurt another woman again. Or, just as importantly, to allow one to hurt him in return. Better to leave now than risk battering their fragile hearts.

CHAPTER SIX

'YOU DO REALISE barbecued food has the potential to kill, or at the very least cause sickness and diarrhoea?' said Alex Morsi.

Ruby almost laughed at her boss as his wife threateningly swiped the air between them with a spatula. Over the last week the couple had often provided entertainment during work hours, but this afternoon they were all attending the practice's annual barbecue in the rear car park, and Kiki had been left in charge of cooking the meat.

'I haven't killed you *yet*.' Kiki smiled not so sweetly at her husband. 'Though if you add any further unhelpful scraps of culinary doom I'm likely to warm to the idea.'

Alex grinned down at his wife, losing his normal serious expression. 'I'm just informing Miss Day of the risks.'

'Don't,' Kiki snapped. 'I'm a very good cook.'

'You are,' Alex agreed, moving nearer to his wife and slipping an arm around her waist. 'I just thought I would tell Miss Day—'

The spatula made another swipe, just missing Alex's nose. '*Don't*, Alex! You know what happens when you "just" something.'

With a final warning glare at her husband, Kiki turned to Ruby with a bright friendly smile. 'Can I interest you in a beef sausage?'

Ruby glanced down at the tasty-looking food on the hot grill, but Alex's remarks still rang in her ears. Edging backwards, in case Kiki decided to turn the cooking utensil on her, she shook her head. 'I think I'll grab a veggie roll from the buffet table. I'm not much of a meat-eater, to be honest.'

Kiki growled at the man at her side and began a torrent of threats that made Ruby wince. Backing farther away, she moved in the direction of the practice and safety, in case Kiki decided to act on any of them. Dog stayed where he was, in front of the barbecue, ever hopeful of snatching something or conning a sausage from the cook.

'Friends of yours?' asked a deep familiar voice from behind her.

Startled, Ruby turned to find Kern, dressed in faded jeans and a dark blue T-shirt. A silly thrill of pleasure ran through her, but she quickly dismissed it. So what if the man was here? It didn't mean anything. Or at least, it shouldn't…

'Mr MacKinley!'

'Kern,' he corrected.

'I didn't realise you would be here,' she said, surprised to see him. Mostly the guests consisted of work colleagues and friends. Kern MacKinley was neither of those.

'Eloise insisted I come,' Kern admitted.

Ruby grinned and teased him. 'So you're here because your aunt told you to come?'

Kern shrugged. 'The woman has a way of making me agree to things when I have every intention of declining. It's a skill I'd hoped she'd lost while I was away.'

Ruby laughed, not believing anyone could make this man do anything he didn't want to. She guessed the real reason he'd come this afternoon was to make his aunt happy. Kern MacKinley might like to act all deep and uncaring, but sometimes he showed glimpses of being a sweet man.

Glancing around, she noticed another surprise guest, talking to Anne's husband, Harry. 'And your stepfather? Did Eloise invite him too?'

'It turns out Fin is friends with your colleague's husband and he invited him along.'

'So an unexpected family gathering for you?' she said, looking up at him to see how pleased he was at the fact. It had been clear during their exchange the other day, and from what Kern had said while clearing out his aunt's barn, that the two men had little time for each other.

'If I'd known Fin would be here then I'd have stayed away, no matter what Eloise wanted. Every run-in we've had since I came back has ended badly.'

'Probably best to just ignore him, then,' Ruby said.

Kern nodded. 'I intend to. Would you like another drink?'

Ruby held up her half-full glass of orange juice. 'No, thanks. I still have plenty.'

She waited for Kern to walk away and find someone else to talk to—someone more interesting—but he didn't. Searching for a different subject, she asked, 'How's Evie?'

Kern grinned, the warm light in his eyes softening his features, taking away some of the tension that seemed permanently to line his face.

'She's much better. I still haven't worked out what magic you used on her, but she's happier in herself and willingly stays in the stables at night. She and my aunt's horse are slowly making friends too.'

Ruby smiled and brushed back a curl that was tickling her cheek. She was pleased to hear that her short session with the troubled horse had helped. 'That's wonderful.'

'It is,' he agreed. 'And it's all because of you and the spell you cast over her.'

She laughed and shook her head, feeling warmth flowing into her chest at his praise, easing some of her awkwardness. 'No spell or trickery involved, I swear.'

He stared at her for several moments, not saying a word, but his eyes did the talking for him. He didn't believe her, and the flicker in their serious depths told her he wasn't done with finding out the truth.

Self-conscious, Ruby touched her neck, wondering if she was imagining things. 'Why are you staring at me?'

'I'm looking to see if your nose grows any longer,' he replied. His eyes narrowed and he leaned forward, closing the space between them. 'No, I think it's as small and pretty as usual.'

Ruby's laughter caused several people to turn their way, but she didn't care. 'I'm not lying. I just spent some time soothing her and talking to her.'

It wasn't a lie. Her healing did soothe and calm. Just like humans, animals reacted to strokes and soft words. Evie was a horse in emotional pain, and normally she would have offered further sessions to help the filly through it, but Kern already suspected some kind of sorcery, so the last thing she wanted to do was arouse his curiosity further. Not when she wasn't sure how he would react to the idea of someone healing by using her hands and her mind.

A lot of people were sceptical about holistic medicines and practices, despite the fact that most of them had been around longer than modern medicine. Many of the old cures had simply been forgotten over time and generations.

'I wish I could work out what you're hiding,' he murmured softly.

Unnerved by his words, Ruby glanced away. If he knew

all her dark secrets she doubted he'd spend any more time talking to her. He'd cut her off without another thought.

It was what had happened in the past, when people had either discovered her gift or learnt the truth about who her parents were and the lurid scandal of a world-famous, much-loved jockey, adored by the public for his humour and talent and his French model wife. They'd been the perfect couple in front of the camera and the racing crowd. Only behind closed doors the marriage had been one full of violence, affairs and cruelty.

She couldn't risk anyone finding out who she really was. They would either hate her for not telling them the truth, view her as being secretive and not to be trusted, or—worse—grill her over her parents' marriage in their quest for gossip.

She shivered and gripped her glass tighter. The old familiar urge to be alone with Dog somewhere secure was returning. But she couldn't leave yet. The party had barely started, and if she did it was bound to cause talk and even offence among her new colleagues.

Kern touched her arm with concern. 'Hey, what did I say?'

She blinked up at him, wishing she had stayed at home instead of trying to join in with the others. She wasn't a people person, preferring her solitary existence.

'Sorry?'

'You seem upset,' he murmured.

'No,' she lied, flashing him a smile she didn't feel. 'Just thinking about something. Nothing important. Why did you leave the other night?'

Raised voices interrupted them. They turned in the direction of the ruckus, which was on the other side of the car park. Eloise and Fin stood several paces apart, glaring at each other. Fin held a can of beer and Eloise a plate full of food.

'Looks like a family bust-up is about to kick off,' Kern sighed heavily. 'Some things never change. I'll be honest— *this* I haven't missed.'

Ruby didn't like the way her landlady appeared about ready to throw her food over the old man. 'Should you go over?'

Kern shook his head. 'I doubt my aunt needs any help. I've known grown men to shake when she gets riled up.'

'Even so,' Ruby said, concerned at the way the old couple were squabbling. 'It's ruining the barbecue.'

Kern grunted 'Okay but if she gets angry with me, I'm blaming you.'

Ruby giggled and shook her head. 'I'll deny everything. Go—before your aunt starts throwing mushroom vol au vents. I haven't had a chance to eat any yet.'

'Fine,' Kern huffed, capturing her elbow and manoeuvring Ruby along with him. 'But you're coming with me.'

'I think I should stay back,' she said, not keen to get dragged into his family's issues.

'No way,' Kern scoffed. 'This is your idea, so if anything gets thrown you can get hit first.'

Ruby gasped. 'Such a gentleman!'

'Oh, I'm no gentleman, Ruby,' he insisted flatly. 'I'd hate you to make the mistake of thinking I am.'

They reached the elderly couple just as their voices began to rise again.

'What's going on?' Kern asked, shielding Ruby slightly behind him despite his earlier comment, his stance both protective and thoughtful.

'Oh, here he is,' Fin sneered, turning his attention to Kern. 'The returning son and nephew. He left with nothing and he's returned with nothing—because he couldn't control a woman.'

'Keep your mouth shut!' Eloise yelled. 'You know nothing about him or his marriage.'

'Enough, both of you!' Kern scolded the bickering pair. 'This is not the time for tossing insults. Go home if you want to do that.'

'Why shouldn't these good people know the truth about you?' Fin continued, not listening. 'You always believed you were better than anyone else—your mother was to blame for that.'

'Don't you speak about my sister,' Eloise interrupted. 'She was an angel—too good for you.'

'She was a money-grabbing waste of time—just like *his* wife.'

Wife? Ruby glanced at the man beside her. Not once had Kern mentioned a wife. Where was she? Did she plan to follow him to Dorset? Why hadn't he ever mentioned her?

She took a step away from the squabbling threesome, the urge to leave returning.

'I said *enough*!' Kern yelled. 'No one here is interested in our family's past and grievances. Now, behave or leave.'

Anne's husband, Harry, moved into the group, his expression annoyed. 'Fin, I think perhaps you should listen to the man and go.'

Fin slammed his beer can down on the buffet table, causing it to wobble. 'Me? Why not them?'

Harry shook his head. 'Everyone was having a good time until this. I won't have Alex and Kiki upset because I made the mistake of asking you to join us. You need to go home and have a good long sleep. You'll feel better if you do.'

'Damn people!' Fin swore. He picked up his drink and pulled a bunch of car keys out of his trouser pocket.

'You can't drive,' Kern said, moving to take the keys from the old man. 'You've been drinking and you're in no fit state to—'

'Give me them!' Fin snatched the keys back out of Kern's hold and hurried away before anyone could react.

'Let him go,' Eloise urged, grabbing Kern arm.

'And risk him killing someone?' Kern asked, heading after his stepfather, who had amazing agility for someone in his seventies.

'Dog—wait!' Ruby yelled after the hound, who had left his pitch near the barbecue and was now intently following Kern out of the rear car park. 'Dog—heel!'

Racing after the trio, Ruby ran down the side of the building and reached the front car park in time to see Kern tugging on the driver's door of a rusty blue van.

'Fin, turn the engine off!'

The old man angrily revved the engine instead, while swearing and yelling at Kern through the half-open window.

Ruby rushed forward, intent on grabbing her dog by the collar before he ran any closer to the vehicle. 'Dog, *wait*!'

For the first time in his life, Dog ignored Ruby. His tail swished side to side as he bounded towards Kern, his focus on the man he considered his new friend.

'Dog! Stay!' Ruby yelled.

Still yanking on the driver's door, Kern turned at her shout and spotted Dog heading towards him. Letting go of the door, he moved in Dog's direction and yelled, 'Stay, Dog!'

The Irish Wolfhound ignored them both and continued to run towards Kern.

'*Dog!*' Ruby screamed, desperate for the canine to halt.

Fin suddenly shot the van into Reverse with a squeal of tyres and slammed into Dog, sending the hound flying into the air with a sickening high-pitched yelp, before he fell back to the ground in a rough-haired heap.

Fear stilled Ruby's blood and her movements. Dazed, she stared at her dog, stretched out in the middle of the car park, her brain struggling to take in what had just happened. Her heart beating loudly in her ears, drowning out all the other sounds around her, she stayed frozen on the spot.

Alex rushed past her and reached Dog first, crouching down to check him over with expert fingers.

'Dog...?' Ruby whispered, tears coating her lips as they ran down her face. As if in a trance, she moved towards her boss and shakily knelt down beside her best friend, dreading what she was going to find.

'Miss Day!'

Alex's urgent calling penetrated the fuzzy buzzing in her head and she stared down at her dog, still not moving on the worn Tarmac. *Was he...? Please, no... Don't let him be...*

Swallowing hard, she glanced up. 'Yes?'

Alex held her gaze, pulling her slowly from the shock that was about to engulf her completely. 'This patient needs our help. He's alive, and that's all that matters right now. Okay?'

She nodded and roughly wiped away the tears. 'Yes.'

Kern crouched down beside her. 'Oh, God, Ruby. I'm sorry. I never meant—'

'Apologies and blame can wait,' Alex snapped. 'Our patient's needs come first. We need something for a muzzle, Miss Day.'

She nodded, reaching out shaky fingers to touch her pet. 'Dog...?'

The sound of ripping fabric barely registered—not until

Kern handed her a long piece of blue fabric that looked faintly familiar. 'Here—use this.'

Without a word, she switched from owner mode to professional vet and prepared to muzzle Dog's mouth. Even the most affectionate and soft-natured animal could turn nasty when in pain. Prevention was better than a bite.

'His gums look okay…'

'He's alert, and seems to be breathing normally,' Alex said, proficiently working his fingers over Dog's rough-coated body. 'His pulse is strong, too.' Alex gently examined Dog's right hind leg. 'There's no obvious wound or breakage, and no sign of bleeding, but…' Dog whined as Alex carefully manipulated the limb. 'I suspect he's sustained a fracture. I can feel the bone through the skin.'

'Anne, we need— ' Alex stopped as his head nurse handed him a blanket.

'Harry's fetching a trolley,' she said.

Alex smiled and took it from his friend and employee. 'What would I do without you?'

'Struggle terribly, of course. I'm indispensable.'

Alex placed the blanket over Dog's body to keep him warm. 'Ruby, you and Kern get down here and support this leg and his rear end while we lift him on to the trolley. No point splintering it for the few minutes it will take to get him inside.'

'Anne and I will take Dog's other end,' Kiki said, kneeling down next to her husband and placing her hands in the correct position to support Dog's head and neck.

Ruby took Alex's place and with Kern's help prepared to lift Dog off the Tarmac with the least disturbance and movement to her pet's injured back leg.

'Right, team,' said Alex, 'let's move our patient.'

Together Ruby, Alex, Kiki, Anne and Kern raised Dog's

limp body on to the trolley Harry had fetched from inside
the building.

'I'll wait out here,' Kern called as the rest of them
moved indoors and through Reception towards the back
rooms.

Ruby nodded, then returned her attention to Dog. She
couldn't lose her four-legged best friend—she just couldn't.
He was all the family she had. Without Dog she would
have no one to love and care for, no one in her life who
loved her back.

'Right, Miss Day, what do we have?'

Ruby studied the two X-rays lit up on the screen, showing different views of Dog's damaged leg, and pointed at
the obvious break. 'The X-rays show a broken femur bone.'

Alex nodded and moved to stand behind her. After a few
moments discussing and reviewing the X-rays, he asked,
'Have you done any femur repairs?'

She shook her head.'

Alex turned away as Kiki wheeled a sedated Dog into
the room. 'Good. I've done plenty, so between us we'll
soon have your boy sorted. This will be your call—I'll
assist, talk you through it and monitor. Is that all right
with you? I'm thinking a pin will work best. What do you
think?'

Ruby twisted round and stared at her boss. 'You want
me to operate?'

Kiki glanced between them, but didn't say anything.

Alex rolled the prepared instrument trolley over to the
table in readiness. 'Don't you want to?'

'Yes, but he's *my* dog.'

Alex glanced across the room at her. 'Would you prefer
I operated on Dog and you monitored?'

Ruby considered the question and realised that she

didn't want anyone else to operate on her pet. If anyone was going to fix his leg, then it was going to be her. 'No, I don't think I would.'

'Good.' Alex nodded. 'I know I wouldn't want anyone else working on my animals, so I figured you'd feel the same.'

'That's because you're a control freak,' Kiki teased. 'Right, you two. Dog's all prepped, shaved and ready for your surgical prowess. Let's get busy, shall we?'

Alex stayed on the other side of the trolley, his gaze still on Ruby. 'When you're ready… Remember I'm here to answer any questions or help overcome any unexpected problems. But I'm sure you'll manage fine.'

'Thanks,' Ruby said, comforted by his words.

She walked over to the trolley, her heart aching at the sight of her anaesthetised dog laid out on the stainless-steel table, tubes coming from his mouth and body. Sucking in a deep breath, she forced all emotions from her mind and gathered her mental strength while Alex placed the surgical drapes over Dog's body. She was very conscious that the operation wasn't going to be finished in a short time.

Carefully feeling the swollen area of the leg, she said, 'I'm going to make my incision now.'

Alex murmured in agreement.

Ruby picked up the scalpel and made a straight cut through the skin and muscle. Using her fingers, she located each end of the broken bone. With gentle manipulation, she managed to realign both pieces of bone in readiness to put them back together.

'Looks nice and clean,' Alex said. 'Should fuse together easy enough once pinned.'

Ruby nodded, and carefully fixed a pin into place.

'Nice…' Alex murmured.

Ruby finished off by suturing the wound closed and covering with dressing, ready for post-op X-rays.

'Good work,' Alex praised her. 'I can see I made the right decision, employing you.'

Ruby grinned beneath her mask. 'Thanks.'

A sense of relief and warmth flooded her heart. Dog was going to be okay, and it seemed as though she had just passed some sort of test where her boss was concerned. Despite the circumstances, a small sense of pride filled her.

'Thanks, boss.'

Alex tugged down his mask and smiled. 'You're welcome, Ruby.'

'How is he?' Kern rose from one of the plastic chairs in Reception, his gaze taking in the exhausted woman dressed in theatre scrubs, standing beside her boss. An overwhelming urge to drag her into his arms and hug her tight gripped him.

'He's stable,' Ruby answered, her voice dry and thick. Suddenly her eyes filled with tears. She shook her head and wiped them away. 'I'm sorry. I guess it's just relief.'

Alex awkwardly patted Ruby's shoulder. 'Time for you to go home and get some rest.'

Ruby shook her head, not wanting to be separated from her best friend. 'I'd prefer to stay and monitor Dog.'

Alex ignored her and pushed her gently towards Kern. 'Take her home, stick her in a bath, and then put her to bed. After she's slept for five hours she can come back and check on her patient.'

Kern gave in to his earlier urge and hugged Ruby close. Liking the feel of her head against his chest, and not at all put off by the antiseptic scent clinging to her, he said, 'I will.'

Ruby sighed into his chest and muttered, 'You're very bossy.'

Alex chuckled. 'That's why I'm the boss. I can get away with bossing you around—at least until my wife corrupts you the same way she has all my other staff members.' Once again he looked at Kern. 'Take this woman home. If you return before the five hours are up, I will fire her.'

Ruby twisted back to glare at Alex. 'Hey, that's not fair.'

Alex smiled. 'Trust me to look after your dog. Now, leave.'

Kiki walked into reception carrying the baby in her carrier and a tray of food. 'I thought we'd eat some of this here instead of carting it home.'

'Has everyone gone?'

'Yes. It started to rain, so everyone grabbed some food and went home. I asked Anne to save you a cheeseburger. It's probably cold, though.'

Alex smile widened and he strolled over to his wife. 'This is why I married her. She's the perfect veterinary nurse.'

Kiki snorted and tilted her head. 'I thought it was for my kisses?'

'They're just a bonus.'

Kern watched the couple and once again felt the loneliness that had plagued him during the last few years rise and hit him harder than ever before. Why did some people find romance easy? When for others, like him, it carried a heavy burden of duty? And wasn't spending time with the woman in his arms now just encouraging fate to wound him all over again?

Stepping into the caravan without the usual boisterous welcome from Dog was too much for Ruby. For the first time in years a cold emptiness hung in the air, as welcoming as a stinging slap.

'Let me help you,' Kern offered, reaching to remove

her jacket when she stood motionless in the centre of the kitchen. His fingers were tender as they slipped over the material and pushed it from her shoulders and down her arms. 'A nice shower and then—'

She touched his chest to stop him from continuing. 'I don't want a shower.'

'You'll feel better,' he soothed, tossing the jacket aside.

She shook her head, not wanting to feel better. Dog didn't feel better, did he? Her best friend was alone, and probably confused, and she wanted to be with him instead of being here. Not once since she'd picked him up from the rescue centre as an overlooked puppy had they spent a night apart.

'I just want to…' Her words died as the ache inside her grew bigger, making her whole chest hurt. Tears hovered, then rolled down her cheeks, falling and releasing the emotions she'd held inside since the accident occurred.

'Aw, Ruby, don't…' Kern groaned, pulling her to him. 'I'm so sorry. I truly am. If I could change what happened so that Fin hit *me*, I would. I promise you.'

Ruby instinctively settled deeper into the circle of his hold, reluctant to move away, needing this moment with this man. No one had held her for so many years, and although she knew she should reject this closeness she didn't want to. She wanted to grasp this moment of comfort, as selfish as that was, and hold on to it for as long as he allowed.

'I'm sorry,' she gulped, between aching sobs. 'I don't know why I'm being so silly.'

Kern stroked the back of her head and soothed her. 'It's not silly. You love Dog and he's been hurt. Cry all you want.'

He manoeuvred them over to the sofa and pulled Ruby down onto his lap, enveloping her once more in his wonderful warm embrace, shutting out everything as she gave in to the feelings she'd kept on hold while she and Alex had treated her beloved Wolfhound.

After a while her gaze settled on the blue-and-white blanket Dog liked to have on the sofa. He'd had it since she'd got him as a pup. Tugging it over, she sniffed at it. 'This is his. It smells of him.'

Kern lifted a corner and smelt it. 'Yeah, that's pure dog. Cheesy paws and all.'

She snuggled the blanket closer and glared at him. 'You think it stinks?'

'It does,' he insisted. 'But I also know that when I lost the horses in my care I didn't get the chance to keep anything that belonged to them.'

'What happened?'

Kern didn't speak for a while, but finally he said, 'My wife was what some might call "highly strung". She suffered terrible mood swings and bouts of depression. Had done since her teenage years. These last few years she became desperate for a child, but it never happened. Physically everything was working fine with both of us, but she just never got pregnant.'

Ruby hugged the blanket closer as she felt the man's sadness fill the caravan. Not sure what to say, she murmured, 'I'm sorry…'

'When the first year goes by without a pregnancy, you start to question if it's going to happen… Two years in, you know something is wrong. But when you seek medical help and the doctors insist there is no physical reason for the lack of a baby, it's hard to take. Who do you talk to then? Where do you turn? IVF gets mentioned, alongside adoption. But Corinne didn't want to deal with either. She had a phobia of doctors, thanks to her father having dragged her to several as a teenager. Knowing her mental health history, they offered counselling, but it never helped. Often she'd miss appointments, or just rip up the referral letters and throw them away. You see, because there was no medical reason, she clung to the hope of one day having a child without intervention.'

'That's heartbreaking...'

'It is when you're the one watching the person you love go through it. Living with her disappointment every month, feeling like a failure for not being able to give her the one thing she craved.'

'She had you,' Ruby pointed out.

Kern gave another dejected smile and continued, 'I'm afraid I wasn't enough to ease her persistent yearning to hold her own baby. Anyway, I'd gone to Doncaster for a race meeting. During the third race the police phoned my mobile. Apparently Corinne had taken the keys for the tractor and driven it into one of the stable blocks. She brought the roof down on the three horses inside.'

'Oh, no!' Ruby gasped, the blurred sensations she'd experienced while working with Enticing Evie instantly came to her mind.

'Evie was in one of the paddocks nearby and she watched the whole thing,' Kern said, unknowingly confirming Ruby's suspicions. 'She must have heard the other horses' cries of fear. Luckily, the other eight horses not racing that day were in another paddock, away from the house. Afterwards, Corinne set the destroyed stables on fire and drove the tractor at Evie. Fortunately, the fire had attracted the neighbours, and one of the staff members I'd left behind, and they called the police.'

'Where's your wife now?' Ruby asked gently.

'She panicked when the police arrived and ended up flipping the tractor onto its side. She was trapped beneath it and died instantly.'

Ruby grasped his hand. 'Oh, Kern. I'm sorry. Why did she do it?'

He shrugged, and his arms tightened around her. 'I think the fragile pieces inside her finally broke. After all the years of depression and disappointment, she just couldn't take any more. Everything built and built in her head until it exploded. I'd tried to get her interested in the business over the years, but she had no real love either for horses or racing. I'd encouraged her to make friends in the village where we lived, but she'd fall out with people after a few months, or grow tired of their company. I'd told myself I didn't have time to cater to her every whim if we wanted to eat and keep our home and the business. Truth is, I ran out of ways to help her.'

'What about her family?' asked Ruby.

'Corinne hated her father, and her sister moved to New Zealand fifteen years ago— not long after their mother died. Her mother never took her role as a parent too seriously, and when Corinne's problems with depression started in her teens, she dropped out of her life for good. She had no one but me. I couldn't abandon her, too. God knows where she would have ended up if I had. We were together for such a long time. She wasn't easy, but you don't walk away from your partner just because your marriage is hard work. I'm not a man who quits.'

'It sounds as if your wife's problems were something neither you nor your marriage could mend,' Ruby said, hoping he wouldn't be offended by her comment. 'Not without professional help.'

Kern was silent for a long time, then he admitted, 'I tried in the beginning—but in the end I'm guilty of just giving up. Corinne had become paranoid about me cheating— I never did. I respected her and my wedding vows too much to destroy either with cheap, easy sex. But according to her, I never spent enough time with her. She resented my work and the horses. She was rude to the owners. Forgot to give me important messages. Our marriage became a mess of resentment and anger on both sides. But although it was hard, and the last few years were a kind of hell, dealing with her mood swings, I did love Corinne once. That love died somewhere through the years, but for a long time she was my best friend and my lover. She deserved my loyalty and I know I should have helped her more—but how do you help someone who doesn't want it and resents you even for suggesting it? How do you get someone to listen when they constantly tell you to shut up or walk away? If I'd given up the business how would we have lived? One of us had to work. It's easy for people standing on the outside to think there are simple answers, but there aren't. Not really.'

'I didn't mean to imply—' Ruby began.

'I know you didn't,' he said.

Ruby sighed and rested her head against his shoulder. His questions were similar to the ones she'd once asked herself. 'I don't know, Kern. How *do* you solve a puzzle when there is no clear, simple solution?'

Stroking a curl back from Ruby's face, he apologised again. 'I'm sorry. I never meant for Dog to get hurt.'

She clasped his cheek and shook her head. 'I know you didn't. It was a horrible accident. You were trying to do the right thing by stopping your stepfather from driving.'

'I don't have a great history of doing the right thing, though,' he muttered. 'Not where women are concerned.'

She squeezed his hand, wanting to offer even the smallest comfort. 'You don't have to hold me.'

He tugged her close, kissing the top of her head. 'I want to hold you. It's been a while since I've wanted to hold anyone. Just for tonight, let's forget about common sense and comfort one another. Tomorrow we'll go back to being each other's bothersome neighbour.'

'It's been a long time since someone held me,' she confessed, snuggling deeper into him.

'No recent boyfriends?' he asked.

'None.' She sighed, wanting to be honest. 'I find it hard to trust people.'

'It's tough, isn't it? Especially when important people have let you down. That's why I've sworn off relationships for life.'

'I doubt I'll ever get married,' she admitted. 'It's not something that's ever interested me that much.'

'It's not all hearts and chocolates, I'm afraid.'

Glad he understood, she squeezed his hand again, wrapping her fingers around his cold ones. For one night she would revel in the feel of Kern and his wonderfully warm hug. Tomorrow they would pretend it had never happened. Slip back into the undemanding roles of acquaintances once more.

'Close your eyes and go to sleep,' he urged, his breath warm against her scalp.

'Okay...'

Some time later, through the fog of sleep, she felt herself being laid down on the sofa. A few seconds later the throw enclosed her body.

'Sweet dreams, Ruby,' Kern whispered, stroking a finger along her cheek. 'I'll be back in a few hours.'

Ruby listened to the sound of Kern driving off, wishing with all her heart that he had stayed. But she had no right to want such a thing. The man's soul was bruised and torn, and he deserved peace and time to heal.

Sadness and guilt had coated every word he'd uttered about his wife—a woman obviously mentally unwell, but too stubborn, perhaps too afraid, to take the help offered.

How tragic for both of them. A horrible situation with no easy remedy. He had been right when he'd described it as something nobody truly understood unless they'd been unfortunate enough to experience the same heart-wrenching pain.

Tonight they had shared some pieces of their pasts, but it made no difference. He was just a client who'd offered her solace and support when she'd desperately required it. A battered man who would one day leave and start a new phase in his life somewhere else.

She needed to make sure she remembered that the only place Kern MacKinley could ever be for her was at arm's length.

CHAPTER SEVEN

'THE PARADE?'

Kern stared at his aunt, certain the woman had gone potty. Why else would she be ranting on about the parade the local town held once a year? A parade she apparently wanted him to take part in.

He trained racehorses. Or he used to. He also had several more boxes to clear out of his aunt's large shed before it got too late, and discussing a parade he certainly wasn't going to take part in was nothing but a waste of his time.

'Oh, stop fussing,' Eloise complained. 'It's half a day— and it will do you good to have something nice to look forward to.'

Kern rested his hands gently on his aunt's shoulders, shocked by the feel of their boniness beneath his palms. Another sign of the passing of time... 'Eloise, I'm not a four-year-old who requires entertaining. I'm a grown man, and I can occupy my time fine.'

'You'll always be a little boy to me,' Eloise insisted. 'Besides, you're not doing it alone. I've arranged for an assistant—not only to help you clean the old cart, but also to keep you company during the parade.'

Wondering which poor sucker his aunt had conned into helping, he asked, 'Who?'

'Your neighbour.'

His heart dropped. 'Fin?'

'I said your neighbour—not your squatter,' she dismissed. 'I've asked sweet little Ruby to help you out.'

Kern swallowed, not sure what to say. He'd avoided Ruby for over a week, since he'd dropped her back at the clinic after her rest. Not because he didn't want to see her, but because whatever he felt for her was best left undiscovered and ignored. He wasn't in a position to offer anything more than friendship to the woman. And a small part of him feared friendship with Ruby would never be enough.

Holding her in his arms, feeling her body against his own, surrounded by her warm womanly scent, did nothing but hike up his unwelcome attraction towards her. An attraction he daren't explore.

'And she agreed?' he asked.

'Of course. Unlike you, she is helpful, and she doesn't complain all the time. You really have become quite grumpy as you've aged.'

Kern ignored his aunt's comment and demanded, 'What did you bribe her with?'

Ruby might be kind, but she also worked full time and shied away from unfamiliar company. He'd noticed her discomfort after watching her at the barbecue before her dog's accident.

Eloise shrugged and admitted, 'I offered to doggy-sit on Saturday afternoon.'

Intrigued, Kern asked, 'Why?'

'I thought she might like to do a bit of shopping or sightseeing. Since the accident she's worked and then returned home each day with nothing else in between. I asked Anne, and apparently she spends her dinner hours going over notes or checking the animals. It's not right for a young woman of her age to have zero social life. I'm just being neighbourly.'

'Hmm…' Kern murmured, not believing his relative.

Eloise clearly had plans stewing in her head, and he suspected the innocent vet would be too polite to refuse his aunt and would end up regretting the inevitable outcome.

'And she said yes, did she?' he asked, irritated by his own curiosity.

What the woman did and with whom was nothing to do with him. If she wanted to date all the men for a mile around, then good luck to her. Ruby was young, pretty and sweet. Any man with more than a handful of brain cells would snatch her up.

Any man who didn't screw up every important relationship in his life…

'Of course. Though I've yet to mention the parade to her. I thought I'd wait and see how you fancied it first. It will be a good chance for Ruby to get to know more people in the town.

'The answer's still no.'

Eloise huffed. 'You've developed a hardness since you left,' she complained. 'It's quite annoying.'

'Yeah, well, life will do that,' Kern replied, retrieving an empty bucket.

It was the reason he had to keep a distance between him and a certain vet. Ruby merited someone who viewed the future as exciting and worth exploring. He saw it as just something to be lived through.

'Is there anything else, or can I get back to work?'

Eloise glanced around the practically empty shed. 'You're doing a good job. Both here and the barn are far tidier. The stables on the farm are looking better too. When do you plan to make a start on the gallops?'

'When I earn some extra money,' he said. 'They're on the list of things to be sorted.'

'I can lend you some—'

'No, thanks,' he cut in, before she made a full offer. He still had a few fragments of pride. Besides, how could he take her money when he planned to move on once he'd got the place tidied up?

'Stubborn—just like your mother,' Eloise complained. 'But it's probably a good thing. Made you strong in mind and nature.'

'I'm still not driving the cart in any parade,' he insisted, not trusting his aunt's compliments or offers of help when she was set on getting her own way. This time he was determined to deny her, no matter what she said or did.

'Think about it, won't you?' Eloise begged. 'You know how to drive it from when your father taught you as a teenager. I'm sure it will all come back to you.'

The memory made him smile—until he noticed his aunt's pleased expression and felt a new wave of resolve grip him. 'No.'

'It'll mean you get to spend some time with a certain Miss Ruby Day.'

His heart kicked at the thought, but he busied himself reaching for several boxes of screws. He was glad for another reason to refuse. Less time with Ruby was better for his head—and a couple of other parts of his anatomy. Parts best left in their customary dormant condition.

'I doubt she wants to see me,' he said.

'I think you're wrong,' Eloise argued, following him to the shed's entrance.

Kern really didn't want to hear any more. He'd already spent far too much time thinking about Ruby, and he refused to do anything further…like develop strong feelings for her. The last thing she'd desire was a man like him in her life.

He sighed and reminded his aunt, 'Her dog has a broken leg because of me. If I hadn't rushed after Fin, poor Dog would be running around just fine.'

Eloise shook her head. 'It was an accident. It's my fault as much as yours, and Fin's really the one to blame. If she's going to be upset with anyone, it should be him.'

'It's also less than a year since I lost my wife, and I feel no desire to form any kind of a new relationship.'

So why do those words feel like a lie, MacKinley? Why do you wake up every damn morning aching to hold Ruby? Why do you feel restless each evening when you glance across the river and watch the light in her caravan window? Wondering what she's doing and how she's feeling. Wishing you could spend the evening with her.

'I'm still getting used to the single life. It might be fun to enjoy it for a year or two.'

Liar. That's how you felt before Ruby. Now you don't know how you feel.

Kern dropped the screws into the bucket with a thud. Where Ruby was concerned, he didn't know what he wanted. Though his excuses wouldn't hold much water with his aunt if she ever knew that he and Corinne had stopped sharing anything meaningful years ago.

He'd offered her a divorce many times over the years, but she'd always refused. Gradually, their relationship and love had faded into monthly sex and a diminishing friendship.

She'd blamed *him* for their lack of children, even though the doctors had insisted they were both capable of producing them. As the years had passed Corinne had convinced herself it was his fault, even though there had been no logic or evidence to support her accusation.

Shaking off the past, Kern glanced at his aunt. 'Ruby deserves to spend time with a man who wants a proper relationship. Someone whose heart is still intact and full of love. That's something mine will never be again.'

Sadness filled Eloise's gaze and she nodded. 'I suppose you're right. She is a delightful young woman. She'll probably meet someone at work or in town. I'm surprised the Baxter twins haven't asked her out. They're both searching for a wife…'

'Maybe you should tell her?' he suggested, forcing each word from his mouth. Despite not knowing the men, he immediately hated them—which was neither fair, nor made any sense.

'I will,' Eloise agreed. 'I'm going to put the kettle on. Come on inside when you've finished here.'

Kern waited for his aunt to leave before he let the bucket drop to the floor. He meant it. Ruby deserved the one thing he was incapable of giving: love. And he'd sworn the day Corinne died that he'd never risk becoming entwined with that emotion again.

Ruby hesitated outside the barn, listening to the bickering voice in her head, one of which insisted that this was a stupid idea. She should never have agreed to help Eloise. But the woman had asked in a way that had made it impossible to say no without causing offence.

As for Kern—she'd not seen him in over a week. The poor man was probably keeping out of her way, for fear she might throw herself into his arms and blubber all over him again.

What a fool she'd been, carrying on in such a way and exploiting his kindness. Too much of a gentleman to push her away, or leave, he'd suffered through her crying session with stoic patience. How cringingly embarrassing for both of them.

The poor man had lost his wife and everything important to him—and despite his admitting that his marriage had been seriously troubled, the last thing he needed was someone using his shoulder as a tissue to sob out her all her relief, worries and woes upon.

With a deep breath, Ruby stopped listening to the squabbling in her head and stepped inside the metal shed. Blinking as her eyes adjusted to the dim interior, she saw Kern standing at the far end next to a large, bulky item covered with green canvas.

'Hi,' she called out, heading towards him.

She refused to show any discomfort or any sign that the sudden fast beating of her heart was making her slightly light-headed. Maybe it was the way his grubby T-shirt hugged his body and showed off his powerful arm muscles. Why did he have to be so handsome, tall and hunky? Good-looking and nice?

A nice man who allowed a woman to dribble tears and a runny nose all over him. A fatal combination for any woman—including her.

Kern slowly turned to her, his smile unnatural and stiff. Ruby's heart nosedived in a sickening spiral to splat somewhere around her heels.

Obviously the snot and the ugly tears really were complete turn-offs and all too much for him.

Ruby swallowed and willed her stupid head to stop overthinking.

The man has no interest in you, Ruby, so get over yourself. So what if you've lost another friend? It doesn't matter. You're used to being alone—deal with it. It's life. Stop whinging and face it like a woman.

Ruby forced a smile in return, then fixed all her attention on the large object behind him. 'Is that the reason your aunt asked me here?'

He nodded and reached behind him for the corner of

the stiff fabric. 'This is her latest project. Or should I say ours? Once I pull this cover off you'll see why I'm not dancing with excitement and joy.'

Ruby lurched forward and placed her hand over his to stop him from peeling back more than a small triangle of the canvas. Warmth rushed over her skin at the contact, and her heart attempted to elevate itself back up to her chest and regain its earlier manic speed.

She blushed at the unfamiliar sensation and at her own unexpected behaviour. When had she become so forward?

'Won't you let me try and guess what it is first?' she asked, her voice husky and rushed.

Kern stared at her for a second, before slowly grinning. 'Fine—but you'll never get it.'

'Bet I will,' she disputed, relieved that his awkwardness had disappeared and the uncomfortable air between them had gone with it. He might not find her attractive, but they could still be friendly.

'Okay. You get two guesses.'

She frowned and rested her hands on her hips. 'Two? Why not three?'

'Because I like the odds in my favour,' he said smugly. 'Shut your eyes and let's start.'

'Must I close my eyes?' she hedged, suddenly unsure.

The man had dumped her in the river before. Could she trust him not to do something just as unscrupulous when her eyes were shut? Though the idea of being in his arms again wasn't unappealing...

His smile turned wicked and teasing. 'Many things are far more fun if you close your eyes, Ruby.'

She raised an eyebrow. 'Sounds dangerous.'

His lips twitched higher and his playful gaze morphed into a dark smoulder. 'We all need a little danger sometimes.'

With a murmur, Ruby closed her eyes and tried to calm

her pounding heart. Suddenly she was happy to experience a little danger, if Kern insisted on it. Her life was so safe and empty of fun…sometimes she hurt from the loneliness of it.

Watching couples from afar, seeing them laugh and play emphasised how little close physical contact she shared with anyone. There was no one for her to discuss the news with, or talk to about what had occurred in the latest TV drama. It made for a staid existence at times. If it wasn't for Dog she'd experience no real happiness and companionship at all.

'Raise your hand,' Kern murmured close to her ear.

His breath tickled and she bit her lip to stop herself from laughing and squirming on the spot.

She lifted her hand and he gently guided her fingers over the canvas and rested them on top. She wrinkled her nose. 'Can I ask questions before I guess?'

He shifted until his chest pressed into her back, his body's heat warming her shoulder blades. 'If you want to—but only two.'

Stroking her fingertips lightly over the rough fabric, she frowned. 'Does the canvas have anything to do with what's underneath?'

'No.'

She frowned harder, searching for a hint from the hard lump beneath her palm. Conscious of not wanting to waste her last question, she asked, 'Is there a connection with horses?'

He chuckled, his fingers twitching slightly over her own. 'Yes, there is. Without a horse this item would be useless.'

Intrigued, she searched her mind for ideas of what it might be. She'd asked about a connection with horses only because of Kern's and Eloise's close ties with the equine world. Other than that, she didn't have any idea.

'Well?' he asked.

'No idea,' she admitted, irritated that she couldn't decipher anything from the bulges, thanks partly to his distracting presence. How was she supposed to concentrate when he enclosed her so completely?

'Do I get a clue?' she asked hopefully.

He laughed dryly. 'No. You've already asked your two questions. Time to guess.'

'You're mean,' she complained.

Kern agreed. 'Open your eyes and let me show you what it is.'

She did, and her eyes immediately took in the sight of their hands still connected on the green fabric—his dark and life-worn, hers paler and softer, thanks to the hand cream she used every night before bed. What would he do if she lifted her fingers slightly and linked them with his? Would he pull away or slip his own into hers?

'Last chance,' he pronounced against the curve of her ear.

With a final glance over the mysterious item's length, she uttered the first thing that came into her head. 'A sleigh?'

'Close.' Kern tugged off the canvas covering to reveal a very old and sad-looking Victorian cart.

'Wow...' she whispered, taking in the two large wheels. Her imagination immediately pictured a young woman on the wooden seat, driving around town, making deliveries or visiting friends. 'It's lovely,' she declared softly.

Kern grunted. 'It's tired and in need of a good clean. Which is what my aunt wishes us to give it. She's nagging at me to drive it in the town parade. This year's theme is Victoria and Albert, apparently.'

'Really?' Ruby asked, visualising Kern dressed like a Victorian farmer, cantering along the country roads, waving and calling out to passing neighbours or grazing livestock.

'My father used to compete in cart driving competitions, and he taught me how to drive this thing years ago. I'm surprised my aunt hasn't sold it.'

Ruby slowly walked around the cart, taking in the large spindly wheels and peeling paint. A piece of wood across the back section had split and required repair, but it was still lovely in a shabby, aged way.

She slipped a hand over one of the long wooden shafts. 'Is it safe to use?'

Kern regarded the antique vehicle. 'It used to be—despite its fragile appearance. I'll give it a good check-over after we brush off the cobwebs and wash it down.'

'Can we pull it outside?' Ruby asked, wanting to get a better look at this relic from the past.

She understood Eloise's wish for her nephew to take part in the parade. She would happily stand on a crowded pavement for a brief glimpse of Kern driving past, looking all dapper and gorgeous.

Kern sighed and handed her the bucket, now minus the screws. 'You fetch the water and I'll move it outside.'

Ruby clapped her hands before rushing towards the door, all her earlier worry forgotten thanks to the cart. 'A new coat of paint won't take long to apply, you know...'

Kern dragged the canvas farther back, until it folded onto the floor in a heap. 'It probably needs woodworm treatment first.'

'Sounds good,' Eloise declared as she joined them. 'There's some black paint in the other shed. You know what else would be good, Ruby?'

Ruby shook her head, her gaze still on the cart. 'No? What?'

'Oh, God…' Kern groaned, convinced he knew where his aunt was heading.

Eloise shot him a glare. 'If you and Kern dressed as a Victorian courting couple and did the parade together. Oh, how wonderful you'd look, sat together on the seat, clip-clopping along… We could twine real flowers on the sides and dress Star in brasses and ribbons. You'd look spectacular.'

'No,' Kern refused, scowling at his aunt.

Until a soft, disappointed 'Oh…' from the other side of the shed reached his ears.

Reluctantly, he turned, and saw that Ruby's expression matched her dejected tone.

'Don't be a nuisance, nephew,' Eloise scolded, sending Kern a triumphant glance. 'Can't you see how excited Ruby is to do it? Are you really so selfish as to deny her?'

Kern glanced Ruby's way again and asked, 'Do you really want to do the parade? Dressing up and everything?'

Ruby grinned and nodded shyly. 'It sounds fun. I've never taken part in a parade… But if you'd rather not, I understand.'

Still feeling cantankerous, but hating Ruby's crushed expression, he sighed. 'All right. I'll help you paint it and I will *consider* taking part in the parade—'

'Wonderful!' Eloise cried. 'Why don't you both discuss it further over dinner?'

'B-but—' Ruby stammered, glancing Kern's way.

The man's face had suddenly taken on an expression similar to that of a person suffering painful cramp.

'Ruby probably has plans,' Kern said, flashing a glare at his aunt.

Eloise ignored him and asked, '*Do* you have plans, Ruby?'

'Well, no…' she answered, not willing to lie, though it

was clear Kern wasn't keen on the idea of spending the evening with her.

'Then Kern would love to take you out for dinner tonight. Wouldn't you, nephew?'

Kern shot another black look at his aunt and cleared his throat. 'Ruby, would you like to go to dinner with me? I can't promise to be great company because it's been a while since I shared an evening out, but I'll try my best.'

'I—I—' Ruby was stammering again, shocked that he was letting his aunt manoeuvre him into asking. But then the woman did have a forceful directness that left a person struggling against her wishes. Feeling sorry for him, Ruby said, 'That's very kind of you, Kern. But you don't have to—'

'I want to,' he said, though his expression indicated the complete opposite.

'Can you afford it?' she asked, wanting to give him a way out.

This time he glared at her. 'Of course I can!'

She glanced in Eloise's direction. 'I don't want you to feel you have to because—'

'I don't,' he interrupted, getting her meaning. 'In fact, the more I think it over, the more I want to take you out. We're friends, aren't we? It will make a nice change from eating a pot of tasteless noodles. Unless you'd rather not spend time in my company? If you'd prefer to refuse, then just say so.'

Feeling reckless and a little mischievous, Ruby grinned. After all, she still owed him payback for that dunking in the river the other day. Why not get revenge and a full stomach at the same time?

'I'd love to,' she said. 'But nowhere fancy. I'm not into anywhere with more cutlery on the table than food on the plate.'

He grunted. 'Good. Because I know the perfect place.'

* * *

She was going out to dinner with a man. No, not any man, but Kern MacKinley. Oh, God, what would they talk about? The weather? Animals? What if she dropped food down the front of her top and spent the whole evening with a large ugly mark on her chest? Though, wearing black, it wouldn't really show.

Not that she cared about impressing the man, but displaying a lack of basic table skills was bound to prevent him from ever asking again. Not that he'd planned to this time. Without his aunt's prodding and interference they would both be spending the evening alone and stain-free.

Going out with a man who, through his work, must have often shared the company of the rich and famous sounded stressful. How lacking would he find her conversation? How soon before he started to rush her through the meal, desperate for an end to the pain of her company?

'Okay, what did he do?' Kiki demanded, slamming her handbag onto the reception counter. The baby strapped to her front giggled and waved her arms and legs excitedly. 'Tell me everything—no matter how bad.'

Startled, Ruby gasped. 'Sorry…?'

'Don't make excuses for him—tell me. Your expression indicates it's pretty mega. Seriously, I've heard it all. You won't shock me.'

'Well, he asked me out to dinner.' The words escaped before Ruby could think better of saying them.

'*What?*' Kiki gasped.

'Dinner,' Ruby repeated, reaching out to stroke baby Neeve's hand. 'To eat.'

Looking as if she was on the verge of either crying or killing someone, Kiki demanded, '*Alex* asked you out to dinner?'

'Alex?' Ruby repeated, not sure what he had to do with their conversation.

'Yes,' Kiki nodded. 'Your boss—*my husband*! The man I gave my *heart* to.'

Ruby slowly shook her head. 'I haven't seen Alex all morning. It wasn't *him* who asked me out to dinner.'

'Then who?'

Ruby stared at Kiki for several seconds, relieved to see the murderous expression had left the other woman's face. Then, licking her dry lips, she confessed, 'Kern.'

'Kern MacKinley?' Kiki cried, loud enough to startle her daughter and make her jump. 'Mr Gorgeous Race-horse Trainer?'

'Yes.'

'Not Alex?'

'No.' Ruby shook her head, not wanting to upset the woman again. 'He's always very kind to me, if a little abrupt. But he would never ask another woman out when he's so in love with you.'

'Those are his best qualities.' Kiki nodded, then grinned. 'In work hours, anyway.'

'Who are you talking about?' Anne asked as she joined them from one of the back rooms.

'Kern MacKinley,' Kiki answered. 'Our local hot and handsome celebrity.'

Anne sat on the chair behind the reception desk. 'Really? Tell all,' she demanded.

Kiki jumped in before Ruby could open her mouth. 'Ruby's going on a date with him.'

'Well…' Anne mused. 'I guess men who smell like horses do have their attractions.'

'He doesn't smell like horses,' Ruby argued, standing up for Kern.

He smelt like sunshine and hard work. Perhaps laughter, cuddles and river water. And if there was a slight horsey whiff to him occasionally, then it added to all the rest in a positive and manly way.

'He's more stallion—all muscle and horny!' Kiki giggled, then frowned. 'So why do you look pensive?'

'Because I have a date,' Ruby repeated, not sure why she'd decided to share with the other two women. She didn't normally gossip or open up about her feelings, but the urge to tell someone had proved irresistible. Though now she was seeing it might not have been one of her best ideas...

Kiki scrubbed at a stain on her daughter's sleeve. 'Why aren't you doing star jumps and cartwheels?' she asked. 'The man's yummy.'

'He's also a client,' Ruby reminded them.

Kiki waved an unconcerned hand. 'Oh, don't worry about it. It's not a no-no for us. Go on the date and enjoy it.'

'But—'

All her doubts returned, stronger than ever. Was it a mistake to consider going out with Kern? Especially as he'd been forced into doing it. Why exactly had he asked her when he obviously hadn't wanted to? Was he really fed up with eating alone?

'But what?' Anne asked gently. 'Don't you like him? If you want to say no, you can. Tell him it's against the rules.'

Ruby dragged a hand through her curls and sighed. 'But Kiki just said it isn't.'

Her boss's wife piped up. 'That's when I thought you were eager to go.'

'I am. It's just...' Ruby hesitated, not sure how to explain the strange see-saw of emotions that had plagued her since she'd agreed to go. She didn't understand it herself.

'You're worried he might be a breast-grabber, aren't you?' Anne asked. 'Or perhaps a bum-toucher?'

'Yuck!' Kiki groaned, pulling a face at the older woman. 'What sort of men did you used to date?'

'Men who soon learnt to stop doing both after trying!' Anne chuckled.

Ruby shook her head, eager to dissuade the pair of that kind of idea. 'Kern's a gentleman.'

Kiki's eyes narrowed. 'You've already spent time with him, haven't you?'

Heat rose up Ruby's neck and over her face, giving her away. Why had she opened her big mouth? Kiki could give terriers and beagles lessons in sniffing out information.

'I checked his horse over one night and—'

'You've been moonlighting!' Kiki accused her. 'Wait until I tell Alex!'

Worried that she might lose her job, Ruby begged, 'Please don't.'

'But I must,' Kiki insisted. 'We've a bet going that Kern MacKinley fancies you, and I intend to win it. I plan to buy six hens with my winnings.'

'You do?' Ruby gasped, not certain she liked the idea of her non-existent love-life being gambled on.

The woman nodded, not in the least repentant at the discovery of her sneaky carry-on.

Ruby blushed once again, wishing she'd kept quiet. What would Kern think if he heard they had discussed him in this way? If the gossip reached his ears, would he think she had instigated it? Telling others that their friendship was more than casual.

'But he doesn't fancy me.'

'Did he ask you out to dinner?' Kiki probed.

'Yes.'

'There you go. He fancies you. That's how it started for Alex and I. Attraction over carrot soup and fresh bread.

Next thing, he's asking to kiss me. It doesn't take much to get my man to pucker up.'

'But—but Eloise sort of pushed him into doing it,' Ruby stammered, then gave up.

Kern did not fancy her. He'd asked her out because he was too kind to come out and say he didn't want to. Probably believed he was saving her feelings.

Kiki snorted. 'From what I've seen of your Mr MacKinley, I doubt he lets anyone push him around.'

'Eloise is very forceful—and I think he feels guilty for staying away so long.'

Anne leaned back in her chair. 'Do you like him?'

Deciding to be honest, Ruby nodded. 'Yes, I think I do—but not in a romantic way. As a friend.'

'Nothing wrong with friendship,' Anne agreed.

'Are you sure?' Kiki asked, sounding disappointed. 'Where's he taking you?'

'No idea,' Ruby admitted.

'You'll need smart but casual wear, then. With some thought I think we can turn your unique style into serious Goth class. You've the confidence to pull it off already.'

Ruby's heart twisted at the other woman's words. If only they were true. Sometimes she felt like the weakest person in the world.

'Let's go shopping in our dinner hour,' Kiki suggested.

Half afraid of the wild twinkle in Kiki's eyes, Ruby searched for a reason to decline.

'Good idea,' Anne encouraged. 'There's a new shop opened at the other end of the high street. Lots of velvet and lace. Just Ruby's sort of thing.'

'Perfect,' Kiki said. 'Don't worry—my taste is excellent. I married Alex, after all.'

For some reason Ruby didn't find that assurance truly comforting…

CHAPTER EIGHT

RUBY GLANCED DOWN at the simple black dress, with a small slit on one side, and muttered a prayer of hope that she wasn't overdressed. She'd teamed it with her mother's velvet jacket and simple silver jewellery. Velvet boots with a crisscross pattern gave her the perfect height, and she'd applied her make-up a little more heavily, coating her eyes and lips in a dark plum shade to match the small handbag she carried.

Standing outside the stables, where Kern had set up a temporary home, she fought the urge to rush inside, cancel, then leg it home.

The earlier shopping trip with Kiki had ended up being a mixture of both fun and embarrassment. The shop she'd dragged Ruby to *did* cater for her taste, and stocked lovely clothes, but the unwanted accompanying pearls of dating wisdom from Kiki had had Ruby cringing in the changing room.

She appreciated Kiki's help and insight, but the trouble was she and Kern weren't dating. Nothing near, in fact. Tonight's dinner was just two people sharing a meal. It didn't mean more than company and conversation. Which was perfect. Brief, safe and easy.

Then why are you nervous?

'Because,' she whispered aloud, placing a hand on her

stomach to stop the nerves darting up and down, 'it feels like a lot more than a meal shared by friends. And even though I know it's best to keep things simple between us, I'm still a little excited.'

Raising her hand, she hesitated for a second, then knocked on the stable office door.

It opened instantly. Kern stood in the space, dressed in a pair of black jeans and a smart black shirt.

He stared at her for several moments before declaring, 'You're beautiful.'

She blushed, ridiculously pleased by his compliment. Warm pleasure swirled through her veins, setting off her nerves again. Silent warnings stirred in her head once more, but she ignored them, too captivated by the man in front of her.

'Thank you.'

He nodded politely. 'You're welcome.'

She giggled then, unable to prevent herself. 'Sorry, but this feels very odd.'

'Why?'

She shrugged, not really sure. Going out for the evening with this man felt unreal. She was just a newly qualified vet and he was a famous racehorse trainer. His world involved horses, wild characters and money. Hers included sick animals, their body fluids and their worried owners.

'It just does. Let's be honest—you didn't really want to ask me out, did you?'

'No, I didn't want my aunt to arrange a date *for* me,' he corrected. 'She seems to think I require help.'

'And do you?'

'No, I can ask a woman out all by myself,' he said, and then did so. 'Ruby, do you fancy going out tonight? I'd really love you to say yes.'

She pretended to consider his question. 'Well, seeing as we're all dressed up and ready...'

Kern laughed, then narrowed his eyes. 'Now we need to change what you're feeling to a more positive emotion.'

'We do?' she asked.

He put out a hand to her. 'Oh, yeah. Give me your hand.'

'My hand?' she repeated, sounding like a confused parrot. She rubbed it against the side of her dress and waited for him to explain.

'Yes—the thing hanging at the end of your arm.'

She presented him with her hand and wiggled her fingers. 'This thing?'

'Yep, that's the one.' He held it and tugged her into the office, kicking the door shut behind them a second later. Not giving her time to speak, he lifted her hand and trailed a finger across the centre of her palm. 'Oh, lookie here...'

Another giggle left her, thanks to the tickling sensation of his touch. And another wash of pleasant shivers raced through her. 'What are you doing?'

'Reading your palm.'

'I thought it was your aunt who believed in all that stuff?'

He glanced up. 'I'm a man of many talents, Ruby. It's not just you and my aunt with undisclosed powers.'

She raised an eyebrow. 'So you're not simply a piggy-back knight?'

'Keep that quiet, won't you? I'd hate to fight back an adoring public, all desperate to experience my special skills.' He studied her hand again. 'It says clearly here that you need to stop worrying about what's going to happen in the next few hours, because fun is coming your way.'

'Is someone else joining us, then?' she asked cheekily.

He glared at her. 'You deserve a second dunking in the river for such a cruel remark.'

'But you're not going to give me one.'

'No, not when you look so beautiful.'

His blue eyes held hers until warmth tickled the back of her neck and oozed over her skin.

Flustered at both his words and scrutiny, she forced herself to act detached. 'I only agreed to tonight as a way of getting back at you for throwing me in the river. I think it's right to be honest with you.'

'So it wasn't the idea of spending time enjoying my company that made you agree?' he asked. His lower lip curved slightly in a disappointed frown.

'God, no,' she dismissed, fighting another smile. 'The bonus of a meal I don't have to cook swung it for me.'

Snorting, Kern returned his attention to her hand. 'Well, right here it says—'

A knock on the office door stopped him from continuing.

Kern glared at the wooden panel and muttered, 'Who the hell is *that*?'

She glanced down at her hand. 'Can't you see the answer in my palm?'

'My talents are a touch weak right now,' he admitted.

'Poor you,' she teased. 'Perhaps it's someone with a remedy for your impotent skills. It sounds like you may need it.'

A second knock filled the air. They both turned to stare at the door, but neither moved.

After a couple of seconds Ruby asked, 'Aren't you going to answer?'

Kern didn't shift. 'I'd rather stay right here, holding your hand, while you continue to enjoy crushing my fragile self-esteem.'

She giggled. 'I must admit it is fun.'

After the third knock, Ruby pointed out, 'Whoever is out there is getting impatient.'

'Their problem, not ours,' he insisted. 'Ignore their rudeness. We didn't invite them, did we?'

Ruby tried to pull her hand from his. 'You should answer it.'

Kern sighed heavily, giving her hand a gentle squeeze before letting go. 'Fine—but if I do, we'll be late for the restaurant.'

'Restaurant?'

His expression turned scolding. 'You didn't think I was going to serve you fish and chips here, did you?'

'I like fish and chips,' she answered.

'I'll remember that for some time in the future,' he promised and opened the door to reveal a small blond man, wearing designer country clothes and a disgruntled expression. 'You must be mad if you believed your last option was to come here.'

Kern stepped away and let the man enter the room. 'It was my *only* option.'

'Because you're too stubborn to call a friend when you need one,' the man complained, slapping Kern on the shoulder. 'It's good to see you. It's been far too long.'

'You too, Jacob. But not right now. You'll need to postpone telling me the reason why you're here, because I have plans tonight.'

'Thanks for the enthusiastic welcome.' The visitor glanced Ruby's way, then returned his attention to Kern. 'God, what a dump.'

Kern folded his arms across his chest. 'Cheers for your tactless opinion on my family property. I'll try not to take offence. I guess you want to stay?'

'Of course. I have a meeting in Lambourne tomorrow. Why pay out for a hotel room when I can bum a sofa off you?'

'I don't own a sofa. All I can offer is a stable full of straw.'

'Good enough. I'm sure I can manage for one night. Won't be the first time I've bedded down in a pile of straw—though usually I'm not alone.'

'Why *are* you here?' Kern demanded, not looking pleased to see his friend.

'Because I intend to talk some sense into your thick head. If you think I am going to let my best friend of sixteen years rot in Dorset, then you need some sense knocked into you.'

Feeling awkward, Ruby pointed to the open door. 'I think I'll go...'

'No, stay,' Kern insisted. 'We have plans for tonight.'

'Yes,' Jacob drawled. 'You two go. I'll stay here and stare at the brickwork. Buy me a pizza on your way home, though. I haven't eaten in hours. Too busy travelling here to see *you*.'

Ruby moved towards the door; the atmosphere was suddenly uncomfortable. 'No, you stay here with your friend. We can go out another night. I'm happy to postpone my revenge for a later day.'

Kern reached for her. 'But I'm not. Ruby—wait.'

She dodged his hand and after a second's hesitation placed a chaste kiss upon his cheek, desperately missing their flirtatious and jokey connection. His skin was rough and firm against her lips and she fought the urge to linger against it.

'Thanks for asking, anyway. Both times. Goodnight, Kern.'

Waving the men goodbye, she rushed from the office and headed back home to her empty caravan. Some things weren't meant to be, and going out to a restaurant with Kern MacKinley was obviously one of them. The man had friends from his past to help him. Did he really need her to clutter up his time? Someone with just as disillusioned a view on relationships and no real clue how to even be in one?

'What the hell are you thinking, returning to this backwater?' Jacob asked. 'Did you think I would let you scurry away and be forgotten? After everything you've done for me over the years? No trainer would have touched me in the early days without your faith in me. There's a few even now who'd think twice.'

Kern closed the door, wishing he could follow Ruby. The last thing he required right now was an evening listening to his friend harp on about the so-called mistakes he'd made. Not when all he wanted to do was rush after Ruby and convince her to stay and spend the evening with him.

'You like to win—there's no shame in that. The best jockeys do. You just need to learn to stay away from unsuitable women. Especially the ones married to trainers.'

'I'm ruthless. Unfortunately, you're too nice—otherwise you would have divorced Corinne years ago. Sorry about what happened with her, by the way.'

'Thanks, but don't start,' Kern warned, still furious at having to postpone his date.

Jacob had always had seriously rotten timing, but tonight was his worst offence. Hadn't he heard of phoning before arriving? Letting a person know he intended to visit?

'Besides, we've not spoken in over a year.'

Jacob shrugged. 'Had a bit of trouble in Argentina,' he admitted. 'Long story. But I met a man out there—a sheikh—and he's keen to start his own yard. When I heard what had happened to you, I suggested you become his trainer. Have all the fun while he foots all the bills. A perfect way to re-enter the game until you can afford to go out on your own again.'

'No.'

Kern refused even to consider the offer. It was one thing to deal with owners who thought they knew everything—another to be completely beholden to a rich man's whim.

'Just think for a minute,' Jacob urged.

Kern walked over to the chair behind the desk and sat down. 'I don't need to. It's not for me, thanks. I'm not even sure what my plans are yet.'

'Well, I hope they don't include the stable girl who just left?' Jacob remarked.

Kern stiffened, not liking Jacob's tone. It was one thing for Jacob to have an opinion of Corinne, because he had known her and their troubles, but he refused to let the man condemn a woman he'd not been polite enough even to acknowledge.

'Her name's Ruby and she's a local vet—not a stable girl.'

Jacob sighed. 'I'm here for one night and we need to talk over this opportunity properly. It's perfect for you. It's the ideal answer to your run of bad luck.'

'I can sort myself out. I don't need any help from rich playboys with too much money and too little care for the horses in their stables. All the man would focus on is the prize money and swanning around with royalty and the upper class. We'd soon fall out.'

'Wrong. The man admires you. And if you want more control over everything, I'm sure you can discuss it with him and come to an agreement which satisfies you both.'

Kern shook his head, keen to change the subject. 'Why don't I order that pizza?'

He pulled out his phone from his trouser pocket and

searched for the number, though his appetite had diminished now he knew he wouldn't be sharing a meal with Ruby.

'So, the woman who just left…?' Jacob asked, settling on a stool. 'The vet?'

Kern gripped the phone and glanced up to find Jacob watching him. 'Ruby? What about her?'

'Anything serious?'

Kern returned his attention to his phone, flicking through the numbers without seeing them. Common sense dictated that he should halt anything serious from developing between him and Ruby, but he couldn't ignore the part of him that secretly yearned for it.

Regardless of his reservations about spending more time with her, and the underhand, sneaky way his aunt had manoeuvred them into tonight's date, he'd started to look forward to it. Had wanted to indulge in one night of her company just for the pleasure of it.

'No,' he said. 'We're friends. She cares for Enticing Evie.'

'Good,' Jacob said. 'I'd hate another woman to screw things up for you. Last thing you need is another heavy relationship.'

Kern turned away, his thoughts still focused on Ruby. Was she angry with him for not taking her out, or as disappointed as he was that they'd had to cancel? Or was she perhaps secretly relieved they'd had to abandon their date?

As much as he hated to admit it, Jacob was right about one important matter. A relationship was the last thing he should contemplate. He might be slowly piecing his life back into order, but he had nothing to offer any woman. No job, no savings—he didn't even live in a proper home. All he had was broken dreams, a tarnished reputation and run-down property. Hardly the stuff a woman dreamed of when searching for a man.

For Ruby's sake he needed to remember just how little he had to offer. He'd already disappointed one woman in his life. Decency determined that he not be selfish and make it two.

CHAPTER NINE

'HE'S LOOKING MUCH BETTER.' Kern crouched to rub Dog's head.

The Wolfhound wagged his tail in reply, but didn't move from the rug he and Ruby sat on beside the caravan. Ruby tried to dodge the frantic whipping of her pet's tail as he tried to crawl closer to their visitor in his desperation to lick his face.

She'd not seen or heard from Kern for three days. Not that she'd noticed his absence, thanks to work. And she certainly didn't daydream about him—much.

'Hey, Dog...' Kern continued to pet the large dog. 'Digging the shaved leg look you're sporting. Bet all the female pooches give you the canine love-eye. Handsome male like you.'

Ruby sniggered. 'I'm pretty sure a Labrador cross laughed at him when we left the practice on the day he came home.'

Kern shook his head in sympathy. 'That, my friend, is women for you. Always ready to mock when we try our best. They're cruel to us poor, innocent males.'

'Huh!' Ruby scoffed. 'You're about as innocent as a sinner hanging out in hell. Is this a passing visit, or does your horse need my expertise again?'

'No, Evie and Mabel Star—'

'*Mabel* Star?' she asked.

'My aunt's renamed her horse Mabel Star after some past ancestor she reminds Eloise of. It's the ears, apparently.'

Ruby shook her head. 'I see…'

'The actual reason for my visit is that it's a beautiful day and I thought you might like to go to the beach with me.'

Ignoring the sudden leap in her stomach, Ruby glanced at her dog with his fresh dressing, knowing she had no choice but to refuse. 'Dog's not really able to walk along the beach with his leg the way it is.'

'My aunt has insisted Dog stays with her for the day,' Kern explained quickly. 'There's a re-run of a murder mystery series she wants to watch on TV, and she figures Dog will enjoy watching it with her.'

Ruby hesitated, torn between staying at home with her pet and going to the seaside with Kern. On such a nice day, the thought of spending time lazing around on the sand sounded wonderful.

'I'd hate to take advantage of Eloise…'

'Sometimes it's good to,' Kern murmured, kneeling on the rug to rub Dog's stomach.

Ruby envied the way Kern's fingers ran back and forth over her pet. How would it feel if the man touched *her* in such an informal and intimate way?

Leaning back on her arms, Ruby forced herself to focus, and stop contemplating irrelevant questions she would never learn the answers to. 'It is?'

He nodded. 'You never know what might happen when you grasp the advantage—what surprises you might discover by doing so.'

Ruby narrowed her eyes, suspicious of his deep, persuading tone. 'Why do I suspect there's more to your invitation than just a trip to the seaside?'

He glanced up and chuckled. 'Because I haven't told you everything and you're a very smart woman.'

She crossed her ankles. 'I've found it best to be smart where you're concerned, Kern MacKinley.'

He sat on his heels and held up his hands in defeat. 'Okay, I'll confess. There's a horse I've arranged to look at and I thought you might like to join me.'

'A racehorse?' she asked curiously. That made more sense than a sudden urge to go paddling in the sea. Did his friend Jacob have anything to do with it?

'Does this have something to do with your friend's visit the other night?'

Kern shook his head. 'No, Jacob called in for another reason. Someone Eloise knows has tipped her off about a colt being a good buy. And to stop her nagging I've agreed to go and check it out. I'm considering him— nothing more.'

'And you'd like my expert eye?' she asked, wondering what his friend had wanted.

'I'd love your company, and although my eye is as expert as yours when it comes to horseflesh,' he replied easily, 'a medical judgement is always welcome.'

'Really? Maybe we should compare notes and see which one of us has the more intensive equine knowledge?'

Kern's gaze didn't shift from hers. 'I'd love to. Perhaps we can reschedule our dinner date?'

'Sounds possible,' she said, her heart racing at his closeness and at his offer. 'You do realise I should charge you for my expert opinion?'

'Dinner not payment enough?'

'Oh, no. That's payback for dumping me in the river,' she reminded him. 'Perhaps I should add interest, seeing as you cancelled.'

'How about I buy you an ice cream?'

'Done,' she agreed.

He stood and stared down at her. 'Eloise will enjoy spoiling Dog and talking his ear off. He'll be the perfect guest. He doesn't answer back or argue with her opinion.'

'You make a convincing argument,' she said, gazing at him.

'Then say yes. You want to. I can tell. And you're already dressed for it,' he said, taking in her dark leggings and black T-shirt.

'If you're sure Eloise doesn't mind?' she asked, worried the old lady might.

'She doesn't,' he assured her. 'You can ask her when we drop Dog off and pick up the basket of food she's preparing for us.'

'A picnic?' she quizzed, delighted at the thought. 'You were that confident I would agree?'

He grinned and reached to help her up. 'No. But Eloise was.'

Ruby stepped onto the soft sand ahead of the man who'd driven them to the secluded cove. The drive in his old horsebox had stirred unsettling memories, but Kern's constant chatter had stopped Ruby from dwelling on them for too long.

Breathing in the crisp, fresh, salty air, she took in the cerulean blue sky, broken only by a distant faint white line of cloud where Nature had dragged her artistic finger lightly across the horizon in a lax attempt to define between the sea and sky.

Turning from the beautiful scenery, she pushed away a curl from where it dangled in her eyes, thanks to the light warm breeze coming off the water, and asked, 'I thought we were seeing the horse first?'

The same breeze ran invisible fingers through Kern's

hair, too. Light and playful, like a lover's caressing touch, ruffling the thick dark strands and causing Ruby's own fingers to want to follow their curious path.

How would his hair feel against her palms? Soft? Wiry? Perfect for tugging playfully when he kissed her?

Kissed her?

She swallowed and turned to the sea again, her mind suddenly confused and muddled. Playful tugging? Kissing? What was she thinking? Nothing like that would transpire between them, so it didn't matter what his hair felt like. He was a friend, and friends did not touch each other's hair. No matter how much they might wish to.

'We are,' Kern answered, his eyes sparkling with a trace of secrecy.

The breeze blew his green T-shirt against his body, outlining the muscles beneath, and the black tight-fitting jodhpurs that encased his firm legs created a truly mouth-watering sight. Kern MacKinley was one attractive man.

Not sure what he meant, Ruby continued to stare towards the expanse of deep blue water. The last time she'd visited a beach there'd been ice creams and buckets and spades for sale. The odd donkey might have hung around, but she'd never seen a racehorse.

'I don't understand,' she said, tilting her head to one side.

She was intrigued by Kern's expression and the mischievous twinkle lightening his eyes. Once again, the sensation that he was up to something raised her curiosity.

Kern rested an arm across her shoulders, immediately enclosing her with his body heat and aftershave. Spicy and light, she liked it. She also rather enjoyed feeling his arm around her.

'The horse's owner recommended we meet him here,'

he said. 'This is a private beach that belongs to his family. What do you say? Fancy a ride along the sand?'

Her distraction at his close presence vanished instantly. Working with horses was one thing, but she avoided occasions for actually riding one where possible. Others carried out the riding and she concentrated on the diagnosing. Just the idea of riding for pleasure alone evoked more memories from her childhood, and not all of them good.

'I'm not sure…'

Kern frowned down at her. 'I didn't think to ask. Can you ride?'

She nodded, then admitted, 'It's been a while, though.'

Relief chased his frown away and he tugged her closer. 'What better location to start again? Come on—say yes. I promise a soft landing if you fall off.'

Insulted at the idea, she snorted. 'I'm sure I can remember how to stay on, thank you.'

She focused her eyes on the gentle sea foam ripples intimately caressing the sand.

Just her and Kern.

Until the owner and the horses arrived.

'It's beautiful here,' she whispered.

The words were whipped away on the wind. But Kern must have caught them, because he answered. 'Yes, it is. Truly stunning. Will you ride with me, Ruby? I promise to lend you some sun cream if you do.'

With lingering reluctance, she nodded, and then smiled when he produced a bottle from his back pocket. 'See— I'm a man of his word and always prepared.'

She laughed and took the sun cream from him.

Kern made her want to do things she normally avoided. All the things she'd purposely denied herself for years.

What would her parents think about her reluctance to do something she'd loved as a child? One of the few things they'd jointly encouraged her to pursue? Would they be horrified that she had taken a different path involving horses, tending to their physical care and well-being, and not the one they'd hoped she would aim for in the show ring? Or would they feel pride that not only had she worked hard to reach her goals, but she was now following her dream career?

'The horses are here,' Kern said.

He grabbed her hand and pulled her towards a man walking along the water's edge with two thoroughbred horses. One grey and one bay. Their coats gleamed in the sunshine.

'Good morning.' Kern shook the man's hand and they chatted for several minutes about the horses' general health and personalities.

Ruby moved closer to the bay horse, offering her hand under its nose.

Kern finished quizzing the owner and asked, 'Need a leg-up?'

She nodded, suddenly shaky. What if she'd forgotten everything her parents had taught her? What if all those riding lessons deserted her and left her bouncing and jigging along like a half-terrified novice? 'Thanks.'

'Ready?' Kern asked, only a second before he grabbed her leg and pushed her upwards.

The strangeness of sitting on a horse after so long hit Ruby hard the moment her bottom settled on the leather saddle. But, like an old pro, she reached for the reins and wrapped them correctly around her fingers. Relieved that she remembered the basics, at least, she waited for Kern to adjust the stirrups, concentrating on slowing her breathing, not wanting the bay to sense her nerves.

Kern mounted the other horse, and with a quick goodbye to the owner they slowly headed along the wet sand, leaving deep hoofprints in their wake.

For several minutes neither spoke, content to let the horses splash through the water. Seagulls squalled above and sunlight reflected from the sea as though crushed glass floated upon the waves.

Halfway along the cove, Kern nudged his horse closer to hers so they could ride side by side. 'Having fun?' he asked.

Ruby couldn't deny it. Everything about this was perfect. The horse, the surroundings and the man. Especially the man.

'What do you think of him?' she asked, nodding towards the grey. By sight alone she couldn't detect any obvious physical issues in his movements or appearance.

'He's nice to handle. Definitely has potential. But he's going to cost a good chunk of my money. I'll be eating crackers and cheese for the next few months if I decide to buy him. How's yours?'

'Wonderful. Is he very expensive?'

'No. Between us, he's ridiculously cheap. But it's still a lot of money to risk when I'm counting every pound,' Kern mused.

'Too much of a risk, then?'

He glanced at her. 'Life's a risk, Ruby. But it's also a reason to get up in the morning.'

'Why's the owner selling?' she asked. If the horse was sound, why didn't the owner want to keep him?

'The man has an interest in several horses already,' Kern answered. 'He wants to offload this one because his trainer doesn't think he has the talent or skill to compete against the best.'

The glimmer in Kern's eyes said differently.

'What do *you* think?' Ruby asked, curious to know

how he viewed the horses. What did a racehorse trainer search for in an animal? Was it purely physical? Or was there more to it than just speed?

'I think with time, proper training and a good dose of luck, this horse has a chance to win some big races. He has talent. It's his trainer who doesn't. I found several recordings of his previous races on the internet last night, and instinct tells me there's more to this horse than he's shown.'

'Sounds like you're going to buy him. Does this mean you intend to start training again?'

Kern shrugged. 'I can do some work with him and sell him on later if I need to. I lost my yard because people stopped trusting me with their horses after the fire. It's hard to come back from a knock like that. I'm not sure I have the drive to do it again, you know?'

In a way, she did. For a long time she'd lived each day with no aim other than to get through it without thinking of her parents and the past. But when she'd decided to become a vet it had given her a purpose, a challenge. A reason to get out of bed, to use her brain, and to indulge her love of creatures who required her help and care.

Animals had never left her feeling emotionally bruised and drained, as her parents often had after one of their many confrontations.

'You've a good seat,' said Kern. 'Who taught you to ride?'

Ruby licked the salt from her lips and answered, 'My parents.'

Kern stared intently at her. 'Why do I get the feeling you're the one holding secrets now?'

She shook her head, and they continued to the end of the cove and then slowly headed back again. Even though Ruby was concentrating on her horse, she sensed Kern glancing at her several times. Was he wondering about her parents? Or perhaps wondering why she didn't ride any more?

When they returned to where the owner waited, the man directed them to the path leading to his farm and stables. There, the next forty-five minutes consisted of both Ruby and Kern giving the grey colt a thorough check-over. After haggling over the price, Kern shook the owner's hand and worked out the arrangements to collect the horse the following day.

'So you own another horse?' she said as they left the yard.

'I do,' Kern said, opening a wooden gate that led back down to the cove.

'Are you sure you haven't come to a decision about your future?' she asked.

For someone who professed not to know, he was committing both time and money to staying at MacKinley farm. And what about his friend Jacob? The few minutes' conversation she'd witnessed had made it clear the man considered Kern mad for coming back.

He shook his head and swung the gate shut. 'No, not yet. But as I said before, I can resell the colt for a profit once I've done some work with him.'

'Why *did* you return to Dorset?' Ruby asked.

What had called him back to the place he'd apparently avoided for years? After making a life elsewhere, why return to the place he'd run from?

'Honestly?' he asked. 'I had nowhere else to take Evie and very little money to keep us both. Desperation brought me home—and a deep need to see my aunt. I've neglected Eloise for far too long. I realised I'd tried to recreate what was here somewhere else, but the truth is, there's only one MacKinley farm. How crazy is that? It took losing what I thought was important to realise that fact.'

'What now?' Ruby asked, pleasantly relaxed despite the slight ache in her thighs, as they wandered back to the beach.

Being on horseback had reminded her of how much she missed it. She didn't want to compete, the way she had as a child, but now the occasional ride might be fun.

Kern shrugged. 'I thought we'd eat our picnic on the beach before returning home. The owner said we could.'

'Sounds nice, but Dog—'

'Is with my aunt—and she prepared the picnic, remember?' he soothed. 'She's trying to matchmake, you know?'

Ruby nodded, suddenly awkward. 'Does it bother you?'

He didn't answer. Instead, he urged, 'Find a nice spot for us to sit and I'll fetch the basket from the van. I hope she's fixed something tasty. I'm starving.'

Ruby grinned as they parted and went in different directions. 'Me too.'

Though she doubted food would satisfy the huge hunger developing deep inside her every time she and Kern spent time alone together.

'Egg sandwiches!' Ruby declared, unwrapping the foil covering the first package she'd retrieved from the old-fashioned wicker basket.

Kern reached over and swiped a sandwich from the pile. 'Great. My favourite.'

She held the rest out of his reach and nodded towards the basket. 'See what else is in there.'

He withdrew two crisp packets, chocolate bars, fizzy drinks and finally a large pork pie. Holding it up, he went to take a bite, but Ruby whipped it out of his hand before his lips touched the pastry and put it in her own mouth.

'Hey!' he yelled.

Munching a large mouthful, she grinned at his shocked

expression, and then took another ravenous bite of the pie. 'Sorry, but I'm starving. Blame the sea air.'

'So am I,' he said, helping himself to another sandwich before she prevented him. 'I never suspected you were a food stealer.'

'It's a bad habit,' she joked. 'I try to resist, but occasionally the urge is too much for me to fight.'

He finished his sandwich and then reached for another. This time she shared without any fuss.

'Can I ask you a question?' he asked.

Wary of his serious tone, she mused, 'Is it personal or professional?'

'Personal.'

She continued chewing her pilfered pie, not sure she wanted the pleasant moment ruined. 'Very personal or a little bit personal?'

'Very,' he answered.

Licking grease from her fingertips, she shrugged. 'Okay. What do you want to know? Though you can only ask one question.'

He leaned back on one elbow and smiled. 'Is this revenge for the other day?'

Ruby nodded, and quoted his words back to him. 'I like the odds to be in my favour. Come on—ask your question so I can get on with stealing more of your food.'

'Did you never learn to share as a child?' he quizzed, tapping her on the nose.

'Nope. Only child.'

'Yeah, me too. But I always share when needed.'

She laughed, not the least bit bothered by his criticism. Taking his food before he could eat it made her happy. Or rather the shocked expression on his face did. A little friendly teasing lifted a heavy soul, and she suspected Kern's was pretty weighty.

'And I appreciate it. The pie was delicious.'

He glared at her for a moment, then asked, 'How long ago did you start wearing Goth make-up?'

Surprised, she considered not answering. But Kern had shared his past with her the other night, so would it really hurt to tell him a little of her own? She wasn't confessing the secrets of her heart—not the deeply hidden ones that lingered among the doubts. Just a small snippet of data.

'When I was sixteen,' she said, reaching for a bottle of drink. She twisted open the lid, but didn't drink from it.

'Do you wear it to hide the scar on your neck?'

His second question threw her completely. She rested the bottle in her lap and asked, 'You've seen it?'

'Yes—the day I threw you into the river. Patches of your make-up washed off and exposed it.'

She fiddled with the bottle's lid. Twisting it on and off. 'Why didn't you ask then?'

'I figured you'd tell me if it mattered. I'm more curious about the make-up.'

Ruby pondered his words, then sighed heavily. Most people would regard her scar as more interesting, but Kern wasn't like other people. Was that because of his own scars? The ones on his heart because of his marriage? Whenever he spoke of his wife, guilt and regret shaded his words. Was he not asking about the scar because he respected the fact that everyone had scars that were often best left alone?

'Don't you like my make-up?' she asked. 'Does it offend you?'

Kern shook his head. 'No, I'm just curious. It seems to clash with your personality.'

She frowned at him. 'What do you mean?'

'You're beautiful, but shy, and yet you wear make-up

which causes people to notice you. Two forces at odds, surely? Who's the real Ruby?'

'I'm not beautiful,' she denied, uncomfortable with his comment.

'Yes, you are,' he insisted, touching her cheek. 'You're very beautiful—and your scar does nothing to detract from it.'

Disturbed by his touch, she blurted, 'I wear it as camouflage. To stop people from recognising my face.'

Why had she said that? Why not tell the man that she loved the Goth look and leave it at that? What had happened to sharing only a vague morsel of information?

His expression tightened as he absorbed her words. 'Are you famous?'

She'd put herself in this hole—now she had to find a way out without confessing more. 'No, not me. My parents were well-known. The scar is from where a bullet grazed my skin. It happened a long time ago. It's nothing.'

Kern's intense gaze didn't flinch. The slight tightening of his fingers against the curve of her skin was his only reaction to her statement. 'Who did it?'

Great. She'd hoped by acting as though it was nothing he'd stop asking questions. Trust Kern to do the opposite.

Gripping the bottle, she whispered, 'My father.'

'Why?'

She sighed. 'He wanted to stop the guilt that consumed him every time he stared at my face and saw my mother's instead.'

'Your mother?'

'Chantel Dainnes,' she said, releasing the name from the secret part of her heart where she'd suppressed it for so long, desperate to keep their connection hidden.

'The French model?' Kern questioned.

She nodded. 'When I wear the Goth make-up I don't resemble her as much. It's enough to stop people from making a connection between us.'

'I see,' Kern replied. He lowered his hand and grasped her own. His gaze searched hers as he shuffled the pieces into sense. 'So Frank Day, the jockey, was your father?'

Ruby sucked in a deep breath, then released it slowly. 'Yes.'

'But didn't he go to jail for trying to shoot his daughter—?' His words dried up. 'Oh, my God. He tried to *kill* you.'

She nodded and drew her knees up to rest her arms on them. Why not tell Kern the rest and give him the truth, instead of risking him searching on the internet, where lies and hearsay waited for the gullible to read and believe? Because of her big mouth, there wasn't any other choice.

'My parents' marriage was stormy. One week they loved each other—the next they hated one another. My father was critical, bad-tempered and controlling. Mostly because he battled hunger daily, trying to retain his weight for riding. Whereas my mother represented beauty to the world, but around my father she became ugly. She made him feel inadequate and small—literally. They were two people who purposely enjoyed wounding each other and thrived on doing it often. Together they played games of spite and point-scoring. They were each other's poison and they never should have married. But to the world they pretended to be faithful and in love. The perfect couple.'

'And *you* were stuck in the middle of that?'

She nodded. 'Oh, they loved me—but each other...? Well, it depended on their mood. One day my mother left home to go on a photoshoot, but returned to the house when she became ill. She searched for my father and found him with the housekeeper, doing the one thing she refused to forgive. She'd endure the fights, the drinking and the gambling, but adultery was her limit.'

Kern reached out and drew her down beside him and into his arms, sheltering her from the wind coming off the sea and the shadows floating up from the past.

Ruby closed her eyes for a second, savouring the closeness.

'She left the house with me in tow, after threatening to drag my father through the courts and destroy him. She drove to my father's agent's house and left me there. Then she travelled to our London apartment and swallowed a ton of pills to numb the pain permanently.'

Kern's hold tightened around her. 'What happened afterwards?'

'I returned to live with my father for a few weeks, but every time we were together he'd cry and yell. He'd talk to me as though I was my mother. Begging, pleading for forgiveness. The one thing I was unable to give because I wasn't my mother. Plus, I *didn't* forgive him. The housekeeper wasn't his first affair—just the first my mother discovered. I knew there'd been others before. His grief and guilt sent him crazy and his behaviour became erratic.'

'Oh, Ruby...'

'One day I was in the stables, seeing to our horses because no one else bothered, when my father appeared with his handgun and turned it on me.'

'You must have been terrified.'

She nodded and gripped Kern's arms, finding the strength to continue through touching him. 'Fortunately, my father's agent turned up unexpectedly, and shoved my father backwards as he took aim. The bullet grazed my chin and neck, leaving me with this scar, but alive.'

'Thank goodness...'

'He called an ambulance and the police while my father wept on the floor. Later my father confessed that he'd planned to turn the gun on himself afterwards, because he wanted us to join my mother. They'd barely managed to live together in life, and yet he couldn't live without her once she was gone.'

'What happened then?'

'My father's agent offered me a home. With no other family, I accepted. I'd known him for most of my life. He supported me through the court case. Stood by me when the newspapers villainised my mother and I—'

'You?'

She glanced at him wearily. 'They wanted someone to rip apart, and I was the only one they could get to. I'd lost all my friends, and hardly left the house. The few times I did, I was followed and offered money to spill secrets about my parents. And then there were my mother's and my father's fans, who accused me of lying because they didn't want to believe they'd fallen so easily for my father's great guy persona and my mother's perfect image. It all became horrendous and suffocating.'

'Oh, Ruby,' he soothed.

'A few months later, although I'd thought I could trust my father's agent, he sold the story of my parents' marriage to those same newspapers. Sold the secrets I'd confided in him because I thought he cared and it was safe.'

Kern kissed the side of her face. 'The man abused your trust. You were a child who needed his protection.'

'That's when I used the Goth make-up for the first time. One day I packed a bag and left the house for good. I walked down the street for the first time in months and no one recognised me.'

Kern cupped her cheek with his hand and gently drew her face to his. 'What a crap hand they dealt you.'

She wrinkled her nose. 'Not a great one, I guess. But

plenty of people deal with worse. I managed, and my life is pretty good. I transferred to a different school, moved on to university, then decided to train as a vet. The best decision of my life.'

'Beautiful and brave.'

She squirmed with embarrassment. 'I just did what I had to. One thing my mother did teach me was that if I wanted something or needed something then I should work for it. So I did.'

'You must hate horse racing and everything about it.'

She shook her head. 'No, I don't. My parents' relationship was troubled because of who they were—not what they did. Everything they did together was destructive, yet they couldn't face being without each other.'

'Not everything,' he said. 'They made you.'

'There's something else you should know,' she confessed, deciding to clear her conscience completely.

'Yes?'

'I can heal animals,' she said. She hated not being honest about her gift, and Kern already had suspicions about what had occurred when he'd left the stables the night she'd tended to Evie. 'What I mean is, I help animals in pain, emotionally and physically, by placing my hands on them.'

Kern gazed at her silently, then grinned. 'You're a healer?'

She tensed. 'Yes.'

He continued to stare down at her, his expression thoughtful. 'Are you saying you put your hands on Evie and made her better? I've heard and read about people who can, but I've never known anyone who actually does it.'

'Do you think I'm a freak?' she blurted out, worried he would see her differently now. People tended to when she admitted to being able to do something unusual. And, despite her trying to keep this man as a mere friend, she knew his opinion mattered to her. It shouldn't, but it did.

'No,' he soothed, softly stroking the outline of her lower lip with his thumb. 'I think you're special and talented and I really want to kiss you.'

She blinked up at him. She could see the tiny bristles over his face and feel the warm breath coming from his lips. 'You do?'

'Yes.'

'But wouldn't that be a terrible idea, considering we're only friends?' she asked, licking her lower lip.

'Yes,' he agreed. 'I haven't wanted to kiss a woman in such a long time, but I can't help wondering how your lips will feel under my own.'

'I keep speculating about what your hair feels like,' she admitted.

He leaned closer and encouraged her. 'Why don't you touch it and satisfy your curiosity.'

She clenched her hands to stop herself from giving in to his appealing invitation. 'But as friends we're not allowed to touch each other in any caressing way. It's a rule.'

'I'm not one for rules…'

She tilted her head farther back and looked him straight in the eye. 'So why don't you break it, then?'

CHAPTER TEN

RUBY LICKED HER LIPS, her breath caught somewhere between racing and suspended in a strange elevation of time, sensation and hope. Would he or wouldn't he?

Did he dare lean forward those last few inches that separated them and place his lips against hers? Kiss her until her thoughts vanished and her nerve ends tingled?

Did she dare kiss him?

Her mouth dried at the thought of kissing Kern. Would he taste the way he did in her dreams? The erotic ones that plagued her in the dark night and left her hot and achy? The dreams she loved to disappear into, knowing he was there with her, doing things she'd never done with anybody else.

He sighed after a moment. 'You're too young for me,' he said.

The logical words sliced through the humming daze of her craving with icy cold reality.

Too young? What did age have to do with this and the way he made her feel? Did age cause her to tremble and simmer with heat until she yearned to douse herself with cold water for some relief? Age didn't make her laugh after a hard day, or offer the comforting safety of his arms. Age had nothing to do with this strange attraction building between them. Age wasn't a concern and he'd no business using it as an excuse.

She smiled and touched his face, slipping her fingers lightly over his rough skin. He needed a shave, but she liked this shadowy appearance on him. It suited his rough-around-the-edges personality. No, she was lying. She *loved* it.

'Why am I too young?' she asked, not about to let him off without explaining. She understood his cautiousness, because of his past, but was he using their age difference as a reason or an excuse?

'I don't mean in age,' he said. 'I mean in life's hardships. You're innocent, sweet and pure, and I am old and cynical. You deserve someone who's not beaten and—'

'Did I not just tell you about my parents?' she asked, curious as to why he perceived her life as being spotless compared to his own when he knew better.

'But you haven't let your circumstances harden you. Your heart is still soft and—'

'That's not true,' she argued. 'I struggle to be myself around people and I'm always worried they'll find out the truth about who my parents are.'

'Would that be so bad?' he quizzed.

'Yes,' she said. 'People loved my parents—or at least they loved the fake image they showed the world. When the truth came out, the public reacted as though it was all my fault. Because I looked like my mother, they blamed me for what my father did. It was twisted and horrible and it didn't make any sense. And it didn't help that my father refused to accept that he'd tried to kill me or that his actions drove my mother to suicide. Do you really think I want to rake all that up again and have it taint what I have now? For the first time in my life I have people who accept me. Work colleagues who treat me as one of the team. I have real friends.'

'And I'm included in those friends?' Kern asked, touching her face again.

She nodded. 'I hope so.'

His hand stilled and he sighed. 'Giving in to this attraction between us is a bad idea.'

'Why?'

'Because I see hope glimmering in your eyes, sweetheart. Do you honestly see any in mine?'

She rested her finger against his lips and smiled softly. No, she didn't see hope. She saw disappointment and pain and so much regret. But she didn't care, because none of those emotions was to do with *her*. What they had was new and clean.

'I like you as you are, Kern. Battered or not. Just shut up and kiss me, won't you? Am I asking you for anything else?'

'But you won't find me attractive for long,' he argued. 'I might infect you with my bad luck. My track record concerning relationships is poor—'

'Maybe I'll melt your bad luck away and replace it with some good,' she interrupted.

Right now, she sought only to try. Everything about this man caused her to wish for more than she'd ever had before. Perhaps hope did still linger in her heart. She certainly longed for his kiss...

'Spending time with you would change any man for the better,' said Kern, slipping his hand into her hair. His blue eyes were thoughtful and serious as he studied her face. 'You're beautiful.'

She wasn't, but under his gaze she felt it. When he looked at her he saw not a Goth or a vet but Ruby. No one had ever observed her with such intensity and need. Not just casual lust, but more a curious hungry desire. As though he craved to consume her slowly. The way a person relished a delicious sweet mouthful they knew they shouldn't indulge in.

'Are you going to kiss me or not?' she asked brazenly, impatient for him to do so. Forget talking—she required full-on lip engagement.

His fingers tightened against her scalp. 'I should finish off those sandwiches…'

She winced. 'Not only too young, but second to your appetite? Man, you're battering my self-worth here, with such unromantic declarations.'

'Is that what you want, Ruby?' he asked, his eyes twinkling. 'Romantic words and verses? I'm not sure I'll be any good at that stuff.'

'No, I want you to kiss me. The rest's not necessary—unless you really want to show me your inner poet. Though, to be honest, poetry kind of bores me.'

'I'm tempted to try,' he said, slowly pushing her backwards until she sank into the soft grains of sand. 'I want to kiss you much more than I want to eat, I swear, but if I kiss you once I'm going to want to put another kiss here on your cheek, and then there on your neck, and perhaps one   '

'Sounds perfect,' she encouraged, melting into the swirling layers of his voice and the shivers that danced like plumes across her skin.

Everything about Kern intrigued her. His looks, his voice… He excited her and scared her. An irresistible combination. She wanted to grab him close and ignore the fear of getting hurt. Wanted him to be the one man she could truly trust and know he would never break that trust.

'Are you nervous?' Kern asked, his tone serious as he studied her face. 'I promise my kiss won't hurt.'

'It's afterwards I'm worried about,' she admitted, brushing his hair back from his forehead. It was soft and thick, exactly the way she'd imagined it.

'Well, if you hate the kiss you can slap my face and wash out your mouth with some lemonade. I promise not to be offended.'

'It's not th-that,' she stammered, unsure how to explain.

She desired his kiss—she really did—but what happened after? Another kiss or three? More than just kisses? Would he want to make love to her here on the beach? In public?'

'Tell me,' he coaxed.

Taking hold of her courage, she did. 'What are you hoping will happen *after* the kiss?'

Comprehension softened his features and a faint smile teased his lips. 'Ruby, if we make love I promise we'll be doing it somewhere private and comfortable, with no risk of a passing gull using my naked butt as target practice. As I'm sure you know, animal mess is no fun.'

She giggled and relaxed. 'In that case, Mr MacKinley, stop being concerned with all the reasons not to, and get on with kissing me.'

He hesitated, as though he still sensed her wariness. 'It's only a kiss. And only if you like it will I do it again. You're in control of what happens.' He rested his forehead against her own. 'Trust me. I know what I'm doing.'

She wrinkled her nose and voiced her last remaining doubt. 'What if you hate kissing *me*?'

He rubbed a soothing thumb over her chin. 'I suspect you're going to be the best kisser who's ever walked this earth. And do you know why?'

'Why?'

'Because this is you and I, and there's strong chemistry between us. It's special and rare.'

'There is?' she asked shyly. His words were reassurance against the last threads of her insecurity.

He nodded. 'Kiss me, Ruby. Throw a spell over me the way you did my horse. Use your magic hands on me, darling.'

He kissed her then, using his hand on the back of her head to draw her deeper into his embrace. His mouth was warm and persuasive as their breath joined and their tongues met for the first time.

Fire tore through Ruby's body, scorching every nerve with its heat, taking their connection from pleasant and hesitant to full-on sizzling, with the smells of the beach and the flavours of their lunch in each breath and taste.

Kern's groan echoed her own as their kiss deepened, until nothing but the pleasure of kissing and touching each other consumed their every thought.

When they finally broke apart, breath ragged, bodies close and smouldering, Ruby opened her eyes and stared at Kern with awe. 'I think I rather liked that.'

Kern grinned and pulled her close again. 'Yeah, me too.'

Kern climbed over the fence that ran along the east side of MacKinley farm and walked towards a huge oak tree. Hundreds of years old, the tree had lived through several generations of his late wife's family.

Sitting down on the bench set purposely underneath the tree's vast canopy, he stared out at the darkening night, broken only by the yellow glow from a single window of the large house in the distance.

Corinne's father was probably sitting in his study, watching history programmes. They'd barely spoken at Corinne's funeral, aware that they shared a common bond neither of them wished to acknowledge. How they'd both failed to make Corinne happy.

A rustle sounded in the darkness…probably a nocturnal animal searching for food—or maybe the spirits of Corinne's family, horrified that he'd dared to trespass on the place where they scattered the remains of their family members and wanting to make their displeasure known.

The family hadn't invited him to witness Corinne's ashes being scattered. But then he'd never asked to be there. That part of his life was over. The ties finally broken so they could all move on.

'What a mess we created, Corinne,' Kern murmured aloud. 'Who'd have thought we'd both return to Dorset? Back to the homes we ran from as stupid kids, concerned only with breaking away from our families.'

An owl hooted in the darkness and the rustling in the bushes ceased.

Kern closed his eyes and continued with his one-sided conversation. 'I never was enough for you, was I? I tried to be, but we both know I wasn't. I loved you for so many years…but perhaps if we'd divorced you'd have found happiness with someone else. Someone who understood you better than I did. Someone whose opinion you would listen to and not resent. Someone capable of giving you a child, or at least easing your pain over the absence of one. I didn't know how to heal that ache you carried inside.'

He tilted his head and stared up at the few stars already showing in the sky.

'Don't you think I ached for a child too? I wanted to adopt, but you always refused to consider it.' He shook his head. 'I guess we were both guilty of never facing things head-on. Of not having that one important conversation. I tried a few times…but when I saw the pain in your eyes I gave up. I used work as an excuse to ignore your unhappiness, and you refused to face the reality of never becoming a mother. I hate it that after all our years together we just grew apart.'

He stopped and swallowed the lump in his throat that the memory caused.

'Do you still hate me? That last morning when I suggested you go and talk to the doctor, you yelled at me that you did. Do you hate me all the way from heaven?'

He closed his eyes and shifted forward on the bench.

'If I had the power to change the last few years, I would. But things were never going to change when you didn't want them to. I think deep down you just didn't know how to take those steps. Steps you had to take alone, to really find peace inside your heart. The only thing your father said to me at the funeral was that a person can only be helped when their troubled soul desires it. And it's taken me a long time to realise he's right. No doctor or counsellor in the world was going to reach you unless you decided to listen.'

He rubbed a hand over his forehead before he continued.

'You left me with nothing, Corinne. I lost it all. The yard, the horses, respect—even the desire to succeed. You finally achieved the revenge you wanted. I sold the trophies and I watched the yard being sold to a man I couldn't stand. Lost our home because I had debts to clear and no other way to pay them. You accused me of not listening to you that last morning, and then you made damn sure I had no choice but to.'

He leaned back again.

'I suppose you want to know why I've come home when I always swore never to? Well, I said it right there. It's home. And when things are rough that's where you need to be.'

He stood up and shoved his hands into his jean pockets.

'Jacob's offered me a job, but Eloise wants me to stay and start over. Why didn't you tell me she'd called several times over the years? Secrets and disappointments are what we became, Corinne, didn't we?'

His thoughts returned to that afternoon at the beach

and Ruby. Even now, hours later, he could still taste her sweet kisses. She was an angel who deserved a man with means and drive. Not an undecided 'has-been' stuck at rock-bottom, unsure how to take the first step to something better. Not a man with lingering connections to a world that had once caused her great pain regardless of her reassurances.

A decent man would walk away from Ruby and the promise of what could be. Trouble was, after kissing her the last thing Kern desired was to be decent.

'I'll always regret the mistakes we made,' he whispered into the darkness. 'But I swear I've learnt from them. I hope someone in the next life can make you happy. As for me—well, I think it's time I made up my mind about the future, don't you?'

CHAPTER ELEVEN

RUBY RESTED HER hands on the cardboard box and eyed the small red-haired boy standing on the opposite side of the examination table with caution. 'So, Jack, who's inside here?'

The nine-year-old stared at her, suspicion twinkling in his grey eyes. He wiped a hand across his nose and sniffed. 'Roger.'

'Roger?' she repeated.

Roger the rat? Roger the snake? Roger the tarantula? Or Roger the boy's baby brother?

Anne had mentioned that Jack liked to play jokes on people. Did he consider the new vet an easy target?

'And who is Roger?' she asked, hoping for a hint of what lurked inside the box.

'He's my best friend,' Jack declared, giving his runny nose another wipe.

Ruby resisted the urge to fetch a tissue from the box on the desk behind her and insist he blow it. Instead, she asked, 'And what species is Roger?'

The boy frowned. 'What?'

'I mean what type of animal is Roger? Am I likely to get my fingers bitten if I wiggle them inside?'

Jack's mum chuckled from the chair in the corner.

'You may do,' Jack said, and then clearly recalled the

first part of her question. 'He's a guinea pig. *My* guinea pig. And he's two years old.'

'Not a vet-eating monster, then?' she quizzed, flashing the boy a grin.

Jack laughed. 'Cool!'

For a spectator, perhaps, but Ruby preferred to keep her fingers and the rest of her body in one piece, safe from unidentified creatures lurking inside cardboard boxes.

'What's wrong with Roger?' Ruby kept her hands on the box, not in a hurry to investigate further until she had more information. Naturally nervous creatures, guinea pigs were best left alone until she'd discovered the problem.

'His teeth are too long,' Jack said. 'He can't eat all his food.'

It was a common issue with guinea pigs.

Ruby softly tapped the box's top flaps. 'I see… And is it just Roger in here?'

'Yes.'

'Okay. Well, I think to make Roger happier I'm going to dim the overhead light for a moment. He's been cooped up in the darkness, so we don't want to startle him with a bright light, do we?'

Jack stayed silent while she took care of the light. Returning to the table, she opened the box and peered inside, to find a brown and white guinea pig twitching its nose and staring at her.

'Hey, Roger,' she murmured softly. 'How are you doing?'

Lifting the guinea pig out, she supported its weight in one palm and carefully checked over its mouth. Yes, those teeth definitely needed some dental work. Far too big for comfortable eating.

'Well, Jack, you are absolutely right. Roger's front

teeth are way too big, and they need filing so he can eat with ease.'

'Will it make them smaller?' Jack asked, reaching out to stroke a dirty finger over his pet's tummy.

'Yes—and I think it might be best for Roger to come back and stay with us for a morning, so we can check his other teeth. Sometimes they grow too big as well, and can make a guinea pig's tongue sore. Let's go and make an appointment with Anne.'

Together, with Roger back in his box, they headed to Reception and quickly made an appointment for Roger to return the next day.

Back in the consultation room, Ruby had turned her attention to clearing up when May, one of the practice nurses, knocked on the door.

'There's a man in Reception asking to speak with you.'

'A man?' Ruby asked. 'Did he give a name?'

'Yeah, Kern MacKinley. Shall I send him in? You've ten minutes before your next appointment. And Mrs Flutter and her Dobermans are always late.'

Ruby nodded. Perhaps he had a problem with Evie? Or wanted to rearrange their dinner date? Maybe share more of his wonderful kisses?

Just the thought set off fizzles of delight inside her stomach. She liked kissing Kern very much. In fact, she struggled not to think about his lips and his mouth and how they'd sent her skin tingling and warmed all her intimate parts...

Shaking some sense into herself, she quickly rinsed her hands under the tap. Drying them with a paper towel, she tried to steady her breathing as she waited for the man who occupied her thoughts to walk in.

'Hi,' Kern greeted her when he strolled into the room moments later, filling the spacious area with his charisma.

The black jumper he wore brought out the blue of his eyes, sending those fizzles into manic spins.

'What's wrong?' she asked, shoving her hands into her white lab coat's pockets.

He chuckled and stepped further into the room. 'Now, why do you think there's something wrong?'

She wrinkled her nose. 'Because you mostly search me out when you want a favour,' she pointed out.

He slapped a hand to his chest in mock pain. 'There you go again—hurting my male pride with your cruel but unfortunately true observations.' He shook his head. 'And it really is true, isn't it?'

She nodded. 'Yep.'

'But what you *haven't* realised is that although I may want something from you—normally your expertise—I always give back in return.'

She snorted. 'Really?'

'Yes,' he insisted. 'The night you tended Evie, I gave you a piggyback.'

She folded her arms and leaned against the cupboards behind her. 'Yes, you did. How silly of me to forget.'

'And when we travelled to check out the horse, I provided a meal—'

'Your aunt did,' she corrected. 'She made all the food.'

'Only because I don't have use of a kitchen,' he said smoothly.

She shook her head and demanded, 'Okay MacKinley, what are you after this time?'

He grinned. 'Your professional skills.'

'Again?' she huffed. 'You *do* realise there's more to me than my job, don't you?'

He let his eyes slowly run over her, visually caressing each and every curve of her body. 'Oh, believe me, Ruby... I am more than conscious of that fact.'

Blushing, she straightened. 'Which horse needs my help this time?'

'I suspect Mabel Star has a blocked tear duct. She has gunk weeping from her left eye.'

Ruby nodded, mindful that her next patient must have arrived. 'Okay, I'll pop in on my way home from work and take a look.'

'Thank you.'

She called out to him as he turned to leave. 'My favours come with a price, MacKinley.'

He glanced back with a strange, almost sad expression on his face. 'I know that, Ruby. Believe me, I know...'

Ruby parked her car on the dirt track outside the MacKinley stables, smiling when she spotted Kern strolling out to meet her. The man's easy saunter always made her stop and take a breath—his loose movements were a sight to relish.

'Hey,' he said, opening her door. 'Thanks for stopping by.'

Ruby slipped out, her heart-rate skipping as she straightened up in the small space between the man and the car. A space Kern appeared in no rush to widen.

'No problem. You suspect a blocked tear duct?'

'Yeah,' Kern said, finally stepping away. 'The discharge from her eye has increased since this morning.'

Ruby grabbed her medical case from the back seat. 'I have everything here to flush out any blockage—except an assistant to help me.'

Kern slipped her case from her hold before she could argue and offered, 'I work well under instruction. Will I do?'

She scoffed and followed him towards the stables. 'Not from what I've seen, MacKinley. I'd say you're a rebel at heart.'

She followed him through the entrance, her eyes flicking to his very nice backside, encased in the usual worn jeans. His blue-and-white-checked shirt sat half untucked at the waistband. Ruby's fingers itched to explore beneath the material. To lift the fabric and slide her hands inside over his warm flesh.

The trouble was his remarks earlier, as he'd left the practice, concerned her.

Was he still struggling with his conscience? Concerned that it was too soon after he'd lost his wife? Worried that people might judge him for moving on? That he owed his wife a decent mourning period even though it seemed their marriage, by Kern's own statements, hadn't included any closeness towards the end. Did the chemistry between them distress him? Or did the difference in age really matter to him?

Friends didn't kiss passionately. So what were they? Not friends with benefits. Surely he didn't see them as such a thing? She wished she knew how he felt, because then she might begin to understand her own feelings.

Did he worry that she wanted more than just kisses?
Did she want more?

Ruby's gaze moved over the man once again, taking in every inch of his firm body and wide shoulders. Yes, she did—and not only physically. She craved Kern's company when they were apart. She dreamt about him at night. She desired his kisses and wanted the right to take one whenever the urge came over her.

She wanted Kern MacKinley. Every single bit of him. And that fact scared her and excited her.

She yearned for the right to pull him close and run her tongue along the curve of his neck. To tug his shirt apart, flick the buttons who cared where and scatter kisses over his chest and stomach.

'Ruby?'

Blinking, she dragged herself from her luscious wondering. 'If you can lead Mabel Star out here into the aisle, where there's more room to examine her, that would be wonderful.'

'Of course.'

She was aware that the procedure for clearing a horse's blocked tear duct could be challenging. 'Most horses hate having the flush done,' she told him. 'She might fidget quite a bit.'

Kern nodded and headed to the rear of the stables to fetch the mare. Ruby sorted through her equipment, pushing all unanswered questions and queries from her mind. Pondering over what Kern thought and indulging in scrumptious fantasies would have to wait. Right now, Mabel Star required all her attention.

When the comforting and familiar clip-clop of hoofs on concrete sounded in the aisle, Ruby turned and waited for man and horse to reach her before she slowly approached the mare.

Examining the left eye, she studied the crusty discharge weeping heavily from the corner. 'Okay, it's probably an obstruction. She hasn't hit her nose recently?'

'Not that I've seen.'

Ruby nodded. 'First I'll flood the eye with fluorescein dye. After five minutes we'll have a clearer idea as to what's going on.'

Kern nodded, and continued to hold Mabel Star while Ruby fetched the dye and applied it. After a few minutes, when hardly any dye had dripped out of the mare's nose, it was obvious the problem was down to a blockage.

'Right, I suggest we sedate Mabel Star, and then place a tube inside the tear duct at the nostril end and flush it out with saline. That should remove any build-up that's inside.'

She stopped when footsteps sounded behind her and Kern's friend Jacob walked through the entrance.

Kern remained holding Mabel Star, but nodded to his friend. 'Back already? Anyone would think you like it here. Two visits in a week?'

Jacob grinned. 'Yeah... Had a call from a friend in Ireland. Thought that as I was passing on the way to the airport I'd pop in and see if you've thought any more about that job offer.'

'I'm considering it,' Kern said, though most of his attention stayed on Mabel Star. 'I've called the man and set up a meeting.'

'Good.' Jacob indicated the horse. 'Problem?'

'Blocked tear duct. Nothing Ruby can't fix.'

Warmed by his faith in her ability, Ruby sedated Mabel Star and gathered everything she needed. Flushing out a horse's tear duct was tricky, especially if the horse resented the intrusion of the tube inserted into the tear duct. And horses always did. Though she didn't blame them. Having something shoved into her nose by a stranger would hardly impress Ruby, either.

Laying a gentle hand on the mare's face, she did her best to reassure the old girl, conscious of Jacob and Kern close by.

Kern nodded at his friend. 'Safe journey. Stay in the saddle and in your own bed.'

Jacob laughed. 'I'll do my best. Seriously, keep thinking about the offer. It's a good one. And give me first dibs on riding your next champion.'

'I will,' Kern promised, glancing Ruby's way.

Jacob nodded to Ruby before leaving the building.

Ruby waited for the sound of Jacob's car being driven away before she asked, 'Your friend has offered you a job?'

'Yes,' Kern confirmed. 'He has connections with someone who's eager for me to manage a yard for him. I've agreed to meet with him—that's all.'

Ruby heart skipped. Neither Kern's bland expression nor his tone gave away his feelings concerning the offer. Did it intrigue him enough to make him consider leaving Dorset?

'Sounds interesting,' she said.

Kern frowned. 'Do you think so?'

She shrugged, only interested in what *he* thought. 'What do *you* think?'

'If I was young and starting off in the game again, I might consider it. But I'm not used to answering to anyone except the odd owner who hasn't learnt to trust my opinion.'

Ruby gathered a thin tube and a syringe filled with saline. 'She may pull and fuss while we do this,' she warned.

'I have her.'

Kern soothed Mabel Star, holding her head firmly. He stroked the mare's ear as Ruby fed the tube into the small tear duct situated inside the nose. Mabel Star tugged for a moment, but settled long enough for Ruby to squirt the fluid inside. Seconds later a mixture of fluorescein dye and saline fluid gushed out of her eye.

'But you've agreed to think about it?' asked Ruby.

Kern soothed Mabel Star again as she tugged and stepped backwards.

Confident the procedure had removed any blockage, Ruby swapped sides and repeated the process in the mare's other nostril. Within minutes both sides were washed out.

'Yes,' said Kern.

Ruby retrieved a wad of sterile tissue from her bag and mopped away the mess around Mabel Star's eyes. 'I suppose it is a way to return to racing…'

Kern snorted. 'At the beck and call of a rich man who

could cut me loose any time he chooses to? What if I went to work for him and then in a year's time he decided to pack it in and invest in racing cars instead? I'd be cast aside and left in the dirt. Same for any staff who worked for me. I've seen it happen before.'

'Yet you're still considering it?' she guessed, sensing his indecision, despite his reservations. 'You must miss racing…'

Kern didn't answer straight away, but when he did, he shrugged. 'What else am I going to do, Ruby? As Eloise once pointed out, I know nothing else. My whole life has revolved around horses. From the time I sat on one to the day I lifted my last winner's cup I've lived and breathed racing. And it's not just about the winning. It's the people, the smells, the kick of seeing a horse you've trained from a youngster and watched improve cross the winner's line to the roar of the crowd. The relief when it's comes home safe and well.'

She stared at the flickering emotions crossing his face as he spoke. A large part of her understood his words. She'd seen the same love for the sport in her father's expression years before.

'You love it,' she said.

Kern nodded. 'I do. But there's a flipside to everything I've mentioned. If I start out on my own again, it will require a lot of work and time—God knows this land needs a small miracle to get it to a half-decent standard.'

'But it would be yours,' she reminded him, confident he could achieve it.

'Yes,' he agreed. 'As well as all the debts and the bills. And all the headaches running a yard involves. Plus the added problem of Fin.'

'You've done it before.'

His eyes met hers. 'What do you think I should do?'

She pondered the question for a moment. Not sure how to advise him. Every career suffered highs and lows. He'd experienced both. 'I think you should consider what you really want deep in your heart. You're in a better position this time because you've done it once and understand what's required.'

'I've also lost everything,' he said ruefully.

Ruby stroked a hand down Mabel Star's face. 'Your wife was sick, Kern. You need to forgive what she did.'

'I do forgive her.' He smiled softly. 'I always forgave her. I think maybe that was the problem. I was weak.'

'For loving someone so deeply? Isn't that what real love is? Not simply the sweet, loving times, but the rough moments too? From what you've told me, you saw your wife as your friend too. And a good friend doesn't let go when things get tough. A friend grips on—even if it's hard, and perhaps the love changes and ebbs—a friend cares enough to shelter a person when they need it. I think Corinne trusted you to do so...trusted you to be her safety. I doubt she meant to do what she did. I think perhaps it's like you said. She hit her final place where everything became too much.'

'So wise...' Kern murmured.

'Your aunt once said we survive trauma and move on. Let Corinne go and do the same. I think it's time.'

'Maybe...' he said. 'I'll put Mabel Star in her stable.'

Ruby reached out and stopped him. 'When do you meet with this man?'

He let out a long sigh. 'The morning of the parade. I figure I've nothing to lose by listening to him. What is there to keep me here? A derelict stable? Weed-thick land?'

Me, Ruby whispered in her heart. *I'm here if you'd open your blinkered eyes and see how much I care for you.*

'So our kisses meant nothing to you?' The question escaped and hung between them. Flushing, she turned away. 'Sorry. I didn't mean to ask that.'

Kern reached for her. 'Ruby, I—'

'Don't!' she snapped, suddenly fed up with his indecision. 'Don't stand there and lie to me. If they were just a way to pass the time, then have the guts to say so. I'm a woman, not a child. I can take the truth.'

'Of course they weren't. I told you there's a strong connection—'

'But not strong enough for you to consider taking it further than kisses,' she guessed, suddenly feeling foolish. She sounded like a teenager, whining because a hot boy wished to dump her.

But she couldn't help feeling used by Kern. One minute she'd believed they were friends and the next they'd been kissing, making her think he wanted to take their relationship further. But now he was talking about leaving and the knowledge hurt. Really hurt.

'Look, it's okay,' she insisted. 'If I was just a bit of fun—'

'Don't you dare insult either of us with that comment. The truth is I desire you. I want to take you to bed right now and love you hard. I ache to kiss every inch of your soft skin. Taste you until I crave no other flavour in my mouth. But I daren't. Because I fail people. I failed Corinne, I failed the owners of the horses who put their trust in me, and I failed my family when I stayed away.'

'You didn't fail—'

'I did. But I swear to God I am not going to fail you. I'm not going to see your respect and affection die because of what I fail to do. Yes, I want to hold you and kiss you, but I won't—because what I feel here in my heart is more than I have ever felt for anyone else. We could never be just friends, Ruby, because I'd always yearn for more. And if we took it further and it all went wrong it would break my heart completely.'

'But what if I want to take the risk?' she asked. 'Don't you care about what *I* want?'

'I refuse to let you take the risk.'

'Coward!' she spat, furious that he thought he could make that decision on her behalf.

'What did you call me?'

'A coward!' she repeated. 'You stand there, all proud and virtuous. Spouting declarations of how you're doing it to protect me. The truth is you're doing it to protect yourself. Because you're a coward, too scared to take a chance.'

'You don't understand—'

'Don't patronise me!' she yelled. 'I understand that you won't give us a chance of a relationship because you're scared. I get that. I was scared for years until I came to Dorset and met you. You've helped me to see that being scared of life is no real life. You've shown me how much I've been missing out on.'

'Ruby—'

'I'm not Corinne. Any relationship we have will be ours. It will be different. Because I'm a different person. You cannot judge any future relationship with the same eyes as you did your marriage. Everyone is unique.'

'I know.'

'So don't use your marriage as an excuse to conceal your fear. If you want to take this job, then go. If you want to stay—fine. But don't bother me unless you meant those kisses and you want to build on them. It takes courage to pick up and start living again. Just make a decision and get on with it.'

Grabbing her belongings together, she rushed from the stables, ignoring the pain in her chest and the overwhelming urge to cry.

'Ruby!'

Forcing herself to keep going, she jumped in her car and drove away. If Kern didn't want a relationship, then it was his loss. Any man she let inside her heart would be there because he wanted her more than anything else in life. If Kern didn't feel that, then it was better to let him go.

CHAPTER TWELVE

RUBY SWIPED THE wet flannel over her face and stared at her reflection in the bathroom mirror. For the first time in weeks, months, or maybe even years, she studied her uncovered features with a critical focus she normally avoided.

Without the make-up she wore throughout the day she could witness her real self. Not the person she showed the world, but the person beneath the concealer, beneath the past's heavy veneer and her parents' scandal. The adult version of the sixteen-year-old who'd discovered that few people around her were trustworthy.

Usually her brain instantly connected her own face with her mother's image, but today, staring at her reflection, she saw herself. She wasn't the child disappointed by her parents and then left alone by one's abandonment and the other's grief. She was a grown woman who'd worked hard to achieve the career she wanted and the life she loved.

When Kern had asked that day on the beach who the real Ruby Day was she'd had no answer. She'd run for so long, wanting to forget the beginning of her life, ashamed and hurt by her parents' actions. Back then, she'd craved normality and peace, but somehow over the years she'd forgotten that she deserved to be herself too.

Leaning forward, she stared harder at her reflection. Seeing her cat's eyes free of black eyeliner and the too-plump mouth. Grabbing a handful of her black curls, she laughed at the image. She didn't resemble her mother at all. She actually looked like herself. Why had she never seen that before?

She was exhausted after years of playing a part and putting on a front. She wanted to roll out of bed and be Ruby. She didn't want to wear make-up all the time. She wanted to let her skin breathe, to undo all the wrappings she'd wound round and round herself, convinced they were protecting her from hurt.

But they hadn't protected her. Instead, they'd suppressed her and hidden away her real self. Suffocating her until she could barely breathe.

And then Kern had come along and gently teased her into wanting to unravel those layers inch by inch, until her head spun and her heart raced and she felt free for the first time in years.

As a grown woman she could cope with life and what the future threw her way without the need for armour of any kind. It was time to be the person deep inside her heart and march into the future as the strong, capable woman she was.

She couldn't accuse Kern of being cowardly and then continue to be the same herself.

Picking up her eyeliner, she swiped a line under her lower lashes and then stepped away. No concealer, no eyeshadow and no lipstick. Just eyeliner and her silver lip ring. She didn't require anything more.

Today, for the first time since the age of sixteen, the real Ruby Day was coming out to play. And she couldn't wait to show herself off to the world.

Leaving the bathroom, Ruby headed to the bedroom. Dog was stretched out on his own large bed for a change, snoring. She grinned and stroked a hand over his chest, her heart full of love for her sweet boy.

Opening the wardrobe door, she withdrew the white lace Victorian dress she'd found online——original, with little wear. She ran her hand over the superb detailed lace-work, wondering about the woman who'd first worn it. Had that mystery lady's heart thumped with excitement and fear as she'd prepared to dress all those years ago?

Slipping the dress off the hanger, she pulled it on, quickly fixing the miniature buttons and ribbon ties around the high lace neck. Lace sleeves had buttoned cuffs, and a matching lace frill draped into a point at the front. The dress fitted perfectly, and for the first time in years Ruby felt feminine in a totally different way.

'What do you think, Dog? Will Kern like me dressed like this? Will he still be talking to me after the way I be-haved the other day?'

Lifting a large white hat, she placed it on her head and pinned it with the long hat pin she'd bought from an an-tique shop. No longer Ruby the Goth. Today she'd be Ruby the Victorian. And tomorrow she'd start living her life simply as Ruby Day, the local vet who could heal animals with her hands.

The violent fluttering in her stomach intensified and she laughed once again. Yes, it was definitely time to be the authentic Ruby—and amazingly, she couldn't wait.

'Ruby you look beautiful!' Kiki rushed over and wrapped Ruby in a hug. 'Utterly charming. I love the dress.'

'Let go,' Alex ordered his wife, sending Ruby an apol-ogetic glance as they joined her and Eloise in a local field with all the other parade participants.

The town had gone full Victorian, and everyone wore outfits suitable for extras in a Dickens adaptation. Several food and beer tents were pitched close by, and a couple of steamrollers puffed and smoked on the other side of the field. A couple of cows complained as their owners pulled them across the grass, and horses waited patiently beside farm wagons and carts.

In the middle of the crowded field was a wagon decorated with a giant papier mâché chicken, which Eloise had informed Ruby was a replica of one pictured in a Dorset newspaper from the 1800s. It shifted precariously, despite its rope fastenings.

'I'm only hugging her,' Kiki insisted, continuing to push the air out of Ruby's lungs.

Alex gently detached his wife. 'No, you're scaring her. Though it would make a nice change for a member of staff to leave because of *your* irrational behaviour instead of mine.'

Panic entered Kiki's gaze. 'Ruby's not going to leave— are you? Please don't. You can have a partnership in the business if you promise to stay. Just say yes.'

'I—I…' She glanced at her boss for help.

'Early stages of pregnancy,' Alex explained, groaning as his wife suddenly rushed off to hug a passing old man. 'She can't keep her hands to herself.'

'Where is MacKinley?'

Ruby glanced around the crowded field, filled with town folk eager to be part of this yearly tradition. 'I don't know. He should be here by now.'

Alex studied her outfit with a deep frown. 'You do look lovely—but you're not giving up the Goth look for good, are you?'

Smiling shyly, she reassured her boss. 'No. But I feel it's time for a change. It's quite nice to wear white instead of black.'

Alex regarded her for a moment before he nodded.

'Good, because you should never change yourself for any-one, Ruby. Anyone decent will want you for yourself—otherwise they don't deserve you.'

Touched by his words and obvious concern, she shook her head. 'I'm not doing it for anyone. I'm doing it for me. Thanks again for understanding yesterday.'

After she'd finished the previous day's consultations Ruby had sought Alex out and explained everything to him. She had told him about her ability to heal animals and who her parents had been. Having recently confessed everything to Kern, telling her boss had come more easily than she'd imagined. And doing so had felt right.

After he'd listened, Alex had leaned back in his chair and asked if she'd be willing to treat some clients for whom traditional drugs weren't helping or working. He'd explained how he wanted to develop the holistic side of their treatments and offer owners a varied choice for their pets and animals.

'You're gifted,' Alex said. 'I'd be a fool not to encourage you to use your talent.' With a wave goodbye, he'd added, 'Be proud of your gift, Ruby. It's an important part of who you are. And maybe we can discuss the idea of partnership in a year or so. With another baby on the way, I'd like to spend more time at home with my family.'

Now Ruby smiled, her affection for her boss growing. Alex Morsi was a very nice man. Professor Handel deserved a large bunch of flowers for insisting that Ruby travel to 'one last interview'. Coming to Dorset had changed not only her fortune, but her life.

'Where's Kern?' Eloise demanded, interrupting Ruby's thoughts.

She'd finished harnessing Mabel Star and putting her to the cart. The sweet mare looked glorious with her plaited mane and shiny coat.

Feeling uneasy, Ruby shrugged. 'I don't know.'

She checked her phone again, but there were still no messages from Kern or anyone else. For the umpteenth time she wondered how his meeting had gone. Had the man persuaded Kern to become his trainer? Had Kern seized the opportunity to go back into the work he loved? Had money influenced his decision? Or the way she'd shouted at him and told him to make up his mind? Did he resent her interference in his life?

'He had a meeting in town this morning,' Ruby said. 'Perhaps he's been delayed, or has stopped to pick up supplies for the horses?'

'What meeting?' Eloise demanded, her eyes narrowing on Ruby.

Ruby sighed, wishing she'd kept quiet. It was one thing for her to worry, but Eloise deserved to hear about the job offer from her nephew. 'I'm not sure…'

'Don't lie,' Eloise scolded. 'You're terrible at it and your face gives you away. Come on—tell me what this meeting was for.'

'A friend of his recently sought him out and offered him the chance of a job training horses for some rich man. Kern told me that he had agreed to meet the man this morning, but that's all he said.'

'I hope he hasn't left without telling anyone,' Eloise said, fiddling with her necklace.

Ruby had noted that she did so whenever she was worried or concerned.

'It's what he did before.'

'He was young then,' Ruby pointed out, not wanting to contemplate the notion of Kern having gone without saying goodbye. 'I'm sure he'd talk to you first. Maybe he can't get through the traffic outside of town. The roads are busy.'

'I hope so,' Eloise muttered, patting Mabel Star.

Darkness crept into Ruby's heart at Eloise's concern. The horrible suspicion that Kern might have chosen to sneak away refused to stay quiet. Surely he wouldn't hurt his aunt again? He had responsibilities both to his elderly relative and MacKinley farm.

But what if this man Kern had met had managed to talk him into leaving and insisted he do so immediately? How long did it take to set up a yard, anyway? Would Kern prefer to go without saying goodbye to her? Did the time they spent together, getting to know each other, mean nothing to him? She knew he wanted her, but was he determined to deny them both?

'Come on.' Eloise sighed. 'If Kern doesn't arrive soon, I'll drive the cart in the parade.'

Giving Eloise's arm a reassuring rub, Ruby said, 'At least you *can* drive it. We'd be in real trouble if I had to do it.'

Eloise paled and admitted, 'To be honest, I struggled to get the hang of it years ago, but I'm sure we'll manage.'

'There's still half an hour until we're due to leave,' Ruby soothed, glancing towards the entrance to the field. 'I'm sure Kern will arrive soon.'

The old woman nodded, unable to hide the tears in her eyes. 'I'm afraid my nephew may have decided not to come. Goodbyes always were a problem for him.'

'Come on. Don't do this to me.'

Kern stared at his phone, silently praying for it to come to life, despite knowing it was a wasted hope. The thing was deader than a medieval skeleton.

His meeting in town that morning with the Sheikh had cemented the decision he'd reached the night Ruby had walked out. After a phone call to one of the men who'd helped him months before, he'd spent the rest of his time making plans. Plans necessary to rebuild his life.

Everything was in place except for one thing. Ruby. The woman he'd been desperately trying to get hold of since leaving the local auction house after dropping off some of his parents' old furniture and belongings. Not precious stuff, but hopefully decent enough to raise enough funds to cover the next six months' bills and expenses.

Shoving the phone into the pocket of his black trousers, he tugged at the blue neck scarf around his throat. With the sleeves of his white shirt rolled up, his traditional Victorian farmer's garb was completed with a plain brown waistcoat.

Already running late, he had no time to linger. Ruby, his partner for the parade, would be waiting. The other half of the Victorian courting couple they were playing.

Only it didn't feel like playing to him. His mind was clear for the first time in months.

When Ruby had called him a coward, he'd balked at the criticism. But once his ego had shifted out of the way he'd faced the ugly truth. A truth she'd told him straight. Denying his desire for her *was* cowardly—and unbelievably stupid when he knew how precious life and happiness was.

With a glance over at Evie, he led the filly outside into the yard. 'How do you fancy a run, girl? I need your help. Don't get jealous, but there's a woman I want to impress and I just hope I can talk her into listening.'

'Where's Ruby?' Kern led Evie over to where Alex Morsi and his wife stood, eating ice creams. Their baby girl gurgled from her pram, looking as though she'd been in a fight with an ice cream monster.

'Where have you been?' Kiki demanded, scooping ice cream onto a small wooden stick.

'I got stuck in town and my phone died when I reached home,' Kern explained.

'She's gone,' Alex said, nodding to the country road going west into town. 'Left about ten minutes ago.'

Kern's stomach dipped and panic swirled through his chest. Gone? Had Ruby decided to leave Dorset after their argument? Surely she'd stay for her job at the practice?

He swallowed hard, and asked, 'Gone?'

Alex nodded. 'The organisers ordered them to line up for the parade. If you listen, you can hear the band playing.'

Kern stomach turned over as another thought hit him. 'Who's driving the cart?'

The other two stared at him, before answering together, 'Eloise.'

The sickening twist inside his body became full-on dread. 'I need to stop them.'

'Why?' Alex asked, following him as he turned to his horse.

Kern mounted Evie again and turned the filly towards the gated entrance. 'Last time Eloise drove a cart she ended up in a bush. Unless she's had lessons since I've been gone, there's every chance they'll have an accident.'

'You'd better hurry!' Alex yelled. 'I don't want to search for another vet. Ruby has talents barely explored.'

Kern grinned at the man's words. Ruby did indeed have talents, and he intended for her to use every single one. That was if she forgave him for his stupidity and gave him another chance.

Riding through the gate, Kern headed in the direction of town. Small groups of people wandered along the pavements. The red, white and blue bunting and flags strung on lamps and gateposts fluttered in the slight breeze.

Up ahead, he caught sight of a vintage tractor, hissing out smoke as it rolled along. Carefully, he eased Evie over to the right-hand side of the road, glad the town council had closed it to traffic. After passing a wagon loaded with children dressed in white pinafores and flat caps, he finally spotted the cart.

Riding along at the driver's side, he called out, 'Taking over my job, Aunt Eloise?'

Eloise sighed heavily. 'Thank goodness. I can't stop shaking—and I'm sure poor Mabel Star can feel it.'

'Pull over in the next lay-by and we'll swap transport.'

Within minutes they'd stopped, and Eloise climbed down from the cart and happily took Evie's reins from her nephew. 'I'll walk Evie back and meet you two at the field after the parade.'

Ruby turned to Kern as he climbed into the cart and reached for the reins. 'I thought you'd taken the job and left.'

Kern grasped her hand and squeezed it. 'Let's do the parade and then I've important news to tell you.'

'Will I like it?' she asked.

'I'm not sure,' he admitted, suddenly nervous.

What if Ruby hated his decision? What if she decided she only wanted him as a friend and nothing else? How could he show her that he was ready to be brave?

With a flare of determination, Kern flicked the reins. Ruby might have doubts, but he was damned if he was going to let her go without fighting to prove to her that if she took a chance on him he'd never fail again.

Ruby's heart thudded harder than the town's brass band's drum as Kern drove the cart away from the crowds and through the countryside. The parade was over, and everyone involved was slowly making their way back to the field to spend the rest of the afternoon relaxing and enjoying refreshment.

Gripping her hands together on her lap, she glanced at Kern and asked, 'Where are we going?'

Kern took a deep breath, before asking, 'Did you really think I'd leave without speaking to you again? Without saying goodbye? I'm disappointed, Ruby.'

'I didn't know what to think,' she admitted. 'The job offer sounded good, and after our discussion I thought—'

'It wasn't a discussion,' he corrected. 'It was our first fight.'

'Oh,' she said. 'Does that mean there are going to be more?'

He chuckled and slid a glance her way. 'I hope so. You're right—the job is a great opportunity for someone. I won't lie to you, I did consider it for a moment. But then we went to the beach and I knew deep in my soul I wasn't going anywhere. Dorset is home. I've missed it and been away from it for too long. This is where I'm going to start over. It's time to get back to work. I owe it to my family. Especially to my mother, who must be cursing from heaven at my endless wavering.'

'You've finally decided?'

He nodded. 'It's time I restored MacKinley farm and the family name. Make the old place a home again. A home filled with a ton of love. Just like it used to be.'

Ruby licked her lips, her heart swelling with hope. 'Sounds like a wonderful idea.'

Kern turned off the country lane into a familiar drive and stopped the cart once they were outside his childhood home. Ruby glanced at the old run-down farmhouse.

Wrapping the reins around the brake, Kern twisted on the seat and stared at her. 'I want to spend time with my aunt and with the sweet, wonderful woman I'm starting to care about. That's if you'll give me a chance?'

Ruby eyes widened. 'Me?'

'Who else?' he asked. 'Ruby, I am everything you shouldn't want, but I'm hoping you'll give us a go anyway. I'm asking for a chance to show you how good we can be. I want to make you happy, Ruby. I want to prove to you that I'm no coward when it comes to our love.'

'Are you sure this is what you truly want—?'

Kern brushed her knuckles with a kiss. 'You're all I want, Ruby. You're the dream I've lived through every night since we met. When I'm with you anything seems possible. You're funny, shy and adorable. I want to spend every day around you, enjoying your company. Since that first day, when you drove onto the farm and ordered me to get dressed, something has happened to my heart.'

'What?'

He smiled and squeezed her fingers. 'It's come back to life. *You* did that. You revived me—brought me out of the coma I'd lived in for so long. If you want to leave and run, then fine—pack your caravan and drive away. But every time you glance in the rear-view mirror you'll see me, coming right after you.'

Ruby grinned. 'Will that be on horseback or in a cart?'

'I'll follow you until you're ready to build a life with me. A better one for both of us. Let me give you a home. Somewhere safe and permanent. Somewhere we can stay for ever. Where you can make long-term friends and find clients.'

'What about Fin? If you intend living on the farm, you'll need to reach a truce.'

'Fin's left and he isn't coming back. I received a solicitor's letter this morning, informing me that he has booked himself into a clinic to get help with his drinking and his depression. The accident with Dog made him realise he needed to change.'

Concern for the elderly man filled Ruby. 'Really?'

'He's also signed over his share of the farm to me. All of this—the land and the house—are mine now. All I need is for you to agree to share it with me.'

'You really mean it, don't you?' she asked, amazed by the love she saw shining from his eyes. 'You really want me?'

'I can't promise an easy time, and there won't be much money for a while, but I'll give you everything you need. I'll hold you in the night and love you through the day. I'll do all I can to make you happy.'

'Kern, come here,' she ordered, beckoning him with a finger.

He leaned nearer, his eyes never leaving hers. 'Yeah?' His loving smile touched her heart.

'Kiss me. We can talk more later, but right now you need to kiss me—because I've never felt so happy and I'm scared it might all fly away.'

'I can do that.'

'I know you can, Kern,' she said, filled with complete faith in the man sat next to her. The man she loved deeply.

And then he kissed her, and Ruby knew that the future looked perfect and she couldn't wait to live it with her man.

EPILOGUE

Six months later

RUBY SLIPPED OUT of the four-poster bed, tugging the top cover off with her. Wrapping it snugly around her naked body, she crossed the bedroom floor to the open door. Hazy sunlight peeked through the curtains, indicating that it was still early in the morning.

As she pulled the door fully open, something shiny on the carpet caught her eye. Pieces of small silver horseshoe-shaped confetti trialled along the hallway towards the narrow staircase. Intrigued, Ruby followed the trail, running down each step to the next, all the way to the lower floor of the farmhouse.

Over the last six months she and Kern had cleaned and stripped the house until it was a basic shell, ready for them to spend the next few years renovating, turning it back into a home—their home.

So far, they'd redecorated the main bedroom and the bathroom. Nothing fancy or expensive, but clean, bright and charming. A small start on the future they'd promised one another.

The smell of toast caused Ruby to pause at the kitchen door. Spying two uneaten slices left on a plate in the centre of the pine kitchen table, she wandered into the room and picked one up. Taking a bite, she murmured with pleasure before heading to the open back door.

Shivering as the early-morning air wrapped around her bare shoulders, she smiled softly as she spotted Kern, dressed only in his jeans, standing next to one of the newly mended paddocks, watching the six horses inside.

Crossing the grass, she stopped behind the man she loved, who over the last months had shown her how good a relationship could be. Not destructive, not bitter, but warm, loving and wonderful. Everything he'd promised and more. Because he was more than she'd believed possible.

Tenderly kissing her favourite spot between his shoulder blades, she greeted him. 'Hey, handsome.'

A deep chuckle hummed through Kern's body as she wrapped her arms around his waist. 'Morning, beautiful.'

'What's with the horseshoes?' she asked.

Kern stole the toast from her hand and took his own bite before turning to face her. Stroking his free hand over her tousled hair, he smiled lazily down at her. 'It's a treasure hunt.'

Her eyes widened. 'I love treasure hunts.'

'I know you do. Somewhere on me there is a gift just for you.'

She frowned and stepped back, running her eyes over his stomach up to his chest, until something dangling from the silver chain around his neck caught her attention. Something sparkly and gold.

Meeting his eyes, she whispered, 'Whose ring is that?'

He kissed her instead of answering. Long and lingering. Finally, he pulled back to speak.

'Marry me,' she butted in, before he could utter a word.

She'd barely managed to get the words out, her heart was racing so much. Shaking, she waited for his answer.

Kern glared down at her. 'That's supposed to be my line.'

She nodded and gripped the bed cover tighter to her. 'I know, but you're taking too long. Marry me.'

He pulled her back against him. 'I can't promise you a family, but I'll try to give you one. The doctors always insisted everything works as it should—perhaps you and I will get lucky.'

'We can adopt if it doesn't happen,' Ruby reassured him, aware how sensitive the subject was for him.

But she didn't need a child to be happy. As long as they woke up together each day, her heart would be full and all her needs fulfilled. She loved this man deeply. He was all she'd yearned for and prayed for in her life.

'We already have Dog and the horses.'

Kern slipped his hand into her curly hair. 'I love you.'

Her grin went from blissful to seductive. 'I love you too. Now, come back to bed and let's celebrate our engagement.'

'Are you intending to seduce me once we get there?' he asked.

She nodded, and tugged him back towards their home. 'Just make sure you do the same.'

'Oh, baby, I intend to—plus more.'

* * * * *

MILLS & BOON

Coming next month

RESCUING THE PARAMEDIC'S HEART
Emily Forbes

The lifeguard buggy pulled to a stop at the bottom of the metal stairs that led from the sand to the tower entrance and Poppy's jaw dropped as a lifeguard jumped out. Tall and muscular, tanned and fit.

Was that Ryder?

She managed to close her mouth as she watched him help his patient out of the buggy and up the stairs.

She hung back, out of the way, as Ryder got the man into the tower and onto the treatment plinth. Jet went to assist, instructing Bluey to keep an eye on the beach. Poppy stayed near the desk by the windows. The lifeguards had a job to do and she didn't want to be a nuisance but staying out of the way also gave her a chance to check Ryder out unobserved. She knew he hadn't noticed her, he was too focussed on his patient.

The last time she'd seen him there had been a hint of the man he would become, of the man waiting to emerge, but he'd still been a gangly teenager. He'd been tall but he'd yet to have a fast growth spurt or develop the muscle definition that would come with adulthood. But all traces of adolescence had disappeared now. Now there was no hiding the man. And no ignoring the feeling of warmth that was spreading through her belly and into her groin. Poppy leaned on the desk, taking the weight off her suddenly shaky legs.

Fortunately Ryder had his back to her and wouldn't be aware of her reaction but she was very aware of him.

He'd grown even taller and he'd definitely filled out. He'd developed muscles where he hadn't had them before. He wore only a pair of black boardshorts with 'Lifeguard' emblazoned across his hips and she had plenty of opportunity to admire the view of sculpted muscles and smooth, tanned skin. His shoulders were broad, his biceps bulging, his waist narrow. He looked fit. He looked healthy. He looked magnificent.

She ran her gaze up the length of his spine and up his neck. She could see where the knobs of his vertebrae disappeared into his hair. He'd always had amazing hair, dark blond and thick, and at almost twenty-nine years of age it seemed he'd lost none of it.

Her gaze traced the line of his jaw. It was strong and square. He looked good, even better than she remembered, and she felt another rush of blood to her cheeks as her heart skittered in her chest.

Her hands gripped the edge of the desk as she observed him, keeping her fixed in place, and she wondered at the involuntary response. Was she stopping herself from crossing the room? While her rational mind might tell her that Ryder's unexpected appearance was of no consequence, it seemed her body had other ideas. Her palms were clammy and her mouth was dry and she suddenly felt like the sixteen-year-old schoolgirl she'd been when she'd last seen him.

When she had kissed him.

And he had kissed her back.

She knew from talking to her girlfriends that first kisses often weren't anywhere near as fabulous as they'd dreamed about but the kiss she and Ryder had shared had been everything she'd hoped for and more. It had been the biggest moment of her young life. It had changed her life.

She'd fallen in love.

First love.

She had only been a teenager but that hadn't made it any less real, any less all-encompassing, any less all-consuming.

And it hadn't made it any less painful when he'd walked out of her life.

Continue reading
RESCUING THE PARAMEDIC'S HEART
Emily Forbes

Available next month
www.millsandboon.co.uk

COMING SOON!

We really hope you enjoyed reading this book.
If you're looking for more romance, be sure to
head to the shops when new books are
available on

Thursday 18th February

To see which titles are coming soon, please visit
millsandboon.co.uk/nextmonth

WE'RE LOOKING FOR NEW AUTHORS FOR THE MILLS & BOON MEDICAL SERIES!

Whether you're a published author or an aspiring one, our editors would love to read your story.

You can submit the synopsis and first three chapters of your novel online, and find out more about the series, at **harlequin.submittable.com/submit**

We read all submissions and you do not need to have an agent to submit.

IF YOU'RE INTERESTED, WHY NOT HAVE A GO?

Submit your story at:
harlequin.submittable.com/submit

MILLS & BOON

LET'S TALK
Romance

For exclusive extracts, competitions
and special offers, find us online:

- facebook.com/millsandboon
- @MillsandBoon
- @MillsandBoonUK

Get in touch on 01413 063232